THE LAST VOYAGE

OF THE

NEW GUINEA TRADER

by   Brent Bateman

Revised 2011 Edition

Sketches by Kahi Chang, Honolulu

ISBN-13: 978-0-9796987-4-3
ISBN-10: 0-9796987-4-X

Dedication

This story is first dedicated to the love of adventure which resides in all of us ... and especially to those of us who dare to actively embrace travel and adventure in their own lives, who dare 'to boldly go'.

As I promise at one point in this true account, I must also dedicate this particular adventure to my high school sweetheart, Jeri Miller and tech-school sweetheart, Angie Harris ... whose tender memories carried me through some very hard times during the voyage.

Foreword

This *is* a true story … page to every page … told by the very guy that it happened to … this is the dinky die truth … I shit you not !!

Of course a few names and other such things had to be changed … to protect the innocent … and so the survivors don't try to sue my butt off … if you know what I mean.

Table of Contents

CHAPTER ONE

Tambu !!

"Mark my words, young man, she is surely destined to a bad end ... my advice to you is not to sail on her!"

I selected a path to the right of the iron rails and wooden ties of the slipway, which sloped gently down from the shoreline of the drydock into the water, and waded out until the tiny surface waves lapped at my chest. The bottom felt sandy to my bare feet and was, surprisingly, clear of debris. I adjusted the goggles which I had borrowed from the New Guinea boy.

"Me like all same glasses belong swim short time, pleez," I had asked in my best pidgin and had motioned with my hands to indicate eye goggles ... the old-fashioned kind with two separate glass-pieces fitted into eye sockets, and joined with a hinged bridge over the nose.

The New Guinea Trader was anchored with her aft transom faced to the shore, about fifty yards out. I gauged where I thought the Captain's glasses had hit the water, below and just astern of the steering house, and pushed off with my feet, free-styling towards the selected spot. The water felt warm, yet refreshing.

Jeeses ... I just know a big-ass shark is about to take a chunk out of me any second!

Reaching the spot, I took a full breath of air, jack-knifed, and dove. Wow ... the visibility was unreal!

A few colorful flat-shaped fish were swimming close by, keeping me to their side and in careful view, and the light tan of the sandy bottom was lucidly visible about fifteen feet down. I couldn't believe my luck ... there were the black-framed glasses, just off to the left. I breast-stroked down easily and scooped them up.

"Now what?" I pondered to myself for a brief second. This was without a doubt the most polluted corner of Simpson Harbor, yet the water was so clear I could see along the entire length of the ship's hull, and could make out a curious bulge on its flat bottom, about midships. I felt the urge to investigate, my curiosity dictating my choice of action, over-riding my fear of sharks, and whatever else. So I surfaced, stroked closer, and dove a second time. The hull and the bulge were thickly coated with barnacles and green-colored growth and it was difficult to make out just what the bulge was ... but it was rectangular in shape, about six feet by twelve, and protruded a full foot from the rest of the hull's surface.

Whatever it is, enough ... I'm out of here! I just know I'm shark bait!

After returning the goggles to the New Guinea boy at the drydock and retrieving my rubber thongs, I rowed the aluminum dinghy back to the Trader. I had noticed a Seagull outboard motor just inside the aft deck's cabin, but I had preferred to row. Too much humbug to rig it up, and those British 'Seagulls' were such temperamental things anyway ... downright primitive compared to, say, an American Johnson. You couldn't even rotate them 180 degrees to reverse. Or so I had been told, anyway.

I secured the dinghy to the Trader's transom, feeling clever completing a 'round turn and two half hitches' with the line, and made my way up to the Captain's quarters, just behind the wheelhouse. As I had hoped, it was too early and he wasn't up yet. Or at least he hadn't come out of his cabin. That part was critical. I was sure he would be firing mad and would be headed straight to Mr. Fitzgerald as soon as he could after waking.

I knocked on his door and heard a muffled grunt followed by a long pause. Without speaking, he opened the door only part way and glared out at me, squinting his reddened eyes and wiping at his long white goatee.

Jeeses, he looks like hell... and that goatee ... bloody ridiculous!

His complexion was gaunt and drained of color, and I was suddenly awashed with the stench of his breath, fouled with the strong odor of cheap rum.

Hell, he smells like he's been at it all night!

"Captain, I have your glasses," and I held them out to him. His eyes reluctantly turned downward and his face flickered with sluggish surprise. I thought I even recognized a hint of approval.

"Well ... thank you ... Chad, it is, isn't it?"

"Yes sir.

I gotta say 'sir' to this guy?

I turned to leave, about to say goodbye. Then I remembered about the dinghy.

"Sir ... Captain, Mr. Fitzgerald wants me to meet him at the hotel at eight. But if I take the dinghy you'll have no way to get ashore. Would you like to come ashore with me now? Or should I make some other arrangement?"

"It's alright, I don't need to go ashore," was his curt reply.

I hesitated, but there was no attempt to detain me, so I simply added, "See you later, Captain," and headed towards the wheelhouse and its two opposing side decks, 'port' and 'starboard' ... I was practicing the lingo.

Well, that's that. Hope finding his glasses helps to patch things up.

It was getting late for the appointment with Mr. Fitzgerald ... no time to lose. I climbed the steel steps to the poop deck above the wheelhouse. Not really steps, more like a ladder. I had been the first to move on board, and with Mr. Fitzgerald's permission had chosen the tiny cabin situated to the port, or left side, of the small poop deck, which was the highest deck of the ship. He had been surprised that I had chosen that particular berth. 'It's not much of a cabin,' he had cautioned. It was nothing but a short passageway beside a narrow seaman's steel bunk, all in all the cabin was no more than four feet wide by eight feet long, wall to wall. But up here I was secluded and on top of it all, so to speak. I changed into a short-sleeved shirt and my usual khaki shorts and started back down again to the waiting dinghy.

I pulled the old blue Hadson into the Cosmopolitan's parking lot.

Well, this is your last day, Charlie!

Walter, my German ex-foreman, was taking her off my hands that afternoon for a lousy eighty dollars. Hell, it was a piece of junk anyway. But Charlie had

8

served me well and with little trouble. The only real problem had been the couple of times the Rabaul cops had stopped me when I was drunk and driving on the 'right' side of the road. Habits long learned are hard to break, I suppose. Especially when the 'ol brain is doused with booze. Couldn't understand why the Pomes and Aussies didn't convert to driving on the 'right' side anyway.

Mr. Fitzgerald was standing outside the hotel's main entrance, under the green dome of the canvas canopy. And there was Harry.

Will I never see the end of this guy?

The red-headed Aussie who worked in the Burns Philip warehouse was standing to one side. He was going to be another quartermaster like myself (that's someone who steers the ship, or at least that's what we'd been told). His name was Laurie ... Harry had mentioned him last night at the bar. And there was Mr. Milner. Taller than the others, just over six feet, I guestimated. This morning Mr. Milner was displaying a stern, no nonsense composure, which awed me slightly, and was even a little puzzling. This was certainly a contrast to his shouting and yelling of last night, I reflected, trying to figure him out. He could certainly be unpredictable, and dangerously mischievous. I wondered how I should let him know I had retrieved the Captain's glasses. Maybe best not to say anything ... not now at least.

I grinned my usual dumb morning grin, the kind that is meant to camouflage a hang-over and by-pass the necessity of having to say anything even remotely intelligent, and said, "Good morning, Mr. Fitzgerald."

"Morning to yu, matey," Harry interjected, out of place, and with the same kind of grin. Mr. Fitzgerald simply nodded.

"Well, gentlemen, we need to get your seaman's papers in order ... for starters anyway. Then I would like to get as many of the crew aboard as soon as possible, although I understand that really won't happen until tomorrow. Can we use your sedan for transportation, Chad?"

"No problem at all, Mr. Fitzgerald. At least for today ... I'm selling her this afternoon." We all loaded into the aging sedan. I had to shuffle a few things from the back seat into the trunk to make room, one item of which was three orange-red, foot-long sticks of dynamite.

Damn ... how did those get left there?

Mr. Milner saw the three sticks and his right eyebrow went up. Way up! Harry saw them as well, and chuckled under his breath.

"Canuck, you're going to be the death of us all yet! Walter's going to love to hear about this." Mr. Fitzgerald and Laurie were busy shuffling into the front seat and missed the exchange.

I grimaced, and motioned frantically with my eyes for Harry to kindly 'shut up', concerned that Mr. Fitzgerald would see them too. But he didn't.

The building where we were to obtain our seaman's cards was on Blanche Street, close to Rabaul's main pier and port, which was several square blocks of single story warehouses and office buildings. The only two story structure in the area, in all of Rabaul in fact, was the Burns Philip warehouse adjacent to their wharf. That was were Laurie worked.

"We shouldn't have any problem getting cards for you, Laurie, and for you two." Meaning Harry and I. "You three are not certified officers ... no experience or certification papers required by Australian maritime law. This is a 'skeleton' crew we're putting together just to get the 'Trader' to Hong Kong ... for a mechanical refit. So excuse us if your cards aren't very fancy looking. We had all heard most of this before when we had agreed to be part of the crew. "But it is necessary to have a certified Captain, First Officer, and Chief Engineer. Their papers are a different matter." We had already been informed about this part as well. I was wondering why Mr. Fitzgerald was making a point of it.

"Mr. Milner, while these boys are getting squared away, you and I need to visit the Harbor Master."

Mr. Fitzgerald took a minute with the clerk, explaining what needed to be done, and I took the opportunity to whisper a message to Mr. Milner: "I fished out the Captain's glasses this morning and returned them to him." He was genuinely startled and took a short step back to appraise what I had said. Several separate reactions passed quickly over his face, then settled to the one I had hoped for, and he answered back in a voice low enough so no one else could hear:

"Good!" There was only the smallest hint that he approved. But it was there. I was relieved, hoping it meant that he was feeling some remorse, even if only a little.

It took only a short time for us to fill out the necessary documents and have our pictures taken. Mine was the quickest because I had my Canadian passport, and the New Guinea clerk seemed to appreciate that. Laurie and Harry had only their Aussie driver's license; they didn't need passports to work and travel in the Trust Territory of Papua New Guinea. Which was a contradiction and a pet peeve of mine, because Australians would not allow Papuans nor New Guineans to enter their country under any circumstances, except for diplomatic purposes and for a few selected students -- all part of their 'white immigration policy' -- even though Papua and New Guinea had been under Australian 'trustee' control since 1919.

Laurie and Harry both announced they were going back to work. It was Friday and their last day at their old jobs.

"Joe wants me to spend the whole day going over the 140. Kind of a farewell to her, I suppose." Harry was referring to the Caterpillar 140G motor grader which had been his baby the last few months.

"Right on, Harry," I answered teasingly. "Try and learn a little about diesel engines while you're at it."

I had touched the magic button. Those protruding ears of his turned dead pink as he retorted indignantly: "F_ you, Canuck ... I know plenty about diesels!"

"Sure you do, Harry." I winked at Laurie, who was looking on in astonishment. "You're going to need to, 'cause the Trader has two great big 'ol Perkins main engines with a White auxillary, and none of them are running!"

"No worries, mate!" Harry was taking his 'I am the greatest' stance. So I knew better ... no sense arguing. You could never win with this guy anyway. This was Harry ... Harry, the great Aussie bullshitter!

Harry had been my next door neighbor at the CDW camp for the whole time I had been there, which had been eight months. I was constantly pissed at him for his B.S. -- I swear he couldn't utter one whole complete sentence without at least part of it being an out and out lie. But then he was so damn likeable -- full of dumb humor and with that perpetual wide grin, like it was pasted on his face forever. And those ears -- pointed and sticking straight out like a panda bear's. And maybe I was being just a little jealous at the same time. For one thing, his 'mari' was Liza. He was 32, she was only 16, and she was the cutest, liveliest thing around the camp. Among the maris, that is. 'Mari' was the pidgin word for 'girl'; of course we used the term to mean only Papuan and New Guinean girls. Yes, Liza was a lot better looking than my Deli. And while I was 21, Deli was 22. Funny thing that -- I'm a younger guy and sleeping with a sixteen year old is definitely out of the question. But with Harry, who is well into middle age, I figure, sixteen was just great. Regardless, I had felt pangs of jealousy more than once when their giggling and squeals and bumping around had woken me up during the night. Sure would like to spend a night with her, though ... just one night!

Oh, oh ... time to see Deli!

"Hey, want a ride?" I offered, trying to change the direction of conversation. "Harry, how's Liza and Deli ... by the way?" I inquired, now that those two were on my mind.

"Aaahh? Feeling horny, Canuck?" Harry was getting even with me.

"Never mind, Harry ... just asking."

"Well ... haven't seen Deli since you moved out. Don't think she'll shack-up with anyone else 'till you're gone. And Liza ... well, you know already ... we're doing great."

"You're talking about your maris, are you?" Laurie interjected.

"Yeh, don't tell me you know them?"

Laurie laughed. "No, but we've heard about you blokes at the CDW camp, and your maris. We're not nearly so raunchy, but we have a few of our own."

"What do you mean *raunchy*?" Harry joked in return. "Just keeping the sap running!"

"Whoa, no offense ... being a 'hoop' is OK by me, mate." Laurie was on the right track. It occured to me that he seemed a pretty decent sort; a straighter, more clean-cut variety of Aussie.

I pulled into the driveway of the CDW compound and stopped in front of the shop to let Harry out. CDW stood for Commonwealth Department of Works, and was the Australian sponsored public works arm for Papua New Guinea.

"Ta, mate ... catch up with you later." Harry immediately headed for his 140 motor grader, which was parked to the side of the shop, all washed clean and looking pretty, her caterpillar-yellow paint shining in the morning sun. I spotted Joe, the shop foreman, coming out of his back office and decided to stop and say a few words of farewell. I didn't have much of a chance three days earlier when I had finished my last day and had boarded the Trader.

"Laurie, mind if I stop to talk to Joe for a minute?"

"Sure, think I'd like to look over Harry's machine, anyway. I've never been around this kind of equipment before."

"Joe ... never had a chance to say goodbye." I stuck out my hand to the man. He was a tall, good looking Queenslander with a soft manner and easy smile. Although we had our foremen in the field, Joe was the guy who hired and fired us operators. But we never heard much from him unless we were really out of line. I liked Joe, and respected him.

"Well, Canuck, off on another adventure I hear."

"I guess ... if we ever make it out of the harbor."

He laughed. "I've heard rumors you may not, or may not make it very far."

"Oh??" My curiosity was all ears.

But to my disappointment he changed direction. "Well, if you do end up back here, you've got a job if you want it. You've been a good operator and we've liked you, Canuck. Even if you are a bit crazy sometimes." A look of knowing and perhaps a touch of personal nostalgia reflected on his face, and he added: "Ahh, but you won't be back! You've got a whole world to explore, right matey?"

I shrugged. "By the way, Joe ... I hear Blue's on my 950."

"Yeh, that's right." He looked at me questioningly.

Blue was a big red-headed Aussie from the Melbourne area. A real red-neck. He was permanently stationed in Rabaul and had brought his Aussie wife and two kids with him. They rented a house in the purely 'European' part of town and I had spent a couple of Sundays visiting there with Harry, drinking beer all day and arguing endlessly about nonsense things that were total bullshit. Blue was a fair all-around operator, but I thought he was too rough on the machines and I really didn't like him all that much because of his arrogant, bone-headed manner. It bothered me that he was operating my Cat 950 front-end loader -- I had been operating her since she was brand new and in my book she was the sweetest machine ever. I was just getting good on her, and was feeling like I could make her truly dance. Blue being on her was like an angry cowboy horsewhipping a yearling mustang into submission.

"Temporary though, right?" There was no confirmation from Joe. "How about putting Samuel on her?" I was being bold. Samuel was a New Guinea boy. No 'boy' really; he was at least 35 years old. He had been an operator for CDW for a long time, and operated the old Hough Payloader, already an antique. I knew that he had wanted the new 950, and felt that he was entitled to her. But I had showed up and Joe had assigned her to me instead. There had been an unspoken, seething friction between Samuel and I ever since. And I had always felt very bad about it.

"Easy, Canuck, you know I can't do that." I was treading on forbidden ground. "You know, at one time we were told by the Morseby office to let you go ... 'cause of the problems they had with you there." Again that knowing look. "But we didn't have those kind of problems with you, so we told them to kiss-off. Just so you know." That revelation stunned me, though I tried not to let it show. I'd had no idea that what had happened in Moresby had followed me to Rabaul.

Then we did shake hands for a final goodbye. As I started back towards the Hadson, he threw me one last comment: "One thing though, Canuck ... how about lightening up on the booze a tad *ehh*,?" He tried to imitatate the Canadian 'ehh', and smiled. My face broke out in that dumb grin again, and because I couldn't think of anything better to say, I countered with: "What, and lose my sense of humor?"

"Must be a lot of fun to run those machines," Laurie inquired, once he was in the sedan.

"Yeh, they are. Guess we operators are just kids at heart. Except that our toys are bigger and a lot more expensive." I chuckled at myself for repeating that worn out cliche. But Laurie didn't indicate that he had heard it before, so it was OK.

"Too bad you didn't work with us." I said this because Laurie looked like he enjoyed physical activity, and being in the sun. In fact, his lower lip had that permanently swelled appearance caused by repeated sunburns, like a surfer's. He was darkly suntanned, and yet I had never seen so many freckles ... huge ones, and they were everywhere. Everywhere I could see, that is. That was unusual ... a fair-skinned person with freckles and yet deeply tanned. He couldn't have gotten that tan here, I reflected. Nobody tanned in New Guinea ... the sun was just too damn intense. Even people who would normally tan dark in a higher latitude went to great lengths to avoid the sun in New Guinea, and skin cancer was a common occurence among those who had been here awhile. Laurie was just under six feet and looked a solid 170 pounds or so ... yes, he would have liked the construction scene.

"Where you from, Laurie?"

"Brisbane."

"Surfer's Paradise?"

"You got it! That's where I was born ... been there all my life until this job with Burns Philip." Laurie laughed. "Well, here's where I get off. Guess I'll see you on board tomorrow."

"OK, and I'm sure we'll have a shit load of things to do. See you tomorrow.”

See, I was right about him being a surfer!

I spent the better part of the afternoon transferring the last of my belongings from the Hadson to the Trader, and cleaning up the Hadson ... for Walter. I guess the Captain heard me moving about, for he suddenly appeared just as I was preparing to return to shore.

"I would like to come ashore with you, Chad."

"Certainly, Captain." I followed him down to the main deck and through the narrow, centrally located cabin-way to the aft deck and transom. He declined my offer of assistance in climbing down to the dinghy. He handled himself quite well, which surprised me, knowing that he had been into the rum. I was considerably more clumsy.

Guess I gotta do the rowing. Hope I can row the thing without looking like a damn fool!

So I spent the entire 50 yards red-faced and fumbling with the oars and trying my best to appear professional. The Captain remained stone-faced the whole time. If he was amused, or disgusted, I was not to know, for he showed no sign of either.

This man is a real trip ... wonder what makes him tick?

Once we were standing upon real mother earth, I offered the Captain a lift, and he accepted, indicating that he was headed for the Cosmopolitan Hotel. Of course, I thought, where else but the 'Cosmos'.

I dropped him off and plotted a course to Walter's house, puzzling over the Captain during the entire route. So far I had seen no sign of a strong will, or any kind of strength in the man what-so-ever. He was well on in years, probably past sixty ... on the tall side, not fat but a bit flabby, and terribly gaunt with light blue eyes that seemed to make his complexion even paler. And he maintained a snow-white goatee, long and pointed, reaching down towards his upper chest, which he habitually stroked with his right hand. His appearance reminded me of a movie I had seen once where a man with a goatee similar to the Captain's was suing another guy for having said that 'he looked like a goat'. In the ensuing court case the defendent brought the first gentleman before the court -- this took place in the southern U.S. and the claimant wore a plantation style white suit -- and brought a real live goat into the courtroom as well, which was also white. The resemblence was of course obvious -- the guy did, indeed, look like a goat -- and the defendent won the case. I think Spencer Tracy was the actor.

Walter wasn't home. His pretty five-year-old daughter, Anita, met me as I got out of the Hadson, and playfully stuck her tongue out at me. She was still holding a grudge for me having said to her: 'you all same number twenty-seven' at Walter's latest party. To express approval in pidgin for almost anything, one called him or her or it 'all same number one'. But I had called her 'all same number twenty-seven'. Her mother and a couple of others had heard me and had roared in laughter and she had been embarassed.

"Hello ... number one!" I was trying to make up, but she thought I was teasing her again. She planted both her fists on her hips, once more sticking out her tiny tongue, and then fled towards the house. Her mother met her at the door. My heart did a flip. Aahh, such a woman her mother was!

I smiled, and asked Anita's mother what I already knew. Walter was at the Returned Servicemen's Club. I was too late. "If it's OK, I'll just leave the car here. Walter can pay me tomorrow. There's a party tomorrow, right?"

"Yes, another party," she sighed, "And it's OK." She was hap-caste -- New Guinean and Chinese. But she showed a lot of Chinese, and she had just about the nicest figure and most vibrant personality I had ever had the pleasure of encountenng. At the frequent parties ... for Walter was a party man ... she was always the gracious host, a gentle yet firm mother, and the first to laugh at anything genuinely humorous.

"Great, see you tomorrow." I had trouble keeping my eyes from lingering ... and wandering.

The sun still hadn't touched the top of Tunnel Hill -- the high ridge running north and south just to the west of Rabaul town -- yet the hotel bar was full. It was Friday. Mike was at a table by himself; I aimed in that direction. I hadn't seen him for awhile.

"Chad, I was sort of hoping you'd be by here. Wanted to say goodbye."

"How have you been, Mike? What's it been ... about three weeks?"

"Yeh, about three weeks. We've been surveying a new road in the Toriu River district. You wouldn't believe the things I've seen."

"Yes I would. You've had some of the most unreal experiences I've ever heard. Nothing you would tell me is unbelievable." I really meant that.

"Well," Mike gestured with his hand to dismiss that line of conversation. "Have you seen Kelli?"

"No, Mike." I switched to serious and sympathetic. "No, I haven't seen her since just before you left on the survey trip." I chose to remain silent after that. This was a tender subject.

"You know I love her ... I ... I want to marry her!"

"I know ... I remember that night."

Jeeses, man, but you can't marry her ... she's a ... whoa there, Chad, what is she ... ??

"Can you get a message to her ... for me? Through Deli?"

I started to say that I hadn't seen Deli for four whole nights, but changed my mind. "I'll be seeing Deli tomorrow ... I'll give her a message ... you want to see Kelli again, right?"

"Yeh," Mike nodded, meaning much more than just a nod. "Yeh, I need ... I want to see her again." Mike was trying his best not to sound like a fool in love, and he was only too aware of what everyone's opinion was about him becoming infatuated with Kelli and wanting to marry her.

"So ... tell me about your experiences in the boonies."

Just about then I spotted Harry working his way towards our table.

What now, Harry ... can't I have just a couple of drinks in peace?

Harry had been sitting with Mr. Fitzgerald and the Captain, a fact which had not escaped my attention. It was just like Harry ... plonking himself down in the middle of it all and bullshitting at ninety miles an hour ... again. Four nights ago we had gone through a similar scene. Harry had come over to where I had been sitting and told me I had a chance to be part of the new crew for the New Guinea Trader, bound for Hong Kong. It was a chance to get out of New Guinea ... he knew I wanted that ... and I could get off the ship in Hong Kong. I had heard something about a New Guinea coastal freighter leaving for Hong Kong, and needing a crew, but I never dreamed I could be part of it. But I hadn't reckoned on Harry ... he had been talking to the ship's representative, Mr. Fitzgerald, and out of the blue I was introduced to the man and offered the position of quartermaster. I had accepted on the spot. I was ecstatic. I could have kissed Harry right then and there, if he wasn't so ugly and annoying. Afterwards I had asked Harry: "What's a quartermaster?" He said it was the bloke who steered the ship. But he didn't sound very convincing at the time, and I wasn't sure he really knew. Anyway, I was a quartermaster. But now the scene seemed about to repeat itself.

Harry ... what are you up to this time??

Harry reached our table and there was that wide, wide grin again.
"What's up, Harry?" I asked apprehensively, even worriedly. I knew he was up to something.
"Come on over, Canuck. Mr. Fitzgerald wants to talk to you. "Then he bent over and whispered: "We need a 2nd Mate, and I told them you had some college. "
"Harry!!"
"Sshh ... just bullshit a tad!"

Harry ... you know I don't bullshit ... (well, maybe a little ...)

I rolled my eyes and stood up. All of a sudden I was very nervous. Mike was chuckling -- he knew my life story, and knew I'd never made it to 'college'. I reluctantly followed Harry back to his table, thinking frantically about how I was going to explain that I had been booted out of high school because I had set a school district record for the number of successful days of playing hooky, but that I did go to a technical school for one year ... and if I ever made it back to Canada I was going to move in with my sister in Utah and go to college.
"Good evening, Mr. Fitzgerald ... Captain." I was holding my breath.
Mr. Fitzgerald went straight to the matter at hand: "Chad, we need a 2nd Mate ... that's supposed to be the navigation officer. Harry tells me you've had a couple of years of college." But before I could stammer out some sort of explanation, he quizzed: "What's a cosine?" My mind was racing. Well, I had taken some trigonometry, but ...
"Uhh, sir ... it's opposite over adjacent!"
There was a pause. I was guessing. It was a long shot.
"Well, that's wrong ... but it's the right idea. So ... you're 2nd Mate. If you want to be 2nd Mate, that is?"
"Of course ... sir." Now I *was* stammering. "I'd be honored."

"Then it's done. Thank you." I was dismissed. A glance at Harry's face stirred my sense of humor. I had actually impressed him. Guess he had no idea about what a cosine was, or any other trigonometric function.

And thus I became the New Guinea Trader's 2nd Mate.

As I turned to leave their table I caught sight of a salty, stern faced figure watching us intently from an extreme corner of the bar ... as far away as one could get in the small Cosmos bar, yet close enough that he probably could have heard most of our conversation, including my 'promotion' to 2nd Mate. His hard eye and the combination of unshaven face and untidy naval-styled jacket and cap caused an uneasy shudder through my upper torso. I ever-so-briefly returned his stare, and was startled by a slight nod of his head in acknowledgement, complemented by a transient wry smile and a humorless glint to his eye. I felt the fleeting sensation of having just encountered a dark character from Treasure Island or some macabre pirates tale. I turned away, reluctant to glance his way again.

I made it back to Mike and prepared to listen to the story of his new adventure. And it was fascinating. But for the first part at least I was only half listening; my mind was on the Trader and the events that were taking place ... and the disquieting exchange with the mysterious stranger, who had since disappeared from the bar.

It was only a short time, or so it seemed, and Harry joined us a second time. And then Laurie showed up, which was unusual because I had never seen Laurie in the bar before. The Captain and Mr. Fitzgerald had left. I knew that the Captain wasn't going back to the freighter. So where did he go?

Sure are a lot of strange things happening!

Harry was the first to speak. "Well, how does it feel to be 2nd Mate?"
Laurie knew only that Harry was referring to me. "2nd Mate??"
"I shit you not!" Harry stole my favorite line.
And so Harry related his expanded version of how that had come to pass. All due to him, of course.
Then it was Laurie's turn. "You know, I just had to find you blokes tonight. I've been hearing some wild rumors. The blokes over at Burns Philip tell me that the sister to the New Guinea Trader, the New Guinea Princess, was run up on a reef four months ago. And the owner, Lancy Shipping Company, collected insurance. They say she was run aground on purpose."
I whistled. Harry was grinning that spectacular grin again. In a way the guy resembled Alan Ladd ... well, maybe ... about the same short height, distantly similar face, short blondish hair combed straight back ... if you really wanted to

think nicely about the guy, that is. But with that grin he was strictly Dennis the Menace!

"There's more. The Trader is headed for the same fate. They say it's never intended to make it to Hong Kong. That's why none of the old crew will even step aboard her. She's 'tambu' -- unlucky and forbidden!"

"Kinda explains our choice of crew, doesn't it." Harry was still grinning.

"So why are you grinning about it?" I didn't understand why Harry was taking this so lightly, and I was starting to become annoyed ... or maybe worried.

"Cause I don't give a shit! That's why!" Harry sensed my irritation and was responding forcefully. "But it's going to be one hell of an adventure, anyway you look at it!"

"Yeh ... if you survive." Mike interjected dryly.

"Anyway ... " Harry was changing direction. "I gotta tell you what I heard from Mr. Fitzgerald and the Captain. Bloody hell, there's a bunch to tell you blokes. First of all, we still don't have a Chief Engineer. The bloke Mr. Fitzgerald hired is a half Maori, half Aussie from Auckland, and they flew him up by way of Cairns. But he never made it. Or at least not all the way. Apparently he's a total alcoholic and, as you know, no booze is served on flights over Australian air space. And he had a several-hour wait-over in Cairns. Fitzgerald reckons he's still in Cairns, on a drinking binge with the advance money they gave him.

"Jeeses!" I rolled my eyes again.

"But that's nothing. Wait'll you hear this ... about our 1st Mate, Mr. Milner. I hear you witnessed an argument between him and the Captain last night, on board the Trader?" Harry was referring to me.

"Yeh, he was kinda unreal," I replied.

"Well, tell us about it."

"Well, he came on board with me, late, and he was drunk. And downright belligerent. He's a different person when he's had a few. Or so it seems. Anyway, for some reason he had it in for the Captain, and went straight to his cabin and started pounding on the door. The Captain came out and they had a wild argument. Most of the shouting was from Milner, though. He was trying to provoke the Captain into swinging at him. The high-light of it all was when he grabbed the Captain's glasses straight off his face and tossed them overboard. He did it just like that." I motioned with my hand to indicate one quick fling backwards, over the shoulder. "I finally got myself between them and cooled Mr. Milner down. Enough to row him back ashore and get him to the hotel, at least."

"The Captain says you fished his glasses out early this morning?"

"Yeh, that's right." I smiled.

"I reckon that's one reason you're 2nd Mate. Those two need someone to keep them apart." Harry snorted. "But what was the argument about?"

"Don't really know ... But come to think of it Mr. Milner did accuse the Captain of being hired to 'scuttle the ship'. Yeh, I think that's the word he used. Fits the rumors, ehh Laurie?"

"Or maybe Mr. Milner just doesn't like Captains!" Harry was squirming with impatience ... he had something else to tell us. "Mr. Fitzgerald mentioned that an 'inquiry' was being held for him. That's the reason Milner hasn't gone aboard yet. Something about Milner being the 1st Mate on a sailing schooner that was brought down from Hong Kong to Lae, and the captain was lost overboard on the trip. The other crew members reckoned Milner had done him in."

That raised some eyebrows!

Harry ... you making this all up?

"But there's more yet." Harry was getting all excited. "The Captain ... I reckon he was getting a little loaded and he finally started to talk. You don't hear him say much ... right? Well, we got a beaut with this one! For the last fifteen years he's been captain of a dredge in Sydney Harbor. Never been out of the harbor in fifteen years! And he said some things about navigation that didn't make any sense at all. If we had to rely on just him alone, I don't think we'd ever find Hong Kong!"

Harry paused to let all that he had said sink in, still grinning that grin. Each of us was chuckling, each of us seeing the humor, or maybe the lack of it, in a different way.

"Hey, you guys ... this is enough for me." And it was. A lot had happened, a lot to think about. "I'm headed for the Trader. See you all tomorrow. You're coming on board, right?"

As I was standing, preparing to leave, Harry turned to Mike: "Hey, Mike, you should be part of our crew. Wanna join us? I could probably fix it up."

Yeh, you probably could, Harry.

But I was already on my way out. I knew what Mike's answer would be. And why.

I paused in the cool night air to clear my head and adjust my bearing. I was just about to start out between the ironwood trees in the direction of the Trader when a shadowy figure emerged from the unlit shrubbery and blocked my path. It was the stern faced stranger from the bar. The light from the hotel behind lit his face, and I could make out his roughened, deep red complexion above the unwashed wiskers, flecked with small purple surface viens, suggesting repeated overdoses of tropical sun and liquor. He touched the edge of his cap's sunvisor in greeting, a blue naval officer's cap -- equally unwashed and deeply stained by many months of sweat and salt spray.

"Might I have a word with you, 2nd Mate ... not to fear ... I only wish to talk to you as a friend, and to give you and your crew a warning." Again I experienced the wry smile and glinted eye, and noted an accent which I guessed to be Scottish.

"What do you mean ... a warning?" I questioned cautiously, taking a step back-wards to keep the intruder at a safer distance.

"Allow me to introduce myself ... my name is Captain Rodney McKay, and I am the former skipper of the New Guinea Trader. . . "

"Former skipper?" I was curious, yes ... but this man was giving me the chills.

"Yes ... and you might be wondering why I'm not with her now, on her voyage to Hong Kong ... am I right?"

"Uhh ... yeh."

"I will make this brief ... it wouldn't be wise for our Mr. Fitzgerald, or someone else, to see us out here talking ... Let's just say I've had a 'falling out' with the owners. It has to do with something I refused to do. But it's more than that ... the ship is, let's say, 'unlucky'. I'm not one to be superstitious, or to give much weight to the New Guinea boy's notions ... but sometimes they seem to have an uncanny foresight ... they say she's 'tambu', and destined for an unlucky fate."

"I'm sorry," I started to chuckle. "But I can't take that serious."

The man shrugged, instantly annoyed that I was about to dismiss his warning without serious consideration. He glanced uncomfortably towards the bar exit, and turned to leave. "There are things about the Trader that you don't know about ... about the ship herself, and her owners ... her cargo ... and the members of your 'skeleton' crew. Mark my words, young man, she is surely destined to a bad end ... my best advice to you is not to sail on her!"

CHAPTER TWO

This is our crew ??

**I can navigate by the color of
the water," he boasted.**

George reached for the phone. "Hello, George Franklin here ....
Fitzgerald!??

Well ... its been awhile. Sure, I'll help if I can. A Mr. Stanley Morris is lost,
you say? But what can I do? You're pretty sure he'd be stoned out in a pub
somewhere, ehh? Sounds like a long shot to me, mate .... OK, OK ... I'll do it.
How can I get back to you ... Roger! ... Got it! Oh, by the way, I hear Lancey's
down to one freighter, and she's out of commission .... Take it easy, Fritz. ... Just
asking. But there are a couple of ugly rumors going around ... Yeh, yeh ... bye."

Stanley Morris, our Chief Engineer, wasn't on the Thursday 3:00 P.M. flight.
It hadn't taken much for Mr. Fitzgerald to confirm that he had been on the
ANSETT flight from Sydney to Cairns, but had never made the connection to the
Air Niugini flight to Port Morseby. "Damn," he cursed to himself," Probably
couldn't handle such a long a gap without something to drink ... oh yeh, I forgot
... flights over Australian air space don't serve liquor. That means he had nothing
from Sydney to Cairns, and the wait for the Air Niugini connection was three
hours ... and no bar at the airport. Must have just about done the poor bastard
in!"

George had to figure out where to look for this Morris bloke. "Couldn't miss
him once I'm in the right pub," he mused, "Not if Fitz's description was at all
accurate." Kind of strange though: only about five stone in weight and 160
centimeters tall, half Maori and showing it, and a full-on alcoholic! "Now, if a
bloke like that was stranded at the airport, what would he do?" George reasoned,
putting himself in Stanley Morris's place. "That's pretty easy to answer: he'd
catch a taxi and ask to be taken to a pub. And where would the taxi take him ...
or better yet, where would he end up? He's a seaman, and Cairn's waterfront
pubs are world famous. So it'd be downtown in the waterfront area. Now, if he

was prone to passing out, there's only a couple of places that would put up with that sort of behavior. Or have a room for him .... I'd put ten quid on it that he's at the old Empire Hotel, down at the end of Abbot Street where it runs into Wharf Street. He'd fit right in with the regulars there, and they have rooms upstairs if he wants to sleep it off or passes out on'em. The Empire it is!"

"Guess Fitz knows what he's talking about after all. For such a small bloke he sure is easy to pick out in a crowd," George chuckled to himself. Stanley ... it must be him, he assumed, from the look of him, was in one corner talking up a storm, entertaining a pair of locals. Maori brown complexion with a definitely bluish-green tint ... Fitz was right on ... a broad, flat nose astride a bushy grey-white mustache, and the little man was so thin and fragile looking that one could surely blow him over backwards with one good puff of bad breath. Mind you, however, you'd have to get past that fiery tongue of his, for it was that part of Stanley's anatomy that the pair of locals were finding so entertaining.

"Mr. Morris, I am terribly sorry to intrude," George interrupted gently, "but you have a plane to catch." George didn't even bother confirming identity, he was so sure.

"The hell you say, matey! And just who in this company of gentlemen might you be? If you can call yourself a gentleman, that is!"

"Sir, please excuse me ... my name is George Franklin, and I've been sent by Mr. Fitzgerald to fetch you and to assist you in making your connecting flight to Rabaul, Papua New Guinea ... you have a ship awaiting you!" George Franklin was playing his role carefully, and all in especially good humor. For one thing, he knew that he would have to win the consent of Stanley's audience. These blokes could get awfully touchy about the rights of their new-found mates. It was a different era, now-days, but this was still Cairns' old waterfront, and the comradeship among sailors meeting here from all around the world ran a deep current indeed.

"You say a ship is awaiting 'fer me?"

"Yes sir. And a fine one it is. The New Guinea Trader herself. And she desperately requires your able expertise as her Chief Engineer."

"Of course I would accept ..." There was a mischievous sparkle to Stanley's blood-shot eyes ... "except that I've just started a good round of drink and I can't possibly leave my new mates here, now can I."

George had read the scene well, and had chosen his words appropriately, for the two locals immediately agreed that Stanley should not turn away from his duty as a seaman and an officer, and such a grand opportunity, despite their selfish desire not to end their socializing with such a fine new fiend. And then George clinched it by adding: "And of course you can continue your round of drink. I'll even join you. And I'll purchase a bottle of Johnny Walker's from the bar and we can continue together until flight time, on the way to the airport." George had been observant enough to note Stanley Morris's drink of preference.

Once settled in George's Mazda sedan, Stanley let out a long sigh, and adjusted his composure. "Thanks for the rescue, mate. Thought I'd never get out of there and back to the airport. Just about out of money too! I'm drunk, but I'm OK, mate."

"This time we'll give you an airlines bag with a couple of bottles of whiskey to carry you over. But you must promise you'll follow through. You've got a couple of hours wait in Moresby too. And the Morseby airport is hell. Think you can do it?"

"Now you just stop right there, matey!! You're talk'in to Chief Engineer Stanley Morris, and I'll have you know I've navigated more airports than you've ever even heard about, young man ... "

George let him ramble on, happy to have directed his fury in the right direction. "Damn, though, the bloke is bloody drunk!" he exclaimed silently to himself.

●   *   *

It had been light for a half-hour or so. I felt full of excitement and surging with energy. Time to get out of this sore-ass bunk and get this adventure *going*! I expected Laurie and Harry, along with Mr. Fitzgerald and Mr. Milner, to be coming aboard very soon. Mr. Fitzgerald would probably have a long list of things to be done in order to be ready to sail. But first, I needed some kau kau. Damn, I already miss those CDW breakfasts. And a 'morning delight' with Deli.

Don't kid yourself, you were almost always too hung over for a 'morning delight'!

Yes, it had been good at the CDW camp. It had been only about a hundred steps from my room to the mess-hall -- and great food. Just about anything a guy could ask for, Aussie style of course. Just loved those morning 'steak and eggs'. Aussies do know how to eat! And for lunch each of us had a cooler which we could load up with sandwiches, fruit, drinks, and whatever else we wanted. The size and weight of that cooler didn't matter either, since each 'white' operator and his machine was assigned a New Guinea boy as a helper. His job was to service the machine, to keep it clean, greased, and fueled up, and generally took care of the operator, which included carting around the lunch cooler. The idea was that we were 'training' these guys, teaching them about basic operations so that some day they could become operators. That would be some day a long ways into the future, was my guess. Maybe training them was the 'plan', but it was total B.S.. We didn't teach them anything. Or even try to. They were just there to be our 'whipping boys'. And while we were paid about a hundred dollars a week, they were paid five. Even Samuel, an experienced operator and a good one, made only ten. It reminded me of what I had heard Mike say one time about the European missionaries: they would pay the New Guinea boys at the mission a half-dollar for a weeks work, then put the fear of god into them at the end of the week and take the half-dollar back! The stories I had heard about New Guinea missionaries ... you could write a book ... they exploited native labor and the local craftmanship for their own selfish gain, and were notorious drunks and lechers, creating little 'empires' out of their plantation mission hide-a-ways.

My boy's name was Tuko. He had told me a few of the things I knew about the missionaries, for he had spent most of his younger years on a Methodist plantation on the western end of the island of New Britain. Tuko was a typical New Guinean: short and lean, with skinny legs and a seemingly over-sized head, and thick lips and black-brown eyes, the whites of which were an unhealthy looking biege color. He flaunted a small pot-belly, as if he habitually enjoyed a dozen or so beers at the end of each work day ... but I knew he didn't. And of course he was black. Very black. With kinky hair cut short and trimmed straight up from around his ears, and the back of his head, so that it looked like he had a round 'birds nest' of matted hair square on top. Newcomers to New Guinea almost always assumed that their kinky hair was wiry and tough, but it wasn't ... it was, in fact, so very soft to the touch, and gently bouncy. I knew that because I knew Deli's hair so well, and because I used to playfully tussle Tuko's on occasion.

Tuko was a joy ... always with a ready, full-on smile (which revealed his fondness for beetel nut) and was a Mr. Johnny-on-the-spot, eager to do whatever I requested. Pidgin was our communicating lingo ... and once I had gotten the hang of it I could understand most of what Tuko said, and could get across just about anything. A few 'non-english' words were necessary, however. For example, if I wanted a drinking coconut, I would say something like: "Hey, Tuko, kiss'em long me all same number one kuulau, pleez." 'Kuulau' was the word for 'coconut'. I would always add please to any request; it was certain to guarantee an instant smile and a quick response. The other 'imported' operators and foremen were not nearly so thoughtful with their boys, except Mike and Walter, but they didn't appreciate them like we did. Too bad. Too bad for the imports.

Anyway, Tuko would jump up ... he was usually squatting on his heels on the side of where I was working, probably bored as hell just watching ... and he would climb a nearby coconut tree in just seconds, with his cane knife clamped between his teeth, and fetch a green coconut, of just the right maturity, with cool refreshing coconut water inside ... not too watery and bland, yet without the strong, dry, bitter taste of a mature nut. I always marvelled at how fast and easily he could scale up a tall tree. If it was near vertical he would resort to 'hugging' the tree and shimmying up with his feet and knees on the side of the trunk. But if the tree had any lean to it at all he would simply walk up the son-of-a-bitch, feet in front of him on the face of the trunk, his arms somehow long enough to reach the back of the trunk. That was Tuko.

I rounded the end of the passageway to the aft deck and stopped abruptly, dead in my tracks. I think I must have gasped or made some sort of funny noise, and my eyes were probably popping out of my skull, for right there in front of me sat this super weird dude just about to poke himself with some sort of giant needle. He looked Aussie, or maybe English, with incredibly thick opaque eye glasses, and was squatting on top of a large steel storage box, which was part of the aft deck. He was poised to inject the inside of his left forearm with the thing -- the longest, largest hypodermic needle and syringe I had ever seen. Or at least that's what I assumed it was. I say I must of made a noise and looked strange, because he was also startled, but then he quickly relaxed and smiled.

"Uhh ... sorry," he raised the syringe and needle a short distance to make it clear what he was referring to, "I'm a diabetic. This is insulin. I have to take an injection every day. Usually just once ... in the morning after breakfast."

"Ohh" My head was nodding slightly, but I wasn't about to accept all this quite yet. Not that I didn't understand about diabetes and insulin shots -- my mother was diabetic. But this scene was just too unexpected and unreal. I still wasn't discounting the notion that he was, perhaps, some sort of heavy duty drug addict, and he was just about to shoot himself up for an all-time high!

"My name's Kevin. I'm your 3rd Engineer."

"3rd Engineer??" Now he had my interest. After an ackward pause, I too sat down.

"My name's Chad." I didn't say I was 2nd Mate; that title was still too new and far too grandiose to announce to anyone, for the time being anyway. But he already knew.

"You're our 2nd Mate, right?"

Okay, the cat was out of the bag. I grinned that dumb grin again. "Yeh, for what it's worth!" I laughed. He smiled, with humor, and I sensed that he knew perfectly well how absurd it was ... me being 2nd Mate, I mean. "Uhh ... do you know anything about diesels?" What I knew about Harry's abilities, and the story about our Chief Engineer ... it had me worried.

"Yes," he answered, with the air of a person who suddenly found himself comfortably back on his own turf. "I haven't had a lot a marine experience, but I think I'm a pretty good diesel mechanic."

"Damn, am I glad to hear that!" And I was. "You see, your 2nd Engineer is my buddy, Harry ... but Harry doesn't know jack shit about diesels. Although he'll tell you otherwise."

Oh yes, he'll tell you otherwise!!

"And I understand our Chief Engineer is a total alcoholic who was hired just because we need a Chief Engineer with papers. Glad to have you aboard. I stuck out my hand. "Where are you from?"

"England. And you? You sound American ... or Canadian?"

"Canadian ... yeh ... I'm from Canada ... western part." It had become a habit of mine to stress that I was from Western Canada, so that no one would expect me to speak French. Not that I had anything against speaking French. I dearly wished that I could. But while everyone else was learning French in high school, like a dumb ass I chose German instead. Especially dumb because my class was full of 1st and 2nd generation German immigrants, and I had one hell of a time trying to get passing grades.

"Well, I need to grab some kau kau. Talk to you later ... How did you get aboard, by the way?"

"One of the Guinea boys brought me over," and he motioned in the direction of our neighboring dry dock.

I nodded. I hadn't thought of that as an alternative.

As I turned towards the transom I noticed the Seagull outboard tied to the railing. It was wet. "Did you get the outboard running?" I asked, turning back to Kevin.

"No ... couldn't get the bloody thing to fire up ... but I'm working on it!"

I shrugged and smiled. That was kinda what I had expected. "Well, it *is* a Seagull. Good luck!" For some reason I had a flashing premonition that this Seagull outboard was going to be a serious problem for us, sometime in the future.

Kevin nodded, glad to see that I understood.

I found something to eat at one of the tiny roadside stands on Kokopo Road, near the intersection with Mango Street. This one was run by an old hap-caste woman, with three pikinini kids running around nearby on the loose ... only the little girl had anything on, and that was only a dirty, one-piece sack blouse. I didn't choose much to eat, just a couple of bananas and a bowl of rice porridge ... more a soup than a 'porridge', with small bits of vegetables and an egg poached directly in the bowl's hot water. It had become a stand-by favorite of mine when I didn't have access to the CDW mess. Like when I had gotten stuck into the booze after work and had ended up being too late for dinner.

I returned back to the dinghy just in time to meet Mr. Fitzgerald and the next segment of our illustrious crew to come aboard, namely big-mouth Harry himself, and Laurie, and Mr. Milner. All four 'gentlemen' were dressed in short sleeve shirts and shorts, and all except Harry wore knee socks, folded at the top just above the calves, and shoes. They looked kind of sharp, the three of them that is, like they were dressed to go to a cricket match or the Sydney horse races. Mr. Fitzgerald and Mr. Milner had both chosen dark blue shorts and a white shirt, which gave them the appearance of naval officers ... very fitting. Laurie had overdone it a bit, with the socks and shoes and especially his shirt -- a brightly colored floral print, the kind that is cut straight at the bottom with no tails and is meant to be worn outside, Polynesian style. Harry and I were the slobs of the group, or were at least the most casual. We were used to having to wear high, heavy work boots on the job, so rubber thongs were a delight and the preferred choice when not working. Our casual choice of clothes was also dictated by what was available in the local shops, which were typically modest little one-room affairs closely fronting the roadway of a Rabaul street and were almost always a part of or just in front of a home residence. All were owned and operated by local Chinese, who were Hokien immigrants from southern China, one or two generations removed. I knew this because I had stayed with a Chinese family for a few days when I had first arrived in Rabaul. Anyway, all the clothes and footwear were Hong Kong made and were only available in a limited choice of colors and even less of a choice of style. Shoes were definitely a luxury. But then again, we were in an out-of-the-way corner of the world, and at four degrees latitude south of the equator our normal garb was the practical choice. For the New Guinea boys as well, if they worked in Rabaul. Of course the lap-lap was the standard in the villages ... usually the waist style lap-lap for both sexes, except that the ladies were now-a-days becoming more modest and preferred the longer lap-lap worn above the breasts. Too bad, because that really spoiled the scenery.

"So, what are you looking at?" Laurie wanted to know. I was staring at his polished shoes. Harry understood what I was thinking, and was of course grinning.

"Ohh, nothing, Laurie." And then I submitted to a mischievous urge, and a way to circumvent the certain embarrassment of exposing my ineptness at the oars: "By the way, I think the quartermaster is the one who does the rowing ... isn't that right, Mr. Fitzgerald?"

"That's right, Chad," he smiled. "If he can handle it, that is."

Laurie only grunted. But he was half-smiling as well, and he promptly placed himself in position to row, once we had loaded their rather large suitcases.

Good move, Chad. See, you're not nearly as dumb as you look ... thank god!

But Laurie surprised us all, for he handled those oars just fine. I was more than just a little jealous.

Once on the Trader's aft deck, Mr. Fitzgerald announced that we would have a meeting in the officer's mess immediately. I was given the job of summoning the Captain and Kevin, which took but a couple of minutes ... the Captain was in his cabin and Kevin was down in the engine room, looking things over.

"Gentlemen, if you haven't already met, please introduce yourselves. This is your Captain, Mr. Frank Patterson, and your First Officer, Mr. John Milner. And of course you all know me – I'm Robert Fitzgerald. I am the agent acting on behalf of the ship's owner, Lancey Shipping Company, and I am responsible for putting the ship's crew together and seeing you off on your voyage to Hong Kong. The purpose of the trip, again I am sure you are all aware, is to put the vessel into drydock for repair and a refit. The rest of the crew will be boarding shortly. For now I would like to make sure that you two, Harry, and Kevin, start working on those engines. One 'head' for the auxillary is being delivered sometime this morning. We need that auxillary running as soon as possible. Without it we have no electricity, no water pressure, no refrigeration, and of course no compressed air for starting the main engines. Your Chief Engineer is arriving today. And I would like you two, Chad and Laurie, to work under Mr.

Milner and survey the ships lifesaving and navigation eaquipment. That's all for now. We'll have another meeting later when the others board."

●   *   *

Stanley Morris wasn't feeling well at all. The Johnny Walker definitely wasn't mixing well with recent events. The wait-over at Morseby had been hell. "What a shit-ass airport," he reflected. It had been hot and crowded and there had been no air conditioning in the terminal building. Papuans and New Guineans had been pushing and shoving in every direction, with no place to sit down, and Stanley had been very aware of the shifty looks directed towards him and his luggage by a few of the 'boys'. He had felt very uncomfortable indeed. And then the plane trip itself was bumpy as hell, with the small Dash 7 prop plane flying low over the mountainous terrain, jostling against the turbulent air.

Even though his stomach was not faring well, and a persistant nausea pulsated from his mid-section, he could not help but appreciate that he was flying over some unusual landscape. His was a window seat and the white, pillowing clouds were scattered thinly, offering full views of the scene below. He observed an open vista of deep-green mountains and clear blue sea, with spots of lighter shades of green to indicate shoals and coral reefs … the shoreline was laced with intermittant bands of light-tan colored beaches or rocky cliffs, and with differing lengths of narrow, flowing white lines to mark incoming surf. He could see that he was flying over a long island with a high mountainous range running along its center. He knew from the Air Niugini tourist map that this was the island of New Britain. It was very long, for neither end was visible, but he could see the deep blue ocean on both sides, and judged that the island couldn't be more that fourty kilometers wide at the most.

"What a switch from Morseby!" he mused. Port Morseby had been little more than an eyesore to Stanley. On the incoming flight from Cairns he had had an unencumbered arial view of the town and surrounding area, and he had been disappointed by the sight of denuded hills and a seemingly treeless city. As far as he could see towards the interior and along the coast in both the west and easterly directions the hilly topography appeared dry and parched. Stanley didn't appreciate that type of countryside, for he was fond of the rich, cool greenness of his native New Zealand. He was half Maori, and all Kiwi, despite the Aussie half of his genes donated by a father he had never seen. Whether returning home to Auckland by sea or by air, which had occurred many times during his long sea-faring career, he had always felt an immense joy when first glimpsing the golf-course-green patchwork of the sheep paddocks and the gentle groves of deciduous trees which so predominated the North Island's rural landscape.

The stewardess announced that they were descending into Rabaul, and Stanley shifted his attention to studying his new port of departure. He urgently needed a more stable environment, and a couple of good, strong drinks, but the panorama unfolding beneath him caught his breath. What he saw was a vast natural harbor on the south-east tip of the eastern end of the island, shaped like an upside-down woman's boot, actually formiing two harbors instead of one. The toe portion protruded more deeply into the green of the peninsula, and he could make out the outline of a town stretched along the shoreline of the 'toes' end. He saw that there were two, three, no, four ships in the harbor. The heel portion of the upside-down boot formed a second harbor, but there was no town on its coastline nor ships anchored in its waters. As the plane descended, details became even clearer.

Everywhere on land was intense green. He could make out large areas of coconut trees near the shore and on the mountain range's lower slopes and plains, and above that appeared to be thick tropical rainforest. The landscape was so dazzlingly green and picturesque that he was almost willing to concede that it might run a close match to New Zealand. Almost! The airport runway became visible, and he could now see that there was actually a third part to the harbor: a small, round body of water that projected out from the forefoot, or front of the ankle of the upside-down boot ... so formed because of a volcano having formed in the harbor, connected to the mainland by a long neck of land. And that was where the airport runway was located. The town itself was fully visible now, and Stanley was surprised that it was laid out so rectangularly, its streets straight and perpendicular to each other and lined with trees. The Air Niugini brochure had named Rabaul "the second prettiest town in the South Pacific", next to Madang. "Reckon Madang must *really* be something!" he whistled to himself.

But it was the marine portion of the picture below that pleased him the most. Despite being a harbor, the water was a lucid blue-green throughout. He could see that the segmented stretches of beach and lines of surf continued well into the harbor's interior. A ship's wharf was clearly visible, and the four vessels began to take on character. Two were tied up at the pier, a third anchored close by, and a fourth farther down the shore next to a couple of small drydocks. That fourth one didn't look too healthy: small and rusty looking, sitting low in the water and with a very definite list to one side. "One of those must be the New Guinea Trader," he whispered to himself again, searching for a clue. "Sure hope it's not the rusty one with the bad list!"

A freckled gentleman of medium height and build, but with an unmistakable air of authority -- and a missing left hand -- approached Stanley just as he picked up his two bags and stepped outside the small baggage claim area of the two-room, single-story terminal.

"Mr. Morris, I presume," spoke the man, not without humor.

"Mr. Stanley Morris it is, and you must be Mr. Fitzgerald," Stanley returned, a little shakily. He was definitely needing a drink.

Mr. Fitzgerald was amused by this strange looking little fellow, but he was a bit perplexed as well. "My God," he thought to himself, "Will he make it? And is he always that greenish color?"

"Mr. Morris, we can stop at the Cosmopolitan Hotel for awhile. We can have a couple of drinks and I can go over what we expect of you. Besides, I need to meet part of our crew there. Our native boys, three of them.

"That'd be fine," Stanley answered, thinking that it would be wonderful indeed.

Mr. Fitzgerald parked the Toyota which he had decided to rent from the Avis agency at the airport, and they entered the bar entrance of the hotel. The bar had an open-air lanai section, which was on the ocean side, and if you sat in just the right corner you could look through the iron-woods of the park-like hotel grounds and make out the New Guinea Trader. She was anchored far enough around the curve of Simpson Harbor to afford a view of her from off her port quarter bow.

"There she is, Mr. Morris," Mr. Fitzgerald pointed in between the tall iron-woods.

There wasn't any question about which vessel Mr. Fitzgerald was referring to.

"Mr. Fitzgerald, it appears to me that your New Guinea Trader has a very noticable list to her."

"Yes, I'm afraid you're right." Mr. Fitzgerald responded without humor.

"She has a full load of scrap iron, which I'm afraid was poorly loaded. But not to worry … the load is secure and the vessel's sound."

Stanley was still not easy about this. He knew little about the ship and its owners, except a reference by an old shipmate he'd had a few drinks with before leaving Auckland. "A fly-by-night outfit, Lancey Shipping Company is," he had warned.

As if sensing Stanley's concern, Mr. Fitzgerald went on. "She's a pre-World War II Dutch tanker -- 500 tons. We converted the tanks to holds and rigged the center mast when we acquired her, some fifteen years ago. This will be her second trip to Hong Kong for a refit."

Stanley gazed at her from the distance. He could see that, yes, she was about 500 ton load capacity, was about forty-five meters in length with an aft positioned, three level cabin structure, and a single mast halfway between the steering house and the raised fo'scle at the bow. Must have two holds, he surmised, the central mast serving both. And the engineroom would be aft, below-decks. Perhaps her design *was* seaworthy, with a high, proud bow. An ex-tanker, though. Probably is flat-bottomed, and tends to roll a lot, he guessed.

Well, never mind, I don't have any choice now, do I, he thought. Jobs came scarce now, and this was better that staying in Auckland, living off the dole.

Stanley was about to order his fourth scotch when three young men entered the bar patio from the outside, visibly ill at ease. They were all dark, but he judged that they were of mixed race, especially evident with the tall skinny one, too tall and fair to be New Guinean, and with straight hair that was cut in a most bizarre fashion ... shaved close to his scalp execpt for about a five centimeter wide strip down the center and to the back of his head, like a freshly manicured mock orange hedge.

"Come and sit down, boys." Mr. Fitzgerald had seen them as well. They hesitated, then came forward and sat at the table adjacent to Mr. Fitzgerald's and Stanley's, still appearing shy and uncomfortable.

There was something about the tall one that Stanley didn't like, more than just his strange haircut.

"I'm sorry, sir," the youngest looking of the three spoke out. "But they usually don't allow us in this bar." He was the shortest of the three as well as the youngest, but he was well proportioned and looked very fit. He was an attractive young man, his complexion almost as fair as the tall skinny one's, and his eyes were almond shaped.

"Oh, I'm very sorry." Mr. Fitzgerald's face reddened slightly and for just a second he lost his authoritative composure. "I'd forgotten about that. But I'm sure no one will mind. Anyway, it's early in the day and we're in the outside patio. We'll only be a minute."

"Stanley, this young man is Joseph, and this is Richard, and Frederick." He had motioned first to the youngest, then to the tall skinny bloke, then to the third -- a man who was older and darker skinned than the other two -- but he had a quiet, knowing look about him and, like Joseph, was solidly constructed and in seemingly excellent physical condition. Stanley shook their hands, again feeling the least at ease with the tall one. Looks like a trouble-maker, if you ask me, he thought.

Mr. Fitzgerald didn't want to test the hotel's acceptance of the newcomers, so at this point he suggested they load the three's luggage into the Toyota and head for the Trader.

Little was spoken en route, and it was Frederick who took up the oars on the dinghy. Mr. Fitzgerald again summoned a meeting in the officer's mess.

The officer's mess was positioned on the main deck in the most forward part of the ship's cabin superstructure, on the starboard side. It was a fairly large room, maybe eight feet by sixteen, and featured a long oval table with a curved, cushioned bench seat stretching the full length behind, and arc'd around the two ends. The woodwork was old and poorly maintained, but was impressive never-the-less, with fine Scandinavian styling and workmanship, done in dark mahogany.

Laurie and I entered together; we had spent the last couple of hours checking out the Trader's two lifeboats. Harry and Kevin were there, already grimy from working on the auxillary. Somehow it gave me joy seeing Harry like that. We jostled each other coming through the narrow doorway, and I gave Laurie a nudge on seeing the fellow who I supposed was our Chief Engineer, sitting behind the table directly opposite the passageway.

Jeeses, can this really be our Chief Engineer?

He was so small looking behind that table, maybe only about a hundred pounds or so, and he couldn't have stood much more than five foot four, judging from the height of his head above the table. Not as old as the Captain, maybe, but he was well aged ... grey showing in his hair and with a brown Maori face, kinda pudgy and with a whitened mustache. And his coloring ... it was definitely not healthy ... sort of a mixture of greens and blues mixed in with the Maori brown.

The three hap-castes were standing to the left. I glanced them over, and was startled by the realization that I had seen the tall one before. No forgetting that Mohawk haircut! His eyes met mine, and there was a fleeting, subtle acknowledgement, but nothing else. He had been one of the 'gang' of hap-castes who had attempted to harass us 'hoops' at Auntie Frietas a couple of times. On one occassion he and several others had thrown stones at the sleeping room where Deli and I were crashing. But Auntie Freita had yelled at them and they had promptly taken off. For some reason she wielded a lot of power over them. So, no big deal. It was OK, I just knew I might have to be careful with this guy.

I didn't recognize the other two, but I felt comfortable with them as a first impression. The shortest and youngest looked like a 'good kid' and the other, the older of the three, had the appearance of an able sort; a hard worker judging from his hands and legs.

Standing there waiting for Mr. Fitzgerald to speak, I thought about our hap-castes. Theirs was a tough lot. Regardless of their mixture, whether it was New Guinean with

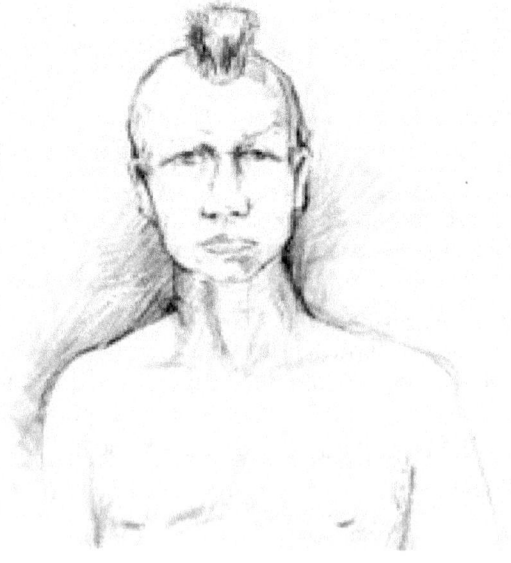

Chinese or with white, they were outcasts from either side. Or so it seemed. Yeh, hap-caste and out-cast could be almost synonymous. They were usually thought of as a sultry, moody lot, with a chip-on-their-shoulder attitude, and they stuck together. I guess it would seem an oddity that you didn't see Chinese-white mixtures. But the Chinese and white males fooled around with the New Guinean 'maris' ... a lot ... but there were no white girls around for the Chinese men to chase after, and the Chinese girls kept very much to themselves and married only Chinese. They especially avoided a white guy if it was known he chased after maris or, in other words, he was a 'hoop'.

Mr. Fitzgerald orchestrated the introductions and went over what he had told us in the earlier meeting, for the benefit of the new arrivals. We all met Mr. Stanley Morris, our Chief Engineer, of course. And we were informed that Joseph and Frederick would be the second and third quartermasters, and that Richard would be our cook. I took a start at that, wondering what caliber of cook he would make. I didn't feel easy about trusting my food supply to a Mohawk haircut. Mr. Fitzgerald then pulled out a written 'punch list' from his briefcase, which was a list of items that we all needed to work on in order to ready the Trader for departure.

"Gentlemen, I want to emphasize that we need to be shipshape and seaworthy. For your own safety and to ensure the success of the voyage. I might also point out that our Harbor Master has made it very clear that he will not allow this vessel out of the harbor until we satisfy him in this respect and he will be coming aboard for inspection. I will post this list on the bulletin board." He pointed to a section of wall at the far port-end of the table. Please return to your work. Of course we don't need 'quartermasters' while anchored in port, so I would like you, Frederick, to give a hand in the engineroom, and you, Joseph, to help Chad and Laurie and later Richard. As for you, Richard, come back ashore with me now and we'll put together some emergency food supplies. Thank you gentlemen."

Laurie and I paused in the passageway at the bottom of the flight of steps leading up to the second deck, waiting for Mr. Milner to join us. He had suggested that we take the ship's two lifeboats out of their 'chocks' and test them in the water, starting right after the meeting. And now we would have Joseph as an extra hand to help us. Harry was right behind us, and stopped to join us, grinning through his newly acquired film of black dirt and grease -- which unfortunately did not interfere with his favorite facial expression.

"Well, Canuck ... we have a full crew now. Hong Kong, here we come!"

"Yeh," I shrugged, indicating that, yes, I guess we do have some sort of a crew. But I was not so sure about reaching Hong Kong.

"Harry, I was thinking about what you were telling us last night." I glanced back towards the officer's mess to make sure no one was coming our way, and I lowered my voice. "I'm a little concerned about the 'navigation' part ... you mentioned that the Captain said some things that didn't 'make sense' ... what?"

Harry chuckled, and leaned closer towards us, also lowering his volume of speech. "Our noble Captain was bragging that he could ... get this ... 'navigate by the color of the water'!"

"What??"

Harry straightened up, and turned to continue on his way to the engine room.

"I shit you not!" He laughed loudly, and disappeared down the steps to the engineroom.

Laurie and I exchanged expressions of disbelief.

Jeeses, I wondered to myself. This is our crew?? Three hap-castes, one with a crazy 'Mohawk' haircut, a diabetic third engineer, a second engineer who doesn't know anything about diesel engines, an alcoholic Chief Engineer who looks like he couldn't hold up the correct end of an double-ended wrench, a navigation officer who doesn't even know what a cosine is, a madman for a 1st Mate, and a Captain who ... navigates by the color of the water!

CHAPTER THREE

Just a whoop'in and a holler'in !

"Time you go long way long sea
Sun or rain no hurt'em me
Me sorry too much long you
Suppose you no love long me no more"

Laurie and Joseph pulled on the two separate block and tackle lines, watching each other closely in an attempt to coordinate their efforts.

'Damn, the bugger's heavy," I muttered to myself, under my breath. We glanced at each other, and Mr. Milner. He had a worried look on his face, but gave a nod. They gave a second, harder pull ... and a third. There was a ripping, tearing sound, and the lifeboat suddenly broke free and jumped upwards several inches, bobbing slightly against the ropes and exposing two narrow bands around the hull where she had sat in her 'chocks' ... the paint not on the hull anymore, but left behind on the wooden supports, leaving bare, damaged wood in view.

I think we're in trouble, guys!!" I couldn't help but let out a worried chuckle as I said it. Mr. Milner did not share my propensity for humor, and turned away from the lifeboat long enough to give me a brief, sullen stare. Not really a hostile expression, more like a subtle admonition to shut up and be thinking about a solution. Laurie just stood there, visibly distressed. Joseph didn't know what to do, or think, and so he just waited solemnly for further instructions.

The two lifeboats were nice looking craft, double-enders with lap-strake hulls in the North Sea tradition, about fourteen feet long with slightly turned up ends and low freeboard at midships. Upon climbing up to the poop deck and removing their protective tarps we had found that they were well stocked with lifesaving necessities, except that items like the drinking water and emergency food rations hadn't been renewed for a very long time. But in each was a compass and riggings for a sail, even a chart of Papua New Guinea waters. Mr. Fitzgerald's instructions had been to put the two vessels in the water and demonstrate their seaworthiness. We had been told that this was a prime concern of the Harbor Master's.

"Well, let's swing her out and lower her into the water and see if she'll stay afloat."

Fat chance, the wood's rotted all the way through in spots!

Laurie and Joseph didn't hesitate, regardless of what any of us were thinking, and so we proceeded to follow orders. Lowering the boat was going to be easy; we had intentionally chosen the starboard side -- the side that the Trader was leaning towards -- for just this reason. Mr. Milner had voiced concern about lowering the port lifeboat. With a 4 degrees list it would be hell keeping the boat away from the Trader's sloping side while lowering her down. For a second I visualized the situation as if we were actually abondoning ship, say in stormy seas or while being tossed about on an unchartered reef.

Jeeses!!

And so Laurie and Joseph lowered the lifeboat to the water -- and then we all watched as it slowly filled with seawater and submerged. That is, submerged except for a couple of inches of her gunwales sticking above the water. After all, she was a wooden craft and had *some* buoyancy.

The four of us were leaning over the rail of the upper deck, peering down towards the water:

Laurie: "Not very seaworthy, I reckon."

Chad: "A little hard to row like that, but might keep the sharks out!

Joseph: He kept his mouth shut.

Mr. Milner: "Damn!"

"Well, let's lift her out of the water, for now ... I've got to check out our navigation equipment. Joseph, why don't you see what you can do to help your mate make the kitchen ready for use. It needs a thorough cleaning."

"Mr. Milner," I started, as Laurie and Joseph proceeded to lift the unfortunate vessel out of the water, "I have an idea. Can Laurie and I do some scouting around?"

"Go ahead, do whatever you like." There was no doubt Mr. Milner viewed the lifeboat's condition as unsalvagable, and a serious setback.

"You know, Laurie, I saw a whole bunch of paint and stuff up in the bow of the ship -- you call that the foc'sle, right?"

"Hell if I know," he replied. He was feeling down

"Now, let's see what we've got. Here's some white paint, maybe for the outside hull. And here's some linseed oil putty ... kinda hard and dry, but we can probably use it. And here's some really thick grey paint. Let's try to patch her up.

Laurie started to understand what I was getting at, and slowly began to show some enthusiasm. "Hey, just might work. Let's give her a try! Wish we had some fiberglass and resin, though. Then we could do a proper job."

"Like repairing a surfboard, right."

"You got it!"

"Trouble is, I don't think there's any materials like that in all of Rabaul." I wasn't trying to be pessimistic, I was just expressing what I knew would be true. Hard to find much of anything in Rabaul. Besides, working with fiberglass and polyester resin was kind of a new thing. "Have you seen a surfshop around?"

Laurie laughed, "No, I guess you're right."

We had just started assembling the various materials together on the upper deck when we heard voices and a lot of noise coming from shore. Six New Guinea boys were loading a bulky metal object into the heavy, wooden rowboat owned by the neighboring drydock. I recognized one of them as the boy who had lent me the diving goggles. Harry and Fred were at the Trader's stern, watching apprehensively.

"Looks like we're getting the head for the auxiliary," I speculated.

We watched for a few minutes, marvelling that they actually got the thing to the Trader without losing it in the water. Harry was almost jumping up and down with excitement.

Take it easy, Harry!

Laboriously, Laurie and I pulled on the ropes to hoist the lifeboat back to the upper deck, where it would be easier to work on. It was wet, so we did what we could to get rid of the surplus water and allowed time for it to dry out. Meanwhile we were able to scrape off the paint and dig out the soft wood in the spots where it was rotten, in preparation for the putty and new paint. Once dry, we first filled the holes and areas we had dug out with putty, applying it from the exterior and trying our best to blend with the original surface. We then painted over our patchwork with the white paint, which was god-awful thick and very old, but it seemed a fairly close match and the result didn't look half bad, especially if you stood back a bit. I had the idea of painting the entire interior with the grey paint, which was even thicker and more ancient that the white. My intent was to give the whole inside a coating to fill any cracks or small holes and block any potential leaks. Laurie went along with the proposal.

We finally reached the point where we felt we could try putting the vessel back in the water … once the paint had dried.

"But you realize that this is only a temporary patch at best, even if it doesn't leak when we set her in the water, right?" I was testing to see if Laurie understood that this was strictly a bullshit repair job.

"You don't think it would hold if we had to use her?"

"No way, guy ... half an hour in the water and that putty and paint would come all apart!"

"But we're never going to have to use it anyway. Right!" Laurie was feeling good about our efforts, and very optimistic about the success of our voyage-to-be.

"If you say so, buddy." His attitude was OK by me and I'm just naturally optimistic anyway.

Yeh, one very optimistic fool*!*

The sun was dipping towards Tunnel Hill once again. There was the evening to look forward to. It seemed everyone had their place of choice to go. Harry and I were destined for Walter's. I was looking forward to a few cool ones, and my eighty bucks ... and watching Walter's wife. We asked Laurie if he'd like to join us, but he had a party to go to with some Burns Philip people, and declined.

"How's Kevin to work with?" I asked, as we started walking the ten blocks or so to Walter's, on Kuanua Street, one block from Queen Elizabeth Park.

"Good. I think he's an OK mechanic, I'll have to admit. And I'm glad we have Fred with us -- he's a fair hand too."

I was feeling better about our engine-room situation already. "How about Mr. Morris?"

At that Harry let out a loud snort: "Huhh!! What a joke that useless piece of shit is!" Harry was now vivid. Very vivid. "You know, he refused to even go down into the engine room. Said he didn't need to. Just asked us what make and model the diesels were ... that sort of thing. Then gave us some horseshit advice. Didn't tell us anything we didn't already know ... then left us and went up to the wheelhouse to dive into the booze with the Captain."

"And the auxiliary? Do you think you'll get it running?" I was thinking about the future of my food supply.

"No worries, mate!! No problem there. We'll have it running sometime in the morning."

"Really, Harry?" I wanted to test whether this was more Harry B.S., or was dinky die for a change.

"I shit you not!"

"Hey, Harry ... quit stealing my lines, OK!" I laughed.

Don't know why I like this dumb ass, but in some weird way I do.

We picked up a couple of cases of 'South Pacific' on the way -- it wouldn't be cool to show up empty handed.

It was about the third beer and the party was OK. Of course that was expected, for Walter was always good company -- a ton of jokes and just plain good humor. You wouldn't expect that from the man upon first meeting him; he was a big, rough-looking guy, standing a full six foot two, with wide shoulders and massive, calloused hands, and moved as if he was always expecting someone to take a swing at him. Beneath that macho exterior, however, was a ready-charged laugh and a soft heart. You knew instinctively that once this man was your friend he was your friend forever, but you had better not cross him.

And of course Harry was entertaining us with more of his usual generic bull. I was still trying to improve my relationship with Walter's five-year-old, but I was facing an uphill battle. Finally, there was Walter's wife to watch ... discreetly of course.

"Hey, Walter!" Harry had pulled out an Aussie Marlboro and was tapping it lightly on the table in front of him, which signalled to me that he had ended one string of B.S. and was about to explore another. "Are you missing any sticks of dynamite?" Harry was grinning at me again. I squirmed and rolled my eyes.

Oh, oh ... shut up, Harry ...just shut up!

"No ... why?"

"Cause Canuck had a few sticks in his Hadson. Now they're on the Trader."

"Bullshit, Harry!!" I didn't appreciate him bringing up about the dynamite sticks. Besides, he didn't *know* they were on the Trader.

"Canuck ... You still have some sticks of my dynamite?" Walter was referring to an incident a month ago when he had asked me to help him with a couple of boxes of dynamite which he needed in order to break up a few boulders we had run into on the Kokopo Road extension. He had asked me to bring them out in my Hadson. So I had casually loaded up the two boxes of sticks and a small carton of caps. He had gone completely ballistic when I reached the job site and he saw that I had placed the caps directly on top of the boxes of dynamite. "You crazy fool," he had exploded in his German accent, "You trying to kill yourself ... and us??" After he had hurriedly removed the dynamite and caps from my back seat ... caps first, carefully ... and had cooled down, he had literally come apart with laughter. For a full week I was his favorite joke ... the dumb ass Canuck who carried two boxes of dynamite with a carton of caps right on top in the back seat of his old Hadson, and had driven for twenty miles on the bumpy Kokopo Road. I was 'one crazy son-of-a-bitch', he would exclaim, the German accent making it sound funny as hell. So I had been a star for a few days.

"Walter, I don't have any sticks of dynamite!" I had decided to play innocent and let everyone think Harry was bullshitting. Shouldn't be hard to do, I figured.

"Chad, don't lie ... I saw those four sticks in your car."

Oh, now its four *sticks*!

"I don't know what you're talking about, Harry. . and besides, 'I don't have to show you no stink'in badge'!"

At that Harry burst into full laughter. "I don't have to show you no stinkin badge!" he repeated. And laughed some more. It was an inside joke … one of Harry's standard lines. He had repeated this particular one to me about a thousand times when we were drinking together at the Cosmos. He claimed it was a Humphrey Bogart line. Something about one of his movies in which he was a Mexican bandito posing as a sheriff. And when his status as sheriff was challenged by the good guy American hero, his reply was "I don't gotta show you no stink'in badge." I really don't know if the scene and the line are for real, or Harry was making it up. I'm lousy with movie trivia, and that one must be pretty old. Only Bogart line I do remember is "Here's looking at you, kid" I used that one a couple of times. It was about as clever as "What's a nice girl like you doing in a place like this?" About as effective too.

Anyway, Harry thought the Mexican bandit line was one of the greatest. And I was searching for a way around this dynamite business. It worked. Harry just had to explain the movie scene. And he cracked up over and over. Walter got bored, didn't know what the hell he was talking about, and walked away with a shrug and a shake of his head. And I grabbed the opportunity to play at chasing after Anita when she had stuck out her tongue again … she raced away, this time squealing with delight, with me running after her just far enough to get away from Harry.

About the time I was looking for yet another diversion, Mike showed up.

"Mike, tell these guys about your recent experience in the boonies," I requested, once Mike had a South Pacific in his hand and had settled in. It took a bit of prodding and a couple of false starts, then he finally got into the meat of it.

"You wouldn't believe the forest we were working in. It was genuine virgin rainforest, with the largest trees I've ever seen" And Mke had seen a lot of New Guinea forest, for he had spent a year and a half in the 'mainland' mountains prospecting for gold. His story was an incredible account of how he and his partner had contracted malaria … his partner had died and Mike had somehow travelled on foot, in a malaria delirium, for over a hundred kilometers through wild forest and untresspassed jungle to finally reach a village on the coast … and some quinine tablets.

"It was like the forests you see pictures of, or read about. The trees were so tall that the underside of their canopy of branches and leaves was about twenty meters from the ground. There was almost no vegetation on the ground itself, except for the tree trunks, and those were far apart, at least fifteen meters or more, so it was easy to walk through. The canopy was so thick that at mid-day it was dark underneath, like it was twilight. It felt safe walking through that kind of forest, because there was no bush or thick grass on the ground ... except that you felt like something might drop down on you from above, like maybe a giant snake. The forest covered a wide area, sort of in groves ... there would be open spots where there were no tall trees and the vegetation would be low, and then the virgin forest would start again. I felt bad about us building a road through there, and destroying part of it." But then he shrugged, meaning that that decision was out of his control.

"But that isn't the best part. One day when we were right in the middle of the forest we were suddenly surrounded by about a dozen of the most hori looking New Guineans you could imagine. They were short, naked except for a small loin-cloth made of animal skins, and they carried spears and bows and arrows. Their hair was long and matted, sticking out in all directions, and they were heavily tattooed and painted."

"Did any have a bone in their nose?" It sounded like a dumb question, and it was, but I could imagine some pretty wild looking New Guinea natives.

"Yeh," he chuckled, "Come to think of it, a couple did have bones in their noses. It was pretty obvious that they were cannibals, and my boys were scared out of their minds. They didn't know what to do, they just bunched together, nervous as hell. But it was the strangest thing ... the cannibals were talking, and making motions with their hands ... they wanted food. So we opened our packs and gave them everything we had. Quickly, I might add! And then the most fascinating thing happened. A couple of them started licking the arms of my boys."

"Licking their arms?" Harry wasn't sure he heard right.

"Yeh, licking their arms. They were starving for salt!"

"Salt??" It was Harry again.

"Yes, salt! As soon as we understood that, I opened my pack to give them my container of table salt. They went crazy over it, passing it among themselves and gobbling up the contents. And I had some of our regular salt tablets, so I gave them those too. You could tell they were grateful, the way they made motions and all, but they took everything we had offered, and just as suddenly as they had appeared they were gone. After they left my boys were all excited, jabbering away with each other. And they wanted to get out of that forest, fast. They were still plenty scared."

"Where do you think they came from? I questioned, again reflecting that this was another dumb question.

"From high in the mountains, most likely." Mike didn't think it was a dumb question. "High up they probably wouldn't have any source for salt. They were probably coming down to the ocean in search of food, and to get salt."

A fascinating place, I was thinking. In many ways I was sad to be leaving this 'land of the unexpected'.

Walter had rejoined us. "Ya, I've heard the same kind of story before. But those horis could have killed you for food, too. You were lucky."

"So, you blokes are leaving on the freighter? Walter changed the direction of conversation, and waited for confirmation.

"Yup, I guess so," I answered.

"So, you are going to throw a goodbye party, then?"

Harry and I looked at each other. We hadn't thought about that one, but I knew what he was thinking. Harry was too tight-fisted to want to spend money on a party. Actually, I was of the same mind. We needed whatever we had for the trip, and beyond. I hadn't saved any money while working for CDW. None at all. I was just living payday to payday. My final double paycheck and the money for the Hadson was all I had.

"So?" I could tell that Walter was expecting us to say yes, and the pause was irritating him.

'No, Walter," I started, "We can't. We can't afford to. We gotta hang on to what we've got. We don't have much, right Harry?" I urgently needed some support.

"I don't have anything to spend on a party," Harry probed cautiously. "Hell, I'm just about broke." I knew that was a lie.

"Walter's irritation was growing, quickly. "What do you mean? You're leaving Rabaul, and you won't give a party. What kind of fuckers, are you." Now he was pissed, and showing it. "You come to my parties -- you think it doesn't cost me money ... now it's your turn."

"Oh, oh," I raised my hands, trying to offer an explanation: "Walter, you gotta understand. We don't know what's in store for us. We might end up stranded in Hong Kong, or somewhere else."

"OK ... OK ... if that's the kind of blokes you are!" And with that he shoved out a wad of Australian dollar bills. "Here's your money for the Hadson ... you two are my friends, but I think you should have a goodbye party ... I don't like it!"

Oh boy!

After that scene I sure didn't want to stay around. So I stuck it out long enough to make an exit gracefully. Hell, I was headed for Auntie Freita's anyway. I said goodbye to Walter's wife.

"Sorry about Walter," she tried to consol me, "You're welcome here anytime, Chad, and goodbye."

I sure wanted to give the lady a kiss. But I settled for a last chase after her daughter, and left ... leaving the echo of the young girl's squeals behind.

"Not good!" I was talking out loud to myself.

Sometimes it's the only way I can get intelligent conversation!

I felt terrible about Walter ... I didn't want to leave Rabaul with a bad feeling between myself and a guy like him. I liked and respected the man too much. He and Mike were the only white guys here that shared my sensitivity towards the New Guineans. That part was important. Their compassion showed in the way they treated their native crews. They spoke expanded pidgin with their men, not the simplified, 'broken English' that guys like myself and Harry used, but real pidgin with a substantial vocabulary of 'Tolai' words (the tribe local to Rabaul and the surrounding area was Tolai, with some Baining). They would joke and play with their 'boys', and were always considerate of their work load and sympathetic to their problems and needs. The result was that their boys loved them, and worked hard for them. And of course Walter had married a hap-caste.

Yes, not good. It seemed that I was repeatedly getting myself into this kind of situation. It reminded me of my time with Dennis. Dennis Macleod, my 'ol travelling buddy. 'Booze is the only answer' Dennis! That was his favorite expression, and that guy could drink! We had a lot of good times together. I left Canada with Dennis. Well, not really 'with' him. We had worked our passage on two separate German freighters, both belonging to the San Francisco Columbus Line. He had been on the Cap Verde, bound for Auckland, our intended destination ... and I on the Cap Finisterre, which left Vancouver six weeks after the Cap Verde, and unloaded me in Sydney. It's a long story about how we ended up on those two freighters, working our passage as 'deck hands', but it had been pretty much my doing ... I had set it up for Dennis, walking the Vancouver docks to find a ship that would take one of us and lending him what money I had at the time so that he could take that first opening on the Cap Verde, while I went to work on a vegetable farm and waited for the next chance. It had established a pattern for our further travels ... at some point I would have to give the heavy drinking and the partying second place and concentrate my energies on working and saving money so I, or we, could continue travelling.

Dennis was a ladies man, and was very good at it ... he was reasonably tall, muscular, with a dark Scottish complexion, and a good looking face which had been roughened by teenage acne that the ladies somehow found attractive. I had been shocked by one of Dennis's secret revelations ... during his last year in high school he had carried on a relationship with Mrs. Johnson, my very attractive neighbor to the back of my parents house in Edmonton, and mother of another of our close group of buddies, Jerry. She was a knockout ... curves all in the right place, and plenty of them, a pretty face and delightful smile. Mr. Johnson would leave for work early, and then Jerry would leave for school. Somewhere in between the time that Jerry left and Dennis had to go to school as well, Dennis would jump into bed with Mrs. Johnson for a morning delight. Even now, thinking about it just pisses me off ... I was shocked!

45

No ... tell the truth, Chad ... your're just plain jealous !!

I often wondered if Jerry knew about that relationship. Anyway, as we travelled, Dennis would end up with the chick, much to my frustration, and I would be the one with the bread-winning job. So he ended up in Auckland, me in Sydney. I worked for a few months for the British Motor Corporation there and became foreman for one of their new assembly sections ... which I was able to do mostly because of my one year of 'mechanical technology' at the Southern Alberta Institute of Technology ... and then gave up the job to join Dennis in Auckland. He was shacked up with a chick, I hitch-hiked to Christchurch and worked. He followed, shacked up with another chick, and I left to become part of a survey crew on the famed Lake Manapuri Power Project -- one of my most cherished travelling memories.

The project consisted of drilling a tailrace tunnel six miles through a mountain, from remote Lake Manapuri ... to empty in Deep Cove, one of the inlets in the incredibly beautiful fjord area of the southwest coast of the South Island. I was on the survey crew pioneering a road to join the two ends of the tunnel, high over a two thousand foot elevation mountain pass through cool, dense rainforest. A de-comissioned trans-Tasmanian cruise ship had been anchored in the cove and set up as a worker's hostel. It was a fascinating location, rich in exotic flora and wildlife, and the fjord scenery was magnificent. There was a sheer cliff on one side of the cove, close to the ship hostel, which soared majestically and ominously straight up for well over a thousand feet, covered thick with vines and ferns. It was truly humbling to pass below in the small ex-fishing trawler that was used to get around the cove, gazing up through the morning haze and driving rain to view the immensity of that magnificent palisade. Our trawler's operator told us that the depth of the water right next to the cliff was again over a thousand feet. On shore the forest teemed with 'axis' deer and strange New Zealand creatures. The deer were so unnacustomed to man and so plentiful that one of the electricians lassoed one from the entrance of his temporary shop one day, and we were treated to venison that evening. We enountered flightless partridge-like birds called 'wickas' which would come and feed from our hand while we stopped in the forest to have lunch. And there were the destructive 'kias', a dark green colored cross between a parrot and a cock-a-too, whose beak was so strong and mischievous that they would curl back the corners of the corrugated steel roofs, the curl forming a complete circle ... or rip a heavy canvas tent to shreads in minutes.

Anyway, I saved enough for both Dennis and I to travel to Australia.

The pattern continued: Dennis shacked up with a 'sheila' in Sydney, she supporting him, and I hitch-hiked to Townsville looking for a warmer climate and another job. After I had been there awhile and was working, and he was

tired of his sheila; he followed with two new Canadian buddies he had met ...
Alan, an old acquaintance of his from Edmonton, and Art, a tall ex-postman from
Vancouver. All three crashed uninvited into the apartment I was sharing with
three Aussies. During one notorious evening I got suckered into a drinking
contest at the downtown 'Commercial' with Dennis ... I should have known
better. After countless beers my eyes finally closed on me and Art caught me in
his arms as I keeled over backwards off the high bar stool. It was a great scene, I
was told later: tall, skinny Art carrying me out of the bar, my limp self draped
across his arms, while Dennis and the rest of the patrons (and barmaids, one of
which I had a terrible crush on ... ouch!) cheered him on, laughing uproarously
at our expense. Later that night I had ended up peeing all over the floor of the
apartment, and Dennis, drunk to the max, had climbed into the neighbor's lanai,
banged on the door, and told the middle-aged gentleman answering the door that
he 'wanted his daughter'. The next morning we abruptly found ourselves without
a place to stay. So we decided to move on to our next destination of choice,
Papua New Guinea. But we were broke. The solution: we drove up to Cairns in
my recently purchased antique Morris pick-up truck, and found jobs in the sugar
mill at Mossman ... the three of us, Dennis, Alan, and myself

Then one night Dennis and Alan got drunk out of their trees and and busted
all the louver glass panes in the two windows of our 'dormitory', just for fun. The
sugar mill fired all three of us. For me this was a turning point, a time to make a
decision. The choice was to go along with Dennis, join in with his heavy
boozing and partying life style -- and give up going to Papua New Guinea -- or to
put my foot down and say no, to put my own interest and goals first and not let
drinking and partying side-track me. So I had gone to the sugar mill supervisor
and explained to him that I wasn't part of the glass breaking episode and that I
wanted to continue working at the mill. Dennis went back to Sydney, and his
chick, I saved some bread working at the mill and finally made it to Port
Morseby.

Maybe it wasn't the same thing, but it was close. I had a choice to make. I
new that I had been drinking heavy the past few months. Too heavy. Rabaul
was the sort of place you could lose yourself. Easily. Like Dennis and I had
joked in our more somber moments ... you felt yourself 'going down the drain'!
So I could spend all my dough on booze and a party, or place getting on that
freighter and out of Rabaul as number one priority. I shrugged. But I would feel
bad about Walter for a long time.

Aunty Freita was about four feet ten inches tall and looked like she was at
least 120 years old, so withered and wrinkled she was. But she could spring
about like a young rabbit in heat, had a rapid-fire tongue, and a twinkle in her
eye. I never knew her real mixture; she would mumble something like German,

Chinese, and a whole bunch of other things whenever I asked. She lived in the predominantly Chinese residential area of Rabaul, and owned a collection of three buildings on a corner location, the three single-story structures forming an L, which naturally allowed for a large patio area in her backyard -- a great place to drink and party. To make the location even better, there was only a large field behind her property, part of it devoted to a vegetable garden and the rest left unused.

Aunty Freita loved to drink. If you went to Aunty Freitas there was only one rule: you brought along plenty of booze. So on the way I stopped at one of the Chinese shops and picked up a case of South Pacific and a bottle of gin -- the gin simply because the beer was too damn heavy, and one case was weight enough. Besides, I was partial to screwdrivers and bloody marys (no pun intended). Aunty Freita only drank beer. And Deli ... well, she drank anything!

I found my way between the buildings to the patio area. Yes, there was Aunty, sitting at a table with a drink in her hand, of course.

"Hello," I set the case of beer and the gin on the table. Aunty Freita grinned her toothless smile, offering a glimpse of beetel-nut stained gums. "Is Deli here?"

She nodded, still grinning, and yelled out "Del--ii" in a high-pitched shrill.

Deli stumbled sleepy-eyed out of the wooden structure on the left side ... it was a large sleeping room which housed about ten cots and was the sleeping place for the women ... and their partners. I could see Deli was happy to see me. I felt good about that. Crazy though it was, I felt a lot of warmth for her ... I really liked this girl.

"Hello, Chad." She spoke with a heavy pidgin accent, with the pronunciation of the original English syllables and their meanings reduced to their bare essence. 'I like' became 'mi lik', 'suppose' became 'sa pos', 'belong' became 'bi lon', 'beer' became 'bia'. That sort of thing.

Deli was from Kavieng, on the neighboring island of New Ireland. I never understood her full history, but there had been a husband who used to beat her and she had run away ... to Rabaul and Aunty Freita. Auntie Freita's was sort of a refuge for New Guinea run-aways, and there were quite a few of them in Rabaul. I had heard other stories of similar backgrounds ... a husband who was a wife beater, or the girl had broken a tribal or village 'tambu', or had been disgraced by infidelity or rape. The patterns were consistent. They would come to Rabaul and Aunty Freita, and work as housemaids or kitchen help, or be maris ... which was often the same thing.

Deli Matak was black. Of course. But maybe she was blacker than most, for New Ireland was the next major island north of Bougainville, which is reputed to be 'the home of the blackest man on earth'. She had a wide face with broad, high cheekbones, and her hair was in keeping with the usual New Guinea style, cut close to the side of the head and straight up, except Deli didn't try to dye her hair blonde, or reddish blonde, like most. And she had a wonderful smile, full and open, and with healthy white teeth surprisingly devoid of the red-orange stain of the opiate beetel nut.

Within a few minutes a couple of New Guinea boys appeared. One was Henri ... he could play the ukulele, local style, and was always available to 'whine-out' a few songs. I say 'whine' because that is just about what it was. It wasn't their style to learn the full, complicated lyrics of a song. Instead they would pick out key phrases and sing them over and over, in a whining, stretched out manner which may or may not have a close resemblence to the original melody.

Then Sika joined us. I think her name was Sika. At least it sounded something like that. She was a slightly younger and taller version of Aunty Freita. But Sika was a pest ... always hovering around like a leech. In fact, she *was* a leech. She could drink like a ... whale, and she was the horniest little 'ol lady one could imagine, or like Mike had once put it: 'she was hornier than a half-fucked fox in a forest fire' -- excuse the language -- forever grabbing a blokes arm and trying to pull him into the sleeping room.

About which, there had been a memorable occassion. A good Marlon Brando flick had been showing at Rabaul's one and only movie theatre, which was a small wooden building on Mango Street, with stairs in the front leading up to double swinging doors, more like an old American Southern church than a theatre. It was one of his old cowboy westerns. At the start of the show Mike and Harry had shown up, absolutely soaking in sweat. I asked them where they had been, pointing to their drenched shirts. They answered that they'd just been to Aunty Freitas and had both 'experienced' Sika.

"What!" I couldn't believe this.

"Chad, you have no idea. That little 'ol lady is fantastic! You can't even imagine the things she did. She was the greatest piece of ass I've ever had!" Mike went on to add a few more details.

"Nah?" This I could not accept.

"I shit you not!"

Seems like everyone is stealing my favorite expression.

But that's only half of why that occassion was memorable. During the movie there was a scene where Marlon Brando's bad guy boss asked him where he'd been, after a night of drinking and dancing and chasing after senoritas. Marlon Brando answered: "Oh, just a *whoop'in* and a holler'in!" Well, that just about brought the roof of the theatre crashing down, cause the entire audience exploded with uncontrolled laughter. They literally come apart at the seams. Up till then I had figured that 'hoop' was a guarded term, known only to those of us who were hard core practitioners. But that night I discovered that everyone in Rabaul, I mean everyone, knew exactly what 'hoop'in' was all about.

Deli was feeling sad. I felt I knew why. I sat close to her, holding her hand and stroking her arm. I really did like this girl. A couple of times I reached up to her face and caressed her tattoos with the back of my fingers. I loved to do that. She had a row of dots on each cheek. Six to be exact, with two added marks in the shape of a crude 'seven' under the row of dots, on each cheek. Tattooing New Guinea style was not sophisticated; I don't really know how they do it … but the result was often raised scars. Or maybe it was only Kavieng style. Could be, because I had seen a lot of tattoos that were heavy lines, but not raised -- usually black but sometimes reddish colored. Anyway, I loved to caress Deli's bumps, on her face, and on her breasts, where there were two vertical lines of dots on each.

Deli was typically built for a girl in this part of New Guinea -- about five feet tall, with kinda skinny legs and a muscular upper body, usually on the thick side at the waist. And with nice full breasts. Healthy tits were important for New Guinea women ... because it was common for them to nurse piglets once the nursing of their own infant was complete. Yes, piglets! Raising pigs was a significant part of their family and village economy. It was only natural to help out with the nuturing of the piglets. You don't believe me? Well, it's the absolute truth ... I used to see them doing it in the villages we passed while

51

working on the roads. And you would see women, especially older ones, with monsterous breasts which would hang down in long cylindrical shapes, often reaching all the way to their navels, and sometimes past. I wouldn't lie about this … I shit you not!

Deli wanted to sing, so Henri was a welcome addition. We whined out a few of their favorites, like 'Picture of my mother on the wall' … don't know if that's the name of a song or just the key phrase. Then she started to sing something I had never heard before; I knew it was meant especially for me:
"Time ... you go long way long sea,
Sun ... or rain no hurt 'em you,
Me ... sorry ... too much long you,
Suppose ... you no love long me no more."

She sang it over and over. I asked her what the second line meant, because it didn't seem to fit. She shrugged … she pretended not to know, and it wasn't important. The essence was there in the other lines. Then I realized that it should be 'me' in the first line, instead of 'you', but she had changed it so that the message was from her to me rather than the other way around. She was telling me goodbye -- in her own special way -- she was feeling sad, and melancholy. I felt very close to her. In my own way, and considering the circumstances, I loved her dearly.

A short while later we retired to the sleeping room. I loved to crash with Deli here … even more than back at my own room at the CDW camp. Here we were in another world … a non-Australian, non-Canadian world … it was *her* world … and we slept under a mosquito net. Oh, how wonderful that was! The bed was a narrow cot – so we were forced to snuggle closely -- and we would drape the white mesh of the mosquito net around and above us, which was suspended by a cord strung between two poles, one at each end of the cot. Once enclosed by the soft whiteness of that netting it was as if we were in a universe of our very own … removed from the anxieties and cares of other spheres, and it was glorious to make love, the barrier gentle, but complete.

Deli was particularly tender and responsive that night, and it was truly memorable.

There was one diversion, however. Just when we were about to drift into a velvety sleep I felt a hand on my arm, tugging at me. I sat up suddenly, startled, and then realized it was Sika again, laying on the floor beside our cot, trying to entice me into falling off the cot and directly onto her. I resisted (of course). Deli giggled.

"Go ... do it!" she insisted.

"No way!" I answered back defiantly. I remembered Mike and Harry's account and felt a kind of urge, which tempted me. But no, especially not tonight. I scolded Sika and slapped at her hand. Deli and I re-positioned the mosquito net and we snuggled together again, falling into a deep, intimate sleep.

"Now, let"s see if your workmanship has solved our problem." Mr. Milner was leaning over the rail of the upper deck, trying to understand what we had done. We had already lowered the lifeboat back over the side, in anticipation of setting her in the water and also because we were more than a little shy about Mr. Milner examining our work up close. From the upper deck railing the lifeboat looked pretty decent. Nearer, however, and he would see what a terrible job it actually was -- the thick grey paint swabbed on the interior, leaving thumb-sized gobs and long, hanging runs; the exterior putty was rough and un-feathered, the new white paint a visibly contrasting color, now that it had dried. The grey paint had been of a honey consistency and was difficult to apply ... we had no thinner and the brushes were stiffened with old, dried paint. And we didn't have any linseed oil to re-vive the dried putty ... we had applied it the best we could.

On Mr. Milner's signal Laurie and I lowered the craft to the water. We waited, peering down from above, expecting the boat to begin filling with seawater again ... but hoping it wouldn't. A couple of minutes passed -- no water. I turned my head towards Laurie, he flashed me an upward turned thumb. We both glanced at Mr. Milner. He was expressionless. We waited a couple more minutes.

"Congratulations, gentlemen. It appears that your efforts did the trick! Now, let's leave this lifeboat where it is and see to the port vessel."

Laurie and I exchanged worried looks.

"Uhh ... Mr. Milner, could we raise the lifeboat out of the water ... uh, the paint isn't quite dry yet." I was pretty sure that if we left the boat as was the putty would start to absorb water, swell, and come apart.

Mr. Milner considered what I had said for a brief second, then agreed. "Alright. Today is Sunday, we'll have the Harbor Master aboard for an inspection tomorrow. That should give the paint ample time to dry. Good thinking, Chad."

But that was only part of the reason behind our anxiety. Laurie and I had seen that the port lifeboat was in even worse condition, although we hadn't attempted to lift her out of the chocks. And we had used up almost all of the putty; it was questionable whether we could repeat our performance a second time. I wanted to explain all of this to Mr. Milner, but didn't dare. Not leaving the first lifeboat in the water was concession enough, at least for now. I raised a questoning eyebrow towards Laurie as we followed Mr. Milner to the right side of the Trader's upper deck, and his answering shrug told me that he was of the same mind. We could only do what Mr. Milner instructed.

The tarp was already removed, and the lifeboats' contents were stacked neatly close by, ready for inspection. We readied the two block and tackle and ropes for the lift, and waited for Mr. Milner's signal. We pulled, once ... no movement ... then a second time, slightly harder ... then a third. On the fourth we again heard what was now a familiar sound -- a tearing and ripping of paint and wood. But before the craft had a chance to break completely free Laurie slacked off on his side and signaled with a free left hand for me to do the same. I obliged.

"Mr. Milner, I don't think we should lift her free." Laurie was taking the iniative; he had something in mind. With that, he proceeded to inspect the damage which had started to take place. "See this," he pointed to one area beside the chock support, where the paint was cracked in a curve several inches away from the cradle member, indicating that a sizeable piece of the hull was about to separate, and would probably leave a hole you could put your fist through. "I think this lifeboat is in a lot worse condition that the first one, Mr. Milner."

"I see what you mean." Mr. Milner agreed with Laurie's appraisal, which surprised me. I had expected him to be arrogantly bone-headed about this. Were we seeing a different side to this man?

Feeling increased confidence with Mr. Milner's more agreeable attitude, Laurie added: "What if we left this lifeboat in her chocks, and painted the interior with that same thick grey paint, and then filled her with water to show that it didn't leak?"

Mr. Milner took awhile to consider this new proposal, his coutenance shadowed, then he laughed. "Laurie, the Harbor Master is no fool. I don't think he would accept that."

But Laurie had more to his idea, and wasn't about to let it go so easily. "Yes, but maybe we could use the excuse that it would be impractical to lower this lifeboat into the water because of the ship's list? Besides, Mr. Milner, we don't have any more putty to repair holes with."

Mr. Milner chuckled, and smiled with humorous approval and a glint of shrewdness. "Laurie, you're suggesting that we try to con the Harbor Master?"

Lauirie shrugged, and grinned.

"OK ... I agree ... it's worth a shot. We don't have much of a choice, do we. . go ahead and paint her, boys. Try to hide those cracks already showing too. . . . By the way, the other boat won't hold up in the water very long either, will it?" Again that shrewd look. I shook my head slowly.

"God help us if we ever need those lifeboats. And once you have our lifeboat problem taken care of, I need you two to survey the entire ships lifesaving equipment -- how many life vests and throwing rings we have, where they are, what condition they're in -- all of that. Make a detailed list. There's paper and pen in the wheelhouse. This will be for our friend the Harbor Master. And our signaling equipment: flares, signal flags ... the whole nine yards!"

Haven't heard that expression for awhile ... sounds kinda strange coming from an Englishman.

"Oh yes, and one more last thing. Check out our radio to make sure it's working properly."

We were just putting the final touches to our grey masterpiece when we heard the sound of the clanging of a bell, loud and piercing.

"What the hell is that?" I wasn't asking anyone in particular, but then Laurie was the only one around.

"Sounds like a cook's bell ... I think we're in for some kau kau."

"Oh, yeh ... right on, I'm starved."

We raced each other all the way down to the officer's mess. But even with our phenomenal speed we were well behind Harry. Kevin and Fred followed a few seconds later. Just then Joseph brought in a large tray full of terrific looking sandwiches -- a mixture of tuna, ham and cheese, and a New Guinea favorite: corned beef. And orange juice. Not bad!

"So what about our officers?" Harry queried Joseph, the question curiously leaving me out.

"They're eating on the wheelhouse deck," Joseph explained.

And so the pattern was set. Our three certified officers would drink and dine up top, and the rest of us occupied the mess on the main deck.

"Are they hitting the booze?" Harry wanted to know, speaking in a low tone.

Joseph just nodded, smiling.

"Have you blokes noticed about Mr. Morris?" Harry was monopolizing the conversation, continuing in his subdued volume. "The bloke lives between the colors of green and blue ... when he hasn't had anything to drink for awhile he starts to turn green, and then when he's loaded and about to pass out he's a full on blue."

We all snickered. I thought to myself that Id have to watch for that, to see if it was for real.

"By the way, Harry?" This was a golden opportunity to tease the dumb ass. "It's lunch time and we haven't heard the auxillary start up."

"No worries, no worries," he rebounded quickly. "We'll have her going lick-ed-dee-split!"

Kevin and Fred looked his direction, both mouths full of sandwich. I didn't think Fred understood Harry's unusual choice of expression.

"Is that right, Kevin?" I asked. He nodded.

"Anyway, who do you think you are, the 2nd Mate or something?" Harry teased back. Everyone laughed.

It took Laurie and I most of the day to put together Mr. Milner's requested list. We were pretty proud of ourselves ... there was a lot of gear aboard this piece of iron, a lot of it old and useless, but a substantial amount relatively new as well. We were in the mess, summarizing everything on paper ... must have been about 3:00 ... when we heard the unmistakable sputter, cough, and ensuing roar of a diesel engine starting up.

"I'll, be damned ... they got the auxillary running!" I was delighted to hear the sound, partly because it was a familiar, friendly sound, reminding me of my Cat 950 loader, and partly because we would now have electricity, and the subsequent luxuries of water, lights, and reftigeration. Plus, we were a big step towards being able to weigh anchor and begin our voyage. Sure enough, the lights came on a few minutes later.

The sun was on its persistant descent towards Tunnel Hill one more time. Someone went ashore to buy a couple of cases of South Pacific, and we started to assemble in the officer's mess. Our engine room crew came in, and I was startled to see Mr. Fitzgerald with them, heavily spotted with black smudges, wiping his one hand with a rag, in a curious self-learned manipulation, wedging the rag between his hand and body. Maybe he's the real reason the auxillary is running, I speculated.

The beer arrived, and a few minutes later some more sandwiches, and we all started to feel a degree of confidence towards this venture, the first time for most of us. We learned that the main engines -- the two large Perkins -- would be running soon. They just needed some tuning up and a filter change. Apparently our engine fuel had become badly contaminated with water ... tomorrow a fuel hose would be rigged ashore and the tanks drained, then refilled with fresh fuel.

We also learned a little about Mr. Fitzgerald. He had a family in Sydney: two teenage daughters and a younger son, and a wife of course. He had previously spent quite a few years at sea and possessed full papers for a Captains ticket, *and* First Mate's. Harry and Kevin let us know that he was also a damn good mechanic -- he knew marine diesels. He emphasized that he was anxious to get back to Sydney, to his family and other responsibilities ... he wanted to see us off as soon as possible!

He seemed like a fairly decent sort of guy, not the kind of person you'd expect to be plotting our demise on a rocky shore or coral reef. I was beginning to form the conclusion that the rumors we had heard were nothing but just that -- empty rumors.

Mr. Fitzgerald didn't stay long, politely excusing himself after two beers -- and a short farewell excursion to the upper deck.

I was into my fifth South Pacific, plus or minus a couple, when my blissful tranquility was brought to an abrupt, crashing halt by the sound of Mr. Milner's loud voice, calling out my name from the wheelhouse deck.

"Oh - oh ... what's up? Be back in a minute ..." Or so I thought.

I found Mr. Milner in a rather excited state. Neither the Captain nor our Chief Engineer were in sight. I wondered if that had something to do with Mr. Milner's present mood. I knew he had been drinking steadily since before lunch and his current hyper state was remeniscent of the night of his wild argument with the Captain.

"Chad, it is time to teach you navigation! You don't mind if I call you by your first name ... if you were a qualified 2nd Mate I would be required to call you Mr. Fletcher. But you're really just a 'trainee' ... am I correct?"

"Yes sir."

So far so good

.

"Now, sit down here ... and let's get started."

I realized that Mr. Mlner was enjoying this new role as a teacher. But I was wondering if I was going to be his new 'star pupil' or more an 'object of abuse'.

Mr. Miner was on his feet, pacing back and forth on the port deck, which faced Rabaul town, and more or less due north if you looked out perpendicular to the ship's side.

"Chad, I am going to teach you the Marcq Saint-Hiliare method of finding a 'line of position'!" He strode to the chart table, which was located directly aft of the ship's 'wheel' -- a wooden, three foot diameter spoked wheel, finely crafted and varnished with a high gloss, reminding one of the sailing ships of an earlier era -- and wrote on a piece of paper.

"It is important to be correct about these things. I've written down the correct spelling of things. Here's a notebook for you to use ... 'line of position'! From now on we will use the normal abbreviation: LOP. I'm going to give you the formula for finding the LOP, and show you how to work it out. It's not difficult. In fact, it's childs' play. You should have it mastered by the time we're ready to weigh anchor!"

I wanted to explain to him that it all sounded kinda optimistic and that I really wasn't very smart -- and so on. But I could see he was not in the sort of mood to be receptive to excuses, so I resigned myself to making the best of it. Besides, I am supposed to be the navigation officer. My response, therefore, was a straightforward and enthusiastic "Yes sir!"

And thus began my series of lessons from Mr. Milner on the subject of celestial navigation.

"Actually, I will be teaching you a simplified, more modern version of Marcq Saint-Hiliare called the H.O. 214 method. We will be using the Nautical Almanac for our reference data." With that he pulled out a large volume from one of the shelves below the chart table and handed it to me. It was a very large volume. "You know some trigonometry, I understand."

I started to say something, but shut up.

"Well, what finding an LOP boils down to is solving a triangle, a navigational triangle. You know that a triangle consists of three sides and three angles.

Correct?"

"Yes." I nodded, pretending I knew that that was correct.

"And you know that if you know any three of these six parts, you can determine the other three, correct?"

"Yes, sir!" My most remote memory vaguely indicated that that might be right.

"Well, in celestial navigation we use that Nautical Almanac, a sextant, and a chronometer to give us two sides and the included angle of our 'navigation triangle', and we then solve for the length of the third side and another angle, and presto, we can plot out one LOP. The 'line' which we have thus plotted on our chart means that our position is somewhere on that line. We can plot a second and third LOP, using different stars of course, and where those lines intersect, well, that is our position."

Mr. Milner was now glaring at me to see if I understood all that. There was no way in hell that I was getting the 'big picture', but I understood the part about the triangle and I figured I could work through a formula if he gave it to me.

"Yes sir. Put like that it doesn't sound difficult at all." I lied.

"Of course there's a lot of incidental 'garbage' that has to be accounted for -- corrections -- but I'll make that all clear to you as we go along."

"Now, allow me to introduce you to the chronometer and sextant." He led me to the chart table, on the side of which was a finely tooled wooden case. A drepressed area of the table top had been built-in as part of its original design, and was contoured to precisely accomodate the wooden case. In this manner the case was well secured, and presumably could not move about. Mr. Milner opened the top of the case, exposing a brass encased clock suspended on gimbals, which looked like a fine instrument indeed.

"This one is one of the best, a 'Hamilton'. I don't understand why this vessel would have it, but then at one time this was a pretty decent vessel. This is a 'chronometer' -- just a fancy name for a clock -- but a chronometer is always set to 'Greenwich Mean Time'. Do you understand what that is?"

This one I knew. "Yes sir ... the time at 0 degrees longitutude, which is in Greenwich Village, England. Just on the east side of London, I understand. It's also famous as a popular musician and artist hang-out."

"Correct." Mr. Milner glanced sullenly at me to let me know he didn't require the extra information about Greenwich. "Now for the sextant."

I kinda knew what a sextant was, I had seen pictures of them. But I had never seen the real thing. Mr. Milner disappeared towards his cabin for a few seconds and came back holding another wooden case. This was also exquisitely constructed, perhaps even better looking that the chronometer case. He set it on the table and opened the lid.

"This is a micrometer sextant, it is a Plath, and it is one of their finest."

I reached towards it, but he stopped my hand. "This is an extremely delicate instrument, and I'm sorry, but I cannot risk you handling it. I just wanted to show it to you." With that he reached under the table and brought out another case, this one rather ordinary looking, and opened it as well. "This one was on board, and you can use it. It's a 'vernier' sextant -- not nearly as fine an instrument as my own, but it'll do. Do you know how to read a vernier scale?"

"Yes, I do." I felt a little more comfortable with this part. I had used vernier calipers for measuring diameters and short lengths; the mechanism was similar. He motioned for me to pick it up, which I did.

"'Be careful, now. Hold the handle in your right hand. You must always keep a firm grip on that handle -- whether you're sighting or just carrying it. Come over here on the deck ..." We walked to the starboard deck, which looked out into the wide expanse of Simpson Harbor. "Now, can you see the moon?"

I certainly could. It was a full moon. Or almost, anyway, shining very bright and high in the sky, its light reflecting off the smooth surface of the harbor.

"Now, hold the telescope eye-piece to your eye, and place your left hand on the index arm, and squeeze the little trigger here. See, that releases the arm and you can swing it along the curved scale, or the 'arc'. OK, look through the telescope and adjust the swing of the index arm until you can see the horizon and the moon come together."

I did so, experimenting. There were two parts to the view -- a double reflection -- and by moving the arm I could bring the moon and the horizon in line together, horizontally.

"Try to adjust the index arm so that the line of the horizon just touches the bottom of the moon. Got it?"

"Yeh!"

"Now swing the sextant from side to side, gently. See how the moon makes an arc?"

"Yeh, this is great!"

"Now, put your left fingers on the screw knob and fine tune it, swinging gently at the same time, until the horizon line and the bottom of the moon coincide perfectly. Got it?"

"Yes."

"Keep doing it. Do you notice that it keeps changing?"

"Yes, I have to keep turning the screw. It's because the moon is moving, right?"

"And the earth turning," he snorted. "You've got the idea." He touched my arm and motioned for me to discontinue. "You understand then, that the angle that you will read on the vernier scale will depend on the precise time that you make the sighting?"

"Yes, I do." I was super impressed. Even estactic. This was going to be fun.

"That, young man, is celestial navigation in a nutshell. Tomorrow we'll take some star sights and I'll introduce you to the formula." I was dismissed.

CHAPTER FOUR

Fare-thee-well

"However, Mr. Fitzgerald, I must be honest with you ... I have very serious reservations about the seaworthiness and

safety of this ship, and your owner's true intentions."

Monday ... day two in Simpson Harbor with the crew all aboard and accounted for.

Mr. Fitzgerald came on board at nine a.m. and announced that the Harbor Master would be making an inspection an hour later at ten.

Laurie and I immediately went to work hustling a water hose and setting it up in anticipation of filling the starboard lifeboat. While doing so Mr. Fitzgerald located us and instructed Laurie to be available to row the Harbor Master from shore. In fact, he requested that Laurie have the dinghy already at the landing, waiting, at a quarter to the hour. I was hurt that Laurie had been selected, and not I. Apparently my lack of rowing prowess had become common knowledge. But then Laurie had mentioned previously that he had met the Harbor Master while working for Burns Philip ... Mr. Fitzgerald was probably counting on a little P.R. from that direction, I rationalized, my feelings soothed a little. Before leaving us he did have one special request directed to me, however:

"And for Christ's sake, Mr. 2nd Mate, please put some shoes on!"

Now my feelings really are *hurt!*

Our Harbor Master arrived precisely at the prescribed hour. There was an excited air of expectancy and apprehension among the four of us waiting for him on the aft deck. Even from the distance of the Trader's stern I could see that he was a big man ... middle-aged and he carried a sizable midsection ... sizable indeed.

Once he had joined us on deck Mr. Fitzgerald made the introductions.

"Gentlemen, this is our Harbor Master, Mr. Murray Holmes. Mr. Holmes, this is our Captain, Mr. Patterson, 2nd Mate Mr. Fletcher, and you have already met our 1st Mate, Mr. Milner."

Our Chief Engineer was absent, having passed out about a half hour before, being about the color of the deep blue sea.

Mr. Holmes seemed amiable, and my hopes were up, thinking about our lifeboat problem. However, I did notice a puzzled expression on his face, just briefly, when I was introduced as the 2nd Mate. In the real world I suppose I just didn't fit the part ... even with shoes on. I was simply too young to have acquired Second Officer status. I wished Mr. Fitzgerald had introduced me as 'apprentice 2nd Mate' or some such thing.

61

Mr. Holmes went straight to the matter at hand, and surprised us with his choice of priorities: "I would like to inspect your navigation and radio equipment first, gentlemen."

Once in the wheelhouse, my already diminishing optimism deteriorated even more, for Mr. Holmes found fault in everything.

The condition of our radio was his first concern, and he especially wanted to know if we could transmit in case of distress and whether or not its direction finder worked properly. Laurie and I had messed with the thing, and we had found that it received just fine, or at least so we thought. But it hadn't occurred to us that we needed to verify that we could transmit as well, let alone knowing how to go about doing that. And checking out its direction finder ?? No one had said anything about a 'direction finder'. We didn't even know what a direction finder was!

"Can you please demonstrate the capability of this radio?"

Laurie and I exchanged big question marks and just stood there, not having the slightest idea of how to proceed. Mr. Milner looked our direction and realized that we were of no help; he stepped forward and began manipulating knobs and mechanisms, but only succeeded in receiving strange noises and garbled transmissions. So, big zero on the radio! We were all standing there, ackwardly embarrassed, especially Mr. Fitzgerald.

"Mr. Fitzgerald, I will not allow this vessel to weigh anchor until you have a properly working radio." The man was visibly irritated. Further observations in the wheelhouse only heightened his irritation. "You do not have adequate charts for your intended voyage. You are specifically lacking charts for your passage through the Philippines and for Hong Kong harbor. And I am going to require that you have your compass checked and re-compensated if necessary and your chronometer adjusted ... by a professional from other than your present crew."

Things were not going well. I was sure Mr. Fitzgerald was as aware as I was that asking Mr. Holmes to inspect our lifeboats at this time was pushing our luck -- but he did it anyway.

"Mr. Holmes, we have our starboard lifeboat ready to place in the water -- for your inspection."

There was a pause on our Harber Master's part and I was sure he was about to decline. I was hoping he would decline. But he terminated his pause with a nod and Mr. Fitzgerald led him the few steps to the side rail of the port deck, where we could see the lifeboat, still suspended on her ropes a couple of feet above the water, below us and approximately fifteen feet towards the stem.

"Mr. Fletcher, could you please take Laurie with you and ..." Mr. Fitzgerald started, but was interrupted by Mr. Holmes.

"That won't be necessary, Mr. Fitzgerald. I'm sorry, but I will require that you not only place the craft in the water, but man her and display the vessel's structural integrity and your crew's ability to manage her. But we simply don't have the time for that now. I must get back to shore and you gentlemen have, I believe, your work cut out for you."

I felt relief. Mr. Fitzgerald was angry. A visual check with Laurie revealed that he mirrored my own sentiments. The Captain and Mr. Milner were practicing their 'stone faces' again.

"Mr. Fitzgerald, can you please have your sailor row me back to shore."

The Captain had taken possession of one of the lounge chairs on the starboard deck and already had a drink in his hand. Mr. Milner and I were waiting for instructions from Mr. Fitzgerald, who was the first to speak:

"Our Harbor Master is going to make it difficult for us, it seems ... Mr. Milner, I would like you to come ashore with me and help me arrange for someone to make the compass and chronometer adjustments. You have some expertise in those matters and can take over that responsibility for me. I have a great deal of other things to be concerned about. Chad, see what you can do about that radio. Find help if you need to, but let's figure the damn thing out. I'm sure it works, you just need to get used to it. You can ask the Captain." He motioned with his head in the direction of the opposing deck, as if to say 'good luck with trying to get any help from that useless drunk'. "Yes, try to get some help from Mr. Patterson. We're going to try to have Mr. Holmes back tomorrow."

With that we parted in our separate directions. I figured that if I was going to succeed in having the Captain help me I had better ask him right away, before he had too many drinks.

"Captain ... sir," I approached the loungechair. "Mr. Fitzgerald suggested I ask you for assistance in trying to get our radio to function." Apparently he didn't agree, or was thinking about it, for there was a long, vacant silence. "Could you please help me, sir." I was feeling desperate. I didn't know jack about that radio. More silence. Then:

"Well, it looks like we have a job to do then, doesn't it?"

And so the two of us attacked the radio. I was delighted. I was grateful for the assistance, but I was also happy to see Mr. Patterson set his drink down and accept the challenge, to get involved.

Just about then our Chief Engineer appeared. He watched us for a few minutes, bleary-eyed, and then, incredibly, he too offered to help. Now I had the two of them going at it.

Right on, there's hope yet!!

The radio was on -- we had power -- and we could receive a variety of stations. It was a good-sized radio, old but with a lot of features and attatchments. It was mounted on a wide shelf above and to the side of the chart table. Laurie and I had already discovered that we could receive on regular frequencies as well as on several short-wave bands. We had picked up a marine weather channel, a couple of aircraft channels, and radio stations in various parts of Australia. Mostly we had been searching for rock 'n roll stations, though. Of course we knew nothing about how to transmit and the 'direction finder' had been a mystery to us.

"Do you know what a direction finder is, Chad?"

Jeeses, the guy can read my mind?

"I'm sorry sir, I don't"

"Umm ... I heard Mr. Milner giving you a lesson in navigation last night -- celestial navigation. Well, we use the radio as an aid to navigation as well." He was turned towards the radio, adjusting a mechanism on the top of the radio that consisted of an arm that rotated 360 degrees horizontally, with a small black box at one end and a built-in compass beneath.

"See this mechanism here? Well, if we can receive on a nearby station, we can use this mechanism to determine the bearing of that radio signal, relative to where we are, or to where the ship is."

"Yes ... sir." I was trying my best to understand.

He then brought out several charts from the chart shelves under the chart table and selected one -- a chart of Simpson Harbor and the surrounding area, including Rabaul town.

"Come and look at this chart. See this right here ... it marks the location of the Rabaul radio station's tower." He pointed to a spot in the Chinese residential section, very close to Aunty Freitas. And I remembered, yes, there was a radio tower near by. "If we could receive on that station, and at the same time use this direction finder to give us the compass heading of that signal, we could plot it on this chart ... it would be one line radiating out from that position. It would be a 'line of position', just like a LOP from taking a star fix. We would be somewhere on that line. If we could do the same with a second radio station, then the two lines would intersect -- and that would be our position. Or the second LOP could be the bearing of a lighthouse or landmark." He looked at me, and for the first time I saw something that hinted of character, a suggestion of strength and purpose.

Nah, it's just the 'teacher' complex again!

"Mr. Milner can teach you navigation by the stars, I can teach you methods for working closer to shore."

See, I'm right! Next he'll be teaching me how to 'navigate by the color of the water'!

After a great deal of turning various knobs and listening carefully for several minutes at a time, we finally succeeded in locking onto the Rabaul radio station indicated on the chart.

"Aahh, we've finally got it. Now to see if the direction finder can give us the correct bearing."

"Mr. Patterson, I see that those two screws are loose … there ... see ... I'll see if I can't find a screwdriver." Mr. Morris was doing his part too. Wonderful!

More fidelling. A screwdriver arrived. I was the one to use it, however -- Mr. Morris couldn't hold it quite steady enough. Guess he was needing a couple of drinks about now. What did Harry say? Oh yes, green was the color when his blood was shy on alcohol. Yes, he is definitely towards the green side!

"Gentlemen, we have a bearing of 50 degrees. Now, let's plot it on the chart." The Captain then proceeded to work out that LOP on the chart.

"Next lesson, Chad. See this 'compass' marked out on the chart."

"Yes."

"That's called a 'rose'." He then removed an apparatus from one of the side drawers that looked like two rulers connected by two brass bands, each riveted to both rulers so that the bands could rotate at their fasteners and the two rulers could be pulled apart or held close together. "And this is a 'parallel rule'.

He then positioned the outside edge of the ruler at 50 degrees on the rose and pulled out the other ruler to the indicated position of the Rabaul radio tower, and marked the line with a pencil. I understood that this was supposed to be our LOP. However, the line didn't proceed anywhere close to where we were anchored, but instead pointed way out into the center of the harbor.

Oops!

"Well, our direction finder is clearly not giving the correct heading." The Captain was distressed.

"Let's adjust it so it does give the correct bearing then!" Our Chief Engineer was brilliant! So I pulled out the screwdriver again, and we did exactly that, the Captain giving the correct bearing of 106 degrees from the chart, which was fairly accurate because the dry dock next to us was clearly marked on the chart, so we knew precisely where we were.

We had just completed this procedure and were contemplating trying to locate another radio station and, following the same sequence, to see if our adjustment would hold true -- when we were interrupted. Mr. Milner had returned, with a second gentleman following behind who was carrying a wooden 'suitcase'.

"Gentlemen, this is Mr. McKenzie ... who's here to adjust our compass and chronometer."

"Good day, gentlemen. Shouldn't take very long to do. A proper compass compensation would take some time, ordinarily, but I understand your engines aren't running and we therefore cannot swing the vessel through 360 degrees. So I will have to rely on my own instruments, an azimuth sighting, and a couple of calculated judgements. Should be adequate, however."

Mr. McKenzie proceeded to open his suitcase, which contained various tools, a chronometer, and a large, expensive looking compass.

"By the way, Mr. Holmes has also asked me to check your radio and direction finder." The rest of us all exchanged surprised glances. I had an inspiration and felt a surge of excitement.

"Mr. McKenzie, we have been checking out the radio ourselves this morning, and we found it to be pretty accurate. In fact, right now the radio is tuned to Rabaul radio and we have a bearing on the direction finder ... which we have plotted on the chart."

Mr. McKenzie looked towards me appraisingly. "Can you show that to me? That would certainly put one concern aside in good order."

I did so, with the Captain's assistance -- he kept a cold, stone face the whole time. I caught Mr. Morris with a smirk. Mr. Milner followed the whole sequence, trying his best to suppress a measure of surprise, and a mischievous twinkle in his eye.

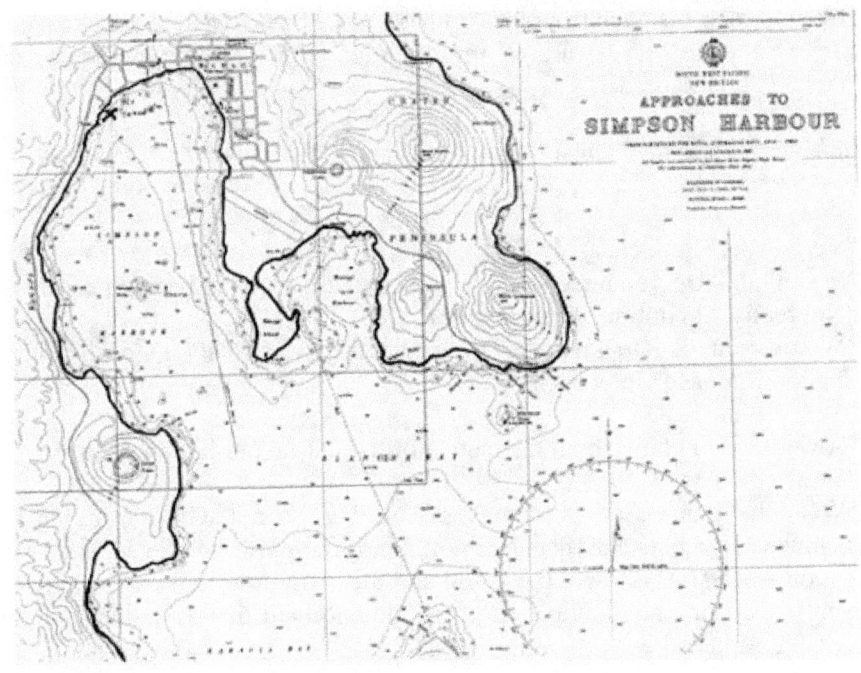

"Alright, it looks OK to me. Now let's have a go at the chronometer and the compass."

The Captain and Chief Engineer returned to their loungchairs, Mr. Morris esepecially happy to do so. Mr. Patterson signaled for me to accompany him.

"Now, Chad, whatever you do, don't touch that radio ... and make sure no one else does ... Is that clear?" he whispered.

"Yes, sir ... but ... sir ... how about knowing if we can *transmit* on the radio?" I had a hard time keeping my voice subdued, and I was grinning my dumb grin again.

"Never mind that! It'll do just fine."

Mr. McKenzie checked the chronometer first ... easily done because he had his own chronometer to compare with. He made a small adjustment. Then he turned to the compass, and started to disassemble the outside casing. I was curious, and wanted to watch. The compass was a large instrument housed atop a separate pedestal just fore of the ship's wheel. I judged it's face to be about twelve inches in diameter with a domed glass cover. Once the housing and glass were removed I could see that the compass was gimballed, and had a pair of cast metal arms attached to the main housing, one on each side. The arms were approximately eight inches long and had small 'weights' fastened on a metal slide, so that their distance from the compass could be adjusted and locked.

Mr. McKenzie was aware of my attention. "Do you know much about compasses?" he inquired.

Ohh oh!! How should I answer that? Let's see ... no one told him I was 2nd Mate. Maybe I can get away with the truth ...

"Very little," I understated.

He smiled. "Do you understand why a compass needs to be compensated?"

"Not really." I continued being honest.

"Would you like to know?" He apparently wasn't about to start a long explanation if I wasn't interested.

"Yeh ... uhh, yes!"

"Alright. You know about magnetic north and true north, don't you?"

"Yes."

"Well, that's one kind of 'compensation', but it's not what I'm doing here. The compensation between magnetic north and true north you do as part of your navigation -- it varies all over the world and the 'variation', that's what it's called, is given to you on each navigation chart. For Rabaul that variation is about 6 degrees, 35 minutes East."

Our Simpson Harbor chart was still laid out on the chart table ... Mr. McKenzie showed me where the 'variation' was stated on the chart 'rose'. It read "Mag. Varn 6 degrees 35 minutes E. (1970), Increasing about I minute annually".

"But it's important that you understand that the compass operates on the principle of magnetic attraction, and points to the magnetic north pole if other magnetic attractions don't interfere. Unfortunately, however, there are always magnetic interferences -- especially when one's vessel is a large metal object in itself "

"Mr. McKenzie, I'm ready for the azimuth shot!"

I had been concentrating on what Mr. McKenzie had been saying and doing and hadn't noticed that Mr. Milner had brought out his sextant and was standing on the port deck, sextant ready for a sighting and waiting for a signal from Mr. McKenzie.

"Excuse us, but we will now take an azimuth shot of the sun, which will in turn give us a calculated true bearing to compare our compass with." Both gentlemen worked together to take the sight reading, chronometer time, and data from the Nautical Almanac needed to calculate their required azimuth. I watched as closely as I could, trying to understand what they were doing.

"Now, where were we? Magnetic deviation can be very complicated, and we use a lot of special jargon, like 'permanent' and 'subpermanent' magnetism, or 'vertically induced' versus 'horizontally induced', and so on. There are interesting concepts like, for instance, each ship has an inherent magnetic character determined by where precisely in the world it was built, and the compass heading of its keel during construction." He looked at me to see if this had caught my interest. It had.

Fascinating stuff!

"That part is usually compensated for when the compass is first installed. But then that compass will need adjustment as it ages and becomes worn. And then we must consider any changes in the ship itself -- changes in construction, or the effect of its cargo. This ship, for example, underwent a major structural alteration when its tanks were converted to holds and that mast constructed." He pointed out the wheelhouse window to the Trader's single mast -- a pretty sizeable piece of iron, with a base diameter of about 2 feet, tapering to a height of at least 40 feet, and with two, say, 10 inch diameter booms attached, one fore, one aft, complete with iron block and tackle and steel cables.

"Our Harbor Master, Mr. Holmes, was mostly concerned about the effect of your cargo, which I understand is a full load of scrap iron. That could have a marked effect on the accuracy of this compass as well. That's what I'm adjusting these magnets for." He pointed to the small metal blocks on the compass compensator arms.

"And, that's about it ... I will write out a complete report for your log, with a copy for Mr. Holmes. The adjustment I made was small ... don't think you'll have any problem. It would have been much better, however, if we could have swung the vessel through 360 degrees, but under the present circumstances that's a luxury."

So, not yet three in the afternoon and we had accomplished a lot! I was trying to think of what else I could do. Mr. Milner had joined the Captain and Mr. Morris.

"Mr. Milner, what else would you like me to do?"

But Mr. Milner was content with his freshly established semi-prone position, had a scotch and soda in his hand, and apparently didn't want to be bothered. The three were enjoying themselves, and I sensed that they were satisfied enough with how events had unfolded thus far, and my participation, and that I could do as I please.

"2nd Mate, please carry on with things as you see fit. Perhaps the cook and our engineer crew could use some of your guidance."

"Yes sir." That sounded so good I could feel my head starting to swell. I decided to take him seriously. After all, I was the 2nd Mate and the rest of the crew *did* need my guidance.

Don't kid yourself... he's just getting rid of you!

I went below to seek out Laurie. With recent events he had taken it upon himself to be our official escort for persons going to and from shore and was just returning from having dropped off Mr. McKenzie. Fred was on the aft deck and I could see Harry on shore. They had rigged a one-and-a-half inch rubber hose from the dry dock to the Trader.

"We've drained the two main fuel tanks ... we're just filling them with fresh fuel now." Fred answered in response to my inquiry.

Laurie had just about reached the mid-way mark from shore, when he was stopped by shouts from on land. Richard and Joseph had appeared, the tailgate of a Nissan pick-up visible over the thick grass behind them. We were about to receive another segment of our newly sequestered food supply. This was the third load.

So I got involved in helping with each operation, and the remainder of the day passed quickly ... we were really making some progress, I felt. The fuel tanks were filled, and the large rubber hose was replaced by a smaller, cleaner looking one to top off our fresh water supply. No fewer than 4 pick-up loads of food goods and miscellaneous supplies came aboard; one entire load was beer -- South Pacific with some Fosters thrown in. I was delighted to see steaks and other meat cuts, ingredients for making bread, plenty of canned items, and even fresh vegetables and fruits.

Richard was glad to have our help, I was sure, even if he didn't indicate it. In contrast to Fred and Joseph's friendly and easy-going style, Richard was markedly stiff and cold. The only real expression was in his eyes, which mostly alternated between cool indifference or a shifty hostility. And of course that Mohawk hedge on the top of his head didn't help. But it was clear that he liked his position as a cook; and he was very definite where and how he wanted everything placed and stored. Once the loading could be under someone else's guidance he left us to prepare a meal -- steak and eggs, no less, with toast and potatoes and orange juice.

"Kinda late in the day for an Aussie breakfast," I suggested teasingly to Laurie.

"Uh - uhh, no way ... steak and eggs and potatoes are great any time, matey!"

Kevin, Fred, and Harry had joined us. They looked pooped, and grimy as hell. Fred and Kevin went through their food in a hurry, anxious to get back to work. Lucky to have them as part of our crew, I thought. Harry lingered ... of course!

"Hey, Laurie, did you notice some peculiarities about what we were loading?"

"What do you mean," he replied.

I glanced around to make sure there were no unwelcomed ears. "For one thing, we sure loaded a lot of rice. I counted 12 ten-kilo bags."

"So?"

"But it's only the three hap-castes that are rice eaters!"

"Yeh, I see what you mean."

"And the vanila ... did you see the vanila?"

"Yeh, I reckon that was odd -- two cases of the stuff, 24 large bottles in each case. That is a lot of vanila ... why, do you think?"

"Guess Richard's going to be cooking a lot a pasteries and pies." Harry suggested, as a joke.

Although we never saw Mr. Fitzgerald until he finally came aboard briefly just before sunset, it was obvious to us all that he had been very busy on shore setting up all the things we had been able to accomplish: the fueling and loading water, Mr. McKenzie, the food supplies, and so on. He wanted to know what we had managed to get done. I didn't offer him any details about Mr. McKenzie's visit, and the radio episode. I was feeling awkward about it all ... I wasn't sure he would approve. After-all, we still didn't know if the radio direction finder actually worked right, or if we could transmit on it, and even the compass adjustment had been marginal because we couldn't swing the ship -- according to Mr. McKenzie anyway. But after talking to our 'officers' he had no questions or comments, so I presumed everything was OK. He then suprised us all with an announcement:

"Gentlemen, I have your seaman's cards. They're not fancy, like I warned you, but they are official and legal.

'Official' and 'legal' I could not judge, but they certainly were *not* fancy! Mine was simply a piece of grey posterboard folded in half to make a 'document' approximately 2 inches by 3, with a black and white photo glued to one inside surface. The minimal information was typewritten on the rough posterboard, and a round, blue seal had been stamped across one edge of the photo -- the only feature to offer a semblance of genuiness. I looked around to verify that those distributed to the rest of the crew were the same as mine. They were. Both Harry and Laurie shrugged, to indicate that they were about as impressed as I was. We smiled graciously towards Mr. Fitzgerald. Our sentiment was shared: 'So what ... no big deal!'

Mr. Fitzgeral returned to shore with the three officers, heading for the Cosmso. The rest of us only wanted to hit the bunks, after a few choice cool ones, that is. Seeing Mr. Milner leave was a relief. That meant no navigation lesson tonight! We started to assemble in the mess after cleaning up and a shower -- our first shower on board, and hot water too. I had to join the others in the crew's shower on the main deck, as there was no facility on my own deck, and the officer's cabins each had their private shower, which of course I couldn't use. But it sure beat taking a salt water bath in the harbor, as I had been doing the last few days.

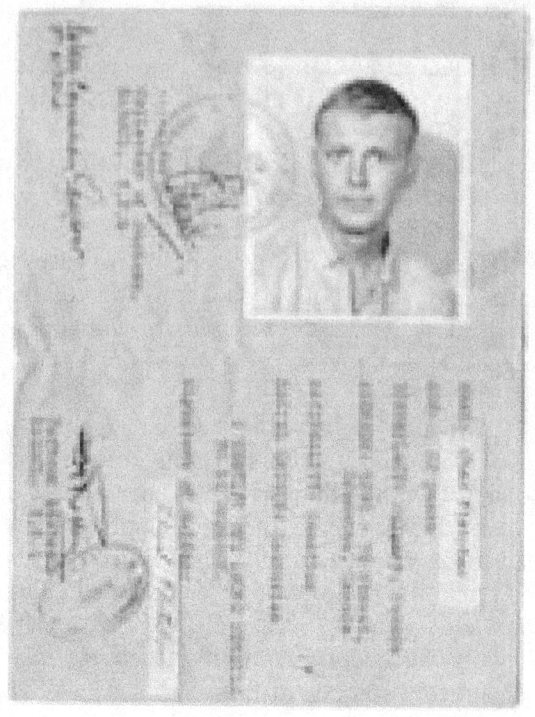

Harry wanted to tell us all about how he was mastering the vital organs of this magnificent vessel. I think he thought he was 'Scotty' and this a Federation starship. Anyway, he went on and on. Kevin was noticeably absent. Fred was quiet, as usual, smiling agreement when required. Harry explained how he had found the fuel tanks not only half-filled with water, but also thick with sludge and a black fungus. He, with Fred's help of course, had cleaned out the two tanks proper like, overcoming impossible obstacles to rig the 4-centimeter hose to shore. And now we had both tanks cleaned spotless and filled with fresh fuel.

"And so when are the main engines going to be running, Harry?" Laurie took the words right out of my mouth -- and with just the right dose of sarcasm.

Harry was insulted. "There you two go again, doubting my capabilities." Harry had just confirmed that I was thinking the same thing as Laurie.

"So, when ... Harry?" Since I was already a part of this, I just couldn't resist.

"They'll both be firing full bore by lunch tomorrow … right Fred!"

Fred was trying his best to be supportive, but Laurie and I both detected a visible measure of panic.

"Harry ... we have a lot to do . . ."

"Right you are, matey ... and it'll be done ... anyone want to wager?"

Well, speaking for myself, I'm not a gambling man. Mostly 'cause I've never won at anything in my entire life ... or maybe it's due to an inherited Dutch sense of thriftiness … my father claimed I was pure Pennsylvania Dutch, from both sides. But Laurie Smale was Aussie, and probably Irish as well, and he couldn't resist the challenge.

"You're on! … twenty dollars!"

This, I was truly enjoying! I knew Harry. And I reflected back to the scene at Walter's. Harry did not want to risk twenty dollars. But his own pride and his propensity to bullshit had placed him between a rock and a hard place.

"High noon it is!"

I just love his sense of the dramatic

Third day, still in Simpson Harbor!

Mr. Fitzgerald was on board early. Very early. I had just fallen out of my bunk and was awakening to the day, and there he was, calling for us to come to the mess. Surprisingly, or maybe not so surprising, Harry was already hard at it. He was even dirty already. He sure didn't want to lose that twenty bucks, I reckoned.

"Gentlemen, we have a lot to do. I want to make sure we are organized and know what each of us have to accomplish.

I just loved the way he was always calling us 'gentlemen'. I suppose it's the standard lingo of a marine officer, but I loved it anyway.

"Chad, Laurie, please take Joseph here with you and be ready to row that lifeboat about. Mr. Holmes will be here at 10:00 a.m. again. I know what you two have done with that vessel … I hope it all holds together … Harry, Kevin, how close are we to having our main engines running?"

"By high noon, sir." Harry didn't miss a heartbeat. "I mean, those engines will be running by noon, sir!"

Harry, you missed your calling … you're a natural born actor!

Mr. Fitzgerald's two eyebrows went up. But he didn't lose a heartbeat either. "Fine, I'm glad to hear that!"

The die is cast!

Laurie and I, and Joseph, had plenty to do.

"Let's take her on a practice run." I suggested.

"Wait a minute, let's think about this … Can we afford to have her in the water very long? And it's going to take some time when Mr. Holmes arrives. I mean, we have to place her in the water, then pull her alongside to where we can board her, and then row her about long enough to show Mr. Holmes. Chad, I don't think we can risk a practice run. Besides, trust me, I can make a good showing of it when the time comes."

"OK, what you say is right, I guess."

"I have an idea, too. How about if we put her in the water just when he's coming across ... so he can't miss seeing us and our 'demonstration'." Laurie was thinking again.

"Uhh - uhh, now wait a minute! You're the best rower, you have to be the one rowing the dinghy."

"Chad, you can handle that!"

"The hell you say! You know I'm a lousy rower!"

"So ... you've got until ten o'clock to improve."

I had to think about this. Laurie was right, I knew. If he and Joseph were rowing around in the water at the same time I was bringing Mr. Holmes across, then he couldn't help but see our demonstration, and that way we had everything in our control ... we wouldn't be caught fumbling with ropes and block and tackle and stumbling aboard, and we could keep her at a distance ... we wouldn't give Mr. Holmes a chance to inspect her up close. But that meant I had to master that S.O.B. dinghy in short order ... in very short order indeed.

"OK Laurie. Let's do it!" I felt a heavy fluttering of anxiety in my stomach.

We discussed the details for a few minutes, then I was off to become an expert oarsman.

Ten o'clock arrived. I was on the small little beach next to our usual shore landing. I had no intention of making things more complicated by having Mr. Holmes wait for me as I rowed across to him. A one-way, one-shot deal was best. Besides, my hands and arms were near worn out by over two hours of continuous practice. At one time I had seen Harry watching from the outside passageway by the engine room, a teasing grin on his face that you could see a mile away.

Mr. Holmes appeared. *And* Mr. Fitzgerald!

Damn, there's going to be two of them!

This was going to be much worse. My stomach was all upside down. I took a deep breath and put on my best 2nd Mate's smile.

"Good day, gentlemen. Are we ready to board?"

Laurie and Fred already had the lifeboat in the water and were positioning her for boarding.

The three of us climbed into the tiny aluminum dinghy, with me in the center, taking up the oars. Mr. Fitzgerald was watching what I was doing, interested and probably a little worried. So was Mr. Holmes ... watching, I mean. I didn't try to guess at what he was thinking. We proceeded to cross.

Joseph and Laurie were now in full control of the lifeboat, rowing her into full view, but keeping a distance. Mr. Fitzgerald saw them for the first time; a look of unmistakeable delight lightening his face. "Mr. Holmes, I believe we have a demonstration in progress. Unexpected, I might add!"

Mr. Holmes turned to see what he was referring to ... he was in the bow of the dinghy, and had been facing away from the Trader. He watched, studying the performance. I thought I perceived a slight nodding of his head at one point.

With their attention focused elsewhere my own performance was improving dramatically. I thought I was doing pretty good, in fact. We reached the freighter's stern without a hitch, and disembarked from the dinghy.

"Mr. Fitzgerald, I have gone over Mr. McKenzie's report; and I find it satisfactory. And you have shown me your newly acquired selection of navigation charts. So there's no need for us to visit the wheelhouse. And I think you have successfully demonstrated the seaworthiness of your lifeboat and your crew's ability to handle it. What I would like to review, however, is your, shall we say, mechanical condition. I would like to visit your engineroom and talk to your Chief Engineer."

The Chief Engineer, you say? Oh - oh!

"Certainly. This way to the engineroom, Mr. Holmes."

Mr. Fitzgerald hadn't batted an eye. Talk to the Chief Engineer? What a joke! I was wondering where in the range of green to blue he would be by now.

Just after ten o'clock in the morning?? ... probably a nice maroon!

The engine room was an all out and out mess. Pails and rags and parts were everywhere, and everywhere was oil and grime. Fred was busy with what looked like super-sized filter housings, cleaning them. Harry and Kevin were both astride one of the main engines.

The Trader was powered by two propellers, each driven separately by a six-cylinder Perkins diesel. These engines were not large by marine standards -- I remembered that the single engine in the Cap Finisterre had six pistons big enough for three people to stand on the top of, and still have room to do the boogie. I know because they had been doing some work on it while we were in Portland, and a side engine access panel had been removed. The panel itself was the size of a regular house door. I had been stoked ... standing there watching the piston go up and down, from below that is ... the access panel was positioned between the crankshaft and the bottom of the huge piston cylinder. The engine had been actually running, yet the piston moved up and down ever so slowly, maybe a complete stroke every, say, 1 to 2 seconds. I felt I could have walked through that panel-way and jumped onto the 'conrod', like it was a medium-sized tree trunk, and hung-on for a fun ride. That's the honest truth!

Well, the Trader's Perkins were nothing like that, but they were still big -- each one about ten feet high from the floor, which was constructed around the bottom of its crankcase, to the top of the heads, and each was about fifteen feet long. A single piston was as big around and long as a 3 gallon cleaning pail, and each cylinder had its separate head, complete with an overhead cam, rocker panel and pushrods. It was the rocker panels that Harry and Kevin were working on.

"Gentlemen," There was that loveable term again.

"This is our Harbor Master, Mr. Holmes ... Mr. Holmes, this is Mr. Fiddler, our 2nd Engineer, and Kevin, our 3rd Engineer." He had placed an emphasis on Harry's 2nd Engineer status.

"Mr. Holmes, our Chief Engineer, Mr. Morris, is unavailable this morning. I'm afraid he's feeling under the weather."

"But I am sure Mr. Fiddler here can fill you in on any details you wish to know. Or myself, for that matter.

Damn, but the man has balls!

Mr. Holmes hesitated, and shrugged slightly. "Very well ... Mr. Fiddler, how is your auxillary running?"

Harry stepped readily into the role: "Sir, she has a re-conditioned head ... we put her on just two days ago, and she runs like a swiss timepiece. We'll certainly have no worries there."

"And your mains?"

"We're working on them, sir. We had a problem with contaminated fuel, and we've had to empty the tanks, clean them, and refill with fresh fuel. We're just now cleaning the engine's supply line and filters, and adjusting her valve clearances. We expect to be running within a couple of hours, sir."

Bravo, Harry! May we please have a round of applause for our new star, Mr. Harry Fiddler, alias 2nd Engineer!

The final line was designed to cut off any more concerns ... and it worked. Or at least partly.

"Alright, Mr. Fitzgerald. You are getting close, but I can't give you a clean bill of health quite yet. I want to hear both these main engines running -- and running well. And I want your Chief Engineer to prepare a full, detailed report on the status of your engines and power train and major mechanical components."

Mr. Fitzgerald was listening, nodding, not liking what he was hearing but not showing irritation either.

"Two more things, Mr. Fitzgerald: I will require you to have an auxillary bilge pump for this engine room ... I suggest you go buy a good centrifugal pump, about a ten centimeter model ... and I want to see that Seagull outboard that's on your aft deck running and powering your dinghy."

"Very well ... sir!" Now Mr. Fitzgerald was revealing a measure of vexation. "As you say ... However, may we have you aboard for inspection again as soon as we have those things in order?"

"I can do that. . . alright Mr. Fitzgerald."

Both men were agitated at this point. I was glad to see that this was the end of Mr. Holmes' visit.

With almost perfect timing Laurie showed up to take Mr. Holmesl ashore. I gave him an upward thumb and a grin when I was sure neither Mr. Fitzgerald nor Mr. Holmes could see.

Lunch was late. I only know because Laurie and I were both watching the time, waiting to see who was going to win the bet. Maybe Harry had something to do with when lunch was ready -- maybe not. It did look suspicious though, because at exactly 12:25 one of the Perkins came to life; and at 12:56 the second made it's rebirth. The lunch bell then sounded 8 minutes later.

Harry was a trip ... I mean he was really something to behold. Kevin and Fred were all smiles and feeling very good about those engines. But Harry -- he was all long face because he knew he had lost the bet, at least technically, but at the same time he too was estatic about the start up of the Perkins and didn't want to lose out in that particular round of glory. So he was a mixture of extremes. Laurie and I had decided to play it real cool -- no smirks, no wise cracks -- just a simple question from Laurie.

"Well, Harry, when do I get the twenty?"

Harry had decided to be stubborn. "Get off my back, OK ... Yeh, the engines were running a few minutes past the hour. So what, you're going to hold a stop watch on this? Besides, if that Harbor Master hadn't interrupted us, we would've had those engines running before twelve o'clock."

"Take it easy, Harry! We're friends, OK? If you don't want to pay up, now, well that's alright with me. I got patience." Laurie was playing out his part in great style.

"Hey, f__ you two. You'll get it when I'm good and ready, OK!"

This was all passed back and forth in reasonably good humor, but orchestrated by Harry so the outcome was uncertain. He had no intention of paying, that was obvious. Laurie really didn't care. But we both enjoyed seeing Harry have a taste of humble pie.

Regardless, the engines were finally running. I felt a lot of excitement ... we were getting close.

As if to confirm my sense of a pending departure, Mr. Fitzgerald instructed Laurie and I and Joseph to return the lifeboat to her chocks, complete with gear and a change of drinking water and food rations. We were told to then 'swab' the entire ship, top to bottom ... to make everything 'shipshape'. Although it was unspoken, the intent was to put forth the best impression possible for Mr. Holmes' next visit, hoping it would be his last.

As we nestled the lifeboat back into the cradle of her chocks, we noticed that our putty work had begun to swell, with the new paint cover starting to form a bubble over several of the patches.

"Looks like it wouldn't have lastest much longer in the water, I reckon." Laurie was worried.

"Bloody hell, hope we don't need it!" Joseph startled us with what was an infrequent exclamation for him, spoken with the hap-caste's curious mixture of pidgin and Aussie English. But he was expressing a deep concern.

Laurie picked up on it and probed: "By the way, Joseph, what do you three blokes think about this trip ... I mean, how about the rumors that the Trader's supposed to be sunk or wrecked on a reef."

"Our families don't want us to go," he answered, seeming to be glad to have a chance to talk about it. "The old crew have put a 'tambu' on this boat, and they say bad things. But they are superstitious, stupid." He shrugged. "What do *you* think?"

"I was worried about the rumors, but I think Mr. Fitzgerald is a good man ... he's trying his best to make sure we'll make the voyage OK." Laurie sounded like he was trying to convince himself as well as Joseph.

Joseph turned towards me, wanting to know what I thought.

"Nah ... this may turn out to be one crazy voyage, but I don't think there's any scheme to see us shipwrecked!"

We were well into the massive chore of 'swabbing down the ship', which had been an adventure of improvision and searching for hoses, scrubbing tools, and detergent, when Mr. Fitzgerald returned. He had two New Guinea boys with him, and what looked like a brand new water pump, painted bright orange and blue and complete with a rigid intake hose and an attached metal filter at the end -- about 4 inches in diameter -- and a roll of collapsable plastic discharge hose. It was the same kind we used as part of our roadbuilding operation, when we needed to pump water out of a trench, or some such thing -- a centrifugal pump with a gasoline 2-cycle engine, probably a five horsepower Briggs & Stratton.

"The Harbor Master required that we have a secondary bilge pump," I explained to Laurie and Joseph. "Uhh ... the bilge is the lowest part of the inside of the hull, where any water drains to." I added in response to their perplexed looks. "That sucker can pump a lot of water. Damn glad to know we've got it."

We labored till the sun was again making its inevitable plunge behind Tunnel Hill. Joseph and Laurie were stowing the hoses and gear, and I was squeegying one last area of puddled water, when we were once more interrupted by a new event, and a new sound. This time it was the sputter-put-put of a small two cycle engine. The pump, I questioned myself? No, too much of a put-put sound.

Aahh, I know what it is!

"Gentlemen," I decided this called for an official announcement from a ships officer: "You are hearing the sound of our mighty Seagull outboard! Do you realize what this means?" I was directing the question to Laurie and Joseph, but I answered the question before they had a chance to reflect on it: "This means that we are ready for Mr. Holme's next inspection, which I have a feeling will be his last."

Now I *was* excited! Our day already ended, we scrampled to get cleaned up and showered. I was thinking about Deli. This might be my last night to see her. And we had been told that the voyage to Hong Kong would take about 21 days. That's a long time without any loving.

"Harry, you wanna go to Aunty Freitas tonight? Bet Liza will be there."

Oops, I had used a bad choice of words, 'cause Harry almost growled at the word 'bet'.

What a sorehead!

"Come on, Harry, this might be our last night."

Harry slowly returned to his normal cheerfullness, which was a relief. "You may be right, mate. Alright, let's relax a bit over a couple, then let's go."

But visiting Deli that night was not to be my destiny, for as we were just finishing our second round I was once again called upon by Mr. Milner. He was in that particular mood of his again, and I was about to receive lesson number two of my crash course in celestial navigation.

"Tell Deli I will see her tomorrow night ... by hook or by crook!"

"What!"

"Just tell her I'll see her tomorrow night, OK??"

"Now, Chad, I want you to find a LOP, start to finish. We won't stop tonight until you've accomplished that ... understand?"

"Alright, Mr. Milner." I could muster only mediocre enthusiasm. I felt the full weight of a depressive gloom. This was going to be a strain. And I sure did want to see Deli tonight.

"First of all, we need to choose our navigational stars ... Let me simplify this for you. The Nautical Almanac lists 57 stars -- all of first magnitude brightness. I think ... I forget. Anyway, it's not important. But for our voyage to Hong Kong we can shorten our list to a select few. Our choice is determined largely by our latitude. We are now at approximately 4 degreees south of the equator."

Mr. Milner was pacing back and forth on the port deck, I was assigned to a chair, with a notebook and pen in hand.

"Do you know where the 'North Star', or 'Polaris' is?"

"Yes sir ... it is at the end of the handle of the Little Dipper."

This I knew readily, for star gazing had been a favorite pastime of mine during my youngest years. And later as well. But it started back when I had inherited my older brother's newspaper route at the age of ten. We were kind of poor ... my mom and dad operated a retail shoe store in the economically depressed hick town of Cardston in southern Alberta, and that newspaper route was an important source of income for me. Every day I would pick up my bundle of newspapers after school, about 4:30 in the afternoon, and trek out on that route. It was a lengthly route, and took me a long time, and the duration would typically stretch out even more because I was such a daydreamer sort of kid, and I loved to play. I would get sidetracked romping with one or two favorite dogs, or in the winter time I would venture out into the fresh snow and trample out a 'geese track' or some design of my own. A 'geese track' was simply a large 'spoked wheel' in which us kids would play tag, being confined to the 'spokes' and 'rim' of the wheel. So I would usually be out on the route till well past dark. Especially in the wintertime, when at that latitiude it got dark about 5:00 P.M. I remember the night sky would be so bright and clear, and full of wonder. During the winter I often spent an hour or so watching the 'Aurora Borealis', or Northern Lights, sitting comfortably in a snow drift, watching nature put on her show. Of course I couldn't do that when it was cold ... and by cold I mean below 0 degrees Fahrenheit. Zero degrees was OK, I was always bundled up with thick layers of clothes. But when it got to minus 20 degrees, or minus 30, or even colder, then I had a hard time. I remember one night when it had been a close call. It was about minus 40 degrees, about the coldest it ever got. Now that's without the 'wind chill factor' which they always add now-a-days, but that's B.S.. Back then the temperature was the still air temperature and everyone knew that if you faced the wind, then of course it was colder, and you also knew to park you car so as to protect your radiator, because at minus 40 the wind would turn the pure anti-freeze in an engine block rock solid. Anyway, that night my feet and hands became terribly cold, so cold they stopped hurting and started to numb. It was the first time I had ever been that cold. I felt tired, so sleepy, and

I laid down in the nearest snowdrift, actually feeling comfortable, and wanting to sleep. Then I jumped up with a start, realizing what was happening, and started stomping my feet and clapping my hands. If I had stayed in that snowdrift I would have fallen asleep and frozen to death. I headed for the nearest house and banged on the door. The old couple living there hustled me inside and took care of me. It was a close call.

But back to the stars. Yes, I knew about the Big Dipper, and the Small Dipper and the North Star, and even Orion. Not much more than that, though.

"Well, you know then that if Polaris is visible, we can determine our latititude easily."

"Uh, not really, sir."

"Umm ... alright. I'll be more basic then. Imagine that you are at the center of the earth ... can you do that?"

"Yes, I guess I can."

"If you are at the center of the earth, then the earth's surface would be a sphere around you, correct? See it as a transparent ball, which is rotating on its axis around you."

"Yes, I can visualize that."

"Then the stars -- and the sun and the moon -- form another sphere around that one, a celestial sphere. OK? That sphere is stationary."

"Yes."

"It is as if you are at the center of the universe. Here, let me sketch this in your notebook." Which he did.

"Now, if you are here ... he pointed to the center of the earth ... and you drew a line from you to any celestial body, then that line would intersect the earth's sphere at a given latitude, right?"

"Got it!" My interest was finally starting to stir.

"Now, if you drew a line from you throught the point where the earth's axis is -- the north pole -- and extended it to the celestial sphere, you would find a point in the sky that would remain stationary while the earth rotates. Well ... it just so happens that we have a star located at that very point over the north pole, which is Polaris. It's off just a tiny bit, no more than 1-2 degrees. Do you understand, so far?"

"I'm following, I think."

"Let's place you on the earth's sphere now. At the north pole the star Polaris would be directly overhead, or 90 degrees. See? If you moved on the sphere, or the earth's surface, towards the equator, then Polaris would become lower and lower in the sky ... until it would be at the horizon when you reached the equator, and would disappear below the horizon once you entered the southern hemisphere."

Mr. Milner stopped for a drawn-out sip on his scotch and soda.

"Unfortunately, we don't have any star directly over the south pole. We only have the Southern Cross, which is rather poorly defined and is pretty well invisible to us this close to the equator anyway, so we won't bother with it. Once we travel north, however, we will be able to see Polaris and it will be useful. Incidently, because Polaris is so close to the northern zenith, its LOP is a straight line lying almost perfectly east and west. That is, it is a line of latititude."

"Now, enough theory, let's get to the real thing. I will give you five stars with which to concentrate on. The first is Sirius, the brightest star in the sky. To find it you first locate the constellation Orion, 'The Hunter'. Are you familiar with that constellation?"

"Orion is the one that has three stars in a row -- the hunter's belt -- right?"

"Yes, can you see it?"

"Right there," I pointed to a location low in the western sky.

"Now follow a line drawn through those three stars on the belt, eastward and slightly south. Can't miss it, can you?"

"Wow, so that's Sirius. It *is* bright!"

"Star number two is Canopus, which happens to be the second brightest in the sky, and is almost straight south from Sirius. See it?"

"Hey, this is neat. Yes, I see it."

"Now we need a couple of more northernly stars. Our third choice is Betelgeuse, which is part of our familiar Orion, and is the brightest star just north of Orion's belt. Got it?"

"Got it!"

"We now have to travel east across the sky. Ahh, we're lucky, we can just see the Big Dipper. See it?"

"Yes."

"Follow the last two stars of the handle, and come a little south. The first bright star is Arcturus, in the constellation of Bootes, 'The Herdsman". See it?"

"I think so."

"The fifth star I want you to know is Vega, in the constellation Lyra, 'The Harp'. But we can't see Vega now, it's below the horizon, to the east. So, you now have five stars, and Polaris. Tonight we will find LOPs' for Beetelgeuse, Sirius, and Canopus. Can you please bring out the ship's sextant."

"I want you to take a shot of Sirius first. And when you have the sighting as best you can, you must walk quickly back to the chronometer, counting seconds at the same time."

"Pardon me?"

"You must have the time exact, right? You can't take the chronometer with you, you have to walk back to where it is. So you must count the seconds that pass and when you reach the chronometer you mark down the time at that moment and then subtract the counted seconds to find the precise time that you took the sighting. Do you understand?"

"OK," I was struggling with this rapid pace. I followed his instructions. Mr. Milner had me repeat the sighting over and over. And then for Beetelgeuse, and then for Canopus. Over and over. I was feeling fatigued. Finally, he had me make a sighting of each of the three stars in rapid succession.

"Well, Chad, I think you've got that part down OK. Now to calculate the LOPs." With that he brought out another notebook in which he had written out a lengthly formula and a table with which to organize the data. "Bring the Almanac and let's go down to the officer's mess."

Once in the mess, he sat down beside me and started to work out the LOPs for the sightings. He had prepared a short outline of the steps I had to follow, which went like this:

1. Make a sighting, noting the name of the body, sextant reading, and the GMT time.

2. Note 'height of the eye above water' and the 'dead reckoning' position of ship at time of sighting.

3. Determine G.H.A. (Greenwich Hour Angle) and d (= Decl. =declination) of the body observed from the Nautical Almanac, corrected to time of sighting.

4. Correct the sextant reading to find Ho (corrected altitude).

5. Apply longitutude to G.H.A. and compute L.H.A. (Local Hour Angle) and t (Meridian Angle)

Mr. Milner completed the first one, explaining what he was doing, I only watched. Then he gave me the second to do myself, with him correcting and guiding me. Finally, he left me to do the third entirely on my own and returned to the the upper deck.

"Bring your third result up to the wheelhouse as soon as you're finished, and we'll plot out the LOPs on the chart.

After a great deal of mental struggle I finally completed the ordeal and brought my paperwork to Mr. Milner. He had already plotted the first two LOPs'. He showed me what he had done, using a theoretical DR., which is an estimated point of position at the time of the sightings. For this exercise he had chosen a location several miles south of Simpson Harbor. His first two LOPs' intersected within Simpson Harbor. Not bad, I thought. The third LOP came close to intersecting the first two lines at the same spot.

"Our results are good. Not bad for a first time, Chad. Of course our DR. was close, so we couldn't be off by too much." I could tell that he was feeling weary of this lesson as well.

"I think that'll do for tonight. You've done well. Thank you."

Jeeses, thank god for that!!

I was leaning against the poop deck rail close to my cabin door, gazing into the harbor and the sky, and measuring the events of the day. I noticed a small, intermittent red glow in the direction of the ship's bow, and could make out a tall, thin sillouette, and the person had short hair. It was Richard, smoking a cigarette. And, yes, sipping on a bottle. No big thing ... he deserves his quiet moments ... and some booze like the rest of us.

But he sure does keep to himself !!

Fourth day, still stuck in Simpson Harbor.

Mr. Fitzgerald was very eager to see us on our way, for again he arrived just after sunrise. Apparently ten o'clock was a popular inspection time for Mr. Holmes ... he was to be on board once again at that hour. Mr. Fitzgerald wanted us all to concentrate on one thing -- getting the ship clean and orderly. He found some faults with our swabbing job, and so Laurie and I were assigned some reworking. Joseph was borrowed from us and sent below with Kevin, Harry, and Fred ... they were to clean the engines and below-decks spotless. Except that Kevin was assigned the special responsibility of also having the dinghy ready for Mr. Holmes, with the Seagull attached and fully operational. And Mr. Fitzgerald had several pages of a type-written report for Mr. Morris to sign. This I know, 'cause I was in the wheelhouse when Mr. Fitzgerald had presented it to him.

"And for Christ's sake, Mr. Morris, will you kindly be sober and presentable at 10 o'clock. You must be the one to hand this to Mr. Holmes."

Mr. Stanley Morris was kinda greenish -- it was too early in the day for him to have had a chance to be otherwise -- and so he answered shakily: "I'll do so, sir ... you can count on it!"

I heard an unhappy grunt from Mr. Fitzgerald as he turned and left. I looked at our Chief Engineer, feeling sympathy towards him, for the first time.

"A couple of drinks and I'll be alright."

What I admired about the guy was his complete honesty regarding his life style and his dependency on booze.

I wonder if 'booze is the only answer' Dennis Macleod will end up like that?

Mr. Holmes arrived. My presence was requested by Mr. Fitzgerald. I wondered why. He probably needed someone to respond to orders in case something needed to be fetched, or done at the last minute. I perceived a different air about Mr. Holmes today. He seemed more relaxed, more amiable. The Seagull had made an early, favorable impression, I am sure. Maybe that was it. And then the Trader was quite a bit cleaner and more presentable this morning, to be sure. That couldn't help but prompt a favorable response. Especially when we visited below-decks. The boys were still busy cleaning, but the restoration already achieved was remarkable. Even I was impressed. And there, right at the bottom of the steps going down into the engine room, slightly off to the right, was the shiny new pump, looking so very pretty. Mr. Holmes smiled and nodded approval.

"I'm impressed, Mr. Fitzgerald ... But now may I talk to your Chief Engineer, and have that report I requested?"

"Mr. Morris is up top sir. Can we go meet him?"

This is where I started holding my breath.

Mr. Morris was on the starboard deck, in his lounge chair as usual, but dressed very differently from what I had seen at any time previous. He actually appeared quite sharp, in a white naval jacket and white slacks -- and there was no glass of scotch and water in sight either. Most noteworthy, however, was his complexion, for at that moment it was neither green nor blue -- it seems there was a narrow middle range somewhere, between the two colors, and he had found it, for the occasion.

"Mr. Holmes, I understand you are needing a report on the ship's engines and mechanical gear. Here it is, sir. I am sure you will find it satisfactory."

We were all impressed. Mr. Fitzgerald was beaming. Mr. Holmes accepted the report almost graciously. Mr. Milner was the exception, however, for I caught a sly narrowing of his eyes and just the trace of a smirk on his face.

Ahh ... this had been Mr. Milner's doing!

However, all this favorable impact was just too much for Mr. Holmes to swallow whole. He hesitated in the wheelhouse for a moment, as if this was all too good to be true and he was searching for fault. Then there was a light on his face.

"Mr. Fitzgerald, I recall seeing only one of your lifeboats in the water. How about the second one?"

Mr. Fitzgerald remained expressionless, but I knew panic lurked just below the surface. It certainly did with me. Mr. Milner broke the silence:

"Mr. Holmes, we have a slight problem there ... You see, our list makes it impractical to lower the lifeboat on the port side ... I have a suggestion, however. We could simply fill the vessel with water while she sits in her chocks -- to demonstrate that she has no leaks."

A dozen separate reactions flickered across the Harbor Master's countenance.

"Mr. Fitzgerald, let's sit down and have a drink. This is a very unusual situation."

The man was showing mental fatigue, and a degree of resignation, yet it was clear that he was reluctant to give-in completely.

"Mr. Milner, please proceed to fill the lifeboat."

That was my signal to move into action. I walked slowly from the wheelhouse to the stairs and out of view, then instantly changed my pace and raced below to find Laurie and Joseph. As quickly as we could we removed the craft's tarp and gear and began filling her up. We now knew how to tap into the ship's salt water system, used for cleaning the decks and which consisted of 2 inch pipes, so we were abe to fill the boat quickly. When she was nearing full I again slowed my pace and climbed below to the wheelhouse.

"Sir, the port lifeboat is filled." I addressed this to Mr. Milner.

Mr. Holmes surveyed the lifeboat, seeing that no water was leaking, and checked the assortment of gear which we had spread out neatly close by. He leaned over the deck railing, imagining the difficulty we would have in lowering the vessel down the outward sloping side. He nodded and shrugged.

"I suppose this will have to do. However, Mr. Fitzgerald, I must be honest with you … I have very serious reservations about the seaworthiness and safety of this ship, and your owner's true intentions. But you have obviously worked hard at getting her shipshape and you have complied with my requests. You may weigh anchor at your convenience and be on your way. And good luck … especially to your crew."

This called for a celebration. No question! But it was Mr. Fitzgerald's idea. As soon as Mr. Holmes was safely removed, we all met in the officer's mess, including our three certified officers.

"Gentlemen, we have received permission to be underway and leave Rabaul. I would like to toast your hard work, and your ingenuity." There was a round of good 'ol boy Aussie 'hear, hear's. "And here's to your success and safety." Another round of hear, hear's, even loader.

Mr. Fitzgerald waited a couple of minutes, everyone having a chance for a few sips of their drinks, then went on:

"However, I feel we must make this celebration brief. I propose we weigh anchor at first light tomorrow morning. But we have several things to do first. Harry and Kevin, you must test your drive train, give the propellers a try. And Mr. Milner, I would like you to form a crew and test the anchor mechanisms -- make sure we can lift and secure our anchor with no problem. Chad, I want to put you in charge of topping-off our fresh water ... which reminds me ... I must instruct you all to preserve your fresh water supply. This vessel was originally designed for a small tanker crew and unfortunately has a limited fresh water holding capacity. I'm afraid that from here on in you must limit yourselves to salt water baths, using the ships salt water piping system. Except for our officers, of course. They will still have the privilege of fresh water showering. Harry, as soon as you can I would like you to somehow ensure that the fresh water supply to the crew's showers is disconnected. I'm sorry, gentlemen. But there is nothing worse than being at sea and running out of fresh water. Finally, I would like you to come on shore with me Richard, we need to complete our food requisition."

We all finished our drinks and then separated to our different chores.

"No way, Harry. I'm going to see Deli."

Harry wanted to go to the Cosmos for some final goodbyes. He had seen Liza the night before, while I had been stuck with my navigation lesson. Everyone was going ashore tonight, it seemed, all saying goodbye.

"But Fitzgerald said first light ... and means that everyone is to be back on board tonight."

Now it was my turn to be a little hard-headed. "Don't you worry your butt about me, matey ... I'm not about to miss this trip ... I'll be back in time."

I picked up as much beer and gin as I could carry, purposefully choosing the shop closest to Aunty Freitas, and headed in that direction. There had been a lot of fussing around on board ... we had all been busy until past sunset, and then there had been cleaning up and having a salt-water shower ... it was already late. My excitement was running high -- because of the adventure that lay before me, and leaving Rabaul, and of course Deli.

Deli was there. News travels fast around this small town ... she already knew we were leaving in the morning. Aunty Freita was there as well, thirsty as ever, and Henri, and even Saki. And there was a new girl, named Mama, who had just arrived from somewhere along the New Britain coast. Young and kinda cute. Reminded me of Liza. We started a repeat performance of two nights earlier, and Deli started again on her new song. I was kind of eager to get her into bed, but I listened patiently while she whined it out a dozen or so times. About then we had a pleasant interruption. It was Mike.

"Hey, guy, glad to see you." I grabbed his hand warmly. This was one bloke I was going to miss ... and remember.

"Chad, I hear you're leaving in the morning ... I was just talking to Harry."

"Yes, tomorrow it is. We're actually going to take that piece of rusty iron out to sea."

"Is it really that bad?"

"Nah, not really. We all feel pretty good about her." I laughed. I related to him all the things that had happened, and we shared a few laughs.

"By the way, Deli, where's Kelli?" He had been wanting to ask that all along.

But Deli looked at him coolly. I knew her well enough to detect sympathy, but she wasn't about to reveal it to Mike. "Kelli no stay ... I no see long Kelli all same long time." She shrugged, then made a strong gesture towards Mama, with whom Mike had been exchanging smiles while I had been telling him about the Trader.

Mike started to talk to Mama ... it was time for Deli and I to head for the sleeping room.

"Mike, here's farewell, in case I don't see you again before sunrise." I winked. "And Mike ... try to forget about Kelli ... OK? ... I wish you were going with us ... you need to get away from New Guinea."

He watched me as I spoke, taking me seriously, but resisting with a sad resolution. It would probably take some time for his infatuation with Kelli to simmer to a level where he could begin to be objective, and to forget her.

Kelli was from the Trobriand Islands, a small group of islands to the south of New Britain. She was taller and lighter skinned than Deli or the local New Guineans, and was comparatively better looking. What was so compelling though, was her great figure: gorgeous high breasts, flat stomach, and a wonderful, full ass. Couldn't blame Mike for finding her so attactive. I remembered the first night I had been at the CDW camp, and had been introduced to hoop'in. Kelli had come to my room first. I had thought that I was about to enter paradise. But it didn't work out. I think I was overly excited, or acted stupid, or maybe it was the heat rash I was nursing at the time and I had applied some foul smelling lotion. Anyway, she decided not to stay with me -- and I got Deli instead.

One night Mike had made a scene that had roused the entire camp. He had caught Kelli in someone else's room and he was in a jealous rage. Right in front of half the camp he proposed to her. Right then and there. Most everyone thought he was nuts. I wasn't so sure. That night I had teased Deli with the same kind of proposal, just to see what kind of reaction I would get. She had suddenly become very serious, and started to explain to me that no, that was out of the question. I was surprised. I thought she would be flattered with a proposal. But she said that she would be my girlfiiend while I was there, but she knew that I would leave someday, and that was OK. "Me be all same girlfriend you, time you stay, and when time you go ... it OK," and she had shrugged. She had gone on to explain that they knew what they were doing, the girls who were the local 'maris' that is, and knew that they were whores. She even explained the drink that they made from the bark of a certain tree that worked as a contraceptive. They did what they did because they wanted to, and had to. They appreciated the dollars we gave them, and our care. What she revealed had been an eye-opener.

"I hope you blokes make it alright," Mike offered as a farewell. Deli and I were on our way to the sleeping room.

"Yeh, me too!"

We snuggled together under the mosquito net. I was feeling hot as hell, sexually that is. This would be our last time together. I wanted to make it exceptional. I caressed her delicately with my fingers, going over the tattoo bumps on her cheeks and breasts. I knew she loved that, and she started to breath heavier. But I was building towards what I really wanted to do. I replaced my fingers with my lips, detouring to suck full and hard on her nipples and to bite them gently with my teeth. I slid down lower ... the mosquito net got caught in my feet and I had to find my way underneath, so that my feet and calves were outside, hanging over the end of the bed. Oh how I loved this part. Deli's pussy was so very sweet; no strong taste or odor ... maybe due to her mostly vegetarian diet. I don't know. She started to giggle and squirm ... it always embarrassed her, until she got fully turned on. I found her 'little man in the boat' with the end of my tongue. At first she would be very sensitive at that spot, so I had to be very gentle, touching only lightly. Later I could grab at it with my lips and tug -- and suck. Her vulva hairs were a special delight, her pubic mass a closely curled mat. But the hairs themselves were lightly soft -- and very fine. I could catch a bunch in my teeth and stretch them out. They would stretch out two inches, maybe three. Then I would let them go, and they would return to their tight curls, not quickly, not slowly either, just softly. I timed my motions and their firmness to her response, sensing her excitement and nearness to climax. If I could get her past the initial sensitive stage I could really turn her on, making her climax over and over. And that's what happened. We went on and on; I brought my feet back under the mosquito net and we transitioned into other kinds and positions of lovemaking, until we had both reached a level of restfull satiety. We finally laid quietly beside each other. I whispered in her ear: "Me all same love long you plenty too much!" She giggled.

CHAPTER FIVE

Mutiny on the Bismark Sea

No one is going to scuttle this ship –
I"m taking her to Australia, where
these scoundrels will be dealt with
properly!

   Laurie was startled from his light sleep by a loud "psst - psst", "psst -psst",
the volume and frequency increasing rapidly ... then it ended abruptly with a hard
knocking sound taking its place -- the sound of a large diesel engine slowly
coming to life. He hurriedly clambered into his shorts and short-sleeved shirt,
anxious to become a part of the events which promised to make this a very
special day. An early morning light was radiating from the pre-dawn glow
emerging over Mt. Kombiu, on the east side of Simpson Harbor, high-lighting
the glass-smooth tops of a series of long, low swells that were advancing gently

across the curvature of the harbor. It was August, a dry time of the year with no strong winds nor heavy rain to disturb the tranquility of this equatorial sea. Laurie theorized that this was an ideal time to begin a voyage north and westward to the Philippines, the China Sea, and finally to Hong Kong. Another sequence of the 'psst - psst' of compressed air being used to drive an engine's pistons gave warning of the starting-up of the freighter's second Perkins diesel, this time the sound subdued by the rumbling of the first engine, already vibrantly operative.

As if not wanting to be left out of the line-up of sounds that would mark the slow awakening of the New Guinea Trader, hopefully in preparation for the raising of her two anchors and the long awaited departure from Rabaul, the loud clang-clang of the cook's bell pricked sharply at the crew's senses, the sound complimented by the stimulating aroma of frying steak and eggs which had already permeated throughout the living areas of the ship. Laurie happily reflected that this was one breakfast favorite he could never tire of.

Mr. Fitzgerald met the crew in the officer's mess again ... he had come aboard before sunrise, as everyone had expected. And once more the three certified officers joined the rest of the crew; all were anticipating final instructions from the owner's representative. An aura of excitement pervaded the small cabin space, emanating mostly from our less inexperienced crew -- it was like we were about to start our first twenty-six mile marathon. For the certified officers this was more old hat ... but even for them the beginning of a new voyage was a special thrill, and the departure of the troubled old Trader was not exempt.

"Gentlemen, I believe we are ready. I've reviewed all the items required for the voyage and I think we're complete. As soon as we've had breakfast, therefore, we will begin weighing anchor operations and you will be on your way. I will disembark as soon I as see the first anchor secured and everything is under control. Good luck, gentlemen. Uhh ... aren't we missing someone?"

Harry came to my rescue.

"Mr. Fitzgerald, Chad hasn't come on board yet ... he went ashore last night to say goodbye to his ... uhh ... girlfriend. But I'm sure he'll be here any minute now."

"Damn!" I half stumbled, half crawled out from under the mosquito net, trying to grab at my clothes and get to my feet at the same time. The dawn light at the window told me that the sun was just about to explode its brilliance over Mt. Kombiu, and that I had overslept. I envisioned the Trader's anchors already secured against the steel plates of her bow, her propellers churning, and her hull slowly making way towards the open sea -- without me!

"Time you go long ship?" Deli had been roughly awakened by my hurried movements.

"Deli, I'm sorry, I gotta go!" I gave her a hastened but delicate kiss on her cheek, and headed for the door. "Goodbye! I love long you plenty too much, all same." I smiled at her warmly ... she giggled. It always made her laugh when I said 'plenty too much'. Don't really know why. Maybe I said it funny -- to her ear at least. But it served to lighten the meaning of a serious statement, and that's what I had intended.

It was about two full miles to the Trader's anchorage. No choice but to foot it ... as fast as I could!

Damn these thongs!

Two blocks to Mango Ave, then the straight shot to Malaguna Road, a left turn and a short cut through the pier area. But all on asphalt paved road or crushed coral gravel ... no chance to take off these rubber thongs and run bare foot. No way -- not with these tender pink feet. That was the one disadvantage to thongs; just too damn difficult to run in them! Pure hell in an emergency.

So it was no four minute mile times two, but I moved as fast as I could. At about the spot where I left Mango Avenue I caught a glimpse of the west side of the harbor. I could see that the Trader was still there ... and I could see her anchor chains still angled down into the water, and taunt ... they hadn't even started to winch in the anchors.

Whew!! But this is cutting it close!

Still, I didn't want to miss a single thing, nor make Mr. Fitzgerald pissed at me ... especially that.

As I rounded the corner at Dawapia Road I was aware of an old battered pick-up truck pulling along side of me, keeping pace with my already fatigued run. I glanced to my right and saw that it was an aged Datsun, with scattered patches of original paint indicating that it had been painted a bright red at one time, but was now mostly rust and grey primer. The driver was my acquaintance of a few nights before: the Trader's previous captain, the mysterious Captain Rodney McKay. Once again he touched the sunvisor of his over-worn blue naval officer's cap in greeting, and once again I endured the wry smile and glinted eye.

"Could I be giving you a lift to the Trader", he offered, in his heavy Scottish accent.

"I'm almost there," I answered, feeling uncomfortable about accepting a ride from this strange man. But then I shrugged, thinking it would be difficult to refuse and wanting to get to the Trader as soon as possible, anyway. So I pulled at the handle to the passenger's side door -- it required two tries before it finally broke loose -- and positioned myself atop the torn and fragmented seat. "But thank you ... we're ready to set sail, and I'm late." I hoped this would serve to hasten our coverage of the short two blocks to the Trader's anchorage, and limit Captain McKay's opportunity to make conversation.

"Yes ... I know ... and I see that my warning hasn't changed your mind."

I didn't answer ... this was the line of discourse I was trying to avoid. But I could perceive that he was determined to continue.

"Well ... if you must insist on being part of her crew, let me tell you that there has been some mischief done ... designed to sink the Trader to the very bottom of the sea, I am sure. Be aware, and keep a watchful eye, and pray that she sinks before you are out of the Bismark Sea."

"Before we're out of the Bismark Sea?" Despite my reluctance to encourage what I considered to be only nonsensical banter, his insistance impressed me, and I wasn't sure I understood what he meant. The Bismark Sea, as I had seen on the charts, was the body of water encirled by New Britain to the south, New Ireland to the east, and Manus Island to the north.

"While in the Bismark Sea you will always be reasonabley close to one or more islands ... but once you have passed Manus Island ... well, there is only the vast open ocean ... and your chances of survival are much less ... much less indeed."

We were now only a couple hundred yards from the landing adjacent to the Trader, and Captain McKay stopped the pick-up.

"This is as far as I care to go, matey. God be willing, and with luck ... I might be seeing you again." He remained with his two hands on the steering wheel, both arms held stiff and straight, and he stared solemnly forward, his gaze centered on the road ahead. There was to be no hand shake, nor any further words of farewell. I struggled a second time with the door, and once out I immediately headed in the direction of the Trader, breaking into a run. But after a few paces I came to a stop, and, somehow feeling an urge to acknowledge this strange man, and to thank him, I turned around towards the Datsun. Captain Rodney McKay was still locked in his motionless stare. I dared a short motion of goodbye with my right hand, sort of a naval salute. But there was no evidence of response from the Captain and I quickly turned away, embarrassed by my attempt.

I raced the short final sprint to our landing, gasping for breath, and was surprised to see that a few people had gathered on the shoreline, presumably to see the Trader off. Yes, I saw that they were members of one or more of the hap-caste families. It was Thursday and a work day for CDW and other businesses in Rabaul, so most of us didn't expect to have anyone sending us off on the beginning of our grand exodus. But yes, the hap-caste boys had their families, and they would be there.

I didn't want to bring unnecessary attention to the fact that I was AWOL, so to speak, so instead of shouting for Laurie I decided to visit our next door neighbor and see if I could con a ride. It turned out to be an easy thing to do.

"Thank you all same -- you all same number one!" The New Guinea boy beamed back widely, and I scrambled from his dug-out canoe to the Trader's transom. I waved at him in appreciation, then directed myself towards the mess ... the tantalizing smell of frying meat and eggs, plus,the fact that no one was in sight, told me that everyone was in the officer's mess and breakfast was being served.

"Chad, we were about to leave without you," Mr. Fitzgerald admonished, between two mouthfulls.

"I'm sorry, sir ... I just ... overslept."

'Don't lie, Chad ... you had to have a final morning delight before leaving, right?" Harry just had to open his big mouth.

"Yeh ..." I grinned, seeing that Mr. Fitzgerald was smiling. If that was an acceptable excuse, fine! Let them think that.

I noticed that everyone was just about finished eating, so I gulped down the plate of food that Richard had brought me as fast as I could. I didn't want to be left out of anything. Besides, I was part of Mr. Milner's crew assigned to working the anchor winches.

The Trader's machinery for lowering and lifting her two anchors was relatively simple. The port and starboard bow anchors each had a sizeable electric-over-hydraulic powered winch which turned a drum contoured and slotted to accomodate the hefty anchor chain. The links of the chain were large, about 4 inches by 6, and the diameter of the steel stock making each link was about 1 1/2 inches -- it would be called a 1 1/2 inch chain. Electric-over-hydraulic meant that each winch had an electric motor which drove a hydraulic pump, which in turn powered a hydraulic motor at the drum, or pulley. It occurred to me that we had to have electric power in order to operate these winches, and that meant our auxillary diesel also had to be running. If it wasn't, we couldn't lower or raise our anchor. Something to consider.

So, what are you driving at, Chad?

Laurie was to take the first shift at the wheel ... as quartermaster, that is ... so he was busy in the wheelhouse, under the direction of the Captain. Mr. Milner was in charge of directing our progress with the anchors, with myself, Joseph, and Fred as his deck hands. Mr. Fitzgerald was watching from the port wheelhouse deck. And of course our below-decks crew had their hands full with the engines. At a signal from Mr. Milner, the Captain pushed forward on the signalling arm mounted on the port side of the ships wheel -- the old-fashioned kind you see in the movies, with one or two brass arms with handles mounted on a waist-high pedestal, and an arcing dial on the side indicating reverse, stop, full ahead, or an intermediate setting. In our case we had two handles, one on each side of the pedestal -- one for each of the two engines. The mechanism was directly connected by cable to a similar dial in the engine room, mounted high overhead in clear view, and each time the arm was moved a bell would ding loudly -- a sound similar to the cook's bell, except higher pitched and faster -- several dings in rapid succession.

I heard the ding-ding of the throttle signal, followed about ten seconds later by the sight of white, churning water at the stem. We had to move the ship forward in order to provide slack in the anchor chains ... soon we would 'overrun' the anchors themselves, forcing them free from the sandy bottom, one at a time of course. The Trader began to move slowly forward and that was our signal to begin winching in the chains ... both at first, then concentrating more on the port anchor, but at the same time not allowing too much slack on the starboard side.

We finally had the port anchor out of the water and lifted to its resting position at the bow, and had locked the chain in position with the bolt-down mechanism provided, Fred using a wrench that he had brought with him from the engine room, intended for just that purpose. At that point Mr. Fitzgerald shouted orders for us to stop where we were. There was another 'ding-a-ling' as the Captain moved the throttle arm to 'Stop', and we discontinued winching on the starboard chain as the Trader slowly came to a stop. It was time for Mr. Fitzgerald to go ashore, Laurie was there, of course, to follow through with manning the dinghy, not being needed in the wheelhouse during the interlude. We all had a few moments to relax, and took the opportunity to meet on the aft deck to wave farewell to our well-wishers on shore. We were now considerably farther from shore than before ... we could only shout a word or two and wave.

"Hey; there's Liza ... and Deli!" Harry nudged me unnecessarily with his elbow, pointing to one side of the tiny cluster of people. Yes, there they were. I felt genuinely pleased that they had come down to see us off. Deli had on a red floral print, mu-mu style dress -- really just a large sack, folded and tucked in tight above the breasts. The dress accentuated the thinness of her legs. I couldn't help thinking that she really wasn't all that attractive.

So ... is it as easy as that ... shame on you, Chad!

But I would miss Deli Matak, and remember her always.

And then, off to the far left side of the group, I could make out a shadowy figure that was now familiar to me, partially hidden admidst the tall grass, and in the shade of a pair of coconut trees. It was the mysterious Captain McKay. There was no mistaking that it was he. I thought I could discern the stained and weathered blue naval cap, the worn and shoddy jacket of the same color and style, and I could even envision the deep red complexion and unwashed whiskers, and the purple veins showing on his face. And the steely glint in his penetrating glare. Such a strange man ... such a ghostly figure!

Laurie was on his way back, the distance covered quickly now that he had the mighty Seagull to power him.

The starboard anchor was raised even easier than her port twin, and the wisdom behind the choice of lifting this one secondly became clear, for as we winched on the chain the Trader naturally swung to the starboard, pointing us straight out of the harbor. As soon as we had secured her chain in place I again heard the dinging of the wheelhouse throttle, followed by a more vigorous agitation by the propellers, and the Trader began to pick up forward speed. .

"Chad, it's time for us to take this vessel in hand and really begin to navigate." Mr. Milner motioned for me to follow him to the wheelhouse.

"Mr. Patterson, you may relax and have a drink now, if you wish ... Chad and I can take this first watch." Mr. Milner was clearly eager to take over control of the ship, even visibly anxious to do so.

"Mr. Milner, you may take the second watch ... I am perfectly capable of taking this vessel out of the harbor and around the end of the peninsula ... Thank you!"

I was stunned by the Captain's sudden. assertiveness. Mr. Milner was startled as well. There was a moment's hesitation as the 1st Mate pondered how to react to Mr. Patterson's words, which was really an order. His expression turned from surprise to brief anger, and then settled on resignation.

"Very well ... sir ... as you wish." With that he sat down on one of the deck chairs, along with Mr. Morris, who was already in his own lounge chair with his third drink in hand. After a moment or so Mr. Milner joined the Chief Engineer with a Johnny Walker's scotch and soda, and seemingly resigned himself to being only an observer for this first leg of our journey, although I perceived a lingering resentment, and a watchfullness.

The Captain was giving Laurie instructions on how to use the compass and keep the Trader on a straight course.

"If I were to give you a compass heading, you would use the 'lubber line' -- that's this line here -- on the forward part of the compass housing, and you would simply keep the compass heading, in degrees, on that lubber line. But for now we'll use only a visual heading. You see those two islands in the center of the harbors entrance?"

Laurie nodded a confirmation. "Yes!"

I was studying the chart of the harbor and found the islands which the Captain was referring to -- more like two jagged rocks than islands, appearing ominous and dangerous, menacingly situated almost exactly in the middle of the harbor entrance.

"Well, the chart indicates that the normal channel is to the east of those small islands, which are named 'Dawapia Rocks'. But we are already well to the west side of the harbor, and the depth on this side of the islands is over 40 fathoms. Do you know how deep that is?"

"I think a fathom is about two meters, sir."

"That's close enough. A fathom is actually 6 feet, in the British system, or 1.8 meters. Our'ship's draft is only 2 fathoms, which is shown by the painted markings on our bow, correct?"

"Yes, sir ... I think that's right."

"So 40 fathoms is ample depth, and we are perfectly safe to plot our course west of the Dawapia Rocks instead of east. Therefore you want to keep the bow pointed half-way between the shore to the starboard and the islands to the port side. Understand?'"

"Yes sir."

"Easy on the wheel, now! Don't overdue it. That's the natural tendency ... to turn too much each time. As soon as you feel or see the bow start to swing, compensate in the other direction ... just a small amount ... and wait ... give the Trader a chance to react. That's it ... the trick is to make small, gentle adjustments ... slowly ... waiting in between ... sighting over the bow."

"I think I have it ... not much different from a small boat, just have to allow more reaction time."

"That's right, Laurie. Now, we don't have any electronic gear on board this freighter to tell us how fast we're moving -- such as a knot indicator. But I can estimate our speed fairly closely. I reckon we're making a bit under 10 knots ... I would say 8 or 9. That means it'll take us all morning to clear the harbor and make our way up the coast to Cape Tawu."

"Later on, once we have left the islands and are in the open sea, we will set up our 'log' to give us an accurate indication of our speed. Do you know what a 'log' is?"

Both Laurie and I shook our heads.

"Well, a log is a simple device, really just a rotor that we drag behind the ship on a long line, its revolutions indicating our speed and distance covered, relative to the water."

"Now, our turning point today will be when we're directly north of Cape Tawu. At that location we will turn to a compass heading of 298 degrees, which is just south of Northwest, to take us between Manus Island and the end of New Ireland, and then on to the Philippines. With luck, that is!"

I felt uncomfortable about the last part of his statement, and was wondering why he had said it. It looked to me like it would be clear sailing from here on in! But then I'm a natural born optimist.

An optimistic fool, *don't forget that part!*

I couldn't help but notice that the Chief Engineer and Mr. Milner were going through glasses of Johnny Walker's at a rather rapid pace. The Captain as well, once he was satisfied with Laurie's expertise at the wheel. The three relaxed in their lounge chairs, mostly quiet ... keeping their thoughts to themselves and watching the Trader's progress, engaging in small talk from time to time.

The Trader passed Dawapia Rocks ... I sighed with a measure of relief and Laurie was instructed to follow the coastline northerly, keeping the actual shore two miles or so to the port side. We must have been some sight to any observer -- a small rusty freighter with an exaggerated list, chugging slowly through the pristine equatorial water, churning a broad white wake to our stern. I was awed to discover that the open sea outside the harbor continued to be mirror-like, the

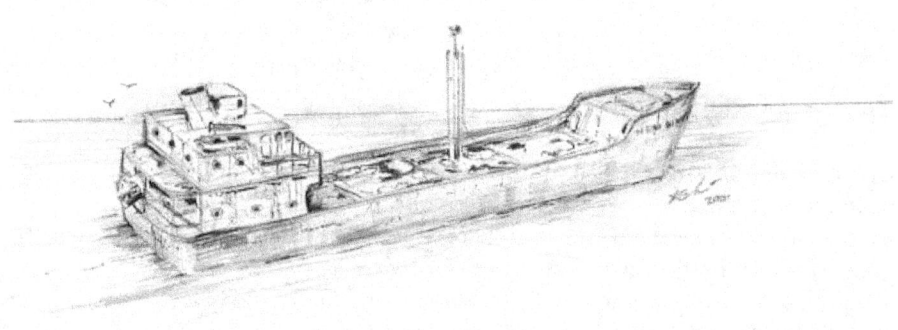

swells flat and endlessly long, seeming to caress the interrupting shores, and the Trader. We were close enough to the coast to be visited by white seagulls and kiris, often swooping down to catch the tiny flying fish which were constantly skipping over the ultra smooth water, sometimes leaving a trail scratched on the surface. I surmised that the passing of our hull and the stirring of our propellers had something to do with the frequency of the flying fish, and the ensuing presence of the birds.

At precisely twelve o'clock we were stirred from our peaceful calm by the din of Richard's bell. Joseph arrived at the wheelhouse a moment later, carrying a tray for the officers ... our mid-day meal was a beef stew, complete with freshly baked rolls.

I offered to relieve Laurie for lunch.

"Right on Chad, I won't be long ... think you can handle her?"

"Are you kidding ... duck soup!" I was eager to try my hand behind that wheel.

It *was* tricky. I was just getting the hang of it when Laurie returned he ... had been gone for only fifteen minutes.

Harry and Kevin were still in the mess, Fred was there too.

"How's things below?" I queried.

"Great!" Harry announced through his food. "This is great living," he added, motioning towards his plate of stew. Kevin smiled and nodded in agreement.

This was the first chance I'd had to talk to Kevin -- he never seemed to be around, or was busy working down below. I suspected his diabetic condition had something to do with that. I remember my mother always being tired and needing to rest a lot.

"Kevin, what part of England are you from?"

"Buckinghamshire," he answered. "Wraysbury, Buckinghamshire," Sensing that none of us had any idea where that was, he continued: "Wraysbury is just northwest of London, a small town ... only thing remarkable about it is that it is Christine Keeler's home town."

At that Harry choked on a mouthful, in the middle of a snicker. "Christine Keeler? The lady who caused such a scandal in Parliament ... a Lord's mistress, I believe?"

I had no idea what they were talking about. Must of been some time ago.

"Yes, that's right. She was a classmate of mine in intermediate school as a matter of fact. Funny, she wasn't much to look at then, from what I remember, anyway."

We had finished our lunch, I wasn't in a rush to go back to the wheelhouse, and neither were Harry and Kevin anxious to return to the engine room. I wanted to ask why. But then I realized the last few days had been hell for them; I knew they were glad to be able to take it easy for a change.

"Chad, what religion are you?"

Wow, where did that *question come from?*

"Uhh ... I'm Mormon, or my family is, anyway ... that's the Church of Jesus Christ of Latter-Day- Saints." It was an unexpected question.

"Yes, I've heard of them ... an American sect, right? ... and they practice polygamy?"

"Wow ... well, American, yes, I guess that'd be mostly right ... the church originated in the U.S. and its background and history is all American ... but ... the polygamy part ... definitely not ... there's a small group that have formed a separate church that still try to practice that, but the Church of Jesus Christ of Latter-Day-Saints outlawed polygamy a long time ago, and even then it was practiced only because during the pioneer days in Utah there was a shortage of men. And what do you mean by 'sect'?"

"Glad to hear they don't practice polygamy anymore ... by 'sect' I mean it's an offshoot of protestantism, started by one man based on his own ideas ... it's not really a separate religion.

"Uhh ... I know a few people who would have a lot to say about that. Have you heard of the Book of Mormon?"

"Yeh, that's their version of the Bible, right?"

"Oh no ... it's a separate book ... no connection to the Bible really ... well, maybe it is in a way ... it's the story of a Biblical people who travelled to the Americas sometime before Christ, but it's written a lot like the Bible, same teachings ... but still a totally different book. So the Book of Mormon makes us separate from other protestant religions ... it's a separate religion, not a sect."

"OK," Kevin was smiling. "It's a separate religion!"

Being a little defensive, ehh Chad?

I was perplexed. "What religion are you, Kevin?"

"Sorry, no religion ... I like philosophy, though."

"Philosophy?"

"Yeh, I really don't need a religion ... I prefer philosophy."

"Don't need a religion??"

"Yeh, a 'religion' means that you have to 'believe' ... you have to believe in a dogma ... someone else's story, or his version of the 'truth' ... and you accept what's right and wrong based on 'faith' ... faith that the other bloke's story is correct, that it is valid and true. I can't buy that. There's too many contradictions."

"What ...?? But we *need* religion!"

"Maybe ... maybe not. The value of religion is that it gives a society ... that is, the masses ... guidance and something to believe in, a framework to hold them together and make it so that they can be productive, maybe even to be able to survive. But I'm an individual ... I don't need all that garbage."

"Well, that sounds kinda cool, Kevin ... but ... excuse me, I think I'd better check up top," I uncomfortably interrupted.

Wow! ... Heavy stuff!

I returned to the wheelhouse, leaving Kevin and the world of philosophy behind, and sensed immediately that something was amiss. Laurie stood tensely behind the ship's wheel, and gave me a side-glance that hinted of a warning. Mr. Milner was discussing something with the Captain ... maybe arguing. But for some reason my presence caused them to discontinue. I didn't know what it was all about, and apparently no one was about to offer an explanation, so I too sat down. Mr. Morris was sitting quietly, a contented look on his face, which was a distinctly bluish color.

"Would you like a beer, Chad? Or a scotch?" Mr. Milner asked.

'Uhh ... no thank you ... I'm OK."

'Umm ... alright."

I was wondering why he asked. Maybe he wanted me to join them in their drinking, to be one of them, so to speak. But it was the strangest thing ... I love my beer, but I had no desire to be drinking at all ... too much was happening, too much excitement. I didn't want to miss anything. Besides, there was a whiff of mischief in the air, and I felt the need to be on guard.

"Where are we, Laurie?"

"I think that's Cape Tawu up ahead. Do you see a lighthouse?"

"Yeh, I think I do."

"That's it, then. Once we've cleared that point I'm to change course to 298 degrees on the compass."

"Umm ... let's see." Our Simpson Harbor chart was on the table, plus another one entitled 'North-East Coast of New Guinea'. The Captain had drawn a line in pencil from just north of Cape Tawu to a point midway between Manus Island and the island of New Hanover, which was really an extension of New Ireland. Just for the hell of it I took the parallel ruler and checked the rose heading of the line. It was 291 degrees. Our 'variation' was just under 7 degrees East, so you add for variation East, and that gives you a 298 degrees heading on the compass. Right on!

"Yes, it checks out!"

The Captain had taken notice of what I was doing.

"Fine, Chad ... carry on!"

Mr. Milner had been watching as well, an interested expression on his face.

Cape Tawu came up directly to our port side, the lighthouse clearly visible. We continued in our northerly direction for several more miles, until the lighthouse was far behind us, just barely visible. The Captain got up from his deck chair:

"Please turn to port, Laurie, and hold us on a compass bearing of 298 degrees."

Laurie complied. The Captain watched for a few minutes ... it took that long for Laurie to get used to holding a course by watching the compass lubber line.

"Laurie, our watch ends at 2:00, which is an hour from now. Joseph will replace you then."

The Captain was following the guidline suggested by Mr. Fitzgerald that morning. We were not in keeping with normal marine practice, but in fairness to the first 'shift' he decided to set the change of watch at 2:00 p.m., 10:00 p.m., and 6:00 a.m., dividing the day into three eight hour periods. Counting Mr. Morris then, we would theoretically have a quartermaster, an officer, and an engineer on duty for each watch. Of course we knew there would be deviations, especially considering our Chief Engineer's shortcomings ... and my own, of course.

Mr. Morris had lasted unusually long today, I noted, going past the time when he normally aquired his desired 'blissful blue' state and crashed.

"'Tis wonderful to be at sea again," he sighed nostalgically.

I had been leaning over the port rail, watching our wake, mesmerized by the churning, swirling patterns of the Trader's trail, a contrast of white froth and bubbling foam against the continuous dark blue of the undisturbed surrounding sea.

"It *is* fascinating," I offered in agreement. "This is only the second time I've been to sea ... and I love it ..." I was reflecting on my time aboard the Cap Finisterre. I had especially revelled in standing at the foremost part of the bow late in the evening, feeling the motion of the freighter and absorbing the wonder of a night sky filled with the familiar patterns of sparking stars, unrestrained in their efflorescence by the lights of man's civilization, the horizon instead a dim straight line dividing a boundless, unspoiled sea and a limitless universe.

"Ahh ... well ... I think I've had enough good 'ol J.W. for awhile."

"You do drink quite a bit of it, Mr. Morris." I was trying to be humorous and conversational.

"Ahh, yes ... 'Tis a slow death, I know ... the liquor, that is ... but then I'm not in a hurry."

I cracked up at that, enjoying a laugh with him. Sounded like it was a favortie line of his: 'tis a slow death, but then I'm not in a hurry!' I like it. Could use that myself, in reference to my beer drinking.

"Gentlemen ... I think I shall rest for a bit," he announced, rising hesitantly from his lounge chair to make his unsteady way towards his cabin.

Yes, today he had lasted till well past noon. His usual 'schedule' had been to divide his day into two drinking binges: one from early morning till sometime before lunch ... he rarely ate ... and then a second in the afternoon till late evening.

Mr. Milner had been listening and had joined in our humor as well. But his participation came across as a strained, forced cheerfullness. I sensed that Mr. Milner was approaching that particular mood of his again. He had been drinking heavy since we weighed anchor, and so had been at it steady for six hours now.

Laurie joined me at the rail. Joseph had come up to the wheelhouse a few minutes earlier, and Laurie had shown him the art of staying on the 298 degree heading. It was two o'clock and the beginning of his stint at the wheel.

"Mr. Milner, you may take over your watch now ... I believe I'll also rest awhile."

Mr. Milner nodded a sullen response, and rose from his reclining chair to join Joseph at the wheel.

"Joseph, what heading are you on?"

"298 degrees ... sir."

Mr. Milner reviewed the chart laid out on the chart table; I noticed he used the parallel ruler to check our course.

"That'll do fine, for now."

"I'm going to get something to snack on." Laurie signalled for me to follow him.

"Sounds like a good idea ... I'll join you!"

Once in the officer's mess, Laurie let out a low whistle and spoke in a low voice: "Chad, you wouldn't believe what Mr. Miner said to the Captain."

"Uhh ... well?"

"The time you came up and they were arguing? Well, Mr. Milner said something like this: 'I know what you and Lancey Shipping Company are up to, Mr. Patterson ... you plan to run this vessel aground on one of the islands to our starboard ... it's your best chance!

"What ?? ... Wow!! ... Was that all?"

"The Captain told him he was crazy ... they argued a couple of minutes, then you came up ... that was the end of it."

"So what do you think, Laurie?"

"Well, I guess Mr. Miner is right about these islands we're passing now being his best chance, if he wanted us to shipwreck that is ... 'cause once we pass between Manus and New Hanover it's all open ocean all the way to the Philippines ..."

Jeeses ... that's just what Captain McKay had said!

"But no way! I don't reckon the Captain has any plan to do anything like that. Anyway, his watch is the morning daylight shift, he won't have a chance to make use of the night to make it look like an accident, and I'd know too ... he'd have to have me steer the ship onto a reef ... no way!"

"Yeh, I see what you mean. We'd better keep an eye on both of them ... glad you told me."

"Well, time for a nap. Standing behind that wheel for eight hours is bloody tiring ... it's going to take some getting used to."

"Yeh, for me too. Talk to you later." As I passed the wheelhouse I saw that Mr. Miner was studying the chart, a scotch and soda close by.

"How are we doing, Mr. Milner?" I attempted some cheerfullness.

"Fine ... fine," he responded, without looking up.

Jeeses, what a moody son-of-a-bitch!

I was stretched out on my narrow bunk, hands behind my head, aimlessly sifting through the deluge of recent events and experiences, and especially the warning by the Trader's previous captain, the ghostly Mr. Rodney McKay, when I felt a change in the movement of the Trader, as if we were abruptly changing course. I waited for additional input. There was a muffled shout, coming from the deck below me. I jumped off the bunk and scrambled down the ladder.

Mr. Milner was standing behind Joseph ... Joseph had an excited, scared look on his face ... and there was another shout from the direction of the passageway to the officer's cabins. I guessed that it was the Captain shouting from his cabin.

"What's happening, Mr. Milner?" I demanded. Well, at least I asked with as much assertiveness as I dared.

It's alright, Chad ... we know you can be brave when the real need arises.

"Mr. Fletcher," he answered, "I am not about to let Mr. Patterson scuttle this vessel on one of these near-by reefs ... I am turning this ship around ... and we are going to Australia!"

"We are what?" I couldn't believe what he had said. I turned to look towards our stern. Sure enough, our white-water wake formed a long arc to the starboard and we had turned almost a full 180 degrees.

"You heard me, 2nd Mate ... I am taking this ship to Australia ... where we can deal with these scoundrels properly."

The man has flipped his lid!

"Mr. Milner ..." I was trying to sound level-headed. "That doesn't make any sense."

No response. I searched my brain for coherent ideas, counter-arguments.

"Mr. Milner, we don't have any proof that the intent of our Captain and Lancey Shipping Company is to scuttle this ship!" I was making it sound like I was on his side.

There was another shout from the Captain. "What the bloody hell is going on? Let me out of this cabin." I hurried to the Captain's door ... and discovered that a good sized Master padlock had been placed in the exteior mounted hinge and clasp.

"I'm sorry, Captain, Mr. Milner has put a lock on the door ... I'll see what I can do."

"Tell Mr. Milner that I will see him in jail for this!"

As I started to retrace my path back to the wheelhouse I hear whispering behind me. I turned ... two faces peered cautiously at me over the crest of the stairs. It was Harry and Laurie, their eyes wide and questioning. I put my fingers to my lips and motioned for them to stay below.

Now, what did Laurie say about how it would be difficult for the Captain to try something like that? Oh yes, now I remember.

"Mr. Milner, the Captain can't possibly attempt to run this ship on a reef without us knowing about it and preventing it from happening."

Mr. Milner only grunted, still standing behind Joseph with his legs spread and hands clasped dehind his back, in solid defiance.

"And heading for Australia is certainly no solution ... where would we go?"

"We will take the New Guinea Trader to Cairns," he broke his silence.

What the hell to do? I could try tackling him. Nah, better Laurie try that tactic. Or try to reason some more with him.

In desperation, and in an attempt to show positive assertiveness, I continued:

"Mr. Milner, this is crazy ... you are mutinying against your Captain ... I cannot allow you to do this ... *we* cannot allow you to do this!"

One thought occurred to me in the midst of all this: I sure as hell didn't want to go back to Australia ... I wanted to go to Hong Kong ... Mr. Milner was screwing up my travel plans!

Mr. Milner was unmoved, maintaining his rigid stance, staring towards the Trader's bow and beyond, over the top of Joseph's head.

I decided it was time to consult with the rest of the crew. Besides, I needed their help, and maybe their muscle.

Everyone was in the officer's mess: Harry, Laurie, Kevin, Fred, and even Richard. Harry was holding a three foot long length of galvanized steel pipe in his hands, about 2 inches in diameter.

Jeeses, Harry, isn't that a little extreme?

"Harry, what are you thinking? With that pipe, I mean?"

"There's only one way to handle this ... we'll have to place Mr. Milner under arrest ..."

"Under arrest?"

"Yes, under arrest ... and lock him in his cabin. This here just might come in handy."

I couldn't believe him ... Jeeses, what an exaggerated sense for the dramatic! I looked at Laurie. I could see he shared my feeling; he was studying Harry, with a smirk on his face.

"Let's go up and grab him!" It was Richard.

I just knew he had a viscious streak!

But it was Kevin who made the most sense, and came to our rescue: "Mr. Milner can't take over the ship all on his own, without our support that is ... he needs us ... so if we all go up and talk to him sensibly I'm sure we can change his mind. He's probably just drunk, anyway."

There was a series of nods.

"Laurie, if we have to tackle him, can I count on you to do the job?"

He shrugged, smiled, and nodded.

"OK, let's go!"

And so the six of us filed up the steps, I dutifully taking my place in front, Harry two bodies behind me, or was it three, still holding onto his length of pipe.

"Mr. Milner, I have the crew here with me. We cannot allow you to turn the ship around. Will you please put the Trader back on course!"

There was a long, silent pause. We were all bunched up on the port deck, waiting for his reaction, ready to do whatever we had to do. I glanced back over my shoulder. Harry's pipe was clearly visible ... he was holding it high and ready. Richard was looking fierce and mean … like a Mohawk on the warpath. In fact, all he needed was a little body paint and he'd look like the real thing. Laurie was poised like a cricket batter ready to spring into a run … only on this occassion he was preparing for an American football-style full-body tackle. We were ready. As ready as we could be, I guess.

"Gentlemen, I already have. We're back on a heading of 298 degrees, bound for the Philippines. You can see for yourselves."

His calm statement caught all of us totally by surprise. We all turned, as one, to see if what he said was true. Unbelievably, the wake trailing our stem once again formed a long sweeping arc, curving in a quarter mile radius, creating a full half-circle. We had all been in such an excited state that we hadn't felt the Trader make a second change of course.

We relaxed a bit. I boldly stepped to the ship's wheel and peered at the brass encased compass, and saw that the lubber line coincided with the 298 degree marking on the compass card. Joseph was turning the wheel, making a small adjustment.

"He's right. I mean ... we're back on course. Mr. Milner, may I please have the key to the lock on the Captain's door."

After a thoughful delay he obliged, somberly unclasping his hands to reach into his right pocket for the key, yet keeping his face and eyes trained straight ahead the whole time.

"Captain, I would like to make a request." I tried to sound as civil as I could.
"Yes, 2nd Mate?"
"Please, let's not try to arrest him, or anything like that right now . I mean, let's give him a chance to cool off and sober up. We all need each other on this voyage."
"Alright ... you're probably right."
I perceived that he was quite happy to accept that as an alternative.
"However, I must put this all down in the ship's log. I have to. It's maritime law. And I will rely on you and the rest of the crew to support me if anything ever comes of this. Is that understood?"
"Of course, sir." What he said about the ship's log interested me.

And so the events of the afternoon simmered towards a calmer setting. Mr. Morris appeared a hour or so later … he had been oblivious to everything that had happened, we discovered … and had slept through it all peacefully. Richard prepared a wonderful evening meal of lamb chops, complete with apple sauce and mashed potatoes. Each of us slowly shifted in the direction of our individual duties and chores. As for myself, I settled in for a long nap … my watch as 'officer on duty' would begin at 10: 00 p.m.

Once again I was able to let my head filter through the latest happenings. Mr. Milner was a complex problem. I could see that I was destined to be a buffer between him and the Captain, and that I would probably be called on to subdue the extreme actions of both. I chuckled to myself, thinking about Harry and his pipe, and Richard the Mohawk, and how glad I was to have more sensible people around like Laurie, and Kevin.

Kevin, now there was a trip! So he was a philosopher. He had definitely caught my interest … what he said about religion, and not needing it. He had touched on a sensitive area, on a problem that happened to be one of my own. I had been raised to be a 'Mormon'. But I definitely had a problem with that. Like a friend in our church 'ward' in Edmonton had once said … a girl it was … 'Chad likes to have fun too much to be a good Mormon'. There was more to it than that though … there had been contradictions. Like once when I was only about twelve I remember a speech by one of our prominent members. He was telling us about the 'dark' side of Catholicism, and that Catholic leaders claimed that, 'Give me a child from when he is born to seven years of age, and he will be a Catholic for life'. I remember reflecting at the time that that was exactly what the Mormons practiced as well -- the same indoctrination from childhood.

Or another time a couple of years later … puberty had finally arrived, and sex had been heavy on my mind, and I had found this book on the subject in one of my mother's bedroom drawers, which was a science based matter-of-fact approach. I had been super intrigued, especially when it talked about masterbation. The author was an MD and psychiatrist, and he explained that 'everyone' masterbated, that it was natural and healthy and not to be ashamed of, and even joked that in surveys 98% of those interviewed admitted that they masterbated, and the other 2% lied. Well, at fourteen I had already entered the Latter-Day-Saint priesthood and had become a 'Teacher', like all good Mormon boys aged fourteen. At one special session we received a lengthly lecture from another prominent church member (seemed like there was always a 'prominent' church member around lecturing us). But this man had been my mother's physician years before and was now a psychiatrist. He delved into the 'immoral' act of masterbation, explaining to us that it was evil and did us great harm and that we should never indulge in such ungodly acts. Well, that lecture really upset me. First of all, he was an MD and a psychiatrist and what he was saying was therefore in direct contradiction with the author of the book I had just read, and the teachings of his own profession. It made me think very poorly of him as a medical professional. Secondly, he was just too damn late! So I resolved at the time that that was one part of church doctrine I would simply have to disregard.

But there had been more much more! For example, there had been a whole assortment of strange oddities about the Mormon religion which I had taken in stride as a young full-on believer, and a holder of the Priesthood, but which seemed mysterious, even bizarre, once I had 'left the fold', so to speak. Don't get me wrong ... I mean I had been in thick and heavy. As an adolescent and a youth I had listened passionately to the stories of Joseph Smith, the Prophet -- and founder of the church. Of how he had been led by the angel Moroni to a stone box containing the plates of gold and the Urim and Thummim. The plates were inscribed with the ancient writings of a biblical people who had travelled to the Americas, and the Urim, and Thummin was a set of two opague stones which could be used to translate the writings. The stone box had been buried on the side of a high, prominent hill named the Hill Cumorah, near the town of Palmyra, New York, the site marked by a curiously rounded, smooth stone. Palmyra was just up river from the future metropolis of Rochester, N.Y., which was located on the south coast of Lake Ontario, which in turn was connected to Lake Erie to the west past Niagara Falls, and the beginning of the St. Lawrence River and the Atlantic Ocean to the east. I had read and studied the Book of Mormon extensively, and on one memorable occasion during my fourteenth summer I had even given a 'Sunday school lesson' to a small congregation in the mountain resort town of Banff, Alberta. Our featured guest at the time had been our visiting church president, Ezra Taft Benson. I remember I had been pissed because my lesson was on the Book of Mormon and I had asked Mr. Benson just one small question and he had stolen my entire lesson. I had been robbed of everything I had prepared to say and had nothing, literaly, to add ... it had been very embarrassing!

As a young member of the Melchizedek Priesthood I had completed numerous 'baptisms for the dead' in the Cardston Mormon temple, which was a truly awesome and mystical building. Mormon temples are beautiful, extravegent structures, designed after the original Temple of Solomon, we were told. As a member of only the lower priesthood, I and my same-age buddies were allowed into only the outer, baptismal area of the temple, but I remember my father and mother discussing the strangely occult and secretive rituals which were carried on in the sacred inner areas of the complex. And there had been the time when my rascal buddy, Jim Hansen, and I had sneaked up into the temple after one session of baptismals, and had witnessed the grandeaur of the inner temple. We had been caught, of course, and severely admonished.

As an impressionable youth the stories and the rituals only intensified the religious commitment. But it had been several years since I had been an active member, and from the increasing distance my perspective had began to shift. It was all so extreme. In a sense, maybe Kevin's description had been fitting -- that Mormonism was a 'cult'.

Travelling had also eroded my propensity for being a true believing Mormon. Other peoples and their different customs and beliefs intrigued and fascinated me. I discovered that I was sympathetic to dissimilar cultures and the various religious persuasions, and I was humbly respectful of their right to follow their own paths, and that I was impressed by the sincerity and tenacity in which they did so. The diversity found in Papua New Guinea had been a great example. In this context I found it increasingly difficult to insist that the Church of Jesus Christ of Latter-Day-Saints was the only true religion and we were right while everyone else was wrong.

So, I wanted to ask Kevin more about his 'philosophy'. Imagine, not *needing* religion!

That night the full moon seemed to have doubled in size, and brightness ... its grey-white radiance unhindered by clouds and reflecting off the glossy surface of the New Guinea sea, hiding the presence of nearby stars as if it was a nighttime sun, its reflection creating a royal path of shimmering silver over the ocean swells, stretching westward from the Trader towards the point on the horizon directly below.

My trusty 'ol wind-up alarm had let me know it was near the time of the beginning of my stint as officer on duty. I didn't carry a wrist watch, which others often thought was an oddity. But to me things like a ring on the finger or a watch on the wrist was such hum-bug and a nuisance ... besides, my sensitive skin and hairy arms made them uncomfortable beyond belief. Or maybe it was my inherited Dutch sense of simplicity and prudence again. Or maybe I could blame the whole thing on my Dutch ancestry, for that's how I acquired the fair, sensitive skin and hairy arms as well! Anyway, I relied on my well-travelled Westlock, a three dollar model, for accurately giving me the time of day ... when I needed it.

The Captain and Mr. Milner were both on deck, and Fred had arrived early to receive a lesson on steering the ship before his and my watch started. Mr. Milner was the instructor this time, this still being his watch, technically. His explanation was careful and patient, much like the Captain's had been with Laurie. Which caused me to wonder ... he could be such a man of contrasts. Right now he was being exceptionally civil and well-mannered, which seemed oddly out of place.

Neither the Captain nor Mr. Milner had a drink in sight, not Mr. Milner's Johnny Walker's and soda nor Mr. Patterson's dark rum and coke. This too was a dramatic change.

"Good evening, Chad. I'm glad to see you here."

I hesitated, not really knowing how I show react to this new courteousness.

"It's a beautiful night -- a fantastic moon," I finally returned, trying to be at least equally civil.

"Yes, tonight is a full moon, unusually bright; it's because of the fine weather and being so close to the equator."

I observed that the Captain was listening, and nodding in agreement.

Such gentility! Something had happened while I had slept. Apparently the Captain and Mr. Milner had formed some sort of alliance, and were actually being responsive and gentlemanly with each other.

"It has been a long day for me ... I think I'll retire ... but before I do I'd like you to practice finding a LOP, Chad ... can you do that?"

"Sure ... uhh, yes sir, I can do that."

"Then go ahead and take a shot of Arcturus and Betelgeuse, along with the chronometer time, and then bring your data and the Almanac down below ... I'm going to find something to eat."

With that Mr. Milner left the deck and I preceeded to follow his orders, first removing the Trader's sextant from its case. The brilliance of the moon made the shots a little awkward ... the stars were difficult to locate and their light subdued enough to make taking a sighting problematic. When I had the data as complete as I thought I could make it, I followed Mr. Milner's path to the officer's mess.

He had found some bread, butter, peanut butter, and strawberry jam, and was wolfing down a couple of king-sized sandwiches. I happen to be particularly fond of the same combination, and so I followed suit.

"Chad, I would like to apologize for my actions earlier today."

At this I was totally astounded. "'Yes ... sir?"

"However," he switched a notch from an apologetic to a more assertive note. "I truly believe there is still a danger that Mr. Patterson will attempt to scuttle this ship ... I need to form an understanding between you and I, and maybe some of the crew. Do you follow me?"

"Yes ... I do." And I did. I could sense what he was leading up to.

"Alright ... now, I can't be on deck all the time ... but if you and Laurie especially, and perhaps the other two quartermasters as well ... if you all would help me ... if you would agree to help me prevent Mr. Patterson from taking a course that would lead us to a shipwreck, then we'll be OK. Do you understand?"

"Yes, I do. I can talk to them." Of course I didn't tell him that we would be watching him as well as the Captain.

"We have an alliance then?"

"Yes ... OK."

"Alright ... the important thing is that Laurie remains the quartermaster during the Captain's watch, and that we never allow Mr. Patterson to take over the wheel and be by himself in the wheelhouse ... I'll leave any other details up to you."

Wow, the plot thickens!

And so the real reason for me taking the star shots and meeting with him in the mess became clear. We finished our peanut butter and jam sandwiches, and Mr. Milner retired. I followed through with the LOP calculations. It was good practice, anyway, plus I had to complete the exercise in order to prevent the Captain from becoming suspicious.

My two LOPs intersected directly on the center of the island of New Ireland. Not too good. Well, maybe I'd have better luck next time.

"Well, my LOPs weren't where they were supposed to be." I explained to the Captain where they had intersected.

Mr. Patterson suppressed a loud chuckle. "You'll do better with practice ... besides, you should always have at least three sights ... the chance of error with only two is too great."

"Yes. Guess I'll have to learn more stars to take sightings on. I only know six, and that's not enough, especially with a sky lit up like it is tonight."

"Yes." An interluding silence followed. "Chad, today was quite a day. What do you think of Mr. Milner ... your honest opinion?" He was talking in a reduced volume.

"Captain ... I don't know ... I think we need him ... he just gets crazy ideas when he's been drinking a lot. What do you think?"

"Well, I think he can be dangerous ... but he knows that he seriously stepped out of line today. He commited mutiny. That's a very serious offense according to maritime law. And it's written in the ship's log. His career as an officer could be destroyed because of this."

"So, what do you think he'll do?"

"He'll want to keep his nose *very* clean from here on in!"

"I see."

'Unless he attempts to do something extreme, that is."

"Such as?'"

"Well, he could attempt to shipwreck us, or kill us."

"What !!"

"It's a possibility."

"Wow, I never thought of that."

"So, Chad, I need you to help me. We must watch him ... make sure he doesn't have a chance to do something radical ... I've already talked to Joseph ... he's been instructed to grab the throttle handle and pull it to 'Stop' if Mr. Milner ever tries something again like today ... if he gives him an order to change course suspiciously."

"And he agreed?"

"Yes. He's a shy young man, but I feel confident he'll follow my order. But I need more help than that ... I can't be on the deck all the time ... I need you and the rest of the crew to be watchful, and we especially must never allow Mr. Milner to take over the wheel by himself, with no one else in the wheelhouse ... Do you understand?"

"Yes, I do"

"We have an alliance, then?" There was that word again.

"Yes sir ... we have an alliance."

Wow, now the plot really thickens!!

With that the Captain decided that he too would retire, and I was left by myself to deliberate on this emerging web of intrigue. We now have three alliances, I summarized: Mr. Milner and the crew to watch the Captain, the Captain and the crew to watch Mr. Milner, and the crew and I to watch the Captain and Mr. Milner. Shouldn't be *too* difficult to keep track of!

CHAPTER SIX

Knocking on Davy Jone's door

I could envision the ghostly Captain Rodney McKay, and I remembered his dark warning: "There has been some, mischief done . . designed to sink the Trader to the very bottom of the sea."

Frederick Yuen was wondering if signing on the New Guinea Trader had been such a good idea. "One crazy bunch!" he muttered to himself. "Mr. Milner locking the Captain in his cabin and taking over the ship ... all same crazy!"

"How are we doing?" I was leaning over Fred's shoulder to verify that we were still on 298 degrees.

"Fine ... sir."

"Sir?" I chuckled. "Oh no, Fred ... you don't have to call me sir. My name is Chad, and that'll do just fine."

"OK." Fred smiled.

"What's your last name, Fred?"

"Yuen ... Yuen is my last name."

"Ahh ... Chinese?"

"Yes, my father is Chinese ... uhh ... was Chinese,"

"He's no longer alive?"

"No."

"Sorry."

"Oh, it's OK. He's been dead for a few years now -- and he lived to be 88. So he had a long life.

"Yuen, that name sounds familiar. Oh yeh, when I first came to Rabaul I stayed with a young Chinese boy and his mother. His last name was Yuen, Alan Yuen it was ... I stayed with them only a few days, before I started working for CDW."

"Yes, I know."

"You know?"

"Yes ... his mother is my cousin. She is my father's brother's daughter ... and we all knew about you."

"Wow, small world!"

A really *small world!*

I had flown in from Lae after having left Port Morseby ... I was looking for another town in Papua New Guinea that would be an improvement over Morseby, which I didn't think should be too difficult since Port Morseby was such a toilet hole, and especially a job. I didn't have a place to stay, and was almost broke, again, so I had left the airport and was walking through Rabaul's Chinese part of town, struggling with a ridiculously oversized suitcase. It was early morning, a Sunday, and I had no idea where I was going. A Chinese boy about seventeen or eighteen appeared out of the blue, walking along beside me, offering to help me with that dumb ass suitcase. He was super friendly, and was a clean-cut, good looking kid, and spoke almost perfect English. I immediately took a liking to him. One thing led to another and I ended up staying in a room at his house, where he lived with his mother. They were so kind to me, and she was a sweet lady, although she couldn't speak a word of English. Ironical that her son could speak English so well but she didn't speak any at all. After I moved into the CDW camp a few days later I lost touch with them.

"I haven't seen Alan since I stayed with them."

"That's because he went to school in Australia ... been there ever since ... he was one of the lucky ones.

"Lucky to be able to go to school in Australia, you mean?"

"Yeh."

"You know, I always wondered, if I had stayed with them ... I mean if I continued to live with them instead of moving into the CDW camp, that things might have been different."

"What do you mean?"

"Well, for one thing maybe I would have met a nice Chinese girl."

At that he chuckled. "Maybe. But you found a mari instead!"

It was my turn to laugh. "Did I have a choice?"

He looked at me kinda funny, trying to understand what I meant.

"Yeh, I suppose I know what you mean. Probably too hard to get to know a Chinese girl ... and you would have to marry her before ... before anything could happen."

"That's what I thought!"

We both laughed.

"But we hoped you would stay with them."

That puzzled me. "What do you mean?"

"Well ... nothing ... I mean, we need good white blokes mixing with us ... being on our side." Fred said this with a lot of feeling.

I wanted to ask him what he meant again, but I sensed that we were entering a sensitive area, maybe a forbidden one, so I left it at that.

"Tell me, how did the Chinese end up being in Rabaul in the first place?"

This question perked Fred's intersest. "Ahh, my father use to tell me the stories. We are Hokien, you know ... or he was Hokien. My mother was Tolai.

The Hokien are from the southern provinces, and Hokien means 'big feet', because they were peasants and the women didn't 'bind' their feet like the northern Han. My father was one of the first Hokien to come to Rabaul."

With that as a starter, Fred went on to tell me of the stories of his father. How they had lived near Nanning, and the people had been devastated by a period of war, by floods followed by drought, and widespread famine. His father had described how everyone around him was dying ... it was like that throughout the entire southern provinces ... and that the only way to survive was to take what you could carry and leave China, to travel south to Vietnam, or Laos and Thailand, or even further to Malaysia, to Indonesia, or the Philippines ... or even to Papua New Guinea. The father's family had mostly died, and the survivors had disseminated and split, ending up in different lands. They had been refugees and illegal immigrants, unwanted everwhere they went. And of course they could not enter Australia, for despite the coutry's vast territory and need for labor and for immigrants to make those lands productive, they had enforced a white immigration policy since the 1800's. It had taken many years for his father and his father's brother to find each other and to re-unite. The brother had brought his Chinese wife with him ... he had been lucky. But Fred's father came to New Guinea alone, there were no Chinese girls available, and so he had taken a native Tolai as a bride.

"What job did you have before this?" I continued our conversation.

"I was a mechanic and welder for the Mango Auto Repair shop."

"Ahh, I know the place. So why did you give up your job for this?"

Fred thought for a moment. "I was hoping for a chance to get out of New Guinea, to find a better life."

"I understand that's pretty hard to do," I offered sympathetically, not realizing that I was touching the tip of an iceberg.

"For you, no ... for me it's bloody impossible!"

"You're talking about the Australian white immigration policy?"

"Yes ... damn the bloody Australians!"

The strength of his statement startled me. We were entering that sensitive area again.

"We are stuck," he continued. "There's no place for us to go. And you know that New Guinea will soon be independent?"

"Yes, I've heard a lot about it. Not so much in Rabaul though. But there was plenty of talk, and action, in Port Morseby."

I was referring to the heightening drive for independence among the Papuans, who were much more politically aware that the rest of New Guinea. There had been a long succession of troublesome incidents -- a riot or two, demonstrations, and a few Aussies being beaten, one recently killed.

"Well, when Papua New Guinea becomes independent, what do you think will happen to the Chinese and us hap-castes?"

Fred was talking excitedly, there was no stopping him now.

"The Chinese will lose everything they have ... the New Guineans will take everything away ... and us hap-castes ... they don't like us either ... we will be below them. And we can't do anything about it ... we can't leave, we have no place to go ... and Australia is closed to us!"

Wow! It was *the tip of an iceberg!*

I was sympathetic with what he was saying, but there was really nothing I could say. I reflected on how absurd I thought the white immigration policy really was. It had been a topic of debate when I had been in Sydney and Townsville ... in New Zealand too, because the Kiwis have the same policy. I remember one party in Auckland: I was just starting to get along with this very nice blond-haired sheila. Dennis and I were celebrities because they loved our 'American' accents and our peculiar Canadian humor ... they kept asking me over and over to repeat "I shit you not". The way I said it cracked them up and they couldn't get enough of it. Then the topic of American blacks and the civil rights movement popped up. Stupidly, I went on the defensive by criticizing their own white immigration policy. Well, needless to say I lost my chances with that blond chick, real fast! Seeing the new Italian immigrants in Sydney had been an eye-opener too. Australians recognized that the country needed new immigrants, but their own policy limited them to seeking immigrants from 'white' countries. Free transportation and $150 on arrival in Australia was offered to prospective European immigrants. 0f course the one group that responded in large numbers were the Italians – mostly the darker complexioned Sicilians. I remember Dennis once joking about them: 'Gee, are they really white?'. The real irony to me, however, was that Australia needed workers, and farmers -- they needed people to cut sugar cane, to work in the mines, to venture out into that vast land and farm it, make it productive. But the Sicilians, at least the ones that I saw, weren't farmers, or even workers ... they were con artists and city dwellers and all ended up in King's Cross, Sydney.

Just my opinion!

But Fred wasn't finished: "The worst thing is that we have no chance to make things better for ourselves. Only students like Alan, who get the very best grades, can go to Australian schools. The rest of us must stay here. There are no good schools, especially technical schools, to give us a chance to advance. The schools that *are* here are at *their* level, the New Guineans. There's nothing higher for us -- the Chinese and us hap-castes.

"So if this ship can take me to a different place ... well, that's why I'm here."

He turned to look at me, as if to say: 'Well, that answers your question, and I'm finished'. I smiled sympathetically, and gave him a firm, short grab on his shoulder.

"Maybe you could've found a nice Chinese girl and taken her away from this place," he concluded. We both smiled.

The moon had become progressively lower in the western sky, finally becoming engulfed below the dark horizon. The contrast was astonishing, for the brilliance of that night 'sun' was replaced by a sudden blackness, the celestial constellations now the rulers of that same heavenly sphere, the stars brilliant in their own right, glittering spectacularly. In my entire life I don't think I will ever become bored with the marvels of the night sky, I mused.

Richard was obviously engaging himself in a contest to make each meal better than the one before. This morning we had Aussie steak and eggs, of course, but it was complimented with a creative yam pie, which was terrific. And another subtle addition -- all at once we had rice: steamed rice, and fried rice, which Fred and Joseph dove into copiously, visibly delighted. I watched this event humorously, smiling to myself. Sly, subtle -- that was Richard -- and he was taking care of his own. Nothing wrong with that, of course. But it wasn't what he did, it was how he did it. But I promised myself I'd have to try and like rice myself … someday.

Our 298 degree heading was still good. Small islands started to appear on the horizon to the east, our starboard side. This was expected, on referring to our chart, and would continue until we were finally north of New Hanover. We would probably see an island or two to the port about that time, which was a string of islands to the east of Manus Island.

I had heard a lot about Manus. I had been told it was the location of some earlier, well known anthropological studies that Papua New Guinea is so famous for; the name that pops to mind is Margaret Mead. It was also the site where the atomic bombs which were dropped on Hiroshima and Nagasaki were first transported to in the western Pacific, brought to Manus on American B-17's, the 'flying fortresses' of WWII. From Manus they were shipped to the Marianas for the final deployment to Japan in B-29's. Manus was the setting of a lot of WWII action, as was all of New Guinea, not excluding Rabaul. Ah, yes, Rabaul. I had spent many Saturdays and Sundays making excursions to the various sites around Rabaul where there were Japanese war relics, or where you could explore the caves and other left-overs of their war efforts. In a grove of trees next to the airport were the remains of several disabled Japanese zero's. Or we would visit the series of small barges still mounted on a section of railroad track inside a huge excavated tunnel at Karavia. And there was the giant Japanese gun mounted on the hill next to the golf course. My favorite, however, was the submarine base on the road out past Monga Hospital. Here the coral reef was close in to the shore and its outer edge formed an incredible vertical drop, a sheer cliff of coral which dove over 300 feet straight down. I would typically spend the day with Harry or Mike, sometimes with Deli and Liza or Kelli, and sometimes not, and we would snorkel our way through the shallow waters over the reef, suddenly finding ourselves past the edge of the precipice, with an endless depth below us and the vastness of the open ocean ahead of us. The water was so clear you could see horizontally for one, maybe two hundred feet, Below, however, everything vanished into a mysteriously inky darkness. The experience was always awesome, but it terrified me. I really do have a phobia about sharks, I guess, because whenever I dared to venture over that edge I would scurry back to the protection of the shallow water within seconds, frightened by the imagined vision of a monsterous killer shark swooping up from the depths to chop me in half, or savor a leg.

After breakfast I retired for a long sleep. It surprised me that I could. I thought sleeping during the daylight hours would bother me. But out here on the open sea we were in a separate world, and it was cool, of course, because we had an eight knot breeze. What really made the difference, however, was the rythmic sounds and vibrations of the Trader itself, lulling me to sleep. It was reminiscient of the Cap Finisterre, the similar combination of a gentle roll and pitch, the vibrations humming through the steel structure of the ship, and the consistent patterns of the rumbling and gentle thumps of the engines, propellers, and other machinery.

The clamoring of Richard's bell awakened me for lunch. At the bottom of 'my ladder' I spotted Laurie and was reminded that I needed to relieve him. Dutifully, I did so, reluctantly downgrading my hunger pangs to second priority, at least temporarily. Laurie returned after a few minutes and I continued down below. Everyone was present, except Laurie and the officers, of course. Richard's meals were becoming popular. Our lunch was a taste of the light side. We had sandwiches and a choice of fruits, and a heavy soup for those of us who wanted something more 'substantial'.
"Richard, my compliments on your cooking," I offered as soon as I had the chance. He actually smiled.
Harry and Kevin were curiously silent, almost moody.
"Hey you two, what's up?"
"Nothing ... nothing!" Harry sounded real grouchy.
I was not about to get any enlightenment, I guessed. Not a good time to find out more about Kevin's 'philosophy' either.

"Well, I think I'll go up top!"
After which I slept some more.

About 3:00 I got up and joined the officers on the wheelhouse starboard deck -- the shady side at that time of day. Laurie had finished his watch and was sleeping, Joseph was behind the wheel. Mr. Morris had recently awakened as well, and was beginning his afternoon shift, already into his fourth JW and ice. Both the Captain and Mr. Milner were present, the Captain lingering after his watch, and Mr. Milner just beginning his ... officially. A pattern was already emerging for the Captain and Mr. Milner, and myself -- we would come and go a lot, recognizing whose watch it was at any particular time, but each being around a great deal of the time. After all, we could only sleep eight hours. And of course each of our new 'alliances' were being implemented, discreetly. The Captain and Mr. Milner were drinking, but less so than previously, I observed. Amazingly, I still had no desire to dive into the South Pacific (the beer, I mean), which was a rare experience for me.

It was about an hour later: Joseph was behind the wheel, and the four of us were on the starboard deck. The three officers were each nursing a drink, and Mr. Morris was already well on his way towards the blue end of his cyclic spectrum. In the midst of this peacefull and tranquil setting my good buddy, Harry, suddenly made an appearance. His countenance was strained, as if he was carrying a heavy responsibility, yet I detected a measure of suppressed pleasure, as if he was enjoying the strain at the same time. Or at least that's what I thought.
Harry approached us as if he was the master of ceremonies introducing some sort of shakespearean tragedy:
"Gentlemen, I have an important announcement to make. May I have your attention, please. I think you should all know that we have been taking on water in the engine room for some time now. Kevin and I have been carefully measuring its rate. We estimate it will reach a height high enough to stop our engines in four hours. I calculate we will sink in eight hours."

Well now, that announcement *did* have a profound effect on our three certified officers. I think it was the Captain who was the first to react -- in a physical sense I mean, for in a burst of movement he was out of his lounge chair, racing to the wheelhouse and the radio, where he proceeded to rapidly turn the many dials, with the microphone in hand, yelling loudly: "Mayday, mayday, this is the New Guinea Trader, mayday, mayday," over and over again.
I'm not sure who reacted next ... that's because I'm not sure when Mr. Morris passed out. Well, maybe it's not important -- he passed out somewhere in the midst of all this, without letting us know. Mr. Milner, within a few half-second's

of the Captain's energetic frolic, also lept to his feet -- to direct himself in a different direction, however ... he literally flew up the ladder to the poop deck and attacked the steel box containing our flares and rockets. On his way he had motioned that I was to follow him. What ensued was truly spectacular. It was like a grand Fourth of July. We shot off rockets, and flares, and anything else that was in that box. And it was a good sized box. I was helping him as best I could -- it was good fun, and kinda pretty too. I did reflect somewhere mid way that we should maybe try and save some of those flares and rockets ... but what the hell.

There was no stopping Mr. Miner anyway.

Of course everyone on the ship was aroused.

Laurie showed up on the wheelhouse, looked around, and then he did a curious thing: he scooped up Mr. Morris in his arms and carried him to his cabin. Mr. Milner had finally run out of flares and rockets ... and apparently energy as well ... and flopped back into his lounge chair. After a while the Captain tired of yelling into the microphone, and he too retired back to a lounge chair. They both poured themselves a drink. I guess they figured they had done all they could.

Now what to do!

I was part of this scene, and yet I felt myself removed, for I had no control and, except for assisting in the fireworks, I had no real participation. I thought it was all kinda humorous, really.

However, it was now time to get involved. I had one clear objective: to corner Harry and find out what this was really all about. As far as I was concerned his 'announcement' was highly suspect.

This reeks of Harry's brand of the dramatic, and B. S.

"Laurie, let's you and I go down below and find out what the hell is *really* going on!" He was with me one hundred percent.

"Yeh, I would like to do that. You know, that almost killed Mr. Morris."

"Really! Didn't know you cared."

Oops, that was a bad choice of words.

"The hell with you, Chad. Don't you have any feelings?"

"Sorry, Laurie ... I didn't mean that."

"OK!"

The ship was sinking. That was the story, anyway. Yet when Laurie and I went below, both Harry and Kevin were in the officer's mess, instead of in the engine room where we expected to find them.

For some non-rational reason we actually thought they would be in the engine room trying to solve the problem.

"Harry, Kevin, what's going on?" I was perplexed to the max. Maybe a little ticked off, too.

"Hey, it's exactly like I told you up top ... we're taking on water ... fast ... and we're going to sink,"

"So where's the water coming from?"

"We don't know ... honestly ... hey, you think we haven't been trying to find out? ... we've been trying ... but we don't know where it's coming from!"

"And what about that brand new 4-inch centrifugal pump?" I couldn't believe this.

"The 10 centimeter pump? It's defective ... it doesn't work ... we tried."

I turned to Kevin. "I can't believe this ... you mean that pump doesn't work?"

"Sorry Chad, we have tried everything we could think of ... it won't work ... yeh, I think it's defective,"

"I don't believe you two." It was Laurie's turn.

"Come look for yourselves." Harry was being defensive ... and defiant.

So we all filed down the passageway ... kinda reminiscent of the day before ... to the entrance of the engine room,

No question about it -- the water was about six inches over the engine room floor, and the pump was sitting at the end of one of the engines, hoses connected, and had obviously been worked on, judging from the smudges and wrench marks on the new paint.

"OK, now what?" I was thinking out loud.

We sifted back into the offficer's mess. Harry was the first to speak.

"Gentlemen, let's review our situation." Somehow him saying 'gentlemen' had an ominous connotation, and he was sounding like a bureaucrat.

What is Harry up to now?

"But before we go any further I want you all to understand that I have first right to the aluminum dinghy."

"What!" It was beyond my comprehension that he had actually said that!

"Yeh ... I reckon that the officers have priority ... right? ... and that the engineer should be the natural officer-in-charge of the dinghy, with its outboard motor and all ... and I'm the highest ranking engineer ... that's sober at least ... so I should be in charge of the dinghy!"

"Harry, you are totally out of your tree!"

"Well, you and Laurie can have the lifeboats," he offered, slyly.

"That's a good one. . those lifeboats won't last ten minutes in the water!"

"Sorry, that's not *my* fault." The man was cunning!

I looked around at the rest of the crew. Everyone was staring at Harry and me passively. Even Laurie. I wanted to get out of there.

Jeeses, what a god damn joke!

Our officers are going nuts, the rest of the crew is fighting over who's going to be aboard our one good lifeboat: the tiny aluminum dinghy. Doesn't anyone have any common sense? I strained my eyes eastward. New Ireland was over there, just beyond the horizon. Ahh, yes, there was a small island ahead, to the starboard, right there. We could try to beach her. Hell, I could almost swim to that island.

And what about the sharks, Chad?

There was some shouting from the wheelhouse deck. I raced up. Mr. Milner was excitingly pointing to a ship on the eastern horizon. We could just make out her bow ... she was heading straight for us.

"I think someone heard us, or saw our flares, they're coming to our assistance." Mr. Milner was exuberant.

The Captain rushed back to the radio, this time trying to sound calmer and more descriptive. "Mayday, mayday ... this is the New Guinea Trader ... our position is 2 degrees 35 minutes South, 149 degrees 34 minutes East ... we are taking on water ... mayday, mayday." He repeated the message over and over, continuing to manipulate the radio's dials.

"I can't believe it ... they're turning away from us!" I confirmed what Mr. Milner was saying … the distant vessel was now showing us her port side and stern ... she was heading away from us.

"I guess they're not receiving our radio message. They must of seen our rockets instead." I suggested.

Mr. Milner nodded agreement. He again flew up the ladder to the poop deck, and again I followed him. But, alas, we had already fired off every single rocket or flare. There was nothing left. Nothing at all.

We watched helplessly and with great despair as the 'rescue ship' disappeared from view. The two officers retreated to their recliners one more time. Again they had done all they could.

I went down below to the open deck to consider our situation one more time. It seemed the ironies and incongruities were piling up. Why had Mr. Milner shot off everthing that first time? Why can't the Captain get that dumb ass radio to work? Why didn't we turn to meet our prospective rescue ship? Maybe seeing our list would have helped. Why aren't we changing course and heading for a shore right now? And why is Harry so reluctant to get back down there in the engineroom and try to find a solution?

Is Captain Rodney McKay's prediction about to come true??

But for some reason I just couldn't seriously believe -- in my bones, so to speak -- that we were about to sink and perish in the middle of this ocean. Maybe everyone else was thinking the same thing. It seemed that we were all waiting passively for some event to save us.

Just about then Fred grabbed my arm.

"Chad, I was looking for you ... I have an idea. Come with me." I followed as he headed for the bow of the Trader, to the foc'sle.

"Chad, these are electric pumps, aren't they?" He was pointing to a pair of cylinder shaped housings mounted on the deck, just inside the foc'sle, which looked like electric motors connected to small centrifugal pumps.

"Yeh, they do ... they are! ... but ..." I didn't understand.

He continued, "This used to be a tanker ... I bet these are pumps that were used to pump whatever the ship was carrying."

I felt suddenly exhilarated. Looking around I spotted two electric switches on the bulkhead close by. "I bet these are the switches ... let's try them."

They were the push button type. I pushed one. Nothing happened. My heart sank. I pushed the second ... there was a jerk and a whining sound ... one of them was running. I quickly turned it off. I certainly didn't want to damage it.

"Fred, you're a welder, can you use our oxy-acetylene torch and cut this one loose from the deck?"

"Sure, I can do that!" We grinned at each other. I grabbed his hand. "Let's do it!"

"I don't know how to wire it, though ... I don't know enough about electric motors to wire them from scratch." I was trying to remember my electrical theory from my one year at the Southern Alberta Institute of Technology. But this was a special situation. I had no way of knowing if the motor was 110, 220 or 440 volts, or whether it was single, double, or three phase, or even if it was alternating or direct current. And it all mattered, because if I wired it wrong I could burn it out in seconds and then we'd be back to square one.

Fred and I managed to locate the torch set and carry the tanks to the bow. While rummaging in the engine room I spotted a roll of heavy three-wire Romex cable, the kind used to wire houses. I showed it to Fred. At the foc'sle, Fred proceeded to cut out the one operative pump. I opened up the electrical connection box, trying to figure out how to wire it from a source in the engine room.

"Fred, can you make any sense out of this wiring?"

"Sorry, I'm not familiar with these kinds of motors. But Chad ... why don't we use that roll of cord and wire it from here, like a long extension cord. That way we don't mess with the connections, just keep them the same."

"Fred, you're a genius!" We slapped open palms together, our comradeship solidified.

Curiously, our actions and noise hadn't caught anyone's attention. Not Harry's or Kevin's that is. I was thinking that they should be here helping us.

But we were in full view of our officers on the upper deck. Mr. Milner had been watching, and now called out, wanting to know what we were doing. I explained our idea, and that the one pump had proven to be operative. He and the Captain were enthusiastic.

"Right on, Chad ... let's hope it works!"

We now had the motor and pump removed, and the wire ready to set up as our extension cord. But the damn thing was heavy. Very heavy. I figured it was time to shake up the rest of the crew and get some assistance.

Harry, Kevin and Laurie were still in the officer's mess. 'I'll bet they're drawing lots for the dinghy', I chuckled to myself. There might even be money involved. Wouldn't surprise me, knowing Harry.

"Hey you three, I need some help!" I announced, with enough volume to make it sound like an order.

"What's up, Canuck?" Harry wasn't about to move one iota without an explanation.

"I think Fred has found us a solution. He's cut loose an electric pump from the foc'sle. We need your help to rig it up!"

The three were genuinely startled, especially Harry.

"What ... a pump?"

"Yes, Harry, a pump!"

Laurie was already on his feet, and Kevin was right behind him. Harry started to move too, he didn't have a chance to hesitate any further. It was almost comical ... I had just popped his bubble.

Sorry to disappoint you, Harry!

We carried the heavy pump to the engine room, and down the steps. Kevin and Harry rigged up the intake and discharge hoses, borrowed from the defective new pump. I strung out the Romex cable and made the connections.

The moment of truth arrived.

"Fred, why don't you do the honors ... go ahead, push the 'on' button in the foc'sle. We waited. It seemed forever for Fred to reach the foc'sle. Suddenly there was a torsional spasm as the electric motor jumped to life, followed a second later by the sound of water rushing through a hose, the limp discharge hose jumped with new animation, changing its configuration to accomodate the passing of pressured fluid.

We all scrambled up the steps and leaned over the rail -- to see the bilge water from the engine room successfully being ejected out the end of the blue plastic tubing, down the side of the Trader and back into the sea.

"It works!" Laurie shouted.

Everyone cheered. Even Harry. When it came down to it, he really didn't want to see the Trader sink either. At least that was my summation. Both the Captain and Mr. Milner were leaning over the side of the upper deck, observing our success, and had both joined in our cheering. This was a good moment.

"Of course the pump is only a temporary measure. We must determine how the water is finding its way through the hull and repair that leakage. Harry, you say you don't know how the water is entering. Is that correct?"

"Yes, Captain, we have tried to find out, but we can't figure out where or how it's coming in." Harry answered.

Harry and I had been asked to join the Captain and Mr. Milner for a review of our situation.

"I wonder if it has something to do with what I saw the time that I dove for the Captain's glasses?"

"And what was that?" Mr. Miner was curious.

"Well, there's a sizeable bulge sticking out from the hull -- on the bottom -- it's about 6 feet wide by 12 feet long and protrudes out about 18 inches."

"Hmm ... sounds like a concrete plug ... a concrete repair to a hole in the hull," Mr. Milner suggested. "It's a common method of repairing a sizeable hole, when a drydock's not available. Yes, that could be the source of our leak."

"Then we must put into a port. We have no choice. Looking over the chart the obvious choice is Manus Island ... they have an Australian naval station there ... they can help us. And it's close. Mr. Milner has done some calculations and he reckons he can place us at the entrance through the reef ... here ... by sunrise tomorrow morning. That's about ten hours from now. Right, Mr. Milner?"

"Correct, Mr. Patterson. I can place us exactly at that location at sunrise ... provided you keep those engines running." Mr. Miner directed the challenge to Harry.

"Well, the water is down, and if the pump holds out we shouldn't have a problem."

"That's it then, gentlemen. Harry, you and Kevin do your best to keep us running. Chad, if you will assist Mr. Milner, we will be in Seeadler Harbor in the morning. This has been another exhausting day for me, I think I'll go lie down for a bit."

Tonight promised to be an attempt at matching the magnificence of the one before, except the moon had passed its peak -- its intensity and apparent size diminished -- yet it was still impressive.

"Do you think placing the freighter at the reef entrance will be difficult?" Mr. Milner was testing my navigational judgement.

I studied the chart, and decided to be bold.

"We're going to have to have some good star shots. We need to make sure we are far enough north to be clear of this string of island and atolls ... they are dangerous to us, especially at night, and there are no lighthouses. But once we are close to the reef entrance, here, we have this lighthouse to guide us." I was pointing the lighthouse marking indicated on the chart, which was on the east side of the reef passageway.

Mr. Milner snorted, agreeing in part.

"Yes, you're right. The star shots will be key to getting around these islands." He pointed to a group named the Los Reyes Islands. "And getting us close enough to be able to sight the lighthouse. But we won't see the lighthouse until we are right on top of it. The star shots are the most important thing."

I nodded, letting him know I understood.

"This is going to be an all night chore ... feel free to rest whenever you like. You've had a full day as well. Thank you for making this possible, Chad."

"It was Fred, really, Mr. Milner. It was his idea and he was the one who knew how to use the cutting torch."

Nah, I'll be happy to take some of the credit!

We waited until the moon had again hidden its radiance below the horizon before we took any star shots. It turned out to be mostly Mr. Milner's baby ... my own shots weren't consistent enough in their accuracy. But a few were close. Mr. Milner stayed with it dilligently throughout the night. I slept off and on. The Captain was present from time to time as well, looking over our shoulder. At 2:30 in the morning we spotted the lighthouse. We had been on a heading of 276 degrees, which was due West (270 degrees plus a variation which had changed to 6 degrees East). The lighthouse was first spotted at a heading of 230 degrees, the heading decreasing steadily as we kept Manus Island to our south, still not visible to us.

Now it was 5:30 and the pre-dawn light was just starting to reveal the outline of an island directly to the south. The crew were all out of their bunks, each anxious to see where the sunrise would find us ... anxious to know whether or not the navigating officers knew their stuff. Harry, Kevin, Laurie, Joseph, and Richard were all on the main deck, towards the bow, searching the morning light

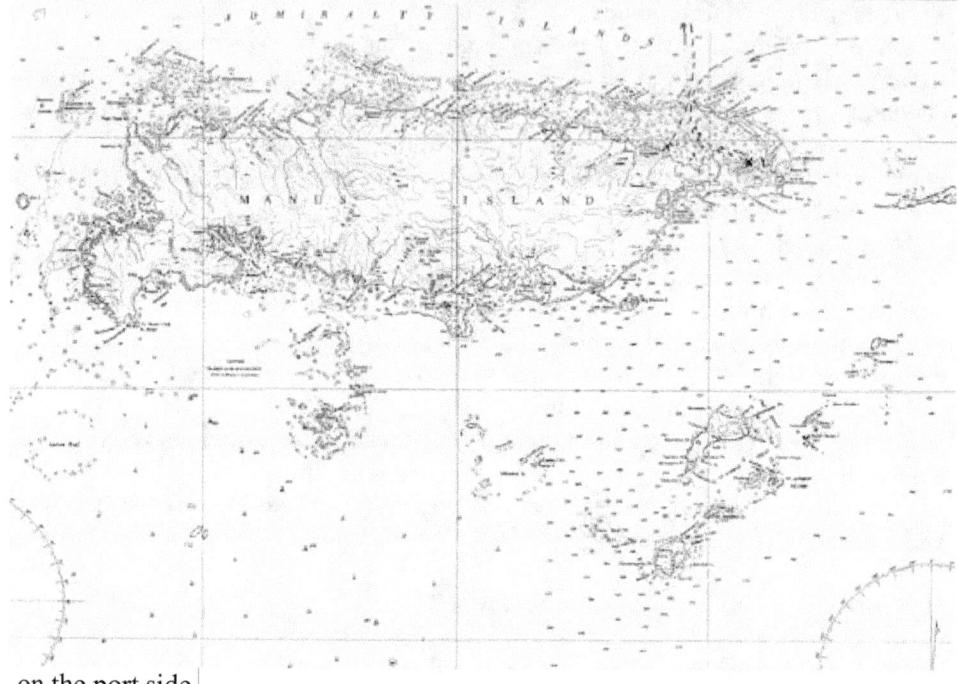

on the port side.

"Look, there it is!" Laurie saw it first, the white water and heightened swell, indicating the surf breaking over a reef, and the huge rusted skeleton of a shipwrecked freighter disquietingly marking the starboard side of the single gap in the reef which was the entrance to Seeadler Harbor, Manus Island.

We were still under way, still at full throttle. This part amazed me. Not only had Mr. Milner brought us to the exact location at the precisely predicted time, but he had done so without resorting to travelling in a circle, or stopping, or even slowing down.

We were poised, and there was no reason not to proceed. We headed towards the opening. It was barely a hundred yards wide, large surf pounding heavily on each side, and the ghostly skeleton of that ill-fated sister only a stones throw away. Dead ahead of us was Lorengau town, with a small harbor of its own, but our destination was the naval station at the east end of Manus, where it joins with Negros Island. We would be required to follow a channel to the port side, which was clearly marked with buoys.

About then Laurie came up to the wheelhouse ... it would be the start of his watch in a few minutes. "How's Mr. Morris?" He wanted to know.

"We haven't seen him since you took him to his cabin, yesterday." I explained.

"Hasn't anyone even checked on him?" Laurie was concerned, and a little ticked at us for being so callous. With that he, proceeded towards Mr. Morris's cabin. I saw him knock, then enter. He returned a couple of minutes later.

"So, how is he?"

"I think he's sick as hell. I offered to get him some food ... soup or something ... but all he wanted was a Johnny Walker's and water."

I shrugged, trying to be sympathetic, but also suggesting that there was nothing we could do. Laurie agreed, silently.

Mr. Milner asked me to bring Joseph to the wheelhouse. Fred and Laurie were already there, of course. He indicated that he had a special assignment for the four of us.

"Now, we will be pulling up alongside a wharf ... I hope to hell it's clear. If not, we will pull up alongside whatever vessel is there. Understand?"

We all nodded.

"I need you four to man the docking lines. Chad, you and Fred will take the bow, Laurie, you and Joseph will take the stem. Use your common sense and do whatever is necessary. You must use the lighter throwing line to pull the 2 inch manila rope with. If necessary, one from each pair must jump onto the wharf, or vessel, to receive the throwing line. Understand?"

We all nodded again.

"Alright ... Laurie, please take the wheel for now, this is your watch ... but when the time comes I'll take over ... OK."

"Yes sir."

We rounded the last part of the channel and yes, there was the naval wharf, dead ahead. We were in luck. Or maybe something else. There were several uniformed sailors on the empty pier, looking attentively in our direction, waiting. Two officers were among them.

"It appears we are expected. Mr. Patterson, your radio message must have gotten through."

It was a straight shot. Mr. Milner took the wheel from Laurie and the 'ding-ding' of the throttle sounded as Mr. Milner signalled for partial throttle, and motioned for the four of us 'deck hands' to take our stations.

We positioned ourselves, ready with the throwing lines. We heard another ding-ding as the propellers were brought to a full stop. We were still a fair distance away from the wharf. We slowed, approaching gently. There was a further ding-a-ling sound, and this time the propellers reacted by turning to the reverse, slowly. The Trader came to a full stop, right at the wharf s edge. The Aussie sailors caught our lines and secured our heavier ropes quickly and efficiently. Mr. Milner had proved himself to be the capable marine officer once again.

The wharf itself was comfortably high, and the Trader comfortably low, so passage from the pier to the Trader was easy. The Captain and Mr. Milner met the Navy boarding party on the main deck, starboard side.

"Sir, I am Lieutenant Gunn, and this is Bosun's Mate Hendrickson. We understand that you are in need of assistance." The Lieutenant was tall and official looking, the Bosun's Mate was much shorter, about my height, with blonde hair and he was built like a … like a 'brick chicken-coup'… he looked like he could plow through six of us without even slowing down.

"Thank you, Lieutenant, I am Captain Patterson and this is my First Officer, Mr. Milner. Yes, we are in need of assistance … we are taking on water from an undetermined source. We managed to rig up an emergency pump, but it is only a temporary measure. We would like to request assistance in pumping out excess water and repairing the leak."

"Yes sir, immediately. The Lieutenant saluted the Captain and Mr. Milner, with both returning the salute. Which, I mused, was kind of a humorous and unnecessary gesture. But it looked great. I was observing from the bow, still standing in position with the docking ropes.

"Bosun's Mate Hendrickson, see to it immediately."

"Sir, there is one more concern ... I urgently need to send a communique to my ship's owner in Sydney," Mr. Patterson requested.

"Of course, Captain, please come with me."

There were shouts, and orders, and we were instantly swarmed by a dozen Aussie sailors. Harry and Kevin could only stand to one side as they took over. A very large pump, mounted on a trailer and wheels, arrived on the pier within minutes, and hoses were set in place. The intake was huge: about 6 inches I guesstimated.

"Wow, a lot of action!" I said to Laurie as he entered the officer's mess. With our emergency well in hand, Richard had let everyone know by word of mouth that we would now have breakfast. I supposed he didn't want to create any confusion with the clanging of his bell. I even speculated amusingly that he might accidently hit on a naval code with the thing and cause a panic ... or some such thing.

Laurie was also looking on the lighter side. "What a reception," he grinned.

Harry exploded through the doorway just then. "Hey, gotta hand it to our sailor boys ... reckon our Aussie Navy's pretty professional, ehh?" He tried to imitate the Canadian 'ehh', again. He did a lousy job. "I reckon we'll be shipshape again shortly. Hope we don't have to go into drydock, though. But if we have to, they can handle it. They tell me there's a large, fully equipped drydock right over there, on the next island, named Negros Island. Reckon our boys can fix anything. Just might have to take out that concrete block you told us about, Canuck."

Aw shut up, Harry!

I just shrugged. Harry was being grandiose again.

The flurry of action continued for two or three hours. And then, all of a sudden, it quietened down. The pump was removed from the pier and all the sailors left except two, who were curiously positioned beside our docking ropes.

I was with the Captain and Mr. Milner at the wheelhouse. The Captain was relating to us about his visit to the communications office.

"It's Saturday, but both Mr. Fitzgerald and Mr. Lancey were in the company's office. Our radio message was heard in many places ... they had received my mayday all the way to Sydney. Mr. Fitzgerald and Mr. Lancey were pretty concerned.

"They weren't hoping we had sunk?" Mr. Milner interjected wryly, out of character with his recent improvement in behavior.

"Mr. Milner, please, do not start that again."

Mr. Milner raised his palms, indicating that he regretted saying that. I sighed an inner relief.

"Sorry."

"Well, I told them we thought the leak was coming from that old concrete patch. Mt. Fitzgerald verified that that is what it was you saw, Chad. It was put in several years ago, after a grounding in Madang."

"What are our instructions?" Mr. Milner wanted to know.

"We are to take advantage of the assistance offered by the Navy. I'm to call them again tomorrow morning at 9:00 a.m.. By the way, just to let you three know, Mr. Fitzgerald was very unhappy about how we handled the situation, I regret to say ... he felt we had acted like damn fools."

"What ... why the arrogant ass!" Mr. Milner was insulted.

"I guess the distress messages ... being broadcast over most of Australia and New Guinea ... it embarrassed the company."

"Harrumphh!" Mr. Milner grunted indignantly. "The nerve of the pompous son-of-a-bitch!"

"Well, maybe we can't blame them. Anyway, it's done. Nothing we can do about it. Let's just proceed."

So, we had embarrassed Lancey Shipping Company ... big deal!

They probably were *hoping we sank! Remember what Captain McKay had said!*

It was at that point that Mr. Milner noticed the slow-down in the Navy's activities, and pointed it out. We were at the deck railing, wondering what was happening, when Lieutenant Gunn and Bosun's Mate Hendrickson were seen walking towards the Trader. We met them on the main deck.

"Sir, may we go someplace where we can sit down and discuss matters."

"Certainly ... uhh ... let's go to the officer's mess. Follow me," the Captain responded.

Lieutenant Gunn was trim and fit, even taller than I had previously estimated, with dark hair and a stern, no nonsense set to his countenance. He spoke well and was actually a good looking man; I speculated that with his attributes he would probably go far in the Australian Navy.

"I'm afraid, gentlemen, that the truth of the matter is that you have made a fool of yourselves, and us!"

The Captain was shocked. Mr. Milner was both shocked and offended.

"What the hell ..." Mr. Milner was reversing character again. I was held in suspense.

"Gentlemen ... please allow me to explain. First of all, your leak was nothing more than loose packings around your propeller shafts. This vessel was sitting for some time, I understand. So the packings were dry and shrunken ... a simple tightening of the packing gland was all that was required. Any experienced naval engineer would know that, and that adjustment should have been done before you sailed, as routine."

The Captain and Mr. Milner remained silent, both faces reddening. I wasn't sure Mr. Milner's reaction was only embarrassment. I was hoping he wasn't about to pop his lid.

"Secondly, there was nothing what-so-ever wrong with your new centrifugal pump.

"What!" It was my turn to be surprised.

"We demonstrated how to operate the pump to your 2nd and 3rd Engineers. They apparently did not know that you had to 'prime' that sort of pump. That is, fill the pump body with water in order to activate its sucking action. I'm sorry, gentlemen, but any engineer, or deck hand for that matter, should know that."

More reddening of faces. And no, Mr. Milner was mostly embarrassed, not angry. I was relieved.

"Sir, I must ask you to please withdraw from this wharf immediately. This is Saturday, my men are all on extra-duty pay, and you are wasting valuable government resources. I must also inform you that a full report will be forwarded to your owners."

With that the Australian Navy departed.

"Chad, please have your crew ready at the lines," the Captain ordered sullenly. "Mr. Milner, what do you suggest?"

"Mr. Patterson, I suggest we take the Trader to Lorengau Harbor and anchor, for the time being."

"Very well, carry on," the Captain quietly submitted. I perceived that this was devastating for him. He had been humiliated and reprimanded twice this morning. First by Mr. Fitzgerald and the ship's owner, secondly by the Australian Navy. I felt deeply sorry for the man. Mr. Milner was reacting coolly, and with clear-headedness. I had to respect him for that.

And yet, I thought as I hurried below to find Laurie and the rest of our docking crew, this does have a certain hilarity to it all ... it had been a comedy of errors ... and the one comical figure in the center of it all was Harry. If anyone was to blame, it was that s.o.b. The packing gland and the pump ... I could hardly wait to razz him.

At the back of my mind, however, a dark notion was starting to form. I remembered the strange Captain McKay, and what he had warned: "There are things you don't know ... about her owners ... her cargo ... and the members of your 'skeleton' crew." And with the second encounter: "There had been some mischief done ... designed to sink the Trader to the very bottom of the sea. Was it possible that Harry had purposely tried to sink the Trader?? No, no .. it just couldn't be. I shrugged the thought away.

Nah ... not Harry!! No way!!

But I wasn't going to get my chance to prob Harry right away. Too many things to do. I did get a chance to tell Laurie about the packing gland, though, as we were getting ready to cast off. Fred and Joseph too. They just shook their heads in disbelief.

Mr. Milner himself went down to the engine room to assess the situation, and to ensure we could run our engines. I imagined there were a few 'other' things said as well. Minutes later they both started up, the 'psst-psst' of compressed air again marking the beginning of the double event.

Our docking crew was ready at the ropes, the two Aussie sailors loosened our lines, and we slowly pulled away from the wharf. Mr. Milner steered the ship in a wide arc to turn us around ... there was ample room. We retraced our path back through the channel, turning to port once Lorengau town and its harbor were in full view.

Lorengau Harbor was a little tricky. We had to swing the Trader a full 180 degrees and lower our anchors, one at a time, so that in the end we were positioned with our stem to the shore and both anchors wide apart, port and starboard to the bow. Once again the ship came to a rest, the two Perkins rumbled to a stop, and all was quiet and still. A small group of people stood or sat at the shore, watching our progress. I wonder what's in store for us now, I pondered, and I watched them in return, giving a wave for the hell of it. I received some waves back. Umm, good sign ... any good looking maris among them?

Stop it, Chad!

Richard's bell clang-clanged us to an awareness that it was a couple of hours past noon, and we were all starved. He had been waiting for our anchoring procedures to finalize before disturbing us with such a mundane matter as food.

Nonsense! Food *can never be a 'mundane' matter!*

"Hello, Harry!" I was looking forward to enjoying this.

"What, you got a problem, Canuck?"

Laurie raised his eyebrows, Fred and Joseph were curious, Kevin was somber.

"Yeh, I got a problem! It has something to do with packing glands and priming a centrifugal pump."

"Hey, bloody bell ... how were we supposed to know?"

"How were you supposed to know? You should have known ... you're the hot shot engineer!"

"How? Kevin and I couldn't have known about the glands ... we've never worked on a ship before?"

"And the pump? It's the same kind we used to use on the road, when we were working for CDW."

"Bloody hell, I was a heavy equipment operator, not a laborer ... I never used one of those pumps."

I laughed. "You know, Harry, if I didn't like you so damn much ... and I don't know why I do ... I don't know ... you just should've known ... the whole thing was such a comedy ... and you ... sometimes Harry, you truly do have shit for brains!"

"Take it easy, Canuck!" He started to laugh too. And where do you find those dumb ass expressions: 'shit for brains', that's a good one."

"Yeh, well it fits!"

At that point Kevin interrupted. He had been silent, troubled. I had thought it was because he was embarrassed by the whole thing, but there was more to it than that. "Harry, tell them about the pump, and what we were thinking."

Harry hesitated, then nodded, and suddenly became serious. "This may seem kind of far-fetched, but you blokes should know that there are a couple of things that are strange about what happened."

"What do you mean,'" I prodded.

"Well, for one thing, the sailor boys didn't have such an easy time getting that new pump to work, like maybe the Lieutenant suggested ... there was a plastic shipping plug in the intake ... you had to remove the housing to take it out. It was the sort of thing you'd expect to already be taken out at the time they sold the pump.

"Yeh, and there wasn't one in the exhaust port, just the intake ... and you couldn't see it, because of the housing and the intake hose fitting, you couldn't tell it was there," Kevin added,

"'So why was it there, or why weren't we told about it ... maybe an instruction sheet, or a manual, or something," Harry continued

Kevin was getting a little excited. "We were thinking about the packing gland too. Why didn't Mr. Fitzgerald or someone tell us that the packing would probably be dry and loose after sitting so long. And maybe ... I'm saying just maybe ... maybe someone backed off the bolts on the packing glands before we left ... on purpose! It would have been very easy to do."

We were all leaning intently towards Harry and Kevin. Richard had joined us too. Their suggestion of intrigue was capturing our imaginations.

Kevin went on: "Another idea occurs to me. If the owner wanted to see the ship sink or shipwrecked, accidently of course, what kind of a crew would they sign on? A Chief Engineer whose a total alcoholic and doesn't even visit the engine room? A second and third engineer with no marine experience? The rest of the crew marginal, as little experience as possible, and maybe a captain and first mate that were a little nuts ... makes you think, doesn't it? No offense to you all, but we're a pretty incompetent bunch. Except you, Richard, that is!"

We all laughed. I think Richard felt good about what he had said.

But, this was all kinda heavy. I brought up my palms and breathed deep to signal that we should hold it there. "Gentlemen,"

Jeeses, I love that opener.

"Let's not get too carried away ..."

"Yeh, the main thing is that we're OK, and we can continue to Hong Kong!" Laurie added sensibly, giving me some support.

"So I'm out of here ... I'm going to talk to the Captain and Mr. Milner ... find out what we're going to do next."

Damn, this whole ship is becoming paranoid!

CHAPTER SEVEN

Escape from Manus Island

It would be an extreme point of view, but one might say we were renegades, maybe even pirates.

"Captain, we have a visitor ... I have no idea who it is."

I had been on the aft deck with Harry and Laurie, lowering our dinghy into the water in preparation for going ashore, when we spotted an outboard-powered craft approaching ... a New Guinea boy was manning the outboard and a European gentleman sat towards the bow. I volunteered announcing his arrival before he reached the Trader, since we were faced away from shore and his approach could not be seen from the wheelhouse.

"Ahh ... thank you, Chad ... please have whoever it is come up."

The Captain was alone on the deck, resting in one of the loungechairs. Mr. Milner had retired to his cabin, sleeping after his all-night vigilance and the busy morning. Mr. Morris had not made an appearance yet, apparently still out of it. That was beginning to worry me.

I returned to the aft deck just in time to welcome our visitor. Laurie was helping him board.

"Good day, sir," I greeted him cordially.

"Yes ... good day to you as well. My name is George Vincent ... I'm one of your agents. I handle all of Lancey's shipping in and out of Manus. May I speak to your Captain?"

"Certainly, sir ... my name is Chad ... and this is Laurie ... and Harry." I didn't bother with our 'official titles' ... it seemed an unnecessary nuisance and the hell with telling him I was '2nd Mate'. "Uhh ... please follow me ... sir."

"Captain, this is Mr. George Vincent ... one of our agents."

The Captain extended his hand: "I'm Captain Patterson, sir ... please sit down.

And what can I do for you?"

"Captain, I've heard about your problems. Both from Lieutenant Gunn and from Mr. Fitzgerald ... and we received your distress signals yesterday. Please understand that the Lieutenant is a friend of mine ... this is a small island."

"Then I assume you've heard of Lieutenant Gunn's poor evaluation of our performance."

Nice choice of words, Captain!

Mr. Vincent responded with a friendly chuckle. "Yes, and Mr. Fitzgerald's!"

That caused the Captain to frown even further. "Then you've talked to Mr. Fitzgerald today?"

"Yes."

"I'm to call him again tomorrow morning at 9:00 a.m.. Are there any new or different instructions from Mr. Fitzgerald?" The Captain was becoming curious as to why Mr. Vincent had taken the trouble to come aboard.

"No ... and of course you may use my office in the morning for your call. Mr. Patterson, the main reason I've come to visit you is to offer any assistance I am able to give, and also to invite you and your crew -- all of you -- to my house this evening. We are having a large party, it's my daughter's first birthday. Maybe we can become better acquainted, get a chance to discuss things. Quite frankly, there are one or two things that are, shall we say, 'special' about your situation. Can I count on your presence ... say about eightish. My house is at the top of the road straight up from the Harbor Park, on the right hand side ... you won't be able to miss it.'"

"Well, I think I can speak for the rest of the crew when I say we'd be delighted. We'll be there, thank you."

I escorted Mr. Vincent back to the stem, this time walking behind. I noticed he walked with a broken stride, like he had a club foot or a similar liability. He was a younger man, maybe thirty-five or so, was exceptionally lanky and stood perhaps three inches above my five-foot-eight. His most noticable feature, however, was his blond curly hair, on the long side, and shaped kind of round, like he was trying to let it grow out to an Afro style. His manner had been straight-forward and friendly ... I had taken a quick liking to him. I was super curious about what he meant when he had said there was something 'special' about our situation. His implication was that he was sympathetic towards us ... 'why' was the question that came to mind. I wanted to ask him ... right there before he got back into his boat, but I held back, hoping I would have another chance later.

Harry was still at the Trader's stern. I was aware that he was checking out Mr. Vincent's vessel, with an envious glint in his eye.

"What, Harry? Bet you'd like to have this one next time we're about to sink!

With good reason -- the craft was a sporty looking power boat, featuring an aluminum hull with lapstrake contouring and a covered section at its slightly turned up and flared bow, and a low, full-width windshield. It even had a steering wheel, but I could see that the cables were disconnected at the stern ... probably because its owner relied on having a New Guinea boy handle the outboard direct, in true colonial style. 'Manus Trading Company, Pty' was painted in large letters on each side. Most impressive, though, its outboard was an 30 horsepower black Mercury!

"That baby can really get up and kick ass, I bet," Harry drooled.

"Yeh ... would be great fun to try it out. By the way, we're invited to a party tonight ... everyone, the whole crew."

"Oh yeh ... where ... when?"

"Mr. Vincent's house, straight up there." I pointed to the street our agent had indicated ... it was clearly visible from where we stood. "But not until 8 o'clock."

"Oh."

That disappointed Harry ... I suspected he was feeling ready to party right then.

"I don't know about you, but I'd like to go ashore now, have a look around."

Damn, this is a new island to explore! Let's check it out!

"Nah, later." Harry wasn't much for walking around.

The word about the party was passed quickly mouth to mouth, and a general concensus developed that we would all find the party at about 8 o'clock, each choosing their own route and own way of passing the time till then. Laurie and Joseph indicated they wanted to go ashore with me. Harry said he'd rather stay on board and rest up for the party, but he agreed to ferry us across and bring the dinghy back to the Trader. So the four of us loaded into our trusty aluminum transporter and headed for Lorengau.

"Well, what do you want to do?" Laurie asked.

"Hey, I just want to walk around, check things out!"

"Sounds good to me." Laurie agreed.

"Me too." Joseph was with us.

Manus Island is a good sized piece of real estate, about 40 miles long by approximately 15 wide, but there's only one main road on the island, which mostly services Lorengau, the naval base, and the airport ... the whole of which occupies only a small part of the eastern end of Manus plus the connecting island of Los Negros. Actually, it is Los Negros that is the home of the naval base and airport, and also the now overgrown airstrip built by the Americans during

139

WWII. The islanders therefore live mostly in isolated villages scattered throughout the rest of the island, accessible only by trails or by outrigger canoe to the coastal areas. Lorengau is the island's one and only town and is the center of commerce and the locale of the island's hospital and main schools. It is also where almost all the European and Chinese residences are. Yet Lorengau is a tiny town, only several street blocks in any direction from its center, which is at the harbor.

It was five in the afternoon, a Saturday. We quickly found the market place area, but as we expected it was already near-deserted. New Guinea market places are a colorful, enjoyable site when in full swing ... where the villagers from surrounding areas bring their goods to sell, the ladies dressed in their long, brightly colored 'lap-lap' style dresses. Typically there's a varied and abundant array of fruits and vegetables, and hand-made items such as baskets and other woven products, and of course beetel nut ... always plenty of beetel nut. Although there were very few real 'tourists' in attendance, the market places seemed to always have an active trade in carvings and artifacts. It had amused me a couple of times before, seeing a European tourist in a market place in Morseby or Rabaul attempting to bargain for a carving or piece of native art, assuming of course that they were on display solely to entice the interest of foreign tourists like themselves, only to find to their surprise that their fiercest competition as a buyer were the New Guineans themselves. Which makes sense: they produce art first for their own purpose and their own enjoyment.

But New Guinea markets are a morning affair; the villagers must make the often lengthly journey back to their villages before dark. And the markets especially closed early on Saturdays, for the teachings of the early Catholic and Protestant missionaries had already become deeply rooted ... Sunday was a day of rest ... there was no market on Sunday ... there was *nothing* on Sunday ... and everyone wanted to get back to their villages early the evening before.

So the market place was deserted. We were kind of disappointed.

"That's too bad, I was hoping to see a cuscus." I tried to sound devastated.

"What ... a cuscus?" Laurie questioned. This was a word he'd never heard before.

"It's a furry little animal that Manus is well known for ... I hear they keep them for pets ... before they eat them." I started to explain.

"You mean you've never seen a cuscus?" Joseph asked both of us, surprised. "There's lots of them in Rabaul."

"Nope, never seen one." I answered. "But I understand they're especially common here."

Joseph chuckled. "Well, there'll be plenty of them in the marketplace on Monday."

Even the huge Burns Philip supermarket was closing … it was a large single story warehouse, piled high inside its single open space with all varieties of goods.

We were turning back after having run out of buildings in that direction, and were passing a collection of a half dozen small Chinese shops, when our path was suddenlty blocked by the figure of a teenage girl … a very pretty teenage girl I might add … the prettiest girl I had seen in a very long time. She instantly reminded me of Walter's wife … only a much younger version, and even more attractive. My heart literally jumped.

"Hello, Joseph." She stood directly in front of him, standing prettily and firmly, looking Joseph straight in the eye. Seeing that her attention was on Joseph, my heart fell. I'm sure his soared. She was all-out to meet Joseph and nothing was going to stop her, that much was obvious.

"What … ?" The poor kid was speechless … he didn't know what to say … he obviously didn't know who she was. He was going to blow it! I felt panic … I'm not sure it was for him or for myself.

"Joseph!" Her expression turned to distress. "I'm Sandie … Sandie Chang!"

Joseph's face exploded with light.

"Sandie … Sandie Chang … it's you?"

"Yes, Joseph Akho, I'm Sandie." Her eyes dropped, it was time for her to be the demure young lady and for Joseph to be the dominant male courter.

Now Joseph was a good looking boy, and we had discovered that he was friendly, intelligent, and a hard worker. But Joseph was also shy. He stammered. I knew he was going to blow it! Something had to be done. Besides, if he hadn't fallen instantly in love with this beauty, I had. So I did what I knew had to be done.

"Sandie … excuse me, my name is Chad … we are going to a party this evening at Mr. Vincent's house. Could you come … be Joseph's guest?"

She looked at me square on. Those gorgeous black eyes saw all. But she knew what she wanted.

"I know about Mr. Vincent's party. Yes, I can come … my family has also been invited … I would like to see Joseph there."

Her English was exceptional … she said all this without resorting to any pidgin whatsoever. I was impressed.

"Joseph?" I was urging him to talk, to at least say yes, he would be there.

"OK … I'll see you at the party!" He finally spit it out.

Sandie bowed … she had a lot of Chinese in her … smiled radiantly, and quickly disappeared into the doorway of the nearest building.

Laurie had a grin on his face that was a yard wide. "You two are something else … Joseph, she is a real beaut! If you don't chase after her … well, I'll be very disappointed … and you, Chad, you'd better lay off."

"OK ... OK ... anyway, I don't stand a chance against this hansome beast." I playfully grabbed Joseph across the shoulders.

We walked in the opposite direction, still staying on the main road, which ran parallel to the harbor shoreline. Like almost every port city I've ever visited, I reflected, the main highway runs along the coast, so the metropolis ends up being long and narrow with all roads returning to the harbor. We soon ran out of buildings in that direction too, and again we turned around.

"Real exciting place, ehh?" I was weary of Lorengau already.

"Well, let's check out the Seaside Lodge then. Maybe we could have a beer or two till eight o'clock."

On the first leg of our excursion we had passed a hotel, or lodge, which we assumed was Lorengau's one and only.

"Laurie, you're forgetting ... their stupid rules won't allow Joseph."

"Even with us with him?"

I looked at Joseph. "What do you think?"

"Well, I don't want anything to drink ... I don't know ... I can go sit in the park."

"Bloody bullshit!" Laurie was mixing his expressions. "We can all go sit in the park."

It was already late and that was actually a good idea, so the three of us found a place to sit in the small park at the harbor, just opposite where the Trader was anchored, and waited for more of our crew to join us,

"So, Joseph, how do you know Sandie?" I was still thinking that I'd love to chase after her if he didn't.

"She's ... a friend of the family, I suppose. My father has a business partner, Sandie is his niece ... I met her a couple of years ago when her family visited Rabaul ... but she was just a girl then ... but now ... wow!"

I was thinking about Fred, and our long conversation a couple of nights before.

"So, Joseph ... why did you want to come on the Trader?"

He smiled, and shrugged. "Adventure, travel, a chance to see the world."

"Yeh, I can relate to that," I responded. Joseph doesn't feel trapped, like Fred, I realized. Maybe he's too young, yet. I wondered about how his future would be if he ended up with a girl like Sandie. Probably OK -- they're both hap-caste, but mostly Chinese, and with families already successfully established in business. I still wondered, though.

"Hey, here come's the dinghy." Laurie's sharp eyes were again the first to pick up on the action. I saw that this load was comprised of our officers, and included Mr. Morris.

"Laurie, Mr. Morris is with them!"

"Yeh, I see that." Laurie turned to me, seeming more worried than surprised.

142

"Chad, I'm concerned about him."

"Yeh, I know." I was being sardonic.

"Forget that ... I mean I really feel sorry for him. And everything that has happened ... well, I can see he might be blamed for it all ... but we know he's not really to blame ... you know what I mean?"

"Not really, maybe he *is* to blame." I was still hung up on my sarcastic binge.

"Come on, you know better than that. It's like he was set up. Fitzgerald and the owner didn't expect anything from him ... so he performed just like expected."

"Wow, Laurie, that's a mouthful. You know what you're saying?"

"Well, I don't know ... I just feel sorry for him ... and I want you to feel some sympathy for him too ... maybe tonight we could, well, give him some support."

I considered that a second. "OK, Laurie, you got it ... but you have a serious problem, you know."

"What's that?"

"You're just too damn soft hearted!"

He laughed. I laughed. Joseph joined in too. We had a good thing going.

It was a bit of a grind up that hill. And a 'few' blocks grew to a couple more. But Mr. Vincent was right about one thing, we couldn't miss the house. We recognized that this area was where the 'better' citizens of Lorengau lived: the properties were spacious, each with a substantial front lawn and flower hedges, and a long driveway leading to a separate carport. The homes were constructed Aussie Queensland style -- single story, raised off the ground, with a row of louvered panels around its lower perimeter to maximize ventilation. There was already a large crowd gathered at the house, most sitting at tables which had been set up for the occasion in the vast front yard; with a spacious tent erected in the middle, for shade and in case it rained, I assumed.

We were a party of six, and in our own small way I suppose we were impressive. Both the Captain and Mr. Morris wore white jackets, Mr. Morris with white slacks as well. Mr. Milner appeared equally naval and aristocratic in dark blue jacket and matching slacks. And Laurie had come to shore showing off his floral 'aloha' shirt again ... he had informed me that that was what it was called. Joseph was neat and respectable, and I ... well, at least I had shoes on.

Mr. Vincent spotted us and rushed to meet us. "Welcome, gentlemen. But there are more of you, aren't there?"

"Two more will be arriving shortly," the Captain explained.

I did some quick counting with my fingers. One person was left out.

Well, the party was just great. There was plenty of South Pacific, and Foster's too. And plenty of people. Except that there were no younger ladies. It was either old farts or young kids ... not much in between. Which caused me to reflect that that was a common characteristic of New Guinea society in the outer provinces. Australians and other Europeans would leave their older children behind at home, or at least send them off to school when they reached high school or college level. Even younger children in the elementary or secondary grades were typically sent to private schools in Australia. Chinese and hap-caste families also sent their children away, the choice for them being the university in Lae or Port Morseby -- the very luckiest going to Australia. And of course the younger 'working set' were eager to leave the small towns to seek better opportunities in the larger centers. The net result was a drain and an absence of young adults, especially European, and secondly among the Chinese and hap-castes.

The exception, however, was Sandie. I didn't realize she was present for several minutes after she had arrived. The Chinese and hap-caste families occupied one corner of the front yard by themselves. I first became aware of her presence through Joseph, for he had suddenly become all fidgety and nervous.

She was truly radiant -- and beautiful. She was wearing a floral dress, in a tight fitting Chinese style, complete with a slit up the side all the way to her thigh, her small yet full breasts accentuating the low cut front.

I drooled, and reluctantly nudged Joseph into action.

"Joseph, get off your ass and go over there." I had to force myself

"That's an order," I chuckled.

To both Laurie's and my amazement, he did it! He stood up and walked over to that section of the party ... we watched him gentlemanly introduce himself to those around Sandie, and he sat down next to her. She was beaming magnificently.

At one precious moment, sometime later, I caught her eye ... Joseph was still sitting beside her ... and I winked. She smiled, I imagined that it was a smile of appreciation. Ahh, I had fullfilled my role well!

Yes, what a true gentleman you are, Chad ... Bullshit!!

Harry had arrived with Fred, both dressed to do some serious partying.

"Where's Richard," I questioned.

"He's staying on board the Trader," Fred answered.

"Yeh, he wanted to stay ... but good thing ... we couldn't leave the dinghy on the beach, and the Trader shouldn't be left without anyone aboard." Harry rationalized.

Now for the serious business at hand, I thought, for tonight I wanted to drink. I mean, *really* drink. The evening moved swiftly, eventually becoming bleary, but was truly enjoyable throughout.

Mr. Vincent and I had a lengthly conversation. That, I remember. He was full of questions, mostly about each of the crew member's background and qualifications. I remember being perfectly honest, which caused him to laugh frequently.

Oh yes, we are *a highly qualified bunch!*

And I recall he was concerned about insurance, specifically the rising cost of insurance, and how they somehow had to put an end to the recent surge in 'unscrupulous claims' which was increasing the cost of trade and ruining the shipping business. It seemed peculiar to me at the time that he had chosen me as his source of information. But then I realized that he couldn't ask our certified officers, nor Harry or Kevin either ... they were the ones he wanted to know about. At one point he was particularly interested in Mr. Morris.

"A strange little fellow, isn't he. You say he has never been below to the engine room?"

"Nope, not even once!"

"That *is* irregular ... And Mr. Fitzgerald allowed that?"

I caught the significance of what he was implying -- a similar conclusion to what Laurie had worked out.

"No, Fitzgerald just kinda accepted it."

"Highly irregular!"

Kevin, our philosopher, had struck up an aquaintance with one of the more extraordinary guests: a tall spectacled gentleman, middleaged but evenly tanned and with sun-bleached light-brown hair. I guessed that he was American, maybe from California. I caught Kevin's eye during an interlude when I was bored, and he motioned for me to join.them. I eagerly did so.

"Mr. Morton, this is our 2nd Mate, Chad Fletcher."

Jeeses, Kevin, why you gotta tell him I'm 2nd Mate?

I was unhappy about him making the introduction like that. Sure enough, once again I had to endure the look of questioning surprise.

Oh, what the hell, at least I'm wearing shoes.

"Chad, this is Dr. Brian Morton, from U.C.L.A.. He's here doing meteorological research to do with the Nina - Nino phenomenon."

"Nice to meet you. But excuse me, what kind of research?" I asked dumbly as I shook his hand.

Mr. Morton chuckled. "Don't feel embarrassed ... not very many people are familiar with the Nina - Nino system. It has to do with the flow of a warm surface current from west to east along the equator, and a counter event of cold surface water flowing in the reverse direction, from east to west."

"Oh ..." I had no idea what he was talking about. Sensing my lack of comprehension, he continued:

"This transfer of surface water seems to have a profound effect on weather, not only along the equator, but world wide. When we have a 'Nina', that's Spanish for 'female child', then the eastern Pacific becomes warmer due to the eastward flow of warm water and, for one thing, we have an increase in the number of hurricanes. With a 'Nino', which means 'male child', the reverse is true."

I think that's how he explained it ... or maybe it's the other way around!

"But what has this to do with this part of the world, especially here in Manus?"

"Well, we think that right here, or just north of here, is where it all begins. We are at 2 degrees latitude south of the equator; the equator itself is just one hundred miles or so away. Here the water temperature is the warmest of the entire Pacific, consistently in the 84 - 88 degree range, Fahrenheit, or 29 - 31 degrees centigrade. That is very warm.

"But how can that effect weather over the entire globe?" I was feeling some effects from the South Pacific myself ... South Pacific beer that is, and his heavy duty explanation was kinda hard to digest.

Dr. Morton continued patiently: "That does get complicated -- it's not easy to explain. But maybe it'll help you envision the wide-spread effect if you understand that hurricane and typhoon systems have tremendous influence, reaching high latitudes, and that a hurricane or typhoon cannot be generated if the surface temperature of the ocean water at that location is below 26 degrees centigrade."

"Ahh, yes ... Now I understand." I didn't, but I pretended I did.

"By the way, you sound American ... are you?"

"Nope, sorry, I'm Canadian ... but I guess we speak the same language.

Excuse me gentlemen, but I need to find another South Pacific. Nice meeting you, Dr. Morton, we'll talk to you again." I had decided that it was better to leave this intellectucal stuff to someone like Kevin.

The pace of the party started to quicken. I remember Laurie saving myself, and Harry, from getting our butts kicked in. For my part a young kid about seven or eight had come up to me with a small red pepper in his hand, which he had pulled off a near-by bush, and asked me if it was OK to eat. It was one of those tiny super hot s.o.b.'s.. Mischievously, I told him: "Yeh, go for it." Well, I guess the kid's mouth damn near caught on fire and his father was all bent out of shape 'cause I had been the 'idiot' who had told him to go ahead and eat it, and so I told the father that his son was a little 'dim' for not knowing better and it didn't really hurt him anyway and that I would appreciate it if he would kindly 'take his bongos and F.O.' Well, the guy didn't understand what I had said, but he knew it involved the 'F' word and he had caught my accent and so he called me a F_ing 'Yank' and some other things, and so of course I had to leap to the challenge. Laurie had to step in between us to prevent me from getting pulverized.

And Harry ... well, he had managed to seek out the good Lieutenant Gunn and had told him about the plastic plug in the pump and also told him that there was a conspiracy to sink the New Guinea Trader and that the Australian Navy was part of it all and that he could lick Bosun's Mate Hendrickson just about any time of the day to prove he was right. Laurie almost had to sit on Harry to shut him up and quell that one down. I thought at the time that Harry was damn lucky that Bosun's Mate Hendrickson wasn't at the party. That guy had reminded me of a bulldozer, about a Catepillar D9L model.

On second thought, I wish he had *been there!*

But it was Mr. Morris who out-shined us all. He had had one hell of a time making it up that hill. And coupled with his already unhealthy state from the day before, well, that had pretty well exhausted him. But Mr. Vincent had included among his choice of booze Johnny Walker's Black Label, and that connoiseur whiskey seemed to have a magical effect on our Chief Engineer, for his vigor and eloquence recovered remarkably ... and then he was on! However, finding an audience was a problem. He finally cornered two junior officers from the naval base, an ensign and something else, and he was berating them severely for having ordered us away from the Navy wharf in our hour of need, making statements about such things as taxpayer's money, who they were really working for, that sort of thing ... plus the need for 'men of the sea' to help one another. In the end the two officers had approached our Captain, Mr. Patterson, and asked if we could please return the Trader to the base pier, in order for them to remedy their ill-behavior of the previous day. About that time Lieutenant Gunn got wind of what was going on, and there was another flash of words. This time Laurie couldn't help, and Mr. Vincent, seeing the writing on the wall, ever so politely suggested that it was time for us to return to the sanctuary of our good ship, the Trader.

What truly amazed me, in retrospect, was that Mr. Milner remained calm and subdued through it all. He had even sided with Lieutenant Gunn, explaining to Mr. Morris that we really didn't need the assistance of the Australian Navy any further. The only plausible explanation I could come up with was that he had slept right up till the time he left the trader to come to the party and that he simply just didn't have enought time to drink.

Good thing!

Anyway, as we all reminisced in the morning over breakfast, it had been a great party and fun was had by all … from our point of view, at least.

It was just after eight in the morning, the Captain was getting ready for his phone call to Sydney. We had all had a reasonably good night's sleep, not counting the hang-overs. Mr. Milner and Mr. Morris were also on deck. A certain air of apprehension prevailed. A lot had happened. In some respects the events had brought us together. And right now we were all super inquisitive about what our owners had in store for us. Laurie was there to take the Captain to shore … they left together.

"Chad, we need to get ready to head out to sea again … can you think of anything we need?" Mr. Milner wanted to know, his eagerness for us to be on our way clearly evident.

"Yes ... there is one thing, Mr. Milner."

"Yes ..."

"Well, we could top off our fresh water supply."

"Hmm ... Are we low?"

"Yeh ... I guess our tanks are kinda small ... and we go through it fast. Yes, we need to top off the tanks. But I don't know how we can do that. We don't have hoses long enough to reach shore. That's quite a long distance."

"There's a fresh water outlet on shore, at the park, right?"

"Yes, I think so."

"If we had a clean 50 gallon drum then we could transport it that way."

"I'm sorry ... but how could we do that?"

"I forget you're not used to sailor techniques," he chuckled. "It's simple: you just fill the drum up till it's a few inches from the top, cap it, and tow it in the water. You only need about three inches at the top to give you buoyancy."

"Wow! Makes sense ... OK ... we'll do it!"

And so the project-of-the-day was going to be topping off our fresh water tanks by using a 50 gallon drum and towing it to the Trader with our dinghy and the mighty 1.5 horsepower Seagull. I envisioned that it would take a lot of manpower to accomplish this, for we had to man-handle the full drum at both ends. So I rounded up all available bodies. The easiest part was going to be towing the drum in the water. Somehow Harry managed to declare himself to be the guy in charge of the dinghy … again.

Of course!

But we needed a clean fifty gallon drum; we had no large drums on board ... and even if we had they wouldn't be clean, for sure.

"Harry, I bet Mr. Vincent could help us find a drum ... let's go ask him."

"Good idea, Canuck."

Laurie had just returned with the Captain.

"Hey, Laurie, so what happened?" I pulled Laurie to the side a moment after he and the Captain had both climbed aboard.

"I don't know ... the Captain didn't say much all I know is we're staying here today ... he's supposed to call again tomorrow morning, same time."

"Hmm ... I wonder why we can't continue on?" I was disappointed.

"Yeh," he shrugged.

I mused that I would have to get more details later. But why couldn't we leave?

"Oh, by the way ... where's Mr. Vincent now? We need a 50 gallon drum."

There was a big question mark on Laurie's face, wondering why we wanted a 50 gallon drum. "Probably still in his office ... about two hundred meters to the right of the park ... just on the other side of Burns Philip."

"Got it!"

So Harry and I took the dinghy to shore, and sought out Manus Trading Company's office.

"Good day, Mr. Vincent." He looked exhausted, probably hung-over.

"God, you two seem chipper this morning ... considering last night."

"Oh ... that ... uhh ... sorry, Mr. Vincent." I tried to sound remorseful, even if I really didn't feel it.

"Yeh ... sorry if we caused any problem for you, George." Harry attempted to be apologetic as well.

I turned our conversation to the business at hand. "What we're here for ... we were hoping you could help us find a clean 50 gallon drum."

"A 50 gallon drum?"

"Yes, we need one to transport fresh water to the Trader."

This didn't seem to be a complete answer for him, but he didn't question any further. I didn't think he was feeling very well.

"Well ... as a matter of fact, we have one or two empty cooking oil drums just out back ... go ahead and help yourselves to one."

"By the way, how did it go with the Captain and Mr. Fitzgerald this morning?"

"Well," Mr. Vincent hesitated. "I'm not sure I'm at liberty to say ... oh, I suppose it's all fight ... you *are* 2nd Mate, and I don't know much anyway ... except that your instructions are to stay anchored here and wait."

"Wait for what?" I decided to push the question.

"Well, to top off your fresh water, for one!" he laughed. "Just kidding ... no, I don't know why." He mused for a moment. "Yes, that's strange, isn't it. Why can't you continue on your way?"

Yes, why can't we continue on our way?

We were about to leave. "George, you don't reckon we could use your boat for towing the drum, do you?" Harry threw out at the last instant.

After last night ... are you kidding, Harry!

Mr. Vincent looked at Harry as if he was crazy, but managed a weak smile. "No, I'm afraid not, Harry ... uhh ... I just can't see doing that."

Harry shrugged, "OK, no worries ... just thought I'd ask."

After we were safely out of the office I cracked up: "Harry, I can't believe you asked him that. Especially after last night. You're a class act, you know that?"

"So, what's a 'class act'?"

"It means you've got shit for brains ... now let's find that drum." I couldn't help laughing.

On the second trip with the drum I noticed Richard rigging some sort of light line, one on each side of the Trader.

"What do you think he's doing, Harry?"

"Awh ... he's setting up a couple of fishing lines ... I heard him talking about it this morning. He's going to see if he can catch us some fresh fish. Have you noticed, this lagoon is just teeming with fish."

"Yeh!"

Maybe big fish too ... the dangerous, flesh-eating kind!

Joseph was helping Harry and I fill the drums, Laurie and Fred helped on the other end. But filling the drum turned out to be duck soup, we simply rolled the drum to the faucet and filled it while it was still on its side, plugging the lower hole, and then rolled it down the beach and into the water when it was full. So when Sandie quietly came into view an hour or so later, shyly keeping her distance on the other side of the park, Harry and I urged Joseph to go spend some time with her.

"Hey, this is a piece of cake ... really don't need a third set of thumbs ... reckon you should take care of your sheila, mate." Harry urged Joseph. It didn't take much urging this time, he was gone an instant or two later.

"Reckon the bloke has really fallen for her, *ehh*, Canuck."

"Shut up, Harry." He was being insensitive.

"What, feeling jealous, Canuck?"

Yes, as a matter of fact! And stop trying to imitate the Canadian 'ehh'*!*

"Up yours!"

The other end, however, was a real challenge. That drum weighed close to 500 pounds. There were four of us the first time, and we even got Kevin in the act to make it five. But we just got into each other's way. It had been a real mother.

But then Laurie ingeniously solved the problem by using one of the lifeboat lifting arms, with its rope, and block and tackle, to lift the drum out of the water. We found we could lift it high above the level of the deck and then insert our one inch hose into one of the openings and syphon its contents into the Trader's filler pipe. It worked great!

There was one part of this procedure which we fought over a bit, however. It was of course convenient for someone to be in the water in order to wrap the rope around the drum and make a sling. On the first run I agreed to be that person, against my better judgement.

"Harry, I don't like this. You know I have a thing about sharks!"

'Don't worry, mate ... we're too close to shore for there to be sharks."

"I'm not so sure about that!"

On the next trip I devised a simple method that could make work without going in the water ... a simple clove hitch with two half-hitches added, looped over the drum just below the higher bulge, or 'ring' formed in the drums circumference. It worked.

The whole procedure was a slow process, however ...we worked at it till late afternoon ... but the tanks were still far from full. Harry suggested we call it quits for the day, anyway. We all agreed.

I was the first to clean up and take my place in the mess, a South Pacific in hand. With things quietened down, almost boring, I felt like a beer.

Kevin showed, I went and got a beer for him too, just 'cause I felt like being a gentleman.

"How's Kevin the philosopher?"

He chuckled. "I'm OK, Chad."

"That was really something ... I mean what that American was saying about 'Ninas' and 'Ninos'."

"Yeh, he was an interesting bloke. He said that there was a long range plan to build huge ocean platforms near here, to monitor the temperature and current, and to even try to control it. Fascinating! "

"Do you remember which was which? Which one was the Nina and which one the Nino?"

Kevin laughed. "We were drinking a lot of beer last night. No, I'm not sure which was which. But I remember that it was the warm current flowing eastward that caused an increase in hurricanes and typhoons."

"So I wonder which cycle we're in now? The Philippines gets lots of typhoons, don't they?" This talk of typhoons made me think about the chance of running into one enroute to Hong Kong.

"Good question, I don't know ... I don't even know when typhoon season is."

Laurie had joined us and was listening to the last part, and was about to ask a question of his own, but Harry noisely interrupted.

"Hey, Canuck, the Captain and our other two officers would like you to join them."

"What's up?"

"Beats me, they just ... requested the pleasure of your company."

"Oh – oh! Put like that means I must be in trouble."

"Oh ... I thought that was your second name."

Take it easy, Harry!

Now what? I was going through the possibilities on the way to the wheelhouse. Our three officer's were in their deck chairs, waiting.

"Chad, glad you could join us," the Captain greeted. "We've been going over our situation, and wanted you to be part of our discussion. What do you make of what's been happening?"

"I'm not sure I know just what you mean, Captain." I was trying to figure out where this was leading to.

"Well, we understand that Harry and Kevin feel that there's an unanswered question or two about the leaking packing gland and the new pump that Mr. Fitzgerald purchased.

"Uhh ... yes ... that's right." I wasn't sure how to answer that question ... I was thinking about all the suspicion that had surfaced between these men.

Mr. Milner sensed my reluctance to talk freely: "Chad, the three of us are trying to understand what the intentions of Lancey Shipping Company are. We are ready to sail, but Mr. Fitzgerald has put us on hold. We are just trying to understand why."

"What does the crew think, Chad?" the Captain added.

"Captain, I think the crew is worried, but everything is pretty much one big question mark. We're just taking it as it comes, I guess."

"Well then, what are they worried about ... *why* are they worried?" the Captain continued.

Hell! Might as well tell it like it is!

"Well. Mind if I sit down? Can I speak frankly?"

"Of course, that's exactly what we would like you to do." Mr. Milner intervened.

"OK ... We're concerned about several things. One is that we were set up, I guess 'sabotaged' is the word. Next, we are worried about either of you officers doing something radical, maybe even following an order in doing so. Sorry if that sounds ... impertinent ... but I guess that's what we really think."

"So Harry and Kevin think that the leak, and not being able to use the pump, was someone else's doing ... on purpose ... a set-up?"

"I don't know how seriously they think that, sir, but they suggested it. But then maybe they were just trying to cover their own butts ... I mean I can see that the blame could understandably be placed on their own incompetance.

"Hmm, I see ... is that all?" the Captain quiried.

No ... What about Captain McKay? And the notion that Harry, or even Kevin, was part of a plot to sink the Trader? Nah . . that is just too bizarre! I had better keep the encounters with the mysterious Captain Rodney McKay to myself.

"No ... now we're concerned that the voyage will be cancelled, or that we'll be discharged and replaced because of our inexperience, or because they think we're incompetent."

This last statement seemed to strike home a bit. The three exhanged glances.

"Hmm ... We noticed that you were talking with Mr. Vincent at length last night ... and you talked to him this morning. Did he give you an insight, anything at all, as to why Mr. Fitzgerald and Mr. Lancey would want us to remain anchored here in Lorengau rather than continue?"

'No sir ... not at all ... except maybe that he was sympathetic towards us. But pardon me ... what do you gentlemen think the reason is?"

The three officers traded glances again. I perceived that my own question bothered them, and they were reluctant to give me an answer. Finally, Mr. Milner ended the silence: "Alright, Chad, I'll answer that, if the Captain and Mr. Morris are in agreement, and you understand that you are to keep this strictly in confidence ... you are not to discuss this with the crew ... understand?"

"Yes sir"

The Captain and Mr. Morris nodded consent for Mr Milner to continue.

"To put it concisely, we suspect that Lancey Shipping Company will discharge some or all of us, maybe even attempt to bring charges against us, or some of us, and will perhaps cancel this voyage altogether."

"Charges? I never considered that ... are there sufficient grounds?"

"We don't want to go into details, and I don't think we should involve you further. Can you accept that?"

"Yes, sir, that's not a problem ... uhh ... I think I'll go back below, then."

"Remember, this has been confidential."

Jeeses, now more complications!

Now it's the officers against Lancey Shipping Company, with me as a confident. One thing for sure, if Lancey Shipping Company were to discharge a few of us, presumably finding replacements, or, worse yet, cancel the voyage, then I don't make it to Hong Kong.

Someone messing around with my travel plans again!

It was much later. After a few South Pacifics and more socializing with the crew, I headed for the poop deck and my cabin. On the wheelhouse deck I encountered Mr. Milner ... he was alone, sitting peacefully in one of the deck chairs, a scotch and soda in his hand. I decided to stop and talk to him for awhile ... I was full of questions.

"Good evening, Mr. Milner."

"Good evening to you, Chad ... It's a nice evening."

"We're in a curious situation, aren't we?"

"Yes. That's probably an understatement."

He was being cordial, almost talkative. It encouraged me to go on.

"I wish we could raise our anchors and leave ... now... right now!"

He chuckled. "Yes, I know what you mean. But we can't."

"Would it really be that serious, to leave against the owner's orders?"

"Yes, it is about the worst offense that an officer could commit. Just about as bad as mutiny." He laughed, long and deeply. I surmised that he was referring to his own actions three days before (or was it four?).

"Chad, I'm afraid that I may be in a bit of trouble."

"You mean because of you taking over the ship and turning us around?"

"Yes, that ... and also because I share some of the responsibility for our 'incompetancy', with Mr. Morris and the Captain. But I suppose it's my own fault, it's the course that I have chosen throughout my life."

"I'm not sure I understand."

"Well, I'm a 'remittance man'. Do you know what that means?"

"No sir, I don't."

"I'll explain then. The Milner family is connected with British royalty, my father is a Lord, we have relatives and ancesters that were or are princes and princesses and dukes and duchesses, and all that nonsense. Now, if a 'black sheep', so to speak, was to pop up in such a high society family, it is customary to ship him off somewhere and pay him a regular stipence to 'remain abroad', not ever to return to England and embarrass the family further. I am, I'm afraid, a black sheep of the Milners, and I hold the distinction of being their most embarrassing remittance man, and the highest paid. My notoriety originally had to do with several ill-conceived affairs with young ladies, one a duchess. I have been adding to my dubious fame ever since."

It was my turn to laugh. "Are you pulling my leg?"

"Not in the least! To use the Aussie expression, it's 'the dinky die truth'. Actually, I prefer the expression which I've heard you use: 'I shit you not'"

We both laughed.

Now I'm beginning to understand this guy!

"It's too bad Mr. Patterson and I, and Mr. Morris as well, couldn't form an alliance and 'alter the record', so to speak. "

There's that word again ... "alliance".

"Why can't you? Then anything that has happened would be 'your word agains theirs'."

"But there's the disress messages, and the report from Lieutenant Gunn, and of course the ship's log. I'm afraid the record is already established."

"Hmm ... I see. But if what Harry suggests has any merit, wouldn't that offset the Lieutenant's report, and the radio messages only embarassed Lancey Shipping Company, they didn't indicate any real wrong doing on anyone's part."

Mr. Milner was looking at me with that sly expression of his again. "Perhaps, but there's still the ship's log." There was an unspoken implication in the way he said it.

"Couldn't it be altered? Or rewritten?" I suggested.

"No ... it can't be rewritten ... but it could be destroyed ... or lost."

There was a long pause between us, neither of us willing to complete the thought, or the suggestion.

"Well, I think I'll call it an evening. I finally broke the silence, feeling uneasy. "See you in the morning, Mr. Milner."

"Good night, Chad." He smiled allusively.

He was about to suggest that I destroy the ship's log! Wow!

Once more I stood at the poop deck rail, sifting through recent events, only this time the setting was Lorengau Harbor. The seascape was different from when we were anchored in Rabaul: the harbor was much smaller, actually a lagoon, with an enclosing reef and string of islands in the distance ... but still with the glistening, pristine beauty of yet another part of New Guinea's unique islands ... and waters. I spotted what was now becoming the familiar red glow of another of Richard's cigarettes, again at the Trader's bow, and yes, the dim reflection as he raised a bottle.

What's in store for us now?

Morning came: there was a lot of commotion on the starboard passageway. I hurried into my shorts and shirt, and leaned over the poop deck rail.

"Bloody hell, look at the size of that sucker!" It was big mouth Harry again, pointing below.

But this time Harry had good reason for making a lot of noise. Richard's fishing fine had snagged a fish, a really big fish. I made it to the main deck as quick as I could to get a better look. Laurie was there by that time too.

"It"s a bloody shark ... pretty good sized ... it's a Tiger shark, I can tell ... I reckon that mother's a full three meters long."

"Shark? ... Three meters? ... Tiger ..." I shuddered, my instinctive dread of sharks causing a wet chill in the small of my back, my adrenalin shooting sky high.

"I knew it, I just knew it. See, Harry, there *are* sharks here, even this close to shore."

"Amazing that the line held!" Laurie remarked.

"Not really," Richard disagreed. "This was the only sugi I could find on board." He held a section of the line across his palm, showing us. "This line is about a 150 kilo line, I reckon."

"So, what are you going to do with it?"

"We don't want it, no good for us to eat ... but I got a buyer for it already," he pointed towards shore, at an outrigger canoe equipped with an outboard headed our direction. "This bloke's going to take it ... we get a couple of big tuna ... in trade ... Hey, we'll have fish for lunch!"

"Right on, Richard!" Laurie praised him, all of us in agreement.

We filtered into the mess after the shark was taken off our hands. Richard had traded for six good sized tuna, each maybe fifteen pounds. We would have fish for quite a few days.

We were missing someone. "By the way, where's Joseph?" I asked no one in particular.

"He hasn't come back from yesterday," Fred tossed off lightly. "He must have spent the night with Sandie's family."

"Oh - oh?" I was definitely suffering a twinge of jealousy, but I was also joking that this looked like a serious relationship in the making.

"Not what you're thinking, Chad," Fred was smiling. "He would have been invited by the family to stay overnight ... in a separate room of course."

"Oh ... I see."

She is delicious! Oh well, just one more lost chance at true love ... in the never-ending series!

Today was our second day of topping off fresh water, and we got stuck into it right after breakfast.

It was about our second trip when Joseph showed. But he was not alone, for he carried a round cage fabricated from rattan, maybe eighteen inches high and twelve inches diameter, and contained inside that cage was a small, delightfully strange creature.

"Well, here's a cuscus!"

Harry and I both rushed to get a closer look. The animal inside was about the size of a house cat, with tight short fur and a small cylindrical snout, and with large brown eyes and short little ears.

"So that's a cuscus?" I was amazed.

"You know, it looks something like a possum ... see its long tail ... and no fur on most of it." Harry observed.

"It's beautiful ... look at it's coloring. I was picking out the greys and browns on it's body, white below its ears, and an orange patch around the eyes. I stuck my finger through an opening, the animal retracted and hissed, drawing its small

mouth open like a dog's snarl.

"Careful, he can bite you," Joseph cautioned. "And scratch too."

I looked at its claws, which were curiously like tiny, skinny, human fingers, four on each limb, with a long pointed 'finger nail' at the end. I imagined it was adapted for climbing trees.

"This one's a male, not yet full grown ... we can keep him if we want. I bought him."

"Keep him ... you mean take him aboard the Trader?"

"Sure, why not? We can always eat him if he becomes a nuisance." Joseph laughed at my expression of distaste. "They're delicious!"

"Hey, I'm in love with this little, guy ... yeh, let's keep him ... but no eating him, OK"

"Yes sir, Mr. 2nd Mate!" Joseph saluted playfully.

So we brought the little fellow with us on the next trip, Joseph taking the cage aboard. Laurie and Fred were curious about our new crew member, Laurie was especially delighted.

"Hey what'll we name him?"

Joseph returned and joined Harry and me. Harry decided that with Joseph back he was no longer needed, and he felt that he had more pressing responsibilities with Kevin in the engine room. I agreed.

"Don't know when we'll receive orders to start up again, Harry. It'd be a good idea to make sure we're ready."

"Canuck, do you know something we don't?"

"No, Harry, but it's a good idea anyway."

I was contemplating on that, thinking that it was a good idea to be ready on a moment's notice, when the Captain met us on the return trip ... he was due for his scheduled phone call. We took him to shore while Laurie and Fred were syphoning.

Joseph and I had a lot of opportunity to talk while waiting for the drums to fill and then be syphoned empty. He told me about his time with Sandie, and her family. It had been great, he explained.

"Her family is very nice ... and Sandie ... she's the greatest! When I come back from this ... this trip ... I want to see her again. We talked about that."

Later, he asked: "Chad, how did you manage to end up in Rabaul?"

"Wow, that's a long story!"

"So, go ahead, tell me."

We had plenty of time, so I agreed. I tried to entertain him with the series of 'adventures' which had led me to Rabaul.

I explained that I was from Canada, and described the cold winters and hostile climate that had prompted me to want to travel to other lands.

"I think the one experience that was the turning point for me, the one that made me decide that I did not want to spend my life in a cold climate, was when I

158

was eighteen and my buddy Don McKeachren and I were just about to take a trip to the 'States' ... to Las Vegas and then Mexico. He had this old Chevrolet, which we had packed full of food and clothes and everything we thought we needed to last just about forever, all from his grandmother's pantry. Well, we got three blocks from his house and one of the rear axles broke. It was January, and it was exactly eighteen degrees below zero, Fahrenheit. I remember that well. We got a friend to tow us back to Don's house, and it was 'ordained' my job to fix that axle, cause I was fairly handy with cars and Don didn't know jack about mechanics. The repair is kinda simple, cause the chevy has a floating axle and you just need to drop out the idle gears in the rear end, remove the snap ring at the end of the axle and pull it out at the wheel. But it was cold and I was working in the snow. Now, you have to understand that steel cannot be touched with the bare hands when it's that cold."

"Why is that?" Joseph wanted to know.

"Because the moisture in your skin freezes to ice, making your flesh stick to the steel. But I had to handle those damn idler gears: they were small and difficult to keep in place ... too small and too delicate a job to use heavy mittens. And the rear end oil was the consistency of thick honey, getting in the way. It was so cold I could only stay under the car for a couple of minutes at a time. I would run into Don's house and warm my hands, then rush out and grab at those idler gears with thin leather gloves, and then give up because my fingers got too cold and I would rush back to the house. Over and over again. Until I finally succeeded in putting that rear-end together. It took me all day. I was so frustrated, and cold, and pissed off ... I swore I was getting out of that country, never to return!"

"So, did you make it to Las Vegas and Mexico?"

"Yes, we did. That's another long story. It was a great adventure. But my buddy Don got homesick and worried about what we were going to do when we ran out of money, so we went back to Edmonton, Canada."

"But you finally left Canada."

"Yes, I'd already decided that I wanted to leave." I told Joseph about working my passage on a German freighter to Sydney, and about New Zealand and the Lake Manapouri Project, and about Dennis, and about Townsville, and the sugar mill, and finally being able to fly from Cairns to Port Morseby.

Joseph was curious about Port Morseby. He had never been there, but it was Papua New Guinea's capital ... he thought it must be a big, modern, wonderful city.

"Joseph, Port Morseby is a hell hole!"

'Really?"

"Yes, it's hot, and dry, with almost no vegetation and very little rainfall, and it's dirty ... dirty and messy ... there's rubbish everywhere ... no one seems to give a damn about it either."

"What are the people like?"

"Well, you know that Port Morseby is the cultural center of the Papuan tribes, which are generally taller and fairer skinned than New Guineans, and that the Papuans in Morseby itself are 'Motu', who are an especially proud people. They have always wanted to make Motu the official native language for all of Papua."

"Yes, I know that, but what are they like? Are they friendly?"

"Well, the Motu are proud, like I said, and kind of jealous about Morseby, so they tend to give other New Guineans a hard time when they come to Morseby, but they are still a very friendly people. You've heard about the movement for independence?"

"Yes, of course, we'll be an independent country soon now, within a few years, I'm sure, even though the Australians say we're not ready."

"The feeling you get in Morseby, if you are Australian or European, is that the Papuans are angry at you, they are a little hostile and suspicious, and you feel that you have to be careful ... Not like in Rabaul"

"Oh ... I didn't know that."

"Personally, I got along with them fine ... maybe too fine." I laughed.

"What do you mean?"

"Well, I got into a little bit of trouble because I was 'too friendly' with the Papuans, I was guilty of 'fraternizing', at least in the eyes of my bosses, and other Europeans, or Aussies."

Joseph wanted to know what that was all about, so I related my series of experiences to him. I had arrived from Cairns on an evening flight. Our plane load of Europeans, mostly Australian, were bussed into downtown Morseby, where almost all of the city's half dozen or so hotels are located. I was very low on cash and really didn't want to check in at a hotel, so I decided instead to take my suitcase with me and go into the bar ... to check things out and see what alternatives I had. That was when I discovered that hotel bars in Papua New Guinea were segregated ... that is, there was a bar for the natives, and a separate bar for the Europeans ... and I, unknowing, walked into the native bar. Jeeses, that was some experience. I was immediately swarmed four-deep with New Guineans, all jabbering at ninety miles an hour. I didn't understand anything they were saying ... this was my first hour in the country! I recognized mixed reactions to me, a European being there in the native bar. No doubt about it, there were a few who were hostile, and a couple were trying to con me into buying them a drink, but most were being very ftiendly and were delighted to see me there. One thing led to another, and I ended up going home drunk with two of them ... they lived in one of Morseby's waterfront 'floating homes' and I slept on a split-bamboo floor, which wasn't particularly comfortable. One, Bak was his name, turned into a lasting fiiend, and that night set the pattern for my whole Moresby experience, and problems.

I applied for a job at the Morseby Commonwealth Department of Works the next day ... Bak had shown me where the office was, and I was given a job on the spot as a heavy equipment operator. My immediate boss was a middle-aged Australian named Art White, who kind of took me under his wing.

He found out right away that I didn't have much experience. First he had me operate a Hough Payloader and found that I didn't know Jack about how to get a load in the bucket or how to load a truck. He spent some time with me, explaining the basics of properly operating a rubber-tired front-end loader, and I started to improve, slowly.

My fiiend Bak stuck with me, from a distance that is. He was unemployed, it turned out, and he explained to me how difficult it was to obtain a job in Port Morseby. He wanted me to hire him as his laundry boy at the CDW camp. I agreed, but immediately ran into a problem, because there were already plenty of laundry boys at the the camp and I was attempting to bring in an outsider. That created a little friction, and somehow Mr. White found out about it.

Then, I had gotten to know a couple of the Papuan operators, going out of my way to make friends with them. One was a middle-aged Motu named Likka ... he invited me to his village for one week-end. That turned out to be another super experience. Again I slept on a split bamboo floor ... I was almost getting used to it. On the Saturday evening I was treated to partying Papuan village style. There had been a giant fire in the center of the village, beer flowed freely and the 'whining' out of songs to the accompaniment of several badly out-of-tune ukuleles continued till late into the night. There had been dancing; I showed off my expertise doing the boogie with a couple of village girls. They had loved it. Of course I couldn't sleep with one of them, I think it was against village rules, and I got drunk out of my stink'in mind and couldn't have handled it anyway. Jeeses, what -a hang-over I had in the morning; the split bamboo floor didn't help matters either.

Likka had talked about Papua New Guinea. He was Motu, like I said, and very proud to be Motu. He felt very strongly that his tribe should be the rulers of the new emerging nation and that Motu should be the official native language. But he of course recognized that Papua New Guinea was comprised of many different cultures and languages, each having their own right to their customs and language. He just felt that the Motu were the most advanced. In fact, he told me of some of the diversity of this 'land of the unexpected'. He knew that Papua New Guinea was comprised of over 700 separate peoples and cultures, each with their own distinct language and traditions. He told me about the Mudmen of Asaro and cannibals who lived in the high mountains, and of a village on the southern coast that was called 'the place where women slap their hair in the water' because the people were strongly polynesian and the women had long straight hair which they washed in the ocean in a ritualistic 'slapping' of their hair on the water.

161

Then I had my first 'affair' with a New Guinea girl, or a 'mari'. Her name was Marie. I thought she was gorgeous. She was a waitress at the hotel which I frequented ... not the same one which I visited on my first night in Morseby ... but she worked in the 'lounge' section. I of course always drank in the 'pub'. But I had taken notice of her at a distance. I had gotten to know John, a young Aussie who was working at CDW in between school semesters ... his father was Mr. White's boss. His family had a very nice house in an exclusive European section of the city, and his parents were often away for the week-ends. We had become friends, and he was looking for a partner in a scheme of his to have a couple of maris over to his parents house for a weekend. It just so happened he was equally infatuated with another girl who worked at the same hotel as Marie. We put our heads and talents together, and with our good looks and ample charm to help, of course, we succeeded in enticing the two girls to the house for a party. We both, I mean we four, had a wonderfid time. He later told me he had been a virgin. I told him I'd been a virgin for awhile too. He said that wasn't the same thing, and I told him 'you wanna make a bet?' Unfortunately, however, his father eventually learned about our use of the house and my reputation as a fraternizer deepened, besides also being on the father's shit list for having led his son astray.

But what finally set the scene for a confrontation with my boss was my continued friendship with Bak. One night I had invited him with me to have a couple of drinks in the CDW mess hall. It wasn't really a bar, just the place where we ate, and sometimes lingered in the evening to have a few drinks. Well, a couple of Aussie's took a strong objection to me bringing one of the laundry boys into the mess to share a beer. A noisy scene ensued, I told them that their whole attitude towards the Papua New Guineans stank, and that they did too, and as far as I was concerned they could kiss my Canadian butt. And then, after Bak and I were thoroughly inibriated, I let him sleep in my room ... on the floor of course.

The next day Mr. White asked to see me. I received a very long lecture on how the Australians were doing their paternal best to nurture the Papuans and New Guineans into the modern world and, eventually, lead them to independence. But of course this would take many years because they are still a 'primitive' people and are like little children, really, and of course they are inferiorly 'black'. Most importantly, however, we must 'keep our distance' and not fraternize with them, especially now when there's a lot of talk about independence, and their 'rights', and disputes over such things as inequal pay. Well, I realized that my job was on the line, and that was important, and at that moment I was terribly hung-over and not very eloquent, so I mumbled some sort of apology, pink faced, and thanked him sincerely for having been so patient with me and teaching me, and for giving me an opportunity to work as a heavy equipment operator in the first place. And then I politely told him that I didn't agree with what he had said and that he could 'take this job and shove it!'.

I thought Lae might be a better place, and so booked a flight.

It seemed I was forever getting off airplanes in a strange place with no money in my pocket and no place to stay, nor a prospect for a job. Well, it had happened again. I lounged around Lae's largest hotel ... I forget its name, it was a spacious single story 'lodge', constructed island style with surrounding bungalows ... and I used it as a base to explore the town. I quickly found out that Lae, despite being green and incredibly pretty, was small, and there was almost no opportunity for finding a job. I spent the night under a set of bleachers at a municipal playing field. Almost comically, I was again discovered by a local New Guinea boy who wanted to befriend me and take me home with him. I declined; instead we sat there under the bleachers while it rained, and we talked, I telling him about myself, he telling me about Lae and himself. He was one of the several New Guineans whom I have met who had lived in a church mission. His had been a Catholic mission on the Sepik River, and the monk used to beat his boys mercilessly and hord large quantities of carvings and artifacts which he periodically transported to Madang to sell for his own profit, mostly for cash to buy whisky, for he was an incorrigible alcoholic ... and he could also trade whisky for more carvings at a great advantage, back at his plantation on the Sepik. The next day I decided that Lae was not a good place to stop, and I chose Rabaul as the next destination of choice.

"Joseph, I just gotta tell you about one memory I have of Lae. It doesn't have anything to do with Lae itself or me coming to Rabaul, but it is one of my star-marked memories."

However, just then we were interrupted by the Captain's return from Mr. Vincent's office.

"I'll tell you about it another time," I promised Joseph.

Mr. Patterson was walking with a lighter stride than earlier and his countenance seemed to have lost some of its cloudiness; I judged that we were about to receive better news.

"How did it go, Captain?" I cheerfully inquired.

"We will be leaving in the morning."

Joseph and I both beamed, and cheered: "Right on!"

"Chad, will you please join the other officers and myself on the bridge when we board."

"Yes sir!"

"Gentlemen, I feel I must explain to you what transpired when I called, and we must make a decision."

We were all ears!

"Go ahead, Captain," Mr. Milner urged.

"Well, I couldn't get through for a long time ... and when I did neither Mr. Fitzgerald nor Mr. Lancey were in the office. However, I did talk to a Mr. George. He explained that he was a junior partner in the company, and he said that as far as he knew we were to wait, although he didn't know why. I talked to him at length, and took the liberty to explain that our 'repairs' were complete, that we were topping off our fresh water tanks and replenishing other supplies, and we were ready to sail. I also added that we were anxious to conserve our food and fuel resources, and of course save on the crew's wages. I ventured the suggestion that waiting was simply adding to the company's cost unnecessarily. With that he agreed that there was no reason for us not to depart immediately. He therefore gave us permission to leave."

"Hmm ... not really official though, it would seem." Mr. Milner was not satisfied.

"Yes. That's quite right. However, Mr. Vincent was present. He can confirm that we were given permission to leave. And he verified that Mr. George was a man of authority within Lancey Shipping Company ... he had dealt with him on numerous occasions."

"Did Mr. Vincent offer an opinion?" Mr. Morris wanted to know.

"Oddly, he did. He felt we should leave before someone changes their mind."

Right on, Mr. Vincent, 'ol buddy!

"Chad, what's the status on our fresh water?" Mr. Milner questioned.

"Just about filled up sir, by the end of today the tanks would be completely filled. But sir, we could stop right now, we have enough ... Captain, Mr. Milner ... why can't we leave now, I mean *right* now ... before someone *does* change their mind."

"We'd have to weigh anchor within the next hour to be able to make it through the reef before dark. Quite frankly, we need some time to make a trip to shore ... to stock up on some supplies. And the fresh water operation should be completed. We should wait until morning," the Captain reasoned.

"Alright, then it's settled, we leave at sunrise," Mr. Milner concluded.

Why do I have this vision of pending doom?

I rejoined Joseph in the dinghy, relieving Fred. We continued loading fresh water. We were only on our third run, at the park loading the drum, when we heard a shout. It was Mr. Vincent.

"Chad, I just received a fax from Lancey Shipping, Sydney. Here, go ahead and read it."

I read it, stunned!

164

"Please inform Mr. Patterson and Mr. Milner of the New Guinea Trader that they are to disregard Mr. George's permission to leave Lorengau. Their instructions are to wait for Mr. Fitsgerald and party to arrive. They are scheduled to arrive Tuesday P.M. We repeat, they are not to leave Lorengau, they are to wait for Mr. Fitzgerald. Please deliver this fax to them ASAP.

Mr. Tom Lancey,

President, Lancey Shipping Company, Pty."

"Wow, thank you, Mr. Vincent."

"Chad, can I trust you to take this to the Captain and Mr. Milner right now."
"Of course!"

"With a message from me. . . "

"Yes?"

"If they decide to weigh anchor now ... within the next hour ... then ... well, I never received this fax until after you were out of the harbor."

I looked at him, puzzled.

"It's what I want to do. And this is a copy, the original is still in the fax machine."

"Mr. Vincent, could you write your message on this fax ... I'm afraid they won't believe me."

"I'm sorry, Chad, I can't do that. It could be used as evidence against me."

I was thinking. I knew the officers wouldn't take just my word. They couldn't, too much was at stake.

"Then how about coming aboard and telling them personally."

"I ... I can't do that either. Look, Chad, I'm sure you can understand ... I can't get involved, I shouldn't be doing even this much."

My mind was racing, how can I solve this dilemna?

"Then can you please wait here for just a few moments and give them a wave as a signal ... as a signal that what I tell them is coming from you."

"It's against my better judgement, but alright ... just hurry!"

That was the fastest trip with the drum all day. I had Joseph take me directly to the transom, and I scurried aboard.

"Hey, tell the guys to unload this pronto ... as fast as they can."

Laurie met me as I was hurrying down the passageway. "What's up, Chad?"

"Plenty, but no time to talk ... but let's get the drum emptied as fast as we can and be ready to hoist anchor!"

"What?"

"No time to explain."

"Gentlemen, I have a fax here from Lancey Shipping ... Mr. Vincent just gave it to me." I handed them the sheet of paper and waited, impatiently ... I needed to explain Mr. Vincent's message ... and his 'offer'. Their expressions were vivid, each displaying increased dismay as they understood the owner's order, and its implications.

"Gentlemen, please excuse my impatience, and interruption ... but Mr. Vincent is waiting on shore, at this very moment, to signal to you ... to verify a message that he has given me, and that message is that if we leave now, right now, then as far as he is concerned he never received this fax until we had already left the harbor."

The three rushed to the deck railing, leaning over and directing their vision aft, towards shore. Mr. Vincent was standing there, and he waved, adding a gesture that left no doubt to the validity of my message: a waving motion with his arm moving backward and forward, as if to say 'go', 'get out of here'. Then he turned and quickly left.

"This sheet of paper is a copy. Mr. Vincent said the original has been placed back in the fax machine."

"Why didn't he come aboard, or have us come ashore?" Mr. Milner quizzed.

"He felt he was really sticking his neck out as it was ... he's afraid to become involved ... I had to plea with him just to wait on shore and wave. I was sure you gentlemen couldn't accept my word alone on such an important message."

Mr. Patterson spoke: "Gentlement, I guess we have a choice: stay and all of us will probably be discharged, maybe some of us even jailed." He tried not to look at Mr. Milner, but a glance slipped through. "Or we weigh anchor immediately and head out to sea."

Mr. Milner let out a low snicker. "It would be an extreme point of view, of course, but if we were to knowingly disregard company orders and continue, one might say that we would then be renegades, maybe even pirates!"

Mr. Morris was visibly shaken up. "But we would have to be in this all together ... can we trust each other?"

Now it was my turn. We were wasting precious time. And their fear of reprisal was going to blow the whole thing. I had to do something.

Jeeses, my travelling future is at stake!

"Do we have a choice?" I glanced towards Mr. Miner, and we exchanged an unspoken communication, an inspiration. This was the time.

"Captain, can you please show me the ship's log."

The Captain looked at me incredulously, then nodded, suddenly understanding. Mr. Milner gave me a sly smile. The ship's log was in my hand a moment later.

"This is the only document that gives incriminating evidence to any wrong doing ... without it it's just one man's word against another ... I propose that I, not one of you, but I ... seal our decision by dropping this overboard, right now ... and then we raise our anchors and be on our way!"

Hesitation hung in the air like a black mist. I walked calmly to the decks edge and held the log out over the rail. I waited. The three finally nodded, one by one. Led by Mr. Milner, of course. I freed my grip on the heavy, hard bound book, and watched as it fell towards the water below and splashed, and sank.

We were all suddenly the picture of pure efficiency. The whole crew knew what was happening. It was like we were pirates about to attempt running a blockade. Adrenalin was running high ... we moved together, quickly. The anchors were up and secure, the dinghy stowed on board ... we kept the 50 gallon drum, a souvenir from Mr. Vincent ... and we made our way towards the harbor's entrance.

The sun was already setting ... we wouldn't have full light for the passage through the reef ... but hell, it was a familiar road to us already. And besides, we had the lighthouse on the starboard side. We passed through without slowing.

We had decided to stick to our previous watch schedule.

"Joseph, put us on 310 degrees and hold her steady as she goes." Mr. Milner stood to the side, his feet firmly apart and hands clasped behind his back. I was watching him from the starboard deck, searching for the proper perspective. I wasn't sure he if looked like an aristocratic English officer, straight and stout and a gentleman ... or a remittance man and a pirate, a Francis Drake just about to direct his corsair off to another plunder, and adventure.

CHAPTER EIGHT

West of northwest ..
by the color of the water

> "By the way, Mr. Morris, what was it
> you gentlemen needed to 'stock up on'
> in Lorengau .. ??"
> "We needed some personal things, of
> course.. and more Johnny Walker's."

"Hey, Canuck, welcome to the 'Main Deck Pub'!"

I was startled to find Harry and Laurie on the aft deck, resting comfortably in two loungechairs, each with a beer in hand.

"I didn't know we had one."

"What do you mean 'we' ... this lounge is for us regular blokes, yours is up there with the 'officers'." Harry chortled.

"Sorry we don't have an extra chair for you, mate," Laurie was grinning.

"No problem, I just wanted to see the last of New Guinea ... to say goodbye. See the outline of those hills ... that's probably the last all three of us will see of this magical place ... doesn't that mean something to you?"

"Not really," I heard Harry mutter behind me.

It was already dark, an incomplete moon was descending in the west, but the dim outline of Manus's central hills were still visible, a dark shadow against the slightly lighter shade of the lower edge of the night sky. This would indeed be my last view of Papua New Guinea, and probably the end of a memorable part of my life. I watched the churning and unfurling of the broad band of frothing white that was our wake, pushing us slowly north and west, away from this enchanting land that had been my home for so many months, and the memories and lessons it contained. Would I ever be back. I felt I knew that I wouldn't. I thought of spectacular views of lush forests and green mountains, of snow white surf and glistening sand, of pristine waters ... sometimes deep blue, sometimes lighter shades of greens and blue-greens, of virgin reefs and magnificent marine life. I thought of Deli and Aunty Freita, of Walter and Mike, of Tuko, of all the wonderfully different peoples and their delightful diversity. Yes, this is goodbye, New Guinea, to the magical 'land of the unexpected', and fare-thee-well!

Richard's bell shattered my melancholy trance. Back to the real world! Like the watchful observer that he was, Richard had again waited for the critical moments of action to pass before he summoned us for a meal. We reached the officer's mess to find Joseph there already, the rattan cage set on the table, our new crew member staring nervously out at us. Kevin was studying him, clearly infatuated.

"So what sort of creature is this?" He queried.

"This is a cuscus!"

"He's a what?" Kevin eyes were wide with astonishment, and humor.

"You heard me, a cuscus!" I was wondering what was so surprising and funny.

"You mean, like c-u-s-c-u-s?"

"Yeh."

He roared in laughter. Which was an unusual event in itself, I didn't think any of us had seen Kevin break out in laughter like that before.

"Let me explain. A few years ago I worked in Libya, for British Petroleum. And 'cuscus' is the name of one of the Arab's most favorite dishes ... it's a stew, made with meat and vegetables and ground, yellow maize, usually served in a large open platter with low sides, and everyone sits around and dips in with bread, and their fingers ... Arabic style."

"And that's what's so funny about this little bloke being called a cuscus?" Harry was thinking Kevin was being strange again.

"No, no ... it just so happens that 'cuscus' means something very different in Farsi, that's the language they speak in Iran."

"I thought Iran was Arabic?" know-it-all Harry cut in.

"Most people think of Iranians and Arabs as being the same people, and that's what makes this so funny. But no, Iran is the old kingdom of Persia, and they speak Farsi, not Arabic."

"So?" I too was becoming impatient.

"OK, let me explain. It's a common joke in that part of the world, but let me tell you how I first heard it. One of my American bosses was an Irishman from Bartlesville, Oklahoma. His name was Vern O'Neil. He worked for Reda Pump Company; I was on loan to him, and we were installing submersible electric pumps in an oilfield south of the Libyan city of Bengazi, called Waha. Well, Vern explained that he used to entertain a lot of Arab visitors at his home in Bartlesville, and his wife had become pretty good at preparing cuscus. One evening they had a couple of Iranian families visiting: wives, children, the whole works. Vern's wife cooked the Arabic favorite again, cuscus, and then walked into the living room and asked: 'Would anyone like to eat cuscus?" Well, every

Iranian face turned crimson red, the wives especially, and Vern rushed his wife into the kitchen. "No, no, dear, these people aren't Arabic, they're Iranians." "So, she retorted back, kinda loudly, don't they like to eat cuscus?" Vern had to place his hand over his wife's mouth, and he whispered in her ear: "Dear, in Farsi, or Iranian, cuscus means pussy!"

Now we understood, and we all bust out in a good laugh.

"So 'cuscus' is what we call this guy, and it is also a favorite Arab dish, and it also means pussy ... and those who eat cuscus are eating pussy! So what do we name him ... pussy?"

Laurie was disgusted. "Come on, you blokes ... don't talk like that ... I mean, 'pussy', and the idea of ---- ugh!"

"Laurie, you mean you don't eat pussy, I mean cuscus?" Harry was grinning mischievously.

"Of course not ... that's filthy!"

"Laurie, what kind of a lover are you?" It was my turn. "Have you ever tried it? I mean really got down there and *indulged*?"

"Hey, knock it off. That's absolutely disgusting!"

"Well, it's up to you Laurie ... be a lousy lover, or enjoy the desserts!"

"Hey," Laurie stood up, palms raised: "Let's just choose a name for this bloke!"

Harry and I both chuckled.

"OK ... OK ... no need to get upset ... so what suggestions do we have?" I helped bring an end to Laurie's embarrassment.

And thus the process started. The name 'Pussy' was out because of Laurie's unreasonable revulsion. I suggested 'Charlie' because it seemed I wanted to call everything by that name, like my old Hadson. Someone proposed 'Sweat Pea' and I objected cause that was a name for a female and it sounded real dumb anyway. We heard half a dozen other ideas, but none seemed to win any sort of concensus. Then Harry suggested one that struck home with me.

"How about 'Walter'," and he grinned in my direction. I understood his connection with our ex-foreman. I liked it. So did just about everyone, for different reasons, of course.

"Alright, our new crew member's name is 'Walter'." It was settled.

Laurie was curious about what a cuscus ate, and could we let him run free, and so on, but my watch started at ten and I needed some shut-eye. I would hear the answers to his questions later.

"Excuse me, gentlemen, but I need a couple of hours rest ... see you all later."

"What's our heading, Mr. Milner?"

"I have us on 310 degrees, compass heading. That points us directly to the San Bernarndino Strait in the Philippines, just north of the island of Samar. Would you like me to show you how I arrived at that?"

"Sure!"

"It's strange that Mr. Fitzgerald didn't give us a chart for this entire area, but he didn't, so we have a choice ... we can use the rose and plot to a location shown on both these charts, trying to arrive at a single heading, or we can simply take our starting and ending latitudes and longitudes and plot out a triangle, to scale, on one rose. That's what I have done. Here's my calculations and triangulation ... try to figure it out on your own."

"I think I understand your method ... yes, let me play with it."

"I'll see you in the morning, Chad. Right now I would like to get some rest. This had been a long and full day. By the way, I think you did us all a service today ... especially me ... thank you."

"Uhh ... you're welcome, Mr. Milner ... but really I guess I was just desperate ... I was willing to try anything to get us on the move."

Mr. Milner chuckled. "Well, for whatever reason, it worked."

"Chad, before you end your watch, we need to set up the log," the Captain instructed, the sun just beginning to reveal its perimeter above the eastern horizon.

"The log? Oh yes, the log. Where do you think it is, sir?"

"It should be in the wheelhouse ... try in that bottom drawer, below the chart table."

"Is this it?" I pulled out a brass rotor, shaped like a pointed cylinder about eighteen inches long and three inches in diameter, with a pair of fins curved around its body. I judged by its light weight that it must be hollow. Attached to the pointed end was a long length of tightly braided dacron line, about three-eighths of an inch in diameter. A second part consised of a brass housing enclosing a dial and a metering device, with a protruding shaft. There were also a pair of exterior clamps for attachment purposes.

"Yes, that's it. Let's go set it up."

"And what is this sir?" I pointed to another length of line with a fairly large lead weight at the end; the line had short pieces of smaller line tied at intervals.

"That's a sounding line and weight ... to measure water depth."

"I see."

I gathered the log line in my arms, together with the rotor, and the Captain carried the dial. We proceeded to make our way to the aft deck.

"We must first secure the dial to the rail. This must run continuously and we must not lose it, so the attachment needs to be positive, and strong. Let's choose a location that's out of the way and is solid."

I found a good spot on the port side, and fastened the dial housing tightly to the rail structure.

"The knot you choose is critical -- it cannot come undone. See the one on the rotor ... that's what we need to duplicate at the dial ... it's called a 'bowline'. But first, let's throw the rotor out behind us and let out this line ... slowly ... make sure we don't lose it, now ... that's it, easy ... alright, let me tie it off ... there it is!"

We now had our log in operation. The line was very long; I estimated it to be at least two hundred feet.

"Chad, we'll need to monitor this line and rotor and record the dial and meter readings at the beginning of each watch, as a minimum. As you know, our 'dead reckoning' position is critical. This log will tell us the speed we're travelling and the distance covered. Right now it's indicating a speed of 8.2 knots ... not bad!"

Richard's bell announced breakfast. I was bushed, feeling I could sleep for many, many hours, and I really didn't want breakfast, but I went anyway. Richard's performance was par excellence and the 'fish and eggs' was a delight, and it was great to visit with Walter, who seemed to be a little more accustomed to us. But I left as soon as I could ... I felt I could 'sleep the sleep of a thousand sleeps'.

Both engines were purring away even though their 'purring' was actually somewhat thumpy ... the sea continued to be silvery and velvet-like, the swells still long and flat, and the miniature flying fish still our constant companions, although they were no longer endangered by swooping seagulls and 'kiris', for we were now much too far from any land mass. It was late afternoon and I had finally replenished my body's urgent need for rejuvenating sleep. Mr. Milner was 'in command', watching the sea ahead of us from his deck chair. Mr. Morris was to my left, in the shade of the wheelhouse.

"By the way, Mr. Morris ... just out of curiosity ... what was it you gentlemen were needing to 'stock up on' in Lorengau yesterday ... if I may ask?"

"Uhh ... well, Chad ... we thought we'd like to go ashore and purchase a few personal items, that sort of thing ... and of course a fresh supply of ... spirits."

"Spirits?"

"Yes, you know ... Johnny Walker's, and rum."

"Oh."

The afternoon slowly transitioned to evening, the sunset a spectacular pattern of varied ribbons of oranges and reds, which caused Mr. Patterson to remark:

"Red sky at night, sailor's delight!"

"Sounds like that's a sailor's rhyme ... is there more?" I asked.

"Yes, but it's only two lines:

Red sky at night, sailor's delight.

Red sky in morning, sailor's warning!"

"I see. Does it hold true?"

The Captain smiled. "I think it depends on what part of the world you're in ... the reddening of a sunrise or sunset is usually associated with storm clouds on the horizon ... if you are in a part of the world where storms usually come from the easterly direction, then the ditty perhaps works. Otherwise I don't think it does,"

"Hmm!"

"However, that doesn't explain the beautiful red sunsets that we are experiencing. I understand that the answer to that has to do with the eruption of Krakatau."

"Krakatau?"

"Yes. Krakatau is a volcano on a small island between Java and the southeastern tip of Sumatra, in the center of the Sunda Strait, in Indonesia. Its eruption in 1883 was violent, and catastrophic, spuing many millions of tons of volcanic dust into the atmosphere ... its eruption has been categorized as perhaps the most voluminous in recent history. We are told that the wondrous red sunsets experienced in these lattitudes and longitudes are due to Krakatau's dust still suspended in the atmosphere."

"Wow ... yes ... we are close to about the same latitude as Krakatau right now."

"That's correct. There's a somewhat humorous footnote to the story of Krakatau as well, and it has to do with your American film making. There was a recent film produced entitled 'Krakatoa, East of Java'. But it's name is Krakatau, and it is west of Java, not east."

"That's amazing, Mr. Patterson ... it seems you are well travelled."

The Captain smiled. "I haven't been on a Sydney Harbor dredge all my life. Before, in my earlier years, I served aboard a number of different vessels and navigated the entire globe many times over. Actually, this voyage holds a great deal of nostalgia for me, as the south-east Asia area was my specialty at one time.

"I see." I nodded, smiling in his direction. "Interesting."

Wow, there's definitely more to this guy than I had yet suspected!

My watch passed dreamily, without incident. Fred and I occasionally engaged in small talk. Mr. Milner had instructed me to plot three LOPs, which I did, choosing Sirius, Arcturus and Beetelgeuse again. The three lines intersected very close together and I was delighted, wanting Mr. Milner to review my results.

The Captain relieved me at 6 a.m. and I excused myself to wait for breakfast in the officer's mess. Kevin was also there early ... he and Harry had worked out an arrangement by which they alternated six hour shifts, dividing the day into four periods. But there really wasn't much for them to do ... everything was pretty much on automatic. For now, at least.

"Hi, Kevin. .

"Good morning, Chad," he answered over his cup of coffee.

"What you said a couple of days ago kind of interested me ... tell me a bit about philosophy."

"Tell you about philosophy?" He laughed. "You mean you'd like me to explain all about philosophy in, say, ten minutes."

"Nah, you can take fifteen!" It was my turn to chuckle. "Why, is there that much to tell?"

"Chad, I could talk to you for days and days and we'd only scratch the surface. What part of philosophy are you interested in?"

"What part? ... I don't know what part ... I guess the part that explains why you don't need religion."

"Ahh ... I understand ... OK."

With that Kevin sort of slouched in the cushioned seat a little, savoring his coffee, and prepared to play teacher, obviously enjoying the role, his thick eyeglasses seeming to fit the guise.

Why is it that everyone gets such a charge out of playing teacher with me?

"Alright, religion is all about trying to find an 'explanation', a way to explain the world around us and what we're all about, and 'why' we're here. Would you agree?"

"Kevin, I don't know what you're talking about!" He was being a little too 'wordy' for me.

"OK, I'll be a little more basic then. Imagine primitive man, going way back ... he's surrounded by things that absolutely terrorize him: things like earthquakes and volcanic eruptions, hurricanes and dangerous wild animals. And phenomenon like daylight and darkness, the sun and the moon and the stars, and mysteries such as eclipses, falling stars, tidal waves, and, very important, the four seasons. And disease and sickness as well. He's terrified ... he desperately needs an explanation, a way to explain all these things, he needs to create order, to have some means of control, or at least the illusion of control ... he needs comfort so he can survive, and propagate, and live without fear. You got it, Chad?"

He was mesmerizing me. The question startled me.

"Yeh, I see the picture."

"Now, modern man has 'science' as his explanation. Science is very good at finding a consistent, workable explanation for the mysteries of the world around us. It even has an explanation for 'how' and 'why' we're here. But earlier man didn't have the luxury of science. So he found his 'explanation' in legend and mythology, and in religion."

"Oh, so now that we have science we don't need religion ... is that it?"

"No, no." Kevin chuckled paternally. "Not at all. Science is just another explanation. Philosophically speaking, that is."

"You've lost me again, Kevin."

"OK ... Let's see if I can explain this. You and I agree, I'm sure, that science's explanation is 'valid', is 'true', just from looking at things on the surface, our day to day experience -- the electricity we use in our homes, airplanes and a man on the moon, our automobiles, and so on. Science has been very successful. Follow me?"

"I think so."

"But if you think about it deeper, you can see that we can't really be sure that the explanation that science is giving us is one hundred percent valid."

"Whoa ... what do you mean by that?"

"Well, at one time we 'believed' in the Copernican system, where the earth was at the center of the universe, and the moon, sun, and stars revolved around us, as it seems it does ... and we developed an entire explanation based on that. But then we decided that the system wasn't 'valid', that there were certain contradictions that didn't work out, and so more recently we believed in the Newtonian system. Now a bloke like Einstein comes along and starts shooting holes in *that* system."

"But it's all still science ... just being improved on."

Jeeses, this dude's telling me that science can't be trusted?

"OK ... OK ... but the point is, we can't be sure. Consider this: I'm color blind."

"Hey, so am I."

"Good, then you can understand this even easier: we are colorblind, we know that because we can be 'tricked' with cards of colored dots."

"I know exactly what you mean, I've been through that test a hundred times."

"Alright. Yet you and I, and Harry, and Laurie, and everyone else ... we all agree that this is blue, this is green, this is red, and so on." Kevin was picking out different samples of colors in the mess cabin.

"Yes."

"We all agree on what we all see, but you and I know that we don't see what they see. Our world of color is different. We agree, yet our perceptions are different, our very worlds are different. They are not the same."

"Wow ... yeh, I can see what you mean ... heavy stuff. But you've just brought us back to square one. We need an explanation, you say, and so a religious explanation *may* be just as 'valid' as a scientific one. That's what you're saying, right?"

"Well ... OK, yes. There are complications to that, because maybe we can find a way to 'measure' the degree of 'validity'. But yes, what you said is basically correct."

"So you've still left me with needing a religion, or an explanation."

"Yes, and no. This is where philosophy comes in ... what if we can talk about it philosophically ... stand back from it all far enough to be truly objective ... talk about it enough so that perhaps some alternatives emerge .

"An alternative to religion?"

"No, an altenative to needing an explanation!"

"You mean, not needing an explanation."

"That's just what I said, Chad ... Yes. If all the explanations, *any* explanation, is suspect, then let's perhaps accept them as being suspect, as being 'possibly not valid', and therefore we don't need to insist on a particular one being the one and only 'valid' and 'true' explanation. In other words, we consider any explanation as being possible, but all of a sudden we no longer have to 'believe' in one particular one. And the need for a 'dogma' and 'faith' and all that other garbage disappears too."

"Wow ... that's almost scarey ... doesn't leave a person with much 'security', does it?"

Kevin smiled. "Yes, you're right. Almost takes us back to the terror experienced by primitive man. I guess that's the trade-off."

"Kevin ... that is really heavy duty stuff. I gotta think about this. Where did you get this from, anyway? I mean, which philosopher thinks like that?"

"If I just rattled off a name, or something simple, it wouldn't be fair. I need to explain the history of philosophical thought a bit ... you got a few hours?"

Richard's bell brought our conversation, and my lesson in philosophy, to an abrupt close, for Fred and Harry entered the mess within seconds, and I excused myself to relieve Laurie ... I could take my time enjoying breakfast later, and the continuation of my 'lesson' would have to wait.

The Captain was working out some calculations on the chart table, using the data from our 'log' that Laurie had given him at the beginning of his watch.

"What has our speed been, Captain?" I was curious to know what kind of progress we were making.

"The log shows that we're making 8.1 knots, relative to the water ... I don't believe we have any current to consider in these waters, so that should also be our net. That means we net 194.4 nautical miles in a 24 hour period. What I'm attempting to calculate is the number of hours, or days, that it will take us to reach the Philippines, then to pass through the islands via the San Bernardino Strait, and finally across the China Sea to Hong.Kong."

"That makes it sound like a very long distance."

"But it isn't, really. Here, I have it ... 7 1/2 days to the Strait, two days to pass through the islands, and three more to anchor in Hong Kong Harbor ... a total of 12 1/2 days from Manus. If we can maintain 8.1 knots net speed, that is."

"Twelve and a half days to where?" Laurie had just returned and had overheard the last part of the Captain's explanation.

"That was 12 1/2 days from Manus Island, it's only 11 days from where we are right now," the Captain clarified.

That sounded like good news to Laurie. "You mean we'll be partying with lovely Chinese ladies in eleven days! I reckon that's great news!"

"Well, keep her steady at 310 degrees and maybe it'll happen ... here, take the wheel ... I would like some breakfast."

"Oh, there's Walter ... hey little guy, how are you?" I was happy to see that Joseph had brought him into the mess again.

"Hsst . . hsst!"

"Real friendly, isn't he?"

Joseph laughed. "They never do get 'friendly', not like a pet cat or anything ... they might get used to you, that's all."

"Oh." I was disappointed to hear that. Walter looked so cuddly ... I wanted to take him out of the cage and hold him, pet him.

"Can we ever let him out ... give him the run of the ship?" I wanted to know.

"We can let him out, but then we'd probably never see him again ... there's a million places for him to hide, like in the hold."

"Yeh, see what you mean. But wouldn't he show up for something to eat?"

"Don't know, maybe he would ... or maybe he'd find his own food."

"Like what? ... what could he live on?"

"Mice, if any are aboard ... or he'd find a way into our supplies ... they're famous for that."

"Hmm ... well, time for me to get some zzz's ... see you gentlemen later ... you too, Harry." I waved a departing gesture and snickered. Harry had his forefinger in the air, straight up.

We were now two full days out of Manus. So far so good. The afternoon sun was again gently lowering itself into the western sea, once more with a gorgeous array of color, the sphere itself was a red hot ball of fiery orange ... you could almost hear the wild sizzling and popping as it drowned itself in the vast coolness of the ocean.

God, I love being at sea!

Mr. Morris was feeling talkative. "The Captain estimates we now have only 5 1/2 days to the Philippines. Maybe we can stop at a port there, maybe before

177

entering the Strait." I caught just a hint of the suggestion that he was trying to solicit support.

"That sounds exciting ... but why would we ... why not just keep on trucking all the way to Hong Kong?"

Mr. Morris snickered: "Well for one thing we are going to be in sore need of some more good 'ol Johnny Walker's ... not to mention rum ... and beer. And of course the 'Filipinas' are among the prettiest ladies in the world."

"Oh?" My mind had abruptly departed from the frivolous question of the whiskey. "Filipinas ... have you been in the Philippines, Mr. Morris?"

"Yes, a few years ago was the last time ... in Manila ... the port is close to an area called 'Ermita'. In Ermita there is block after block after block of bars – all strip bars -- with about the lovliest young sheilas you could ever find ... and any one of them yours, if you pay their bar fine and something for themselves ... maybe cost you fifteen dollars."

"Oh?" This man had definitely captured my untethered attention. "Bar fine, you say?"

"Yes, you had to pay the bar in order to take her out, then the young miss was yours until the next day, and you made your own arrangement with her. I remember this one sweet thing singing to me, with her heavy accent:

You are my sunshine, You pay my bar fine,

You make me happy, I give you baby,

You'll never know dear, If it really was yours

Please don't take my sunshine away."

"For real?"

"It's the dinky die truth!"

But then I remembered my concern about the whiskey and the other booze, but the whiskey most of all.

"So, Mr. Morris, do we have enough whiskey until the Philippines?"

"No problem, matey ... if it's only 51/2 days . . ."

The last part drifted off ... Mr. Morris had just passed out again. I thought I'd better go tell Laurie. Oops, Laurie's sleeping. What the hell, Mr. Morris will put himself to bed after awhile. No way I was going to carry the guy to his cabin.

Another dreamy watch. Tonight Mr. Milner didn't bother giving me LOPs to work out. And I just didn't feel like doing them without being ordered to do so. Fred and I talked some more small talk, but mostly I just gazed at the sea, and the night sky, and fantasized about Filipina girls. I wondered if what Mr. Morris had said was true. Really no reason to doubt him, I concluded. Earlier I had seen Richard at the bow.

The Captain and Laurie were right on time at 6 o'clock. I went below early to wait for Richard's bell. Joseph showed, then both Harry and Kevin, and Fred. The bell sounded and I left to relieve Laurie.

I returned to find the same four leisurely finishing breakfast. Our pace was visibly slowing. We were all more relaxed, becoming a little bored, and lazy.

"Chad, how about telling us about that experience in Lae that you had . . the one you started to tell me about?" Joseph was hoping I could entertain them. I looked around at my company. This was going to be tough. But what the hell!

"It's really nothing . . I was telling Joseph about Lae, and I was about to tell him about the most beautiful woman I had ever seen ... I mean, absolutely the most extraordinary and most beautiful woman I have ever seen in *my entire life* ... but we were interrupted." I waited.

"So, tell us then." Harry was impatient, I had snagged his interest.

"Well, as I said, it happened in Lae. You know, Lae is an exceptionally pretty place: green and picturesque, almost as lovely as Rabaul. A nice setting to meet the woman of your life. I saw her at a hotel I was 'staying' at." I winked at Joseph, who knew I hadn't been staying there at all, but had slept under a park bleacher instead. "I was in the lobby of the hotel when she walked through. That was the first time I saw her. She was without question the most remarkably elegant and tantalizingly beautiful woman I had ever set eyes on, and truly the most exotic. I asked one of the male clerks at the recption desk about her, where she was from, anything. I had just fallen in love. He explained that she was with her husband ... he was a teacher attending an international teacher's convention in Lae. She was incredible. Right then it didn't even matter that she had a husband. Once having seen her, I was mesmerized, totally enraptured.

She was tall, easily five foot ten ... oh ... that would be, let's see, 167 centimeters, ehh, blokes. Anyway, she was tall, and she carried herself so very straight and graceful, and with incredible poise, her head held high and proud. One of my first thoughts was that she belonged to royalty, that she was without doubt a queen, not by right of birth necessarily, but a queen by the right given her because of her extraordinary natural beauty and sophistication. Her features were finely cut and unusually sharp, and clean, and her eyes were shining black, with perfectly clear whites. Her skin was delicately smooth and totally free of blemishes, even glowing, radiant. The styling of her hair was exquisite, piled fashionably high, which added to her elegence and straightness; it was a style perfectly suited to the tight curls of her coal black hair."

I looked at my audience. They were listening dreamingly ... hah, now for the coup de grace!

"The clerk had told me she and her husband were from Thursday Island." I paused, letting that sink in.

"Hey," Harry was the first to react. "Thursday Island is part of New Guinea."

"No, Harry, it's not. Thursday Island is at the tip of the Cape York Peninsula, Queensland, and is part of Australia, although it also borders the New Guinea islands."

"But Thursday Islanders are black!" He continued.

"Yes ... she was black ... *very* black!"

Harry and Kevin both laughed, Joseph and Fred joined in, all realizing what I had tried to do.

"Did this really happen, or are you just making some king of a political or social statement?" Kevin quizzed. I could almost see those intellectual gears grinding away.

"Hey, it really happened ... I shit you not !! But, yeh ... it was a turning point for me, I guess ... in my own thinking. Damn, you're too smart for me, Kevin."

But the philosopher wasn't satisfied. "So why was it a turning point? ... what kind of turning point?"

I squirmed. "Wow ... OK ... Let me see if I can answer that. You know, you can *talk* about not being racially prejudiced, you can be intellectual about it, and you think you don't have a prejudiced bone in your body." I glanced at Fred and Joseph to make sure it was OK to talk like this. They were smiling ... we were good friends and it was alright.

"But all that doesn't mean jack until you *feel* it, until you feel it on a *passionate* level. That Thursday Island lady spun my head around. To me she was truly beautiful ... I felt it ... here and here." I pointed to my chest and somewhat lower. "I felt lust for her, plus I was in love with her ... and her blackness was a part of her beauty ... it matched and accentuated everything about her, and yet her blackness was completely beside the point in every other respect. Seeing her was the first time I felt deep inside that black was nothing more than one choice among many of the color of the skin, that socially it is culture, and education, and attitudes that make the real difference."

"That's pretty good, Chad." Kevin was smiling. "I mean, you expressed that pretty well."

Harry was snickering. "Canuck ... let me ask you something."

"Yes, Harry?" I was instantly wary.

"Have you ever made it with a white girl?"

"Harry ... *kiss my butt*!"

"You bare it ... I'll kiss it."

I was undoing my belt when Fred said: "Yes, I've heard that Thursday Islanders are tall, and almost as black as the people of Bougainville, and are good looking too."

Joseph was nodding in agreement.

"And that they can travel or live anywhere in Austalia they want, because their island 'belongs' to Australia, while Papua New Guinea is only a 'trust territory'."

So I re-tightened my belt and decided to get back at Harry in another way.

"Yeh, Harry, what about that? Why can Thursday Islanders live on the Australian mainland while New Guineans can't?"

"Beats me!" he answered slyly. He wasn't about to be drawn in on the wrong side of this one.

I was suddenly feeling tired and didn't have the energy to push the argument any further. Anyway, it was a lot like beating a dead horse, especially with Harry.

"It's past my bedtime, guys, talk to you later." I got up to leave. "But Harry, it does strike me as kinda strange that the 'traditional' people of Australia are black, yet you P.O.M.E.s decide that you can only allow white trash into the country." I turned and ran, leaving the echo of 'Don't you dare call me a POME' behind. I would surely hear more about that later. But for now, sleep.

"You calling someone a POME?" Laurie snorted as I passed the wheelhouse.

"Only Harry ... only Harry." I replied, not stopping.

"Chad, I'd like to show you our plotted course."

I rose from the deck chair and walked over to join Mr. Milner at the chart table.

"You see here that I've worked out that our true heading should be 304 degrees 30 minutes, but that with the variation of 5 degrees 50 minutes East added, this gives us a compass heading of just over 310 degrees. Understand?"

"Yes sir!"

"You can see that this gives us a clean track all the way to this point here, just north of Samar Island, which is the turning point to enter the San Bernardino Strait. Right?"

"Yes."

"The only land mass we will even come close to is the island of Palau ... here. Our track is a safe, open shot!"

"Yes."

"That is why I'm not too concerned about star shots, for the moment at least. It also occurs to me that we could always head for Palau if we were in trouble ... I'd like you to be aware of that."

"I understand." I was aware that Mr. Milner exuded a strong odor of Scotch whiskey; he had been drinking heavy. He left and I studied the chart for a while. Palau was about half way between Manus and Samar. It also occurred to me that one of the more southerly islands of the Philippines would be close as well. Mr. Milner's track placed us west of Palau.

My stomach told me it was approaching dinner time. I had settled into a routine where I slept through lunch, so by the time late afternoon arrived I was famished. I made my way towards the mess, and, hearing the sounds of voices, decided to pick up a South Pacific on the way. All of us not on duty were in the mess, including both Harry and Kevin again.

Jeeses, we are *slacking off!*

Remembering my parting remark about Prisoners Of Mother England, I decided I had best be prepared to divert Harry to something else if he decided to unleash his wrath in my direction. Being called a pome was a sensitive issue with Harry. He used to tell me that it was the people still living in England that were the true 'prisoners of mother England'. He thought that was such a great joke and he would laugh and laugh. I had a diversion in mind.

Walter was on the table, and was the center of attention. Fred was trying to get him to eat a piece of raw fish, but apparently fish was not part of our friend's preferred diet. We thought that was unusual, cause he had ravished everything else we put in front of him. He was clearly omniverous, because he would eat vegetables as well as almost any kind of meat, and he loved eggs.

There was a lull in the conversation, Harry was grinning in my direction. Oh -- oh, now was the time for a diversion.

"Jeeses, I sure miss Deli ... you know, I even had a wet dream about her."

Harry snickered. "What kind of a wet dream, Canuck?"

"Well, Deli and I made passionate love twice, and we were about to go at it once more, but I fell asleep."

It was an old line, at least between Harry and I, but we all laughed. All except Laurie, that is.

"What did you say?"

Harry continued to chuckle. "You heard him, he was 'floggin the log'."

"Bloody hell, but you two are disgusting ... you mean …?”

"Yeh, I mean …” Harry was making the appropriate motion with his right hand.

"You *are* right-handed, aren't you Canuck?"

"Come on. . ."

Harry and I had caught us a good one. It was my turn.

"Laurie, you don't mean to say you don't …”

"Of course not!"

"Oh, I see, you believe that old wive's story about it making you go blind if you do it?"

"What ... ?” Laurie thought we were both crazy.

“I think it's true!" Harry cut in. "I remember once when I was about fourteen .... well, my father caught me in the act one time, and he scolded the living hell

182

out of me, saying, 'don't you know, son, that if you do that you'll go blind?" You know what I told him, Laurie?"

"No, I don't know what you told him, Harry."

"Well, I asked him, 'Dad, then can I at least do it until I need glasses'."

We all laughed, or at least most of us laughed, I made a point of staring at Kevin, and his thick lenses.

"When are you going to stop, Kevin?"

That made everyone crack up again. Even Laurie. He had finally caught on to what was happening.

"Which reminds me of a story ... Harry, you'd like this one."

"Shoot!"

"Before coming to New Guinea and working for CDW, the only real heavy equipment operating experience I'd had was operating Euclid S-14 scrapers back in Edmonton, Canada, just for two summers. Laurie, you know what a scraper is?"

"No, what's a 'scraper'?" He was watching me warily, expecting me to try and trick him into something again.

"It's an earth-moving machine, with four huge rubber-tired wheels, the engine and operator are in front, a large 'can' or bucket is connected behind, and the machine 'articulates' in between. That means it swivels. The machine is loaded by using a bulldozer to push from behind, and the operator of the scraper lowers the cutting edge of the can into the ground, and the can fills up ... then he lifts the can up, an 'apron' drops down over the front, and off you go. When you want to dump, you raise the apron and activate another hydraulic cylinder that pushes the load out. Very versatile, quick machines, and pretty much 'all terrain'. Can you picture the machine?"

Laurie nodded. "Yes, I think I've seen those machines ... they're pretty big, aren't they?"

Fred and Kevin nodded. Harry of course had to show that he was an expert on the subject. "Yeh, on the Snowy Mountain project we had a fleet of thirty of them, mostly Caterpillar 631's, but we also had six twin engine beauts -- 657's -- they could carry 57 cubic meters in one load! But those Euclids you're talking about are pretty small."

What he said wasn't quite right, but I let it pass.

"The important thing is that you understand that the operator lowers or raises his can to load or travel, or unload. Well, I was working for this guy named Ken Gaunt. He was a big half Ukranian and he used to holler at us all the time.

Ken had a fleet of small Euclid S-14's ... yeh, you're right Harry, they are kinda small ... which he used on city contracts to cut out roadways ... kind of a specialty. We would mass out the roadway and another contractor came behind us to place rock aggregate, put in the utilities and curbs and gutters, and so forth.

Anyway, this one job we had required that we transport our loads across a field and then over a railroad track to dump in another field on the other side. Crossing that railroad track was critical. It was the main line between Edmonton and Calgary. Ken was scared shitless that one of us would hit that railroad track with our can and that would be the end of his contracting career. So he had all of us -- six altogether -- bring a load to the railroad track and he guided us and yelled at us and we carefully dumped our loads to make a ramp over the track. He only allowed his one favorite operator to fine grade that ramp. I remember his name was Rick. Then he had us all climb down from our machines and he yelled: 'Now, for Christ's sake, go slow and keep your cans as high as they can go and whatever you do, don't let the can's cutting edge catch that track, understand.

So, we all loaded our next load and each of us in turn headed off across the field towards the dump site on the other side of that track. Now I'd had a particularly good time the night before, and a drinking buddy had told me this rhyme that went: 'A bird in the hand is worth two in the bush ... and then it went on. It had been funny, but damned if I could remember the rest of it. Of course I was badly hung-over and my head was sore like hell. And I was coming across that field, heading for those railroad tracks. And I was trying to remember the rest of that rhyme. Then, all of a sudden, I remembered. It went:

A bird in the hand
Is worth two in the bush. But if, in the bush,
A young maiden you should push,
Then a push in the bush
Is worth two in the hand."

Everyone broke out laughing.

"Wait, wait ... that's not the end. And so, just as I was rejoicing over remembering that rhyme, there was a loud 'clunk' and my S-14 jerked to a sudden stop. My can had caught that son-of-a-bitch'in railroad track."

"Oh shit! " Harry gasped.

"Yup, that's just what *I* said at that moment ... and I turned to look behind. Ken was already on his way, a cloud of dust behind his pick-up, his flashing yellow lights on the top of his cab going full blast. I didn't know whether to shit, go blind, or turn the page. All I could think of was 'now the shit is *really* going to hit the fan'. The idea did occurr to me, however, to get off the machine and just start walking away in the opposite direction," I paused.

"So what happened? Did he fire you, pound you into the ground, what?"

"Well, it was the strangest thing, but he never said a word to me, not even one word. He had Rick hook onto that track with a cable, and he pulled the track back as straight as he could. Next day a railroad crew came along ... a gang of about ten men, each with a long, heavy steel bar in their hands ... and they finished straightening it out. Just like they did in the old railroad days ... a foreman stood down the track a ways and sighted down the rail, the men lined up, spaced apart, and the foreman would yell 'heave' and they would all push together with their bars. Ken told me a couple of months later that no one had ever said anything to him about the incident and he had never received a bill. I was relieved to hear that, but I was pissed that he had waited so long to tell me, because for those two months I was one worried and embarrassed son-of-a-gun."

"How did that rhyme go again?" Laurie wanted to know.

I repeated it for his benefit. We all laughed again.

"See what you've done, Canuck. Now that we've got him past *that* inibition, maybe we can get him to eat 'cuscus'."

As if Richard had been listening and had picked up on the word 'eat', his bell's clang-clang abruptly changed the direction of our interest.

For the third time since passing through the reef at Manus, the sun set in a golden array of splendor, into a sea that was still glossy smooth and unperturbed by wind or rain. Mr. Milner didn't require that I take any star shots tonight either, he was so complacently confident in our direction and progress.

Later during my watch, at about 4:00 a.m., I began to feel a chill ... a chill in my body, in my muscles, like the chill that accompanies the onset of a bout with the flu. Damn, I thought, this is no time to be getting sick. It got worse, rather quickly. When the Captain and Laurie showed at 6:00 I excused myself and went directly to my cabin. I was shivering uncontrollably with a deep chill, yet sweating profusely at the same time.

Damn, this is one hell of a case of the flu!

After about two hours I suddenly felt a great deal better, it had been like a passing squall, and I slept.

Richard's bell woke me at noon. I was hungry. Very hungry.

"Hey, Chad, what happened this morning ... you weren't feeling well?" Laurie queried as I reached the bottom of the ladder to the wheelhouse deck.

"Yeh, I was sick as hell, a one day flu, I guess ... feel OK now, though ... would you like me to relieve you?"

"Nah, Fred usually relieves me for lunch. I'm OK."

I had something to eat, we kidded around some more, and I returned to my cabin, feeling like I could use some more rest.

I had woken, or at least I was partly awake, and I was thinking about Kevin, and what he had said during his 'philosophy lesson'. He made sense, and had massaged an area that I had trouble with. One of the questions that bothered me most about being a Mormon, or not being a Mormon, was that if I was to decide that I no longer wanted to be a member of the church, then which religion would I convert to. But a problem that had nagged me was the realization that no other religion was any better. In fact, the Mormon church was pretty good, considering its strong emphasis on family and high morals. And I didn't want to be an atheist. In a way that was a religion too. The word 'agnostic' had come to mind a few times. Withougt even realizing it, I was looking for a path where I didn't need to chose a religion, any religion, and Kevin had just described how to do it. Maybe I can be a philosopher. Even as I thought about it, it struck me as kind of funny, I had to chuckle out loud.

Just as I had reached this conclusion, I was startled out of my meditation by the loud 'ding-ding', 'ding-ding' of the ships throttle signal, dinging continuously. I lept out of the bunk and slid down the ladder. The Captain was still 'ding-dinging' back and forth on the signal arm, a look of desperation on his face. Laurie was tensely holding fast onto the wheel, eyes glued to the sea ahead.

"What's happening?" I yelled.

The Captain, hearing me, discontinued his clamor with the signal arms, and brought both to rest at 'Stop'. Almost simultaneously I felt the propellers stop churning, followed by the quietening of the two Perkins as they were brought to an idle. It had taken Harry and Kevin a couple of minutes to react.

I'll bet neither of them were in the engine room!

"Bloody hell," the Captain yelled. "Look, we're over a reef, or shoal!"

Mr. Milner rushed into the wheelhouse, followed a few seconds later by Mr. Morris.

"Why are we stopping?" Mr. Milner was shouting too.

"Gentlemen, we are over a reef, or a shoal. Please, let's check our chart!" the Captain suggested, his voice calming to a lower note.

"Our dead reckoning position should be here." Mr. Milner pointed to a small 'x' he had just placed on the chart, after having done a quick calculation.

"But the nearest shoal or reef would be here, named the French Frigate Shoals," the Captain concluded, studying the chart. "That would indicate that we are over a hundred nautical miles off course, and not nearly as far from Manus as we had estimated. What do you make of this, Mr. Milner?" the Captain asked for his opinion, with just a hint of admonishment.

Mr. Milner searched the chart. Laurie and I took the opportunity to take a look over the side. We were directly over a flat coral formation, which extended as far as we could see ahead and to our starboard. The depth of the crystal clear water was difficult to determine, its clarity creating the illusion that the different colored coral and diverse marine plants were just inches away. I looked around for something to toss into the water.

"How about a coin?" Laurie suggested.

"Yeh, sure, like I just happen to be carrying some loose change out here in the middle of the Pacific?"

"Well, I have ... how about a 25 cent piece ... never know when you might want to buy something out here." Laurie chuckled and flipped the coin into the water ... we watched it slowly pursue it's irregular path down to the coral.

"That's surprisingly deep, I reckon ten meters."

"Yeh, or at least seven ... anyway, we're plenty safe." I returned to the Captain and Mr. Milner to let them know of our finding.

"I think you must be right, Mr. Patterson. It's the only plausible location." Mr. Milner concluded.

"Laurie and I estimate we have at least seven meters of water depth here." I offered.

"Alright ... Let's come to port and get off this shoal. The chart indicates that we have ample depth, for this flat bottomed design at least ... and you say you estimate 7 meters, or almost four fathoms. Chad, do you recall finding the depth sounding line and weight in the drawer here?"

"Yes, sir ... oh, yes, I had forgotten about that."

"Please go with Laurie to the bow and be prepared to take periodic soundings."

Laurie and I hurried with the weight and line to the bow and, on the Captain's signal lowered the lead weight into the sea. We discovered that the small pieces of line tied to the main one were at intervals of fathoms, or just under two meters apart, and our depth at the bow was five fathoms. We relayed the information to the wheelhouse. A moment later we felt the engine speeds increase slightly, and the propellers start to turn. We moved forward slowly, swinging to port. We could see the coral formation clearly ... the depth of its surface seemed uniform. Mr. Milner signalled for additional soundings. The readings were consistent. The edge of the formation became visible and we passed over its precipice. It reminded me of the Japanese submarine base site back at Rabaul, the water instantly returning to a dark blue, the ocean bottom invisible beneath the diminishing light of many hundreds of feet of ocean.

"Captain," I interrupted his deep meditation as he studied the ocean in front of us, resting after the afternoon's trauma and the termination of his watch. "How did you know we were over a shoal?"

"Easy ... very easy, Mr. Fletcher ... by the change in the color of the water!"

Jeeses, he had done it! He had navigated by the color of the water!

From the calm of the doldrums . .
to chaos and certain doom

"It seems that everything that could go wrong has gone wrong. But surely there must be more that could be added to the list."

The dial hand rested on zero, umnoving. 'Damn, we forgot about the log!' I swore under my breath and pulled on the dacron line. Sure enough, there was only a slight resistance … our rotor was no longer trailing dutifully behind. I continued to draw in on the braided rope, forming a small coil on the deck at my feet, until I reached its frayed end.

"Mr. Milner … I have what's left of our log's rotor. We forgot all about it when we were on the shoal."

Mr. Milner examined the end of the dacron line. "No doubt the rotor dropped down into the coral when we stopped, and became snagged. We should've thought."

"I'm sorry, sir … I should've known."

"No, no … any one of us should have realized … it's not your fault."

"Chad, while we're on the matter of navigation, however, I've been trying to sort out why we are so far from our estimated location … I'm afraid I've been negligent in not keeping up with noon sun shots and star LOPs."

"But why would we be so far off, Mr. Milner?" I asked inquisitively.

"One reason is that our magnetic variation has been changing dramatically, which I didn't take into account … see here … we happen to be in a part of the world where the variation changes very quickly ... the variation shown here on the Manus chart is 5 degrees 50 minutes East, while it is 0 degrees 10 minutes West on the chart of the Philippines. That's a difference of 6 degrees even -- a substantial difference. As we left Manus and got closer to the Philippines, we should have been altering our compass heading. That would account for a lot of the error."

"Why does the variation vary so much, sir?"

He chuckled. "You're asking a difficult question, Chad. Variation changes from place to place. We have developed an empirical understanding, meaning we have plotted the observed variation at just about every place on the globe. But why it varies is another matter. Current theory is that it has to do with earth mass. Magnetism varies with the variation in the mass, or thickness of the earth's crust. So large continental masses will have a different effect than the thin crust under the oceans."

"I see ... but then why is the change so great here?"

"I was just thinking about that, and maybe I have an explanation that fits the theory. Right now we are sailing along the eastern edge of the Marianas Trench. ... have you heard that name before?"

"Only from geography, in school … I think I remember that the Marianas Trench has the deepest ocean in the world."

"That's right. Very deep indeed. I think the deepest part is …" Mr. Milner

"I'm not sure ... 27,000 feet?"

"Twenty-nine thousand is what I recall ... and that's from sea level, not Just the bottom of the mountain slopes. So ... that means you could drop the whole of Mount Everest in the Marianas Trench, right here, and still have a vertical mile of ocean over its peak."

"Wow, that *is* something! So the ocean is especially deep here, but where's the heavy land mass to create such a contrast? The Philippines are only islands."

"Ah - hah ... not so, Chad. That's what most people think. But the Philippine Islands are actually sitting on the main Asian continent ... look here ... see the depths through the islands, and even out into the China Sea. These seas are actually very shallow. The eastern edge of the Philippines is actually the edge of the huge mass that is the continent of Asia itself. You see what I'm leading to?"

"Yes, I think so ... what you are saying is that we are travelling from a deep ocean trench which has the light mass of a thin ocean crust to the heavy mass of the edge of a major continent ... all in a very short distance."

"You have it, Chad! However, I'm afraid that doesn't explain all our error. I'm wondering if we have also been influenced by a current. But the only one I'm aware of in this region would be the beginning of the Japan current, but that would be minimal at this latitude, and would be helping us along in precisely the direction we are headed."

"Current?" An idea flashed somewhere in that opaque mist I claim for a brain. "Maybe we are in a 'Nina', or would it be a 'Nino'?"

"A what?"

"Mr. Milner, do you remember the American gentleman at Mr. Vincent's party?"

"Yes, I think I do ... the tall tanned fellow with glasses, who was talking to Kevin."

"Yes, that's the man, Dr. Morton. Anyway, he was telling us about a major equatorial current that starts here and sometimes flows west to east, sometimes east to west. He called them a Nina or Nino, meaning female or male child in Spanish."

"So you're saying that we could have been pulled by a current travelling in the easterly direction?"

"According to what he said, yes!'

"Hmm ...”

"One thing, though ... if there is an easterly current, then according to Dr. Morton that means warm surface water is flowing from west to east, and we can therefore expect an increase in the number of hurricanes ... or typhoons."

"Oh?"

"Mr. Milner, the Philippines gets hit by a lot of typhoons, isn't that right?"

"Yes, that's correct."

"When is typhoon season?"

Mr. Milner expired a sardonic snort. "It starts right about now."

“Oh.”

I think I'm recieving a premonition!

"But enough theory for now. You and I need to get down to some serious navigation. I'll take some star shots tonight ... I'd like you to do the same. And I will take a noon shot of the sun each day as well. Do you see anything different about the sky recently, Chad?"

"Yes, the moon is setting earlier, and changing phases."

check."

Mr. Milner and I took separate sightings, me with the Trader's vernier sextant, he with his 'Plath', and then worked out the calculations together. We ended up in pretty close agreement with a latitude of 5 degrees 20 minutes North, which, incidently, placed us just northwest of the French Frigate Shoal.

Mr. Milner took three more sightings, with three LOPs. The plotted lines crossed closely together and matched our Polaris latitiude check. Later, after Mr. Milner had retired to his cabin, I took three shots of my own ... my calculations worked out reasonably close to Mr. Milner's. We now knew where we were, at least.

Just when I was wrapping up the plotting of my LOPs, Fred broke the silence:

"Chad, do you hear something different with our engines?"

I stopped what I was doing, taking a moment to listen, and to feel the vibrations of the engines. "Not really, Fred. You think something's different?"

"Yeh, I think one of the engines is missing on one or two cylinders."

"Oh - oh ... let's hope it goes away ... tell me if you think it gets worse."

Fred hadn't said anything more about the engines and I was dreamily watching our night sky ... the early morning and the end of my watch were approaching. Then, within a matter of only a few minutes, the same chill I had felt almost exactly 24 hours earlier hit me again, only more severely. I started to shiver visibly, breaking out in wet perspiration at the same time.

"Chad, you feeling a fever again?" Fred questioned, a concerned look on his face.

"Yeh. I don't feel good at all."

"Go lay down, Chad. It's OK, I can handle this on my own ... Anyway, Laurie and the Captain will be here soon.

I took him up on his suggestion, but first roamed around the main deck, looking for a blanket, or blankets. I found two and made it to my cabin. During the day I had dug into my suitcase and found my set of athletic sweat shirt and pants, which I now put on, and curled in a fetal position on the bunk, with the two blankets both wrapped snugly around me. I felt freezing cold, yet the sweat was rolling off my body in beads. 'One hell of a case of the flu,' I cursed. I had had plenty of experience with bad colds and influenza, a lot of times just one day affairs ... but never anything like this.

I was aware of the sun having come up, and I vaguely heard the 'clang - clang' of the breakfast bell, but I couldn't react to either. I couldn't move, and my head was buzzing painfully.

Then it was over. One minute I was in a feverish frenzy, the next I was laying on my back on the bunk, cool but not shivering, suddenly clear-headed, and *very* hungry.

"Richard ... you got something to eat ... how about soup?"

"Yeh, Chad ... I got canned chicken soup ... how's that? And some sandwiches ... hey, you look like hell!"

"Yeh, thanks Richard ... for the compliment too!"

"You had a fever ... but now it's gone? Same thing yesterday?"

"Yeh, Richard ... yes."

"I know what it is ... you'd better find some quinine tablets, fast, brother ...

I stepped into the mess to wait for the soup and sandwiches. Walter's cage was on the table ... a large ragged hole exposed on one side ... it was empty.

"Hey, Richard. What happened? Where's Walter?"

"Gone ... he got out last night ... reckon we'll never see him again!"

"Oh no ... hope he'll be alright!"

Damn, seems like everything's going wrong!

Just the thought of things going hay-wire made me immediately aware that something else was wrong. Richard showed with a bowl of chicken noodle soup.

"Is it just my imagination, or are we only running on one engine?"

"Hell, man, your fever was bad ... we've been on only one engine since just after breakfast. Yeh, that's why you don't see Harry or Kevin around," he smirked. "They're down below working on it."

With some food in my stomach I now felt very sleepy.

"Chad, so you had a fever again?" Laurie stopped me at the wheelhouse.

"Yeh."

"I'm worried about you, matey. Doesn't sound good."

"Yeh, Richard says it's malaria!"

"Wow ... Yeh, he could be right. Do you have any quinine tablets?"

"Nah, I haven't taken any for quite a while."

Quinine tablets and salt pills were openly offered on a table at the CDW mess hall, and we had all been encouraged to take both regularly. I did for two or three months, then found that the salt pills didn't agree with me, and I just stopped taking both. There hadn't been any rumors of malaria being around for a long time and it was just too much humbug. And of course I didn't ever think to stock up on them.

"Well, maybe you'd better find some ... for your own good ... I guess we're not worried about getting it from you ... no mosquitos out here!" he laughed. "But I understand you can carry it around for a long time without really knowing ... then all of sudden, bamm!"

Oh?

"Yeh, maybe I'll ask around. Hey, I understand we're only on one engine?"

"Yes, that's right ... since about eight this morning."

"But we're still on 298 degrees?"

"Yeh, why?"

"Mr. Milner had mentioned that our closest landfall right now would be Palau, in case we got into trouble."

"Palau? ... But Harry and Kevin reckon they'll have us back on two engines in a few hours."

I decided to look at the chart for a minute. "After today we'll actually be closer to the Philippines than Palau, anyway ... I was just wondering."

The soup and sandwiches had a welcomed effect ... I was feeling much better, but the fever had left me weak, and I still needed rest. My blankets were damp and, along with my sweater and pants, sure as hell needed airing out ... they were rank with body odor ... so I took the time to hang them on a clothesline I had rigged up several days earlier, strung across the aft side of the poop deck. I was shocked that the effort tired me.

But that means I slept only one hour. But I feel OK, and hungry. Guess I'll go get some more to eat. I stepped out of the cabin, the sun was in my eyes, low and to my left.

Low, and to my left ... the west? Something's wrong, Chad!

The sun was very low, to the west ... it was about to set! Damn, the sounding of Richard's bell wasn't for lunch, it was for dinner! I had slept through the lunch bell and all through the afternoon.

I said 'hi' to Joseph on the way to the mess. Everyone else was present, but there was a noticable lack of cheer in the air. I looked around. Apparently my questioning showed on my face.

"Matey, we have some sad, sad news." Harry's face was very long and he was terribly unhappy.

"So, spit it out, Harry." I prodded.

"We're out of beer!" His appearance reminded me of a man having been sentenced to hard labor in prison, just an hour before.

"The hell you say?"

"Cross my heart and spit to die, matey!"

Laurie explained: "Even Richard didn't realize it ... he thought there were a few more cases in the back of the pantry ... but we're out, no more South Pacific, no more Foster's."

A world without beer ... this is not good!

I started to laugh. The whole scene was just too much. If I had ever wanted to get at Harry, I now realized that this would have been his worst punishment ... to be in the middle of the Pacific, days away from anywhere, and run out of beer. For myself, I didn't really care. Not for the moment, anyway. And I don't think it would be any sort of a death blow for Fred and Joseph. Kevin and Laurie would definitely miss their evening 'brew', but they would be OK too. But Harry ... Harry was in for a rough time.

"Well, so we're out of beer! Any other bad news?"

"Yeh ..." It was Harry again.

"Yes, Harry ... what else?"

Jeeses, Harry, this just isn't your day, is it?

Kevin interjected, Harry was taking too long, still fretting over the beer. "We've got major problems in the engine room ... water in the fuel again. And that black, gooey stuff ... that's why the one engine is down. The lines, filters. injectors, injector pump -- everything is full of water and plugged up with the black fungus. It's a major job to go through everything. And we're draining the filters on the other Perkins and the auxiliary every hour, to keep *them* running."

This new piece of evidence just served to confirm the absurdity of our situation. I started to laugh again. "Sorry for laughing, gentlemen, but this is absurd ... it's as if anything that *can* go wrong *is* going wrong!"

"Well," sneered Harry. "You're right about that ... it *isn't* funny!"

So we now have a serious problem with the engines. I thought it was interesing how this had been related to me ... I mean which of the two issues were priority: the beer or the engines?

tablets.

"Richard, I don't think I have malaria. But OK ... I'll take a couple anyway ...thanks." I took out two tablets and swallowed them, using the water as a chaser, then attempted to give the bottle back to Richard.

"No ... you keep the bottle ... you're going to need them."

So I kept them, more so as not to offend him than for any other reason.

Upon visiting the wheelhouse deck a few minutes later, I was astonished to discover a very different scene, one that was in stark contrast to the one I had just left below. Our three officer's were lounging together, each with a full drink in their hand. Joseph was behind the wheel, and he motioned for my attention.

"What's up, Joseph?" I whispered, pretending to make a check on our heading.

"They're all drunk like hell!" He sneered under his breath, just loud enough so I could hear.

I suddenly had a dark premonition. What would happen if our travel time to the Philippines was extended, and these three gentlemen ran out of whiskey and rum? So, with one engine down, why are they now drinking so furiously?

Like it was their last bottle?

"There's an extra deck chair, Chad ... sit down. Would you like a drink?"

"No, no thanks, Mr. Milner ... I'm still feeling funny from my bout with the flu." I excused myself.

After a moment or so, I added: "The boys have just discovered that they're out of beer!" I was curious to see what effect that news would have.

"Yes, we know!"

"Hmm ..." I nodded.

Now the situation *really* puzzled me. They knew we had run out of beer. But instead of that reminding them that they should perhaps conserve their own booze, they're consuming it at an accelerated rate. Are they afraid that they'll have to share their liquor? Or are they in a panic?

Mr. Morris had passed out hours before. The Captain had retired to his cabin. And Mr. Milner was sound asleep in his loungechair, snoring loudly. We had taken a series of star shots, and Mr. Milner had the results of a noon sun shot as well. Our position was well established. I noted that the northern coast of Samar, with a couple of possible ports to choose from, was now closer than Palau, and as close as any landfall on the eastern coast of the Philippines, for we were approaching in a west of northwest heading, and the Philippine coastline fell away in a southwesterly direction. It also appeared that the eastern coasts of the islands of Mindanao, Leyte, and Samar were treacherous, with no good ports in which to seek refuge.

Some time before my watch had officially began, I once again saw the on and off glow of a cigarette being enjoyed at the Trader's bow. It was Richard again. I was watching dreamily, when I caught the ever so dim reflection and silhouette of a bottle being raised. The realization didn't strike me for a few seconds, then:

"Hey, Fred ... I thought we were out of beer ... but Richard's got a bottle with him now ... at the bow ... "

"Ohh ... yeh ... didn't you know ... that's not a beer he's drinking ... uhh. Richard's a vanila addict."

"A what? You mean he's been drinking *vanila* ... to get a high ... and that's

They call it the 'snowball effect'!

It was 3:00 a.m. I know because I had checked the chronometer, adjusting for local time by adding 9 hours, of course. The same chill of the previous two nights returned once more, abruptly and without warning. The speed of its return and its rapidly increasing intensity told me I was in trouble. For the first time I took Richard's diagnosis seriously. Why hadn't I done so earlier? In that instant I recognized the chill and impending fever for what it was. The symptoms fit, especially the short term attacks spaced almost exactly 24 hours apart, which was a well-known characteristic of malaria fever. Again my shivering was obvious to any one close by.

Now, you're in for it, Chad!

"Chad, you know you have malaria!"
"Now I do ... Richard was right ... I'm going to take the rest of those tablets right now."
I found a coffee mug and managed to fill it with drinking water, and gobbled the ten or so tablets remaining in Richard's bottle. I was shaking violently, sweat running off me in rivers, my head felt like it was being crushed by a steel vise, and my vision was blurry. With a great deal of effort I managed to climb into my bunk and curl up with the two blankets grasped tightly around me, shivering and sweating. I knew I was fading into a delirium, but there was nothing I could do about it.

Laurie heard the sounds of loud cursing, spoken with a heavy pidgin accent, coming from the direction of kitchen ... or the pantry room next door.
"What's going on, Richard?"
It was only 5:00 a.m., and like each previous morning since Manus, Laurie had gotten up early to have a coffee, take a reading from the log, and prepare for his watch. Except, of course, we didn't have a log to read anymore.
"Bloody hell ... that damn cuscus ... look what the little bugger's done ...
"He *does* like eggs, doesn't he!" Laurie stood over the mess of egg cartons and egg shells, with egg whites and the yellow of the yokes everywhere. Walter had managed to climb into the special egg basket constructed as part of the pantry shelving, and had dug down into the stacked egg layers, shredding the corrugated separators and breaking into every single egg ... not a single one was left intact with a complete shell.
"Well, can we have scrambled eggs?" Laurie tried to impart a measure of humor. It was ill-received, however.
"He went through the last of our fresh vegetables too ..." Richard scowled.
"How did he get in?"
"He found a way through the screen on the door ... see ... the little bugger pushed back the screen ... here! As soon as I can make a trap, we're going to eat cuscus!"

"Where's Chad, Fred?"
"Chad is very sick, Laurie. Now we know he has malaria."
"Hell .... you reckon he's OK?"
"He took the rest of the tablets that Richard gave him ... but he's going to need more ... and I know he needs more blankets, I was going to find some as

Noon, the sixth day out of Manus.

"Reckon we may have to shut down the second engine ... before it shuts down on its own, Captain ... Mr. Milner." Harry reported ... the problem with the contaminated fuel was severe enough that he felt he had to discuss the matter with the officers.

"Does it do any more harm if we run it until it does stop?" Mr. Milner inquired.

"Not really, sir, but I thought I had better let you gentlemen know, and leave the decision to you."

"Harry, you say the source of the problem is water and fungus in the fuel tanks?" Mr. Morris asked, making a strained effort to concentrate on the problem at hand, yet clearly not really wanting to.

"Yes ... it's the same problem as before, in Rabaul. Apparently the fuel tanks are leaking seawater from outside ... both of them. And that black, gooey fungus substance is plugging everything from the lines all the way to the injectors." Harry answered, visibly annoyed with his Chief Engineer.

"Can't you somehow drain the water out of the tanks?" Mr. Milner interjected.

Mr. Morris, however, struggled to maintain his professionalism, and anwered for Harry: "Yes, Harry, you have a serious problem. Ships' fuel tanks are built low into the structure of a vessel, obviously to keep the weight low, and can only be emptied by pumping. If we are leaking seawater from outside ... that presents a problem ... fuel to the engines is drawn by the engine pumps from the bottom of the tanks, where the water is. And that black fungus thrives in the fuel and is especially a problem here in the tropics ... it is mostly on the surface of the fuel, but easily gets mixed due to the agitation caused by the movement of the ship."

"So what do we do?" Harry was becoming more and more irritated by this Chief Engineer who could so nicely restate the problem, but not offer a solution. What Harry needed was a plan of attack, a way to overcome the problem.

"Gentlemen, I recommend that we run the engine as long, as possible." Mr. Morris concluded, his eyes heavy with drunken sleepiness. He was on the verge of passing out again.

"Mr. Milner, and Captain, I am worried about Chad. He's sick ... very sick. We think he has malaria. I just went to check him. He's totally out of it ... in a delirium, with a high fever."

"Malaria, you say ... I was afraid of that, yes, his symptoms fit, I have a full bottle of quinine tablets ... I always make sure I have them when I come to the tropics. Have him take about a dozen as soon as possible. Here, let me get them for you."

The Captain returned from his cabin with a bottle in his hand. Laurie didn't tell him that Chad had already taken about a dozen tablets. He figured Chad needed more. Fred had said that he'd seen people take a whole bottle to kick the fever, meaning a standard bottle of thirty tablets.

"Thank you, sir."

He and Fred had been keeping a vigilance out for Chad, one of them checking with him every hour or so. Laurie made sure a mug of water was in the beverage holder beside Chad's bunk, along with the bottle of quinine tablets, to be there when he became conscious enough to take them. Mr. Milner and the Captain said they would extend their own watches to cover his absence.

Laurie was in the officer's mess for dinner. Harry and Kevin were there as well, both covered with greasy smudges and diesel fuel, looking tired and

As Harry predicted, the number two Perkins came to a floundering, spasmatic halt about 9 o'clock. The Captain and Mr. Milner came down to the officer's mess and asked for everyone to join them.

"What's our situation, Harry?" the Captain wanted to know.

"You all just heard number two quit. That means her entire fuel system is probably plugged up with water and fungus. That means its injectors, the injector pump, the fuel pump, the filters, and all the lines -- they all have to be removed, taken apart, and cleaned -- and then reassembled."

"And engine number one?" the Captain quizzed.

"The same with number one, except that we are about half-way through."

"Can any of the crew help?"

"You bet ... I can use all the help I can get."

"Well, you have our three quartermasters: Laurie, Joseph, Fred ... let's get to it. Harry, you arrange the coordinating."

"Yes sir." was repeated around the table.

I have no idea when it was. I only remember opening my eyes and vaguely seeing the bottle of quinine tablets, and the mug of water. I knew I was dying.

I had never felt anything like this ... had never been so sick. My body throbbed with pain, everywhere. I especially wanted someone to find the handle on that vise and let up on the pressure to my head. Cold -- I was *so* cold. In my feverish nightmares I had envisioned myself back in Canada, when I was young, delivering newspapers in the snow ... that one night when I had almost frozen to death. I was so cold, so very cold. And yet I knew I was wet with sweat ... soaking wet. It took a great deal of effort, all I had, but I opened that bottle and dumped its contents on my left palm, and tried to get as many in my mouth as possible. The mug of water was trickier. I didn't know if I had succeeded or not ... I crashed back into the terrible nightmare that was the fever, certain I was going to die ... *wanting* to die.

Oh no, Chad, you gotta be tougher that that! Hang in there!

The Trader bobbed up and down gently, riding the easy swells, rolling slightly, for the swells met the Trader's hull broadside. Only the sound of the auxiliary broke the stillness of the tropical night, four hundred miles from the nearest land mass, surrounded by only the endless sea.

Dawn arrived, marking the beginning of our seventh day from Manus. Breakfast was a welcome event. Harry and Fred were exhausted and encased in grime. They had spent the entire night working on engine number one. Kevin, Joseph, and Laurie were ready to take their place ... they had divided the manpower into two twelve-hour shifts.

"How's Canuck doing?" Harry asked , genuinely concerned.

"He is one sick mother! I just checked on him. He must have woke up, or came to briefly, because the bottle of quinine tablets I had left for him was open and the mug smashed on the floor. Counting the spilled pills that I could find, I reckon he got almost the whole bottle down. Is there anything else we can do?"

"If he's taken that many quinine tablets, maybe he'll be all night. Nothing we can do ... except make sure he's well covered. Maybe a cool pack on his forehead." Fred suggested.

"Do you really think that would help ... the cool pack?"

"Well, thank you very kindly, Mr. Milner ... I reckon that I do care for another." Mr. Morris responded in a drawn out slur ...

"Mr. Patterson, may I bring you anything to go with your rum?"

"No, Mr. Milner, I have my bottle right here, and we're doing just fine."

Mr. Milner unsteadily sauntered to the wheelhouse where the bottle of JW was, along with the bucket of ice. After considerable fumbling he returned with the two glasses.

"There you are, Mr. Morris."

"This is a most peculiar situation we find ourselves in, don't you gentlemen agree?" Mr. Morris was feeling talkative again, and a little giggly. "It's almost ... humorous," he chuckled, mostly to himself.

"Well, we've certainly had a few things go wrong the last couple of days. I don't know about it being 'humorous', though."

"Yes." Mr. Morris turned towards the Captain and Mr. Milner. "What else do you reckon could go wrong?" he giggled. "It seems that everything that could go wrong has gone wrong. But surely that must be more that could be added to the list? Let's think now."

At that very moment the sound and small vibration of the auxiliary diesel engine abruptly ceased. In its wake was a deadening silence.

Mr. Morris giggled. And then he giggled again, louder. Both Mr. Milner and the Captain sat up in their loungechairs, alarmed that the auxiliary had suddenly stopped running and perturbed by Mr. Morris's giggling.

"Well, I guess that answers my question," Mr. Morris slurred. "We could lose the auxiliary as well. Of course -- its only logical." With that the little man eased back in his lounge chair and passed out.

"Hey, mates ... eat up!" Richard barked loudly, being slightly out of character. "With no electricity, no refrigeration … our food's going to spoil fast ... real fast. Eat now while it's good."

"Can't we cook it in advance, or do something to preserve the meat?" Laurie queried. "There must be something we can do."

"Yes, I'll cook as much as I can ... but that'll only keep a couple of days in this heat. And anyway, we really don't have that much. We didn't stock up in Lorengau. It's been twelve days since Rabaul … we were supposed to be in Hong Kong tomorrow.

With no electricity and no lights nothing could be done in the engine room during the night. Everyone slept, and resumed with mounting ill-humor in the morning.

"Hey, it's not *my* fault we don't have any eggs!" Richard snapped.

"Bloody hell, what's your problem, mate?" Harry flashed back.

Breakfast was steak and eggs, only without the eggs, and not quite enough potatoes to go around. There was, however, plenty of rice. Harry had scowled,. and Richard had reacted with lightening speed.

Fred and Joseph watched as Richard left.

"Take It easy on him, Harry, he's going through a rough time." Fred tried to soothe Harry's ruffled edges.

"What do you mean, rough time? Because we're running out of food, *he's* having a rough time?"

"No, it's something else."

"What the hell. Reckon we're all having a rough time ... reckon we'll die of

My body was not mine. There was no control. The pain was there, yes, but it was coming from a part of me not attached, from a distance, and was separated from what was going on in my head … where a thousand memories, distorted and ugly, wracked me convulsively and nightmarishly. I relived every past fear, every anxiety, only each was twisted horribly to multiply the terror a hundred times. Central to the visions was the repeated appearance of the ghostly figure of Captain Rodney McKay ... and his ominous warnings of impending doom. Over and over again I was tortured by the picture of his unwashed, whiskered face, and the blue naval officer's cap with the short sun visor. Of his ruddy complexion and purple surface veins, and his wry, taunting smile and hardened glint, laughing and jeering at me, as if to say 'I warned you … I told you this would happen'. Over and over I envisioned the Trader being driven mercilously onto a rocky shore, of being torn apart by crashing waves and an unforgiving shoreline. This swirled with flashes of ghastly scenes where we were all being swept mercilessly into an angry sea. I felt the panic of being drowned, of being immersed in horribly cold, salty water, my lungs filling with seawater and being unable to breathe. All of this went on and on for an eternity.

And then I felt the hands of someone loosening the tightness of that steel vise, just a little.

Thanks, Laurie ... maybe he's going to make it!

Laurie thought the Trader surely must have somehow entered a world of black magic and a cursed doom. Each day a new addition was made to the lengthening list of things 'going wrong'. Today's entry, he felt, must be the scene he was just now witnessing. It was late afternoon, and the three officers were in their loungechairs, all three so drunk they could barely make it to the deck's edge to pee. Which they seemed to be doing a lot.

"Mr. Patterson, I really don't understand how you can enjoy this stuff ... it's horrible," Mr. Milner offered his critical assessment as he threw back the glass of rum.

"I quite agree … 'tis terrible indeed! " And Mr. Morris emptied *his* glass.

"Gentlemen, I have an announcement of the utmost importance to make ... could I please have your undivided attention?" the Captain pleaded.

You may," answered Mr. Morris.

"Of course," said Mr. Milner.

"Well, we have just drank the very, very last of my precious rum …"

Mr. Morris was drunkenly melancholy, and began muttering a series of trivial, nonsensical statements:

"All good things must come to an end …

What goes up must come down …

For Auld Lang Syne …

'Tis a slow death, it is indeed, but then I've never been one to be in much of a hurry."

And then he giggled softly, shifting his fragile body to a more comfortable position … and quietly passed out, a benign smile fixed on his face.

Laurie scooped him in his arms once again, and took him to his cabin.

Irritability was running at a peak.

"Harry, I'm almost afraid to ask, but what is our situation with the engines?

"Good, Harry ... I'll pass on the information."

Richard entered the mess with a plate of re-cooked meat and steamed rice, which was the complete evening meal. Laurie noticed that his hand shook as he set the plate down.

"Don't tell me Richard's got malaria too ... he was shaking kind of badly." Laurie whispered to Fred,

"No, Laurie, it's because he's run out of vanila."

"Vanila? My god, you mean ... he's going through cold turkey?"

"Yeh."

Laurie looked across at Harry, and thought of the three certified officers one deck up. 'There's going to be a lot of that going on', he judged.

The second night without the auxiliary; again everyone slept, unable to work on the engines during the dark. Laurie lay in his bunk, going over in his mind all the things that had been happening. What chaos! What utter chaos! Everything had been so calm and in place, before the French Frigate Shoal, and everything since then has been nothing but increasing chaos.

CHAPTER TEN

For Auld Lang Syne ... ketchup and rice

"If this storm continues, and we don't have engine power, it is ineviatble that we will be driven straight into the rocky coast of Leyte or Samar, and shipwrecked!"

Breakfast, the ninth day out of Manus.

Richard was a mess. His face was gaunt and sullen, and he seemed twice as skinny as before. Joseph volunteered to bring the plates of rice and twice-cooked meat into the mess, to save Richard the embarrassment of showing his shaking hands.

Harry was just plain grouchy ... he grumbled about someone trying to force him to eat rice, which he refused to do, and re-cooked meat was definitely not OK with him.

Fred had an announcement to make: "Blokes, I just checked our fresh water tanks and we are getting low ... real low. Laurie, can you maybe tell the Captain and Mr. Milner?"

"Oh - oh! Yes, I'll tell them. How can we conserve more on our fresh water?"

"Uhh ... I think the officer's have gotta stop taking fresh water showers." Fred suggested, reluctantly, knowing that the idea was not going to be received well by the officers.

"Hmm ... you're right. Well, I just have to tell them, that's all!" Laurie concluded.

He found the Captain and Mr. Milner in their loungechairs, sullenly and expressionlessly gazing out into the Pacific.

"Gentlemen, Fred has just checked our fresh water tanks and we're low ... " He paused to let the news sink home.

"Damn," Mr. Milner muttered. Mr. Patterson remained silent.

Laurie waited, but there wasn't going to be any further response. He knew he had to let them know of Fred's suggestion. Finally, he broke the silence.

"Sirs … one suggestion is that we all discontinue taking fresh water showers."

"What!" the Captain barked, affronted by Laurie's seeming impertinence. "We will not discontinue our showers!"

The Captain had said this so forcibly that Laurie didn't attempt to continue the conversation, instead he decided to check on Mr. Morris and Chad. Mr. Morris was sleeping, peacefully he surmised, judging by the smile still on his lips. Chad was a different matter: his forehead was burning hot and his body was wet. He was no longer in a curled position, but lay flat on his back, his face sallow and lifeless, the outline of his body quivering. Laurie shook him by the shoulders, hoping he would respond. But all he received in return was a tortured groan … he was still in a feverish delirium.

Laurie checked the engine room. With two helpers Harry and Kevin had ample manpower … he could see that they were even getting into each other's way, and Harry was cursing continuously.

Twice that day Laurie heard an attempt to start the auxiliary. Once it actually ran for three minutes or so, then died.

With no one really needing him, he made his way to the bow of the Trader, which was pointed almost due east, a conclusion he made by judging from the position of the afternoon sun. Laurie gazed into the Pacific, and gradually becoming aware that the sky was different from at any time since leaving Rabaul: there was a substantial amount of cloudiness, mostly concentrated in the east. Not black clouds, or even dark, just a lot of them, and a change from round, puffy clouds to ones that were larger and which tended to accumulate in tall combinations. He was curious, and decided to talk to the Captain and Mr. Milner.

"Captain, I notice that today the sky seems to be clouding over … from the east. Do you think it means anything?"

The Captain was smoking on a shiny black pipe, something that Laurie hadn't seen him do in the past. Mr. Patterson lowered the pipe.

"Mr. Milner and I have been watching those clouds, Laurie. We reckon there's rain in store for us in a day or so. Which reminds me, maybe we can rig the tarps covering the holds in such a manner so as to catch rainwater. But not now, let's wait and see how those clouds develop."

"Fred, how are we doing down there?"

It was late and everyone else had crashed, leaving only Laurie and Fred in the mess, both sipping on a cup of coffee. That was one thing we had lots of, Laurie reflected. Coffee and rice. And still some canned foods. Neither himself,

201

nor Harry and Kevin, would venture so far as to eat rice. Not yet at least. Laurie waited for Fred's reply.

"We've almost got the auxiliary running again ... but it keeps plugging up. I think Harry's gotta do something different."

"Like what?"

"We gotta change the system so that we somehow get the water and fungus out *before* it gets to the engine filters."

"How?"

"I don't know ... wish Chad was better. Between him and I, bet we could figure out something. He's pretty smart when it comes to mechanics."

"You're pretty smart yourself, Fred ... try to figure something out."

"Yeh."

Now Laurie was becoming worried about Mr. Morris. He had been out of it for over 24 hours now. He checked his cabin again, only to find him still asleep, a light snore emitting from his nose, and still with that silly smile on his face. Except his color was different ... a lot greener now.

My first step to consciousness was the gradual diminishing of the nightmares, the visions becoming more tolerable, more sensible. Then the beginning of a sleep, a real sleep, in which my body seemed to come together and be part of me again ... the pressure on my head relaxed, the shivering and sweating lessened, then stopped altogether. Finally, I opened my eyes; my vision was surprisingly clear, and my eyeballs and sockets no longer ached. 'Wow', I said out loud. I remembered the events of the day before I had been overwhelmed by the fever.

How much time has passed?

Jeeses, was I hungry. I tried to sit up, but fell back down, weak and exhausted. Gotta rest awhile yet. After a couple of hours of intermittent sleep I tried again. 'Alright!' I muttered. I still had the sweater and sweat pants on, no need to change clothes, and I stepped out of the cabin. It was dark. It was then that I realized that there were no sounds, and no vibrations. Neither our auxiliary nor a main engine were running. And no lights. I slowly worked my way down the ladder. There was no one in the wheelhouse, nor on the decks.

Jeeses, maybe no one's on the ship ... maybe I'm on a ghost ship!

What has happened? Is the ship deserted? Has everyone abandoned ship ... or died? I chuckled out loud at my own morbidity. Then I heard a distinctive snoring sound coming from Mr. Milner's cabin.

No, we still have life on board!

I completed the manuever of making it down the passageway and the steps, then towards the kitchen. Damn, no lights … don't know where anything is. I groped around. My fingers suddenly found themselves in a pot of cold steamed rice. I wolved down the contents, in the darkness, for the first time ever thinking that maybe rice did taste OK. I opened the freezer door. It was only slightly cooler inside, and almost empty. But my fingers again found something ... meat ... and that also went straight to my mouth. It was beef steak, kinda hard and dry. I found a jug of drinking water. Damn, I was thirsty. Now what? The hell with trying to go back to the cabin, the bench in the mess will do just fine. I'll rest there till breakfast.

Laurie was aware of the dim pre-dawn light at the two portholes in the cabin, which were their only 'windows' to the outside of the ship. The crew's quarters were two separate cabins at the extreme aft of the main deck, opposite to each other -- one to port, one to starboard. Each cabin had four bunks, a pair of upper and lower ones on each side of the cabin space. Harry and Kevin shared the port cabin with him, while Richard, Fred and Joseph occupied the opposite one. A four-stall shower and 'head' was next, on the port side, and opposite to that was the pantry and kitchen.

Nothing was going to happen until full light, when Harry and the blokes could continue working on the engines, and Richard had light to prepare breakfast. But he was already used to getting up at this time, and so he thought he'd go check up on Chad, and Mr. Morris.

First Chad. Upon reaching the top of the steps to the passageway adjoining the officer's cabins, he heard loud snoring coming from the direction of Mr. Milner's quarters. The last time he had checked on Mr. Morris he had been snoring as well, only lightly. But the recollection caused him to pause at the Chief Engineers door and listen. But there was no sound.

'He's probably turned on his side and isn't snoring any more', he rationalized. He'd be back in a couple of minutes, after seeing to Chad.

Laurie stood there, frozen, staring at Chad's empty bunk. And he wasn't on the floor. What happened? Maybe he's up, and resting in a loungechair on the wheelhouse deck … he just hadn't seen him. He relaxed a little with the thought and hurried back down the ladder.

But one thought nagged at him as he reached the bottom of the ladder … everything that could go wrong *had* gone wrong. It was like they were all trapped on a jinx ship, doomed, everything in chaos. Chad wasn't on the wheelhouse deck, neither side. Laurie's chest was pounding with panic. What happened? Did he maybe somehow get out of his bunk and ended the madness of his delirium by jumping overboard? 'Bloody hell!'

And Mr. Morris, what about Mr. Morris? He rushed to the Chief Engineer's cabin door, and entered. Mr. Morris was still on his back, with his lips still pursed in that silly-smile. But there was no sound of snoring. Even in the dim light the man's complexion was visibly green. Laurie moved quickly to his side. There was no movement whatsoever -- no rising and falling of the chest, no quivering of the nostrils or lips to indicate breathing. Laurie touched his face, then his hand. Mr. Morris's flesh felt cold, and without life … the man was quite dead.

Laurie gasped in shock, and ran into the passageway, trying to decide what to do. Mostly as a reflex reaction, he started pounding on the Captain's door, and Mr. Milner's. Both officers shouted, there was the sound of cursing and the rustling of clothes, and each burst into the passageway at almost the same instant.

"What the bloody hell ... Laurie?"

"Captain, Mr. Milner ... Mr. Morris is dead ... and I can't find Chad. I'm afraid he's lost overboard."

Now there were three in a state of panic. Mr. Milner hurried to Mr. Morris's cabin. Our Captain rushed to the deck rail, shouting below: "Man overboard, man overboard!"

Everyone was up!

"Who's overboard ?"

"Chad, it's Chad ..."

Harry did not appreciate this unnecessary disturbance to his final few moments of rest. Someone's overboard? 'What the bloody hell is going on?' he cursed to himself. Laurie was running down the main deck passageway.

"Chad's thrown himself overboard ... and Mr. Morris is dead."

"What?" Harry reacted slowly.

I woke with a start ... the shouts and curses and the heavy sound of running feet had woken me from a very pleasant sleep. I had been dreaming of Jeri. Jeri Miller. Hell, I hadn't dreamnt about her in a long time. I had always thought of Jeri as my high school sweetheart, although we hadn't lasted very long together. But I had been dearly in love with her, and I figured she had been the best looking girl in Strathcona High. I wasn't alone in that judgement, either. She was truly the 'girl of my dreams'. Along with Angie, that is. Ahh, yes, Angie Harris, the girl I had gone with while at S.A.I.T. in Calgary.

Jeeses, now I'm dreaming about both *of them!*

So now both of them are on my mind. Ahh, such sweet memories. But what the hell is all the noise about?

204

"Hey, what's happening?" I yelled at Harry's back as he was scurrying along the passageway in the direction of the aft deck.

"Chad's overboard ... and ..." He stared at me, then broke into that dumb ass wide grin, and walked towards me, holding a finger to his lips, telling me not to say anything.

"Hi, Chad, glad to see you're over your fever ... you alright?"

"Yeh, fine."

"Let's sit down in the mess a minute, OK."

"Sure ... so what's going on ... what did you say just a second ago?"

"Oh ... nothing very much ... Mr. Morris just died ...

"What?"

"Shhhh!" He held his finger to his lips again.

"And everybody's looking for you. They think you jumped overboard." Harry was starting to snicker ... a long continuous snicker.

"What ... Harry ... hey ... we gotta go tell them.

"Nah ... take it easy for a minute.

"Harry!"

Just then Laurie appeared at the doorway.

"Harry, will you give us a hand ... Chad! It's you ... isn't it?"

"Yeh, Laurie, it's me."

Laurie sat down, and did nothing, and then started to chuckle, and then caught himself

"But it's really not funny ... Mr. Morris died during the night."

"Yeh, Harry just told me."

Harry was still snickering. "Well, we lost Mr. Morris, but we got you back. I reckon that's a pretty good trade."

"Bloody hell, Harry ... that's callous as hell ... you've got no sense of compassion, you know that ... none whatsoever!"

Then he slumped down in the seat and started to chuckle again. "But good to see you're OK ... and I guess it *is* kind of funny."

The three of us laughed ... it *was* humorous, in a morbid way.

"But how can we laugh when Mr. Morris has just died."

"Well, it's not like we all expected him to live to a hundred. Reckon he was one foot in the grave when we first saw him in Rabaul," Harry reasoned.

Fred was on the main deck near the officers mess, and heard the sound of laughter. 'Bloody hell', he thought, 'This ship has gone totally mad ... our Chief Engineer is dead and Chad's overboard, and someone's laughing about it'.

Just then Laurie came out of the passageway.

"Fred ... Chad's here in the mess ... and he's fine ... let everyone know, OK."

Richard had hot coffee for everyone, a few pieces of re-cooked meat -- our last -- and plenty of steamed rice. The Captain and Mr. Milner came down to the mess to join the rest of the crew.

Mr. Patterson raised his cup of coffee: "Gentlemen, here's a toast to Chad's return ... uhh ... his return from malaria fever, and from being lost overboard."

Everyone was smiling and in good humor.

"However, we do have the matter of Mr. Morris's death to deal with." He paused to allow time for everyone to switch to more somber thoughts. "Mr. Milner and I feel that we can't keep his body on board and wait for a landfall, especially in this heat and especially since we don't know how many days away that landfall is, due to our engine problems. Therefore, we feel that we should have a funeral service for the gentleman, and bury him at sea, as soon as possible ... later this very morning, in fact. Does anyone have an objection to that?"

The Captain waited for responses. No one was against the plan ... it was, afterall, the practical and expedient thing to do. I personally shuddered at the thought of Mr. Morris rotting in the heat; we didn't even have a freezer we could have perhaps stuffed him in, since we no longer had refrigeration.

"Good ... then I propose we hold a service at 10:00 a.m. ... we could use some help there ... we should have a plank or some sort of board to lay him on, a flag to cover him with, and someone to say a few words. Oh yes, and someone to prepare the body ... prepare it with a weight, that is. You see, his body will have a tendency to float. That wouln't be a problem if we were under way, perhaps, but since we're dead in the water ... sorry, that's probably a bad choice of words. Well, you can see what I mean."

The Captain was having a hard time with this; Mr. Milner came to his assistance: "First of all, we need a volunteer to prepare and handle Mr. Morris."

Laurie raised his hand. "I can do that, sir"

"Fine. Now we don't know a great deal about Mr. Morris but I understood that his religious affiliation was with the "Church of Latter-Day-Saints", something like that ..." Mr. Milner paused, hoping someone could help him."

My eyebrows went up at the mention of 'Church of Latter-Day- Saints', as did Kevin's.

"Ahh ... the Church of Jesus Christ of Latter-Day-Saints, or Mormons as they are called. It just so happens that Chad is a Mormon." Kevin explained, selling me down the river.

But it made sense. The Church was popular among the Maoris of New Zealand, and a good percentage were Mormon. And Mr. Morris's mother was Maori and he had been raised by her, as a single parent, in Auckland.

"Chad, so you are of the same faith?" the Captain inquired, delighted that he had found someone to pass on the chore of ministering the funeral.

"Yes, but ..."

"Good, then we'll trust you to provide us with the appropriate religious message."

Your mother always did want you to be a missionary, Chad!

Damn, how could I get out of this. I'd only been to one funeral in my entire life -- my grandmother's, when I was five years old, and even that one wasn't a Mormon service. And I had thought it was such a morbid, distastefull affair. I had shunned funerals even since. I had absolutely no idea what to say.

"Now, Mr. Milner and I are very concerned about the survival of this ship, and the remainder of this crew. Harry, can you please give us an update on the engine situation."

"One of the Perkins is ready to start, sir, but we don't have compressed air to do that with, without our auxiliary running. But we think we are close to having it going again ... right, Kevin."

"Yes ... but we are going to have a continuous problem unless we figure out a way to remove the water and fungus before it reaches the engine filters." Kevin explained.

I was curious, and I noticed Fred was looking at me, as if he thought I could help. "So our problem is water and fungus in the fuel?"

"Yup, that's it!" Harry tossed out, a little unhappy about needing to explain this one more time.

"But so much that the filters get plugged within a couple of hours." Kevin clarified.

"So you need to get the water and fungus out *before* it reaches the filters?"

"Yeh ... that's the solution all right ... but how?" Kevin implored, to no one in particular.

I shrugged. "I bet we can figure something out."

"Gentlemen, please put your heads together and let's find a solution as soon as possible," the Captain interrupted, challenging us to find a solution.

"Another thing you all need to be aware of, gentlemen ... we have a storm coming our way. And if we're hit with a bad storm without at least one engine operational ... well, we may be in for a very rough time."

With the mornings excitement none of us had noticed the change in the weather. The build-up of heavy clouds was now general across the entire sky, and in the east the bottoms were dark grey, suggesting rain. And the swells were no longer mirror smooth, but instead were now ruffled by a strengthening breeze. I thought about Dr. Morton, and what a typhoon might be like.

Or being sunk by one?

Organization of the particulars for the funeral took place on the wheelhouse deck, where Laurie, Joseph and myself met with the captain and Mr. Milner. Harry, Kevin, and Fred could not, of course, be spared from their vital function in the engine room.

I did not envy Laurie's part of the ordeal ... the very thought of handling Mr. Morris's dead body made me shudder with revulsion.

Jeeses -- a green corpse!

But Laurie didn't seem to mind. With Harry's permission he had procured a spare or broken part of something from the engine room, which was a piece of cast iron weighing about twenty pounds. He fastened the weight securely to both Mr. Morris's ankles with a piece of rope.

There was a problem with obtaining a board or plank on which the body would be placed ... nothing could be found.

"How about taking off a door to one of the cabins?" Laurie suggested.

Joseph had been chosen the person in charge of providing this crucial item. "That's a big job to take off one of those doors. And they're all steel ... heavy like hell."

"Yeh, I guess you're right. Hey, why don't we just use one of the loungechairs. We can set it on the deck rail and tip it up, just like we would a plank." Laurie proposed.

"That's a great idea," I intervened. "It would be kind of fitting too, since that's where he had spent most of his time, anyway."

Joseph snickered. Laurie frowned at both of us.

"How about the flag, Captain?" I had a problem with using our Australian flag, which I had found with an assortment of other flags in one of the drawers below the chart table.

"Yes ... what about it?"

"Well, the only Australian flag we have is kind of small ... and it doesn't seem fitting, anyway, since he was a Kiwi, not Aussie ..." I was thinking that if it was me I sure wouldn't want an Australian flag used. But then again, I wouldn't want that thing that looks like somebody had a nose bleed in a handkerchief used either, I mused, remembering that that was the standard reference joke used when Canada had changed its national flag from a British Union Jack to a large blood-red mapleleaf on a white background, with two outside bands of more blood-red.

"I see what you mean ... well, can we just use one of his white sheets?"

"Sure, I don't see why not!"

"Fine."

Now the matter of who was going to be the spokesperson for the funeral and what was to be said ... I sure wanted out of that role!

"Mr. Patterson, I have a real problem with this ... I have no idea what to say. I've never been to a funeral in my life, since my grandmother died when I was only five, and I've never been to a Mormon funeral. I have no idea what they say."

"Well ... I'm sorry, Chad, but I'm not much good at this either ... I'm afraid I'm not a very religious man. How about you, Mr. Milner?"

"Sorry, Captain, I believe I'm probably even less religious ... one of the reason's I'm a remittance man is because I was charged with slandering the Church of England at one time ... sorry."

This was a problem. I really thought it was the duty of a Captain to conduct a funeral at sea. That's the way it was in all the movies I'd seen, at least. Errol Flynn came to mind -- one of his'pirate' movies. Which in turn reminded me of Errol Flynn's 'New Guinea connection' ... more about that later. Anyway, how could I switch this around? I waited, hoping that one of the two officers would offer an alternative.

Can you think of something that is special to your religion that would seem to fit the occasion anything."

"Let's see. Well, I do remember the Mormon 'Articles of Faith' ... there's thirteen of them."

"Go ahead, say them."

"Alright ... the first is 'We believe in God, the father, and in his son, Jesus Christ, and in the Holy Ghost'."

"OK ... that's good enough. How about if I say a few words on his behalf, and then at the very end say 'In the name of God, the father, and ... how did the rest go ... and then we tip up the chair ... and off he goes."

"Mr. Patterson, that sounds just great to me."

Whew! Sure am glad to get out of that one!

"Can you please write that down for me ... and Laurie, Joseph ... when I say 'In the name of' ... that's your cue to lift up on the chair."

So it was arranged.

Fifteen minutes before the hour Harry, Kevin and Fred came up from the engine room and started to clean up and get ready for the solemn event. Laurie and Joseph moved one of the loungechairs to Mr. Morris's cabin. The Captain was rehearsing his line.

Ten o'clock arrived, and Mr. Patterson let Joseph and Laurie know that it was time. We were to hold the service and 'burial' on the main deck, port side ... which was the leeward side to the now strengthening breeze. I noticed that the Trader had naturally held a position so that the wind came over the starboard quarter bow. Why did it do that, and what significance did it have, I wondered.

Mr. Milner and the Captain took their position on the deck, and the crew began to gather around.

Meanwhile, in the Chief Engineer's cabin, Laurie and Joseph laid Mr. Morris gently onto the loungechair and carefully covered his body with his cleanest bed sheet. But then they encountered a problem at the doorway and passageway. They tried every angle, every direction, almost tipping Mr. Morris on the floor at one point. I had just come up from the main deck and was watching from the passageway. Laurie was becoming frustrated to the max.

For Christ's sake, you guys, don't drop him!

Laurie finally gave up on that particular scheme, exasperated. "Hell ... this just isn't going to work, Joseph ... here, you bring the loungechair!"

With that Laurie picked up Mr. Morris and slung him over his right shoulder, white sheet and all, and quickly carried him down to the main deck, me hurrying along behind him adjusting the sheet so as not to expose the very green Mr. Morris underneath and Joseph following us with the loungechair.

It was one of those aluminum chairs, lightweight and rather flimsy, and the kind that folded up or extended out, depending on how you applied pressure to different parts. Laurie and Joseph succeeded in placing our dear Mr. Morris on the chair, with the white sheet spread over him, tucked under to prevent the wind from blowing it off, but tied to the chair frame at the top, so that when the moment of delivery came the sheet would stay behind with the chair. No sense in wasting a good sheet, I supposed. Besides, that's the way I had seen Errol Flynn do it.

The first attempt at lifting the chair and Mr. Morris almost resulted in both being folded in half ... they had tried to lift at the wrong locations. Finally, the loungechair and Mr. Morris were perched on the deck rail, somewhat precariously I observed, with Laurie and Joseph each standing to one side, ready to lift the inboard end, which would allow Mr. Morris to slide down and into the sea, with the twenty pound cast iron weight to ensure his continued journey to Davy Jones's Locker.

Mr. Patterson was clearly not cut out for this sort of role. Perhaps he had never been required to do this in his previous years of service. All our sympathies were with him.

"Gentlemen. We are gathered here ... ahem ... to pay our last respects to our fellow crew member, and officer, Chief Engineer Stanley Morris ... who ... uhh ... has departed us ... who did not survive this troubled voyage ..." He stopped for air, and to gather his thoughts, glancing nervously at the rest of us.

We were all standing quietly, and reverently, listening and watching the Captain, yet with our heads bowed respectfully. Even Harry was graciously ceremonious. We were the very picture of reverence and respect.

"We didn't know Mr. Morris very well, for he has been with us for only ... two weeks. But in that short time we came to know him as a fine gentleman, an able and dutiful officer, and a wonderful individual."

That part was a little hard for Harry to swallow. He shuffled his feet, and made a small noise to clear his throat. Everyone glanced in his direction.

Joseph was becoming a little tired, and shifted his position slightly.

"Dear Lord, we humbly ask that ..."

There was a scraping sound, aluminum on iron, as Joseph's side of the loungechair slid a few centimeters. But it was enough to upset the balance and the stability of the chair and its contents. Mr. Morris started to slide. Laurie, seeing what was happening, figured that he had no choice but to move his side in alignment and let Mr. Morris go ... otherwise he would go anyway, but off on Joseph's side rather than straight off the end, as intended.

The Captain, realizing that Mr. Morris was already on his way skipped immediately to his rehearsed ending:

"In the name of God, the father, and in his son, Jesus Christ ..." He paused to read the slip of paper I had given him.

But Mr. Morris was going fast. Or at least so it seemed. But then his downward sliding movement suddenly stopped. Laurie watched, horrified, as the cast iron weight got caught on the tubing of the chair's frame ... he could see that a part of the cast iron object had snagged the end cross-piece of the chair. His first thought was to reach out and release the iron weight, then realized it was too far to reach. Joseph mis-interpreted his movement, and at the same time heard a multered scowl ftom Mr. Milner, who stood behind him: "Let the whole bloody thing go!"

"... and in the Holy Ghost."

... as chair and sheet and cast iron weight and Mr. Morris all tumbled together to the sea below.

Harry snickered, kinda loudly.

"Bloody hell!" exclaimed Laurie, expressing both astonishment at what had happened as well as disgust for Harry's snickering.

The Captain sighed deeply, without expression, just glad it was all over.

Mr. Milner scowled.

Joseph was shocked, his face contorted by panic.

Fred and Richard just stood there, startled, not knowing what to do.

Kevin's eyes went skyward, as if to say 'This is absurd!'

I walked to the edge and leaned over, curious about what I would see, what had sank and what didn't. I saw only the last of the white sheet, as the chair pulled it under. "Goodbye, Mr. Morris," I said.

For Auld Lang Syne ... !

The breeze had turned into a full force wind, maybe twenty-five knots, the swells were now higher and more narrow, white cascades showing at intervals on each swell, the water's surface jagged with small waves. The sky had become generally overcast, and a light, biting rain began to fall.

"Laurie, Chad, this is the time to see if you can retie the tarps on the holds so as to catch rain water." Mr. Milner instructed.

"Hey, I'm sorry, blokes, but that's all we got left!" Richard barked in response to the general dissatisfaction felt by all at the table.

"How the damn hell can we eat just rice," Mr. Milner grimmaced.

As soon as Harry and his crew had their fill of steamed rice they returned below decks. The Captain and Mr. Milner went topside. Laurie and I were the only ones left.

"Laurie, let's you and I go hunting for food, before we work on those tarps."

"What do you mean?"

"I mean let's start searching ... everywhere. Maybe we can find something."

"Sure, but it sounds like a long shot."

So we started. First the pantry. Then the kitchen. Nothing!

"Hey, Chad ... the seats here come off ... what's underneath?"

Laurie had just discovered that the cushion seats to the bench behind the mess table were removable, revealing a storage space underneath.

"I'll be damned ... ketchup!" There was no less than six unopened boxes of good 'ol Heinz ketchup.

"This is a goldmine!" I was estactic.

"A gold mine ... ketchup ... ?? What's so great about ketchup?"

"The great thing about ketchup, my good buddy ... is that it makes steamed rice almost ... delicious!!"

"What?"

"Wait till dinner time, then try it ... I guarantee … try it, you'll like it!"

Laurie and I had done our best to tie the canvas tarps that covered the two holds in such a manner as to catch the rain, but our resources were limited. We had no timbers to lay down on the edges in order to form a trough, nor something by which we could raise the corners, and we were afraid that if we altered the shape of the tarps too much we would destroy their effectivenss in keeping water out of the holds, which was becoming an increasingly important concern because of the storm. In the end Mr. Milner decided that it was more important to be secure against storm waves than to capture rain water.

We exerted extra effort to make sure the tarps were snug and strongly tied, then sought refuge in the mess, and a cup of coffee.

"Laurie, you saw the condition of the tarp over the forward hold, didn't you?"

"You mean the way it was tied down before ... or *not* tied down?"

"Yeh ... strange, like someone had purposefully left it so it would come untied by itself."

He smiled. "Like another example of sabotage?"

"Nah, you're right . . . just a lousy job of tying."

What about Captain McKay's warning, Chad?

"Or ..." a thought flashed across my mind. "Or it was left poorly tied after someone had opened it to obtain access to the hold, and had been in a hurry to leave."

"What?? ... what do you mean, Chad?"

"Laurie, I've never told anyone else about this, because it made almost everyone suspect, but I was given a warning by the Trader's previous Captain, Mr. Rodney McKay, and he suggested that there is something mysterious about our cargo.

"What?" Laurie repeated.

With that I swore Laurie to secrecy and explained my two encounters with the strange Captain Rodneyy McKay, and his departing words: 'There are things about the Trader that you don't know about ... about her owners ... her cargo ... and the members of your skeleton crew,' and his warning not to sail on her. Then his second warning: 'there has been some mischief done -- designed to sink the Trader to the very bottom of the sea'. I even included the far out notion that Harry and/or Kevin could have had a playing hand in the matter of our 'leaking packing glands'.

Laurie whistled, and I could tell that he was not a hundred percent ready to accept all that I had told him.

"Chad, it could have been that your Captain McKay was just carrying a grudge towards Lancey Shipping Company, and was trying to get revenge by scaring off any potential new crew."

"Yes, Laurie ... and you're right ... but he was awfully convincing and there's still the chance. It makes you wonder."

And it's our very lives that are at stake!

This had been some day, with Mr. Morris's funeral and all, and I was still weak from the fever and felt a need for more sleep. But I decided to stop at the wheelhouse on my way to my cabin. The wind was now much stronger. I had to bend myself in its direction to hold against it. The sea was no longer characterized by long rows of waves, but instead there were only short groups of shorter individual waves, each forming its own shape and crest, the wind ripping off the tops to reveal white frothing foam, which the waves spit into the wind. It was now a very troubled sea.

"Can we weather a storm without our engines running?" I asked the two gentlemen in the wheelhouse.

"Fortunately, our basic design keeps us swung with our quarter bow pointed to the wind. It's a classic 'heave-to' position, caused by the resistance to the wind offered by our large aft superstructure first, and our raised bow second. The wind is presently from the southeast, which keeps our bow at a heading of about 100 degrees. We are drifting with the wind, however, to the northwest."

"So it's good that the waves hit us on the quarter bow?"

"Yes, that's the best angle ... but God help us if the wind comes from a direction different from that of the waves."

"Can that happen?" I had to talk loudly in order to be heard over the sound of the wind.

"In a typhoon situation ... most definitely!"

Nice thought!

Richard's bell was barely audible over the noise of the storm. The Trader was now rolling from side to side as each wave passed, pitching heavily as the bow lifted high to meet each crest, and then plunged into the depth of each trough.

"Gentlemen ... I am pleased to announce that Laurie and I have found the solution to our food supply problem. It is in the boxes on the floor under the table."

Harry was the first to grab at one of the boxes: "What ... this is only ketchup!"

"Yes ... ketchup!"

"Big deal!" he grunted, disappointed. I noticed his complexion was somewhat sallow. So were several others around the table.

Jeeses, everyone's becoming seasick!

"Big deal, nothing! You don't understand, Harry. Place this Heinz specialty on top of your steamed rice and, presto, you have instantly converted that white mound of tasteless carbohydrate into a delightful delicacy ... try it!"

I watched with great satisfaction as each of our non-rice eaters tried the combination, each in turn deciding that it did indeed make the rice more palatable. Maybe it also had something to do with hungry stomachs and lack of choice, but I discounted that line of explanation. I felt we had just solved our food crisis.

"Chad, we need to have someone in the wheelhouse at all times. Can we divide the night into three four-hour watches, you taking the first.

Later, Mr. Milner came to keep me company for short time.

"I'm worried, Chad. This wind is driving us towards the northwest, which is close to our intended direction, but we can also be driven straight onto the east coast of one of the Philippine islands too ... if the storm continues and we don't have power.

The Captain relieved me at 10:00 p.m.

"Chad, go ahead and get some rest. What's our heading now?"

"Seventy degrees, sir ... it changed from 100 degrees over the last two hours."

"Hmm . .

"What does that mean, sir?"

"That is both good news and bad news ..." He chuckled at his own choice of words. "I don't mean that humorously. We are now in the lattitudes where typhoons are usually generated and usually travel westerly, eventually changing to a more northerly direction and wearing out as they reach cooler waters at higher latitudes or encounter a land mass. Typhoon winds circle in a clock-wise direction in the northern hemisphere. A few hours ago the winds were from the southeast, now they're coming from a more easterly direction. That would be characteristic of a typhoon travelling towards us, its center lying almost due east, or perhaps a little to the north. So the bad news is that the storm is probably a typhoon and the center may be heading straight for us, and the good news is that its center *may* be to the north of us and we will only be hit by the storms southern edge. When, or if, the wind changes so that it is coming from the northeast, then we know that the center has passed."

"You can tell all that by the wind direction?"

"That and knowing something about typhoons."

Opening the wheelhouse door was now becoming difficult, the wind and driving rain so strong. The Captain gave me a hand. The Trader's movement was now more exaggerated, almost violent. The heavy rain came at us at a sharp angle, and even in the blackness of the night the white of the waves off our starboard bow was briefly visible as each wave approached, the very tops of a few managing to scale the main deck rail, the volume of water rushing in a torrent across the deck and the canvas tarps covering the holds.

Jeeses ... if one of those tarps were torn loose our holds would fill with seawater very quickly ... especially if it was the one covering the forward hold.

The tempest raged through the night, worsening with each hour. I could only sleep in short intervals, and I was required to hold firmly onto the 'bunk board' to prevent being literally thrown out of the bunk altogether. I now realized why Mr. Fitzgerald had said my cabin was the least 'comfortable'. What he had meant was that because it was high up on the poop deck, the rolling and/or pitching motion of the ship was the most extreme at my location.

I remembered that at one moment during the night I was startled from my sleep by what I thought was the vibration and screeching sound of metal against metal. I wasn't sure I had actually heard it, or just dreamed it. There was no further sound, and I had gone back to sleep.

It's probably only the ship starting to come apart!

There was a dim light entering the porthole glass ... I was aware that dawn must have arrived. I forced open my cabin door, and was surprised by the effort required. The wind was fierce, and the rain stung my flesh through the fabric of my shirt, now being driven almost horizontal. In the brief seconds it took to reach the ladder I was thoroughly drenched. I had to move carefully, gripping tightly to one hand hold after another.

The wheelhouse door was much more difficult to open than the one to my cabin, for my access from the poop deck to the wheelhouse deck was only on the starboard side, which was now directly exposed to the wind. Mr. Milner was inside, and helped me with the door.

"Good you're here, Chad ... I need you to go below and get Harry and the rest of the crew working on those engines ... we must have propulsion ... you might even say we are at a point where it's a matter of life or death. Don't tell them that, of course .

"Yes sir."

"Let me briefly explain why ... we really don't know our position. But you can see by our compass heading that the wind is from the east. Without power we are being driven due west and are being carried as much with the typhoon as it is passing us. If this continues it is inevitable that we will be driven straight into the east coast of Leyte or Samar, and shipwrecked."

"Yes sir ... I will do what I can! By the way, Mr. Milner ... I thought I was awakened once last night by the sound of something moving ... the sound of steel against steel."

"Yes ... that was a couple of hours ago ... I'm afraid our load of scrap iron shifted ... but with this storm I can't really tell."

"There are things about the Trader that you dont know about ... about the ship herself, and her owners ... and her cargo*"*

'Time to put some pressure on the boys,' I muttered under my breath as I carefully ascended the stairway to the main deck. I had been thinking about the water and fungus problem and had some ideas. The trick was to get them to be receptive to a new idea, even to make them think it was their own ... especially Harry.

Fred, Joseph and Kevin were in the mess. I explained what Mr. Milner had said, and was just finishing when Harry and Laurie joined us. I repeated it for their benefit. So now we were once again talking about the possibility of being shipwrecked. They were concerned. The storm was making us all afraid, and seasick.

"The bottom line is that if we can't make headway against this storm, we may be carried with it right to a rocky shore on Leyte or Samar, and shipwrecked."

"OK ... OK ... we're trying our best." Harry scowled. It was apparent that all five were seasick to some degree. I wondered why I wasn't.

"Mr. Milner also asked me to organize a discussion ... to see if we couldn't find a solution to the water and fungus problem." I lied.

"What do you mean?" Harry sighed, seeing this as an intrusion into his area of control.

"Just that maybe we could talk about it, see if anyone has any ideas."

"If we could just get the water and fungus out *before* it reaches the filters." Kevin exclaimed, repeating what he had said the day before.

"Yeh, but how?" Harry queried in a negative tone.

"How is the fuel drawn out of the tanks?" I quizzed.

"By a long tube that goes in from the top of the tank to the bottom, bolted to one of the tanks 'battens'." Fred explained. Then his face lit up and he continued. "The water is mostly settled on the bottom of the tank, and the fungus is mostly floating on the top of the fuel ... maybe ..."

"That's it, cut the tube short!!" Harry interrupted, nicely claiming the idea as his own.

Harry, we can count on you every time, can't we!

"Harry, that's a terrific idea!" I winked at Fred as soon as I was sure Harry wouldn't see. Fred smiled.

"But that's not quite good enough though ... there's still going to be a lot of water and crap sucked in. I think we need another idea." Harry had just crashed his own idea. But now he was at least thinking positive.

"Harry, remember our Cat machines at CDW ... we always had a water and fungus problem too."

"Yeh, but Joe had us put a chemical in the tanks that killed the fungus, and we had water separators. But we don't have any chemical, and we don't have a water separator." Harry was starting to be negative again.

"Hmm ... how did those water separators work ... ?"

"Simple, it was just a rectangular glass bowl on the fuel line ... the water would settle to the bottom and we drained it out every morning, from a drain cock at the bottom."

"Hmm ... too bad we couldn't make something like that ... a big water separator?"

"How big?" Fred was thinking.

"Hell, the bigger the better ... those two Perkins together go through about a thousand gallons a day, I reckon."

"Then a 50 gallon drum's not too big?"

"Why not?" Harry snorted. "Hey ... Fred, do you think you could weld some fittings ...? Whoa, wait a minute ... the fuel pump would have to suck fuel from the tank through that drum ... nah, no way ... everything would have to be perfectly air tight ... and we'd have to fill the drum up by hand to get it all started." Harry once again lost faith.

"Fill it up by hand, you say? ... so what's wrong with that?"

"Hell, we'd have to lower a pail into the fuel tank and take fuel off the top . . then that top fuel would have all the fungus shit floating on top, and we'd have to strain it somehow when we filled the drum."

Kevin's face lit up, and so did Harry's. They both had the idea at the same time.

"So why not ... we keep the drum full by hand loading with a pail ... and we filter it through ... cloth, a sheet." Kevin was excited.

"Have a drain cock at the bottom of the drum to drain the water that settles ... and have the line to the pump at, say, half way up the drum." Harry completed the idea.

"Now, the drum idea will take some doing to construct ... how about cutting the tube in the fuel tank for the short run?" I was aiming for a short-cut, we desperately needed the engines running asap.

"OK ... we'll think about that one. Hey, let's get to work ... we got a ship to save. "

Damn, Chad, you're such a diplomat!

All of a sudden there was new hope ... there was a light at the end of the tunnel.

Just hope it's not the light of a freight train about to run us down!

"Mr. Milner, I think we have the guys motivated ... and they have a new idea on how to solve the contaminated fuel problem."

"Good, Chad ... good."

I studied our chart, noting that the eastern coast of both Leyte and Samar were strewn with tiny islands ... it was a windward coast and the edge of the continent, I judged that those tiny islands were probably jagged, barren rocks.

The Captain joined us; I gave him an update on the engine and fuel situation. The three of us watched as wave after wave crashed over our starboard bow, the ship was now violently pitching and rolling, the sea around us utter chaos.

"This must be hell for the guys working in the engine room!" I yelled.

"Yes ... but then the motion is the least where they are ... in the bottom of the ship, near its center." Mr. Milner yelled back.

"Still!"

I wasn't sure the sound I heard was our auxiliary running, or not, such was the clamor of the chaos around us ... but yes, it was."

"Captain, Mr. Milner, our auxiliary's running."

A moment later the lights in the wheelhouse came on. Even though it was approaching mid day, the interior lights noticably increased visibility within the wheelhouse, so dark was the raging storm outside.

About a half hour passed, the three of us anxiously listening, then we heard the unmistabable 'psst - psst', 'psst - psst' of compressed air, followed by the endearing rumble of our Perkins number one.

"Chad, can you please confirm with Harry that we can power our one propeller, and fetch Laurie ... we are about to be under way!"

Harry signaled to me from the bottom of the stairway that we were ready to roll, that dumb ass grin of his spread wide across his blackened face.

"Laurie, the Captain would like you to take over the wheel ... we're back in operation."

"Right on! ... I'm already on my way."

"Harry says go for it, Captain."

We happily suffered the loud ding-ding of the throttle signal, and all four of us cheered when we felt the unmistakable rumbling as number one propeller started to churn at 'full ahead'.

"It's simple, Laurie," the Captain instructed. He took over the wheel for the moment. "Just steer so that each wave hits us just slightly on the starboard bow. We're already pointed in that direction now. We prefer the starboard side because of our list, which has now increased to about 5 degrees ... our cargo of scrap iron shifted last night. This way our list helps us ... we actually lean into each oncoming wave. We are now pointed more into the wind and will no longer hold the position automatically. Your bow will want to swing to port as you crest the wave and the full force of the wind hits it ... you've got to find the right wheel position so that it swings back to starboard when in the trough. That's it ... keep it up, Laurie."

"Why don't we take the waves straight on, Captain?"

"Then we would plow into the wave instead of rising with it, and would then sit on top each crest with our bow or stem out of the water ... very hard on the structure of the vessel ... not to mention the violent motion.

Almost everyone was seasick. I went below to the officer's mess, and smelt the odor of vomit in the passageway. Richard was in the kitchen, leaning against his table, and holding onto it firmly, his head down, looking very sick, indeed. Kevin and Joseph were in the officer's mess, Kevin especially looked near death. I was still wondering why I wasn't feeling the motion sickness like they were.

"Where's Harry and Fred?"

"They're finishing up with the drum." Joseph muttered weakly. Kevin couldn't speak.

"So the drum idea is working?"

"We cut the tubes ... while we were setting up the drum."

The afternoon passed slowly, each rising and falling of the ship, accompanied by a corresponding roll, first to port, then to starboard, seemed to take forever, the loud din of the howling wind and driving rain smothering all other noises.

I checked with Mr. Milner in the wheelhouse ... we had returned to our watch schedule.

Mr. Milner ... hasn't the wind direction changed ... isn't it from the northeast now?" Our compass heading was due east, with the wind coming over our port bow.

"Yes, you're right Chad ... it started shifting three hours ago. And the wind strength is beginning to diminish ... can't you tell?"

"I guess I can ... that's great news."

"Chad, I want you to get some sleep, and relieve me early. We have to stay on top of this. We'll have to be ready to change our heading and our tactic continuously. Can you relieve me in, say, three hours?"

"Sure ... I can relieve you right now, if you wish."

"Yes, that would be even better. Alright. But don't hesitate to fetch me if conditions change. I've instructed Joseph to keep the waves on the starboard quarter, even if the wind changes."

I stayed in the wheelhouse with Joseph, then Fred came to take his place, and Mr. Milner showed a while after that. He had slept for over four hours.

"Good, Chad ... go ahead and get some rest ... I think the wind must be ten knots less now that before. It'll be over soon. I think this was a pretty nasty typhoon, but we were lucky enough to catch only the southern edge."

I settled into my bunk, my tired legs and arms wedged against the wall and bunk board. Yes, the movement of the ship was less now. I fell asleep.

I slept long and relatively uninterrupted, especially near the end. I awakened to what seemed a fresh new world. The Trader rose and fell with a moderate gentleness. Sunlight flickered at the porthole. I quickly climbed out of the bunk and opened the cabin door. It was early morning, and the sky was spots of blue in between soft white bulbs of clouds, moving rapidly, as if all playfully racing to a finish line somewhere over the horizon, for we still had a brisk breeze. The sea had not quite settled it's dispute with the typhoon, frequent white caps still spewing at the crests, but the high vertical walls were gone, and the long continuous form of regular swells had returned.

Both Mr. Milner and the Captain were in the wheelhouse, the wind yet too brisk to allow the doors to be left open.

"Good morning. Well, looks like we made it!" I greeted them cheerfully.

"Yes, Chad, but barely. Let me show you." Mr. Milner motioned me towards the chart table. "I was able to take four star shots just before dawn, and I have just now completed the calculations. We are right here ..." He pointed to where four LOPs nicely intersected together, and waited for my reaction. The point was just off the east coast of the island of Samar, perhaps 25 nautical miles from the coastline.

"When the waves had calmed down during the night, I altered our heading to 15 degrees, just east of due north ... which is a heading directed slightly away from the Samar coast. That means we must have been very close to that treacherous shore earlier ... maybe only ten miles. Gentlemen, we were that close to being shipwrecked." He held his thumb and first finger a centimeter apart to emphasize his point.

That is *close!!*

"Laurie, please take us to a heading of 322 degrees. Captain, we need to hold that heading until we reach here ... then change to 288 degrees to take us within site of the lighthouse on the northern tip of Batag Island. What do you think our present speed is, Mr. Patterson?"

"Hmm ... I reckon we're right at 5 knots."

"Alright, then we'll stay on this heading for 14 hours. We change our heading at 8:00 p.m.. Gentlemen, I would like to get some rest."

"Yes, Mr. Milner ... I'll take over ... and thank you."

Mr. Milner turned and paused, then smiled. "You're welcome, Mr. Patterson."

"Chad, look at that chart and tell me where we should plan our landfall." Mr. Patterson instructed.

I studied the chart for several minutes, noting that our choices before entering the San Bernardino Strait were pretty well limited to the northern coast of Samar, the closest being Laoang, then San Jose further down the coast.

"Sir, should we choose a port before the Strait, or after?"

"Before, Chad ... definitely before. Once we enter that Strait ... well, that's another matter."

"Then it's either Laoang or San Jose, I would think."

"Yes, you're right ... Mr. Milner and I have chosen Laoang."

"Then we're very close ... let's see ... Batag lighthouse ... we should be able to enter Laoang Harbor early tomorrow morning."

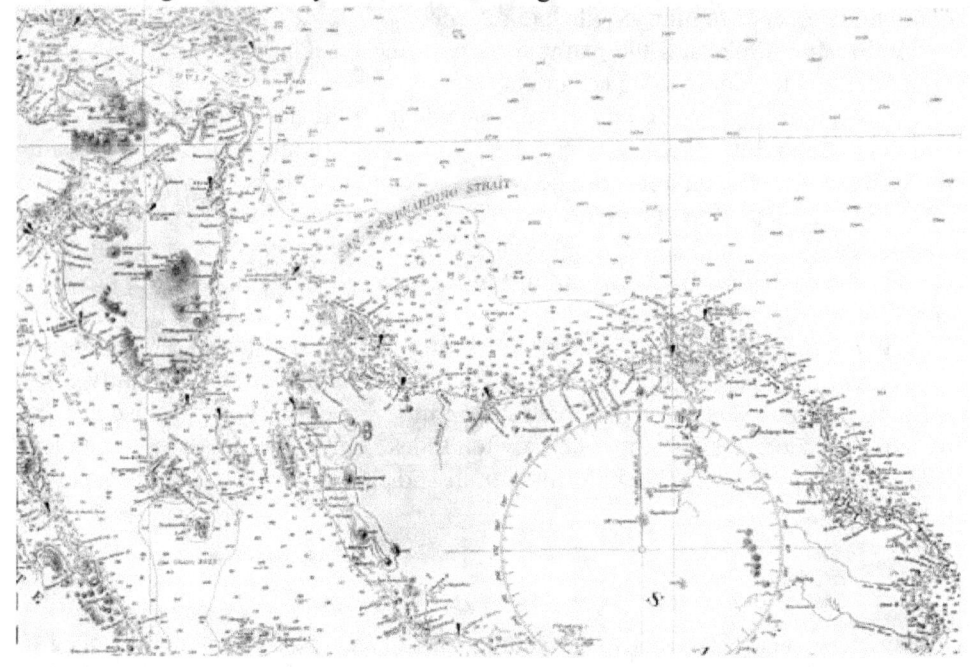

"Would you like to know why we preferred Laoang?"

"Sure."

It's closest, of course, and that's important. It is also a very well protected harbor. In fact, Laoang, or Palapag, is a well know port in naval history. It is where the Manila Galleon used to stop for fresh water on its journey between Manila and Acapulco, Mexico."

"Manila and Acapulco?"

"Yes, Manila and Acapulco. That was during the age of Spanish colonialism. For almost two hundred years the Spanish Galleon sailed with a fleet of protecting warships between those two ports, making one round trip every year. The Manila Galleon would be heavily loaded with riches from China and the Far East in the one direction, and with gold and silver on its return. And

222

Laoang was their main stopover. This area has a long and infamous history, filled with tales of piracy and the sinking of ships, and hidden treasure. We should find our stop at Laoang to be very interesting."

"The rest of the crew will be happy to hear the good news."

And Im thinking about Filipina girls!

Richard's bell was long and especially loud. But no one was in much of a rush. Our breakfasts had been rice, rice, and then some more rice. We expected more of the same.

We all fell into our usual seating pattern, and I started to tell them the news of our narrow miss and our chosen landfall. But before I could finish Richard appeared with his platter. Yes, there was the pot of rice. How nice. But then to our astonishment he set down a delightful looking plate of meat delectably prepared in a tomato sauce. We all dove into it, each of us being very conscious of how much he, and the next person, claimed as his portion, for the plate was not all that large.

"Hell, Richard, right on! This is just great!" Harry was elated.

"Tasty. ." remarked the Captain.

"Dee--licious!" said Laurie.

"Wow ... pretty tender too ... but I thought we were out of meat ... is this a can of something you found?" I quizzed, curious.

Fred and Joseph started to snicker. I looked at them, wondering why the humor. I took another bite. The two of them were watching me, now grinning. I suddenly became warily suspicious. I looked towards Richard ... he turned his back towards me and started to walk into the passageway. Then I understood.

"Richard ... are we by any chance eating cuscus?"

Laurie's head jerked up. "What?"

Harry and Kevin stopped cold.

The Captain and Mr. Milner paused very briefly, then continued, not really have been a part of the cuscus episode, and not caring anyway.

Fred's and Joseph's snickers turned into full-on laughter.

Laurie jumped up from the table and ran out of the mess and onto the main deck. We heard the distant sound of him spewing his mouthful over the side.

Harry and Kevin looked at their plates, hesitated, then shrugged and resumed eating.

I too hesitated, much longer than Harry or Kevin, though. Walter had been such a cute little fellow. But then he had robbed us of a major portion of our food supply, too.

"Aw what the hell!" I scooped another forkfull. "This is just about the best tasting cuscus I've ever eaten!"

At 8:00 p.m. we altered our course to 288 degrees, and at 1:00 a.m. we recognized the white three-second flash of the Batag lighthouse ahead, just off our port bow. Mr. Milner had once again brought us through with his fine navigation.

CHAPTER ELEVEN

Land of the Waray

And we have a tide here, Mr. Milner .. even our most novice sailors know that the proper time to bring a vessel like yours into the harbor is at high tide, not low tide.

"We will round the north end of the island and enter the channel to the harbor ... here ... at sunrise." Mr. Milner pointed to a narrow waterway separating the west side of Laoang Island from the Samar mainland. "The chart doesn't give us much information, but it appears to be straight-forward ... the channel depth is five fathoms ... not very deep, but enough."

It was still my watch, but of course the navigation was too critical to be trusted to me alone. Earlier Mr. Patterson had explained that we were entering the transition from the vast Pacific to the narrow San Bernardino Strait, where tidal waters were forced to converge, creating a waterway bedeviled with countless currents and riptides, and even whirlpools ... some of the currents moving much faster than our current top speed of five knots. And the exposed northeasterly shores of Batag Island and Laoang were particularly rocky and unforgiving.

The pre-dawn light was chasing us from behind, inevitably successful in its pursuit, despite the gallant effort or our one Perkins. Even though we were without food and fresh water, morale was at an all-time high ... we were all in good health, we had survived two tragic deaths, malaria, mechanical collapse, and the typhoon of the century! We felt we had endured, and could go forward to take on just about anything. And of course there was the thrill of coming to a new place, with new opportunities for adventure. Might even have a chance to

meet a lovely Filipina maiden or two.   Or maybe more than just meet them.
Wonder if Mr. Morris was right?

Yeh, Chad ... who knows ... you might even get lucky ? ?

Mr. Patterson joined us. "How are we doing, gentlemen?"

"We're coming up the western side of Laoang right now, Captain ... the channel is straight ahead," Mr. Milner replied.

The chart showed the island of Laoang to be small, maybe twelve miles long, and narrow, with perhaps three miles at it's widest point, it's topography implying that it was really one long hill, with a maximum elevation of less than five hundred feet.   Laoang Island's length ran pretty much north and south, nestled between Batag Island to the east and the towns of Mapno and Palapag to the south and Rawis to the west ... all three towns being part of the the mainland of Samar.   Laoang Harbor was situated mid-way on the island's western shore, in the passageway between the port towns of Laoang and Rawis, but we had no indication of how large the harbor was, nor the towns, nor any information about wharfs or anchorages.   We would just have to wait and see.

Mr. Patterson was watching the waters ahead.

"Damn!" I heard him mutter under his breath. "I had forgotten!"

"Captain?" I inquired, concerned.

"I had forgotten, Chad, that in this part of the world the 'color of the water' often loses its significance."

"What do you mean, sir?"

"In most of Asia the delta and inlet waters are browned by silt carried down the rivers ... silt caused either by a de-nuded landscape or simply by the fact that the river water has travelled through countless rice paddies on its journey from the mountains to the seas." he elaborated.

"Captain, you sound like National Geographic."

He chuckled. "Sorry -- it's an old theme ... but what it means for us now is we can no longer judge the depth of a channel by the 'color of the water' because the damn water is all the same muddy brown."

"Hmm ... I see."

In the distance beyond our bow I thought I could see an a transition -- almost a straight line -- where the clear blue ocean waters abruptly ended and the opague tan-colored river water began.   I supposed that was what the Captain was referring to.

But for the moment we were still afloat in pristine blue ocean, and I marvelled at the beauty around us.   It was remininscent of New Guinea.   On our port side we were passing a long expanse of sandy beach, with an occassional cottage spotted among the trees behind, and a dozen or so outrigger fishing

225

canoes pulled up high onto the sand. I picked out two small clusters of villagers standing at the vegetation line, watching us. That was surprising, considering that it was just a little past six in the morning, our time adjusted to GMT +8, of course. I thought I could make out a couple of younger ladies, and I remembered what Mr. Morris had said about Filipinas being among the prettiest ladies in the world. For a fleeting second I wanted to ask Mr. Milner if I could borrow his binoculars.

Not now, *Chad!*

I thought I would certainly have to visit that beach asap!

We reached the transition line, and the Trader was abruptly surrounded by waters heavy with suspended silt. Far ahead of us on the starboard side we could see a collection of shoreline buildings and assorted structures, which we assumed was the town of Rawis. But there was no sign of a town on our port side yet, our distant view being blocked by a short peninsula jutting out into the channel.

Mr. Patterson reached for the throttle arm.

'Ding-ding, ding-ding." He brought the arm to rest at 1/4 speed.

We were now motoring around the end of the peninsula, and we were startled by the sudden appearance of white houses with red and brown roofs, spaced close together and terraced up the steep incline of the island's natural topography. As we progressed slowly forward we could make out more details, and could see where the town ended abruptly only a few hundred yards past where it had begun, which was equally abrupt. The streets were pleasingly straight and laid out perpendicular to each other and to the shoreline, the houses and commercial buildings constructed in wood, or in stone and mortor, with distinctive Spanish styling, and were mostly finished in bright white; while the roofs were of red and brown tile interspersed with corrugated iron and frequent traditional thatching. At the top of the hill, crowning the buildings on the slope below, stood an ancient Catholic cathedral, standing dominant and sentinel to the town and harbor.

The harbor, however, was a disappointment to our two certified officers. Its shoreline facilities consisted of approximately one hundred yards of a concrete wall with wide steps leading down to the water's edge, the entire length crowded with outrigger canoes closely packed together, their double bamboo outriggers overlapping each other. Beyond that was a concrete wharf of similar length, with one ship already berthed: an old rusty coastal freighter looking remarkably like the New Guinea Trade itself. The waterway between Laoang and Rawls was perhaps only a quarter of a mile wide, suggesting that manueverability and anchorage opportunities were limited.

"Laoang is not much of a harbor, it appears, Captain," Mr. Milner observed critically, not at all thrilled by what lay before us.

Mr. Patterson had a worried look on his face. Both men studied the scene before them, analyzing the situation ... should we seek an anchorage or could we pull up to the wharf?

"I don't reckon we're going to be met by a pilot or customs vessel ... to be sure," the Captain added.

The Trader was now moving slowly, perhaps only two knots. There was a commotion on shore ... three men were running along the beach towards us, waving and shouting, but they were too far away for us to understand their intent.

"Well, at least the locals are friendly," I remarked, deciding to interpret their actions as a welcome.

"Unless they're not just waving at us, but are trying to tell us something," Mr. Patterson questioned, just as the Trader's forward motion suddenly braked, causing the three of us to lurch forward, grabbing onto hand holds for emergency support. The Captain seized the throttle: "Ding-ding, ding-ding," and brought the arm to 'Stop'.

"Bloody hell!"

"Damn!"

We had just run aground on the muddy bottom of the narrow channel.

Jeeses!

"Five fathoms my ass! ... and how did that other freighter get through?" Mr. Milner scowled.

Mr. Patterson glanced at his 1st Mate.

"Makes us look like damn fools ... we should've had Chad and Laurie taking soundings," he added.

The Captain reached for the throttle signal again. "Ding-ding," he moved the arm to 1/4 reverse, the channel water to our stem agitated in white froth and swirling whirlpools ... but with no movement.

"Ding-ding," Mr. Patterson pulled the lever all the way to 'Full Reverse'. The Trader shuddered as the propeller increased its rpms, the water to our aft became darker with mud stirred up from the bottom, mixed with increasing churning and agitation. But still no movement.

"Captain ... it's no use. Judging from the water marks on the shoreline we are at or close to low tide. We need to wait for high tide." Mr. Milner prescribed, clearly infuriated by our dilemna.

Mr. Patterson nodded, and the signal arm was brought back to 'Stop'.

While the Captain had been trying to free the Trader I had been watching the activity taking place on the shore. One of the three men was a European, and he was now in an outrigger canoe with the two Filipino men, making way towards us. A second outrigger had just left the center of the main waterfront, also directed our way.

"It looks like we're going to have visitors." I pointed out the two outriggers to the Captain and Mr. Milner. "One of them is a European," I continued.

Fred and Laurie were both on the port deck, Fred's watch just ending and Laurie's about to start, but the Captain had displaced both by taking the wheel himself.

"Hey, let's greet our visitors," I suggested to both of them, and motioned for them to follow.

We met the first outrigger ... our three visitors all had broad smiles, partly in greeting and partly, I surmised, because we had allowed ourselves to become part of the channel bottom. The European was at the bow of the canoe, and grabbed our ladder with visible ease and agility, indicating a familiarity with boats. His two companions waited in the outrigger.

I watched the man as he scrambled up the ladder and onto the aft deck, interested, because his appearance was so unusual. His feet were bare and he wore cut-off blue jeans, faded and frayed, with a colorful floral print shirt fashioned in an open-chest style, and a bright-red handkerchief wrapped around his head in ... a turban style? ... no ... like a pirate? As he approached I saw that he also wore one large gold earring.

Jeeses, the man really does looks like a pirate!

I was strongly tempted to greet him with 'Good day to you, Captain Blood', but I refrained.

Ooops ... reminds me of Errol Flynn again.

"Ahh, good day to yu' ... mateys ... the name is Bobby ... Bobby Mundy!" He pronounced his last name as if it was Mund*ee*, and he stuck out his hand. I grabbed it immediately, shaking it vigorously. I instinctively liked this guy.

"Uhh ... my name's Chad, and this is Laurie, and Fred." More hand shaking. I observed that his eyes scrutinized everything, especially Fred. "Mr. Mundy, let me take you up top to meet the Captain and 1st Mate."

Our second visiting outrigger had almost reached the Trader as well.

"Laurie, maybe you can greet our second party."

"Sure thing, 2nd Mate!"

I didn't understand why he added on the 2nd Mate, but he did. It caused Mr. Mundy to cock his head to one side and reassess me, a grin on his face and a gleaming twinkle in his eye.

He reached for my arm. "I don't think we need to meet with your Captain and 1st Mate ... you have an 'official' port representative coming aboard right behind me ... Mr. Billatmor. Best save your formalities for him. Suffice for me to tell you that low tide is in another hour, and high tide will of course be after lunch. Our tide here is over two meters ... you will be able to float off in, say, 4 to 5 hours. And the 'Alexander' berthed at the wharf there is due to disembark at eleven o'clock ... you should be able to take her place, provided you have permission from Mr. Billatmor. But that shouldn't be a problem. Can you remember all that?"

"Of course ... I think ... thank you, Mr. Mundy."

"Just Bobby, matey ... and we'll see you all on shore when you're properly berthed. Maybe we can all enjoy some stories over a jug of 'tuba'." He started back down the ladder. "And maybe you could tell me how you came to be 2nd Mate," he added, with a wide grin.

"A jug of what?" I wanted to know, ignoring the question about being 2nd Mate.

"Tuba! ... see you later mates." He waved a farewell and his outrigger pushed off just as our second visitor arrived.

Our second visitor was not nearly so agile, nor so friendly. He was a Filipino gentleman, dressed in brown slacks and a white shirt, and wore glasses. I judged him to be an official of some kind from the port ... maybe an immigration or customs officer. He was watching our first visitor, Mr. Mundy, with a frown on his face.

I waited for him to be comfortably on deck, then reached out my hand. "How do you do, sir? Our Captain and 1st Mate would like to welcome you on the bridge. Please follow me."

We shook hands and I turned to lead him down the passageway, sticking out my tongue to tease Laurie as I did so ... the hell with introducing him, or myself, if it meant I had to suffer that 2nd Mate B.S. again. I smirked to myself. On the way to the wheelhouse I realized that the gentleman hadn't offered his name. 'Hmm, unfriendly sort of guy', I mused.

"Sir, this is our Captain, Mr. Patterson, and our 1st Mate, Mr. Milner." I paused on purpose ... let the guy make his own introduction, I reasoned.

"Good day, gentlemen," he greeted, with a heavy accent that was new to my ears. "My name is Villamor Panganiban ... I am here to welcome you on behalf of the municipality of Laoang ... and to our harbor ... I am also the customs and immigration officer."

While they were shaking hands I reflected on the man's name. No wonder he didn't introduce himself to me, with a handle like that. But our new friend Bobby had said his name was something else ... Mr. Billatmor or something like that. He must have been using his first name and had said Mr. Villamor, I concluded.

"Of course, I will need to see your papers, and that sort of thing, but now I would like to invite you to our Mayor's home ... she would like to meet you, and offer you breakfast."

She? The town has a female mayor?

"Thank you," the Captain answered in return. "We appreciate your kind offer, but we do have a more pressing problem for the moment, I'm afraid. You see, we are grounded in the channel."

"Yes, yes, of course ... but there's nothing you can do now ... you are here for at least four hours ... and then you will be able to float off easy."

"But ..."

"Think nothing of it ... it happens all the time. It's not even low tide yet ... you are going to be stuck even firmer in an hour. But afterwards ... and if we time everything right, you can take the Alexander's place at the wharf. They are scheduled to leave at 11: 00 a.m.."

"Well ... alright ... but we will lower one anchor as a safeguard first. Uhh ... how many of our crew can accompany us?"

"Oh ... you and your officers ... I suppose."

Laurie and Fred and I made short order of lowering the starboard anchor. Mr. Milner had Harry and Joseph ready the aluminum dinghy as well. Mr. Panganiban visited with the Captain in the meantime and inspected the ship's papers and our individual seaman's cards. A general scramble ensued for a last minute clean-up of our immediate persons, and we all finally converged in the officer's mess, as the Captain had requested. Mr. Panganiban had returned to wait for us in his outrigger.

"Gentlemen. There's a few things we need to go over before we go ashore. First we must have at least one person stay aboard ... and the same person to bring back the dinghy."

"No problem there, Captain ... Fred's not too keen on going ashore ... not now anyway ... he just asks that we bring some food back." Harry explained on Fred's behalf, the two of them exchanging signals of agreement.

"Good. Now, the reason we're going ashore is in order to meet with the mayor ... we need to fill our fresh water tanks, we need food supplies, and we perhaps need assistance with our engines ... we are hoping we can get some sort of cooperation from the Mayor. One of our most critical problems involves payment. I must contact Sydney and let Lancey Shipping Company know what has happened. One last thing ... I don't know how many of us are actually invited to the Mayor's home for breakfast ... let's just play it by ear. But remember, we are gentlemen."

With Mr. Panganiban's outrigger and our own dinghy we could all make it to shore in one trip. As soon as it became apparent to Mr. Panganiban that this was our intent and that there were eight of us, his countenance took on a darkly somber appearance, which he maintained all the way to the shore landing. Once we had unloaded and were gathering on top of the pier, he pulled himself close to Mr. Patterson, and whispered:

"Captain ... I'm afraid eight is too many!"

'Mr. ... uhh ... Paniban ... most of us are officers ... plus ... well ... I'm afraid we've had a very rough passage and we lost our food supplies several days ago."

I was standing directly behind the two gentlemen and heard all.

Right on! Bless your heart, Captain!

Mr. Paniban didn't know what to say. Finally, he shrugged, and waved with his hand for everyone to follow.

We approached a pair of astonishingly unusual motorcycles parked with their drivers standing to the side, in the area where the landing joined the street running parallel to the waterfront. The drivers watched us with obvious expectation. I went ahead of the others to get a closer look. These vehicles must be some sort of miniature taxis, I guessed, for attached to the right side of each motorcycle was a structure designed to carry one or two passengers. The 'cage' was constructed of tubular steel, with an outside wheel of its own, and a roof. Most striking, however, was the paint job and the 'christmas tree' assortment of add-ons. Each motorcycle was a show-piece of dazzling color, of basic blue for one and red for the other, with pin-stripping and wider stripes, and chrome and reflectors and added lights, and a great variety of things that could be attached and let dangle ... especially around the edge of the roof and near the driver. I leaned over the handle bars of the closest machine and observed that from a point on the roof nearest the driver hung a Christian cross, a figurine of the Virgin Mary, a picture of his wife (I presumed) and a separate one of his two children, an artificial flower lei, and a rabbit's foot. Or at least it looked like a rabbit's foot. Anyway, the driver was well protected!

I supposed they were expecting to transport us, but either our numbers overwhelmed them or Mr. Panganiban's budget was too restricted, for instead he led us straight past them and continued walking up the opposing street. I wondered how far we were intended to go on foot, for the street proceeded up the hill at a sharp incline and the top seemed a long ways away ... this was not going to be easy. But along with the same thought I was also enjoying the charm of the street: the white Spanish style architecture, the narrow, concrete paved street, the buildings nestled close to each other, and the steepness of the roadway, flattenning out at each cross-street. I realized that it all reminded me of a similar place, very far away.

Hey ... this is just like San Francisco ... maybe like it was a hundred years ago!

I reflected back to my time on the Cap Finnisterre when we had stopped in San Francisco for three days. I had walked all over the city: all through Chinatown and even over the Golden Gate to Sausalito. Yes, this was very reminiscent of the hilly steets in the oldest section of San Francisco.

At the first corner we passed, on the left had side, was a commercial building with an office fronting the street and a sign above the door which read: SAMARTEL, INC, Telephone Service.

"Captain, here's where you can call Sydney."

"Yes ... I saw it ... later, when it opens."

It was still early, only 7:00 a.m., but a few of the tiny shops lining the street were beginning to open. We were a curious sight to their operators, and their one or two customers ... they stopped their labor or shopping to watch us as we passed. I heard words like 'American' and 'Australian' ... I guessed they didn't know what to make of Joseph and Richard. Especially with that Mohawk haircut.

We were all puffing heavily from the effort of scaling the hill, when after three blocks of what seemed like a near-vertical climb we were saved by a right turn and were able to catch our breath on an almost level street. I estimated that we were about half-way up to the cathedral at the top of the hill. With less effort devoted to walking I was now even more enraptured by our surroundings. I remembered Mr. Patterson telling me about the Manila Galleon. Guesstimating, I judged that the town must date back to the 1600's, perhaps even earlier. We passed a street on the right that was cut through a 'bump' on the side of the main slope that was the town, the street continuing past the excavated section down to the waterfront. I could see the harbor and the town of Rawis in the distance beyond. The hundred yard long excavation looked like it had been dug by hand -- a very long time ago -- and was very narrow, perhaps only ten feet wide, with the sides perfectly vertical, and the height perhaps fifty feet at its extreme. Despite the sheerness of the earth walls they were completely green with vines and moss which, with the shaded darkness, exuded an eerie impression of great antiquity.

We finally reached our destination and stopped in front of an exceptionally pretty house, somewhat larger than most of those we had passed, well maintained with a yard full of flowers and hedges, an outside patio, and the exterior proudly showing off a recent coat of bright white paint. Mr. Panganiban went ahead of us into the house, politely asking us to wait on the patio. The sound of many voices came from within the home, children's voices as well as adults.

We were all looking around curiously, especially Laurie, who ventured to walk to the end of the patio, off its end, and around the comer. The sound of a feminine squeal of surprise immediately followed. I was close to the end of the patio as well, and poked my head around the comer to investigate. There had apparently been an unexpected clashing of bodies, boy walking straight into running girl, and Laurie now stood holding a wondrously beautiful Filipina girl by the shoulders. Both were stone still, Laurie finding himself looking down into dark brown eyes, and the girl spell-bound by a red-headed giant with green eyes and a fully freckled face.

It seemed that neither moved for minutes, but of course it was much shorter than that ... she finally came back to life with a start, roughly pushing Laurie away and quickly contorting her face into an admonishing frown. "Arai!" she exclaimed, then turned and fled.

"Captain, could you and your first and second officers please join us inside. If the rest of your crew will please stay here we can accomodate them."

Mr. Milner motioned with a jerk of his head for me to join them, and the three of us entered the home ... into a dining room where a large breakfast table had been arranged, an elegant woman with marked aristocratic bearing sat at one end and two middle aged gentlemen faced us to her left. Mr. Panganiban supervised the introductions:

"Gentlemen, this is our Mayor, Mrs. Angeline Dulay-Quibal ... and this is the Captain and his first and second officers from the New Guinea Trader."

"How do you do, ma'am ... I am Captain Patterson. This is my 1st Mate, Mr. Milner, and 2nd Mate, Mr. Fletcher."

Once again there was the questioning rise of eyebrows.

Oh, how I endure! But at least this time I get a free meal ... so it's OK!

Mr. Panganiban completed the introduction: "And this is the Mayor's brother, Elias Dulay, and our Vice Mayor, Mr. Claudio Mendosa."

We sat down and were immediately served by several young ladies, one of which was the girl who had already met Laurie. I noticed that a table was being set-up on the patio, and the rest of the crew was being served there. It seemed that Laurie's new acquaintence devoted most of her attention in that direction.

"Well, Gentlemen," Mrs. Dulay-Quibal started, "Welcome to Laoang. We don't get very many visiting ships here, and yours is ... shall I say ... a little unusual." Her English, although strongly accented, was excellent. She was truly a captivating woman ... she must have been a beauty in her younger years, I speculated, for she was still well-figured and very attractive; I guessed her age to be in the late forties.

"Unusual because of our vessel's name?" Mr. Milner surprised me by taking the initiative. I sensed a defensiveness in his tone and manner, coupled with an aristocratic bearing of his own.

"Perhaps ... I assume that you have come from Papua New Guinea ... but for other reasons as well. For one, all local shipping has been ... ahh ... 'grounded' ... if you will excuse the expression ... because of typhoon 'Denance' which has just passed our area and is now causing great destruction in northern Luzon. Luckily, it's center was to the north from here and we were spared serious damage. Another reason is that you arrived very early in the morning, completely unannounced, and then went about to choose a most unorthodox anchorage."

Mr. Milner bristled at her words, the Captain squirmed, visibly uncomfortable.

Oh - oh!

"I suggest, Mayor, that you dredge that channel if you wish to maintain your port. This was once a famous port, and our charts indicate you have a depth of five fathoms in that channel."

Mayor Angeleine Dulay-Quibal smiled loftily, yet gently, at our 1st Mate: "A famous port? Laoang has never been a famous port, Mr. Milner. If you're referring to the Spanish colonial era and the 'Manila Galleon', their 'port' was at Mapno, across from the southern end of the island on the Samar mainland, and the entrance was via the deep passage on the other side of this island, between Batag and Laoang. And we have a tide here, Mr. Milner ... even our most novice sailors know that the proper time to bring a vessel like yours into the harbor is at high tide, not low tide.

I expected Mr. Milner to be red with fury, but instead he nodded to our host, with a smile that said *tu-she'*(sp ?). The Captain, however, was now even less comfortable.

"Gent ... ahh ... please, Mayor ... we have come to ask for assistance. Yes, we know about the typhoon ... we came throught it. At present we are without food and water, and we need mechanical repairs. We are taking the Trader to Hong Kong for a complete refitting ... as soon as we can resolve our needs we will be on our way."

"Those three things should not be a problem, Captain ... assuming of course that you have the means to pay for them?"

"That may be a problem, ma'am. I will phone our owner's office in Sydney this morning. We passed a SAMARTEL office on the way up the hill. But I'm not sure of the outcome. We may not have any funds available."

Mayor Angeleine Dulay-Quibal smiled, and then laughed softly. She turned to her brother and assistant, and to Mr. Panganiban.

"Villamor ... can we help these gentlemen?"

"Mayor ... I don't see how the municipality can ... we have no resources for such assistance . ."

"One thing at a time, perhaps ..." Mr. Milner intervened. "Can we first of all berth at your wharf. Just that would be a great help. Mr. Patterson can contact our Sydney office and determine the availability of funds. But we need to start filling our fresh water tanks immediately. May we tap into your municipal system?"

Mayor Dulay-Quibal again blessed Mr. Milner with her smile. She paused to carefully assess him. I thought I recognized a hint of interest that went beyond the present conversation. Why not? I weighed the possibility: Mr. Milner was, after all, an attractive, intelligent man.

Jeeses, in port only one hour and already two encounters with potential!

"Mr. Milner, Laoang is a poor municipality, and we have been struggling to provide even basic services, such as a water system. In your countries not having a municipal water supply would be unthinkable, I am sure. Six months ago I would have had to say I'm sorry, but we don't have a water system. You see, four years ago we laid a network of pipes, built a concrete reservoir, dug two wells and installed pumps. But we couldn't get enough water from those wells to make the system operational. However, six months ago our community prayers were answered. An American firm, named Reda Pump Company, from the state of Oklahoma, re-dug one of our wells to a much deeper depth and installed a new kind of pump ... an 'electric submersible pump', I believe they call it. It was part of an American assistance program. We would never have been able to pay for it on our own. So now we have a chance to repay that assistance ... in a small way, at least ... I assume your 2nd Officer is American."

She turned to me for verification. I was about to say no, but just then I received a sharp kick against my ankle from my neighbor, and I appropriately answered with:

"Yes, ma'am."

Then it occurred to me that someone else at the table knew that I was not American. Mr. Panganiban had examined our seaman's cards. I glanced at him, expecting my lie to be exposed on the spot. But Mr. Panganiban returned my glance with what I had come to assume was his normal lack of any expression ... with just the slightest hint of a smirk, however.

'Reda Pump Company' sounded familiar. I was wondering where I had heard it before, then remembered Kevin's narrative about 'cuscus' and he having heard the story from an Irishman who worked for a company of that name.

Ahh ... such a small world!

With all this talk going on food had been receiving secondary attention. At our table at least. But now was the opportunity to pay more attention. We were all very hungry ... and starved for anything except rice. The crew on the patio had been wolfing down all that was placed in front of them. Even the rice, for Richard and Joseph were there to take care of that item. Two of the three girls servicing us had been scurrying back and forth, surprised looks on their faces. One of them was, of course, Laurie's encounteree of the fourth kind. I could now see that she was unusually pretty, with a knock-out figure ... lots of curves in the right places. I caught a glimpse of muscled calves, a tiny waist, a firm, rounded, and protruding posterior, breasts that were substantial for her petite stature, high and also firm, and almost waist-length glossy black hair. It created an inner joy to watch her run back and forth.

My wandering eyes must have been kind of obvious, for at one point our host stopped her.

"I would like you to meet my niece, Bernadita ... she's Elias's daughter."

We all said hello, and I tried to capture her shy glance exclusively, but alas, even then I knew that the only one of us she had eyes for was Laurie. So, I lose out again, I thought.

Damn ... once again I lose out ... what's the matter? Do I have, a giant wart covering half my face or something?

I was immediately aware of her father's watchful eyes. Mr. Elias Dulay was clearly very protective of his beautiful daughter. 'Hmm', I mused, Laurie had better be careful ... and this is strong Catholic territory, where virginity is still considered a virtue.

How silly can you get?

But back to the food. The assortment in front of us was varied, and lots of it. But the choices were unfamiliar; I realized that we were being treated to genuine Filipino cusine. I perceived that rice was the mainstay with everything else an accessory ... but those were plentiful. Mr. Mendosa especially took delight in introducing some of the dishes. One fried fish that looked like a dark colored carp was 'talapia'; there was a dish of pork stewed in vinegar and soy sauce and a variety of spices which Mr. Mendosa called 'pork adobo'; another fish plate was barbecued 'bangus'; I was told the over-sized eggs that were a mystery to me were 'duck eggs', and then another egg -- a chicken egg -- was fertilized and when opened exposed a chick fetus. That one was a shock to me, and my expression of disgust caused everone to laugh. It was 'balut' and was supposed to be very nutritious. I didn't believe them. Finally we had a sweet made from coconut called 'malagkit'.

Our meal came to an end. We knew we had to get back to the Trader, to be ready for the rising tide, and it was clear that the Mayor and the three gentlemen wanted to begin their day's duties. Our host graciously brought our quest and the breakfast to an end:

"Mr. Panganiban will assist you in whatever way he can. Our resources are limited, but we will help as much as we are able. Please contact me at my office if you need anything from me directly."

Retracing our path back down Laoang's sloping streets, we came again to the Samartel office.

"The rest of you can go ahead ... this may take some time. Mr. Milner, you may need to berth the Trader without me," the Captain instructed, waiting for us to walk down the hill a ways before he entered the telephone office.

"Well, Laurie, looks like a certain young thing has an eye for you," I teased.

"Hell, reckon she's something else ... don't you?"

"No question ... no question at all. Just remember that we're in a Catholic country, though. I saw how her father was watching over her." I cautioned him.

"Yeh, yeh!" He laughed.

Upon reaching the landing we waved to Fred on the Trader, signalling for him to bring the dinghy. Several outrigger canoes were tied near where we were standing, and the operators of two of them started soliciting their service as a taxis. It seemed that a standard crew was one adult and two young boys ... they were chattering noisily to us, partly in broken English, but mostly in their Filipino dialect. Mr. Milner was about to take one of them up on a taxis offer, but just then our friend Bobby Mundy showed with a companion in another outrigger. And Fred was on his way as well.

"Hey, mateys ... can we give some of you a lift ... jump aboard."

He brought the bow of the canoe right up to the bottom step of the landing. I for one decided to take him up on the offer, and stepped up onto the short covered bow and then into the canoe proper.

"Come join us, Mr. Milner ... I'd like to introduce Mr. Bobby Mundy." I made sure I pronounced the *ee* at he end of his last name. Mr. Milner obliged, and followed me aboard, with Laurie and Harry right behind. Kevin, Richard, and Joseph opted for the dinghy.

"Mr. Milner ... Bobby is the one who tried to warn us this morning."

Mr. Milner and Bobby exhanged expressions of greeting, each appraising the other carefully ... like two experienced 'men of the sea', I surmised.

The design of the outrigger intrigued me. They were traditional in shape, or at least so I assumed, with a long, narrow, deep hull equipped with double bamboo outriggers. But the construction also included more modern touches, with plywood used for construction of the hull, and the vessel was powered by an inboard gasoline engine, very similar to the one on our new centriffigal pump.

Very similar!

Bobby noticed me studying the craft's construction. "They call these 'pump boats' and they're just about the standard mode of transportation throughout the islands."

"I notice they get in each other's way a lot, with those cumbersome outriggers." I had observed.

"Yeh, but that's what makes them so seaworthy ... impossible to flip them over."

"Still ... there's gotta be a more practical design ... maybe a catamaran."

Bobby just looked at me funny like.

The 'pump boat' reached the Trader.

"Mind if I come aboard with you mates? Maybe I could help you berth ... there's some sandbars and shallow water ahead to avoid."

"That would be helpful ... sorry, but we can't offer any payment ... not even a drink. At the moment we are dry and broke!" Mr. Milner replied.

"No problem ... glad to help a fellow sailor ... no payment required."

Mr. Milner replied with a soft grunt, and a nod of his head. More 'seaman's language', I supposed.

Mr. Milner insructed us all to stand by and wait for the 'Alexander' to take leave of the harbor before we raised our anchor ... there was no sense in us floating around with no place to go. In the meantime I took Bobby on a grand tour of the Trader, and he visited with Mr. Milner at the wheelhouse for awhile. Although thoroughly sympathetic, he laughed many times as we explained the sequence of events which led to our present situation. And I even related how I came be the 2nd Mate. At that part of the story he laughed the heartiest, and slapped me vigorously on the shoulder.

At 11: 00 a.m. sharp we observed activity aboard the long grey hull that was the Alexander, and on the wharf next to her as well. Our 1st Mate called us together in the officer's mess.

"I just want to make sure we understand our docking procedure ... it'll be the same as at the Navy wharf at Manus. It would be nice to have two of you already on the wharf to receive our docking line. But that's a luxury ... we don't have the extra manpower ... "

"Let me help you with that, Mr. Milner. Without waiting for an answer Bobby disappeared to the aft deck, where his companion was still standing by with the outrigger.

"Alright, then we'll have you, Chad, and Fred at the bow, Laurie and Joseph at the stern, starboard side. Harry, Kevin, please be ready in the engine room."

We watched as the Alexander's docking lines were re-drawn, and the water at her stern began to turn white, eddying ferociously. She began to inch forward, gradually pulling away from the concrete pier. Mr. Milner had decided that we should stay where we were and allow her to pass. As she came alongside we could see that she was remarkably similar to the Trader, except that she was a little longer, and her aft superstructure was designed slightly different, with a wide, fully enclosed bridge rather than a narrow wheelhouse with an open deck on each side, and her stern curved up in a 'canoe' style instead of having a flat transom section like the Trader.

As soon as the Alexander had passed, Mr. Milner gave the signal and Fred, Joseph, and I raised the anchor, again securing the chain with the bolted locking mechanism. Our plan of approach was to bring the Trader up the channel as far away from the wharf as possible and then swing around to berth with the bow pointed out of the harbor. Bobby was with Mr. Milner in the wheelhouse, and was pointing out the areas of shallow water.

"Be careful you don't come too close to that area over there, to your starboard ... see the marked-off area ... that's a mud bar ... they fish for prawns in the shallow water." Bobby pointed to a line of poles sticking out of the water, delineating a large triangular extension of a peninsula jutting out from the Rawis side of the channel.

Mr. Milner handled the wheel, signalling to Harry and Kevin in the engine room for the appropriate amount of propellsion. The Trader moved slowly past the wharf, then circled around, finally coming alongside the wooden 'fenders' that were used to cushion contact between the steel and the concrete, our position almost precisely the same as the Alexander's had been one hour before. True to his word, two of Bobby's Filipino companions were on the wharf to receive our lines. I saw that Mr. Patterson and Mr. Villamor Panganiban were also on the wharf, watching our manuever. The Captain had a strained, problemed look on his face.

I'd wager we have bad news ftom Sydney!

"Oh - oh ... there's Mr. Billatmor again. Be careful with that bloke ... he can be a sly one." Bobby addressed Laurie and I ... Laurie had come forward to join us at the bow.

"What did you call him?" I quizzed.

"Mr. Billatmor."

"But I thought his name was Mr. Panganiban, Villamor Panganiban."

Bobby laughed. "It's a local joke ... He's a real womanizer ... and 'bilat' in Tagalog means 'pussy' ... his name is Villamor, so I call him Bilat-more! "

I snickered. "Oh no, not more of this ... Laurie, his name is Mr. Cuscus!"

Bobby looked at me funny like, again.

"I'll explain that part to you later, Bobby. It's a long story."

Captain Patterson came aboard, and called a meeting in the officer's mess. Bobby invited himself along. The Captain took note of his presence, but didn't say anything, and it was OK with Mr. Milner ... Bobby had already done us a valuable service in helping to pilot us to the wharf, and I obsersved that the two had established some sort of friendship.

Hmm ... interesting!

"Gentlemen ... I have some disturbing news, perhaps even strange. You all know the circumstances under which we left Lorengau, and we therefore could expect Mr. Fitzgerald to be a little unhappy with us. Well, I'm afraid he's more than a little unhappy, or at least the owners are. He says that it is very difficult to get funds to us, because we are in a remote part of the Philippines and they have no established channels to forward monies or obtain credit. He explained that he personally was concerned for our welfare and would like to help, but indicated that Lancey Shipping Company was not so sympathetic. The bottom line, as he put it, is that 'we are bloody-well on our own'." He paused, letting that sink in. The general reaction, as I looked around the table, was 'so what do we do now?'.

"Therefore, I propose the following: Harry and Kevin, we must have both engines running in order for us to successfully navigate through these islands, and so your mechanical efforts have first priority. We cannot use outside help nor purchase any parts or pumps, or whatever ... we must make do with what we have. The rest of the crew, however, is available to you for assistance. Secondly, we have permission to take fresh water from the Laoang municipal system, which the Mayor has graciously allowed ... which in turn has something to do with Chad's national affiliation," be smiled. "We should be able to accomplish that this afternoon. Then, for food I am asking that we pool our resources together and form a fund. Hong Kong is only five days away if both engines continue to run, so we're not talking about a large amount of food." Again he paused.

"Will our money be reimbursed?" Harry wanted to know.

Mr. Patterson had difficulty answering that question. Finally, he said "I'm sorry, but I can't guarantee that. Quite frankly, the owner's attitude is puzzling. I don't really understand their position. It is as if we are, in a sense, an unwanted liability ... they seem to want to abandon us."

"Is there a question of us being paid our agreed on wages, as well ... when we reach Hong Kong?" Harry was being persistent. But he was asking the question for all of us.

"Again, I'm sorry ... I just don't know." Mr. Patterson replied honestly. Which I thought was commendable ... he could have just as easily made false promises.

"Then the bastards have left us up shit creek without a paddle!" Harry scowled.

"May I make a suggestion?" Our new friend Bobby Mundy interrupted. "Your predicament may require a little ingenuity and improvision. What if you were to, let's say, use the company's assests to create your own 'credit'?"

"What do you have in mind, Mr. Mundy?" The question was directed by Mr. Milner, who was watching Bobby, a sly smile on his face, once again.

"Well, I did happen to notice a brand new centrifugal pump in the engine room which, if you could spare it, might possibly be worth enough to put food on your table for awhile."

"Now wait a minute," Harry jumped up. "We haven't reached Hong Kong yet ... we may need that pump again."

I was doing some fast thinking.

It doesn't come easy, does it Chad?

"Harry, maybe we don't really need that pump ... after all, we did without it in our most critical hour of need before. And maybe Mr. Mundy could find a way for you to obtain a hand pump for pumping fuel from the fuel tanks to our improvised water separator, as part of the deal ... so you don't have to use a three-gallon pail any more."

I had managed to touch Harry where it counted. I had heard him grumbling about the hardship of transferring several hundred gallons of diesel a day with an open pail, and the idea of having a hand pump for the job appealed to him greatly.

"Could you do that?" Harry asked Bobby, his forehead creased in a question mark.

"Matey, anything is possible. Just leave it to Bobby Mundy!"

"Wait ... not so fast, gentlemen. What are the pumps worth, and how much will we net?" Mr. Milner quizzed.

"I reckon that big pump is worth two thousand Aussie dollars, at least, and a hand pump would cost about four hundred." Harry guesstimated quickly, his figures biased to his advantage I suspected.

The Captain and Mr. Milner directed questioning looks to Bobby, who grinned widely and shrugged his shoulders.

"It will have to be sold as a second-hand item ... but I will do the best by you gents as I can. Now, if can trust me, I have another proposal to make: I know you all need food right now, so I am willing to loan you five hundred dollars right now, and deduct that from the proceeds when I sell your pump." He waited for approval.

"Captain, I think we should take Mr. Mundy up on his offer ... all of it. We don't have much of a choice. And like the man says, it's using the company's assets to solve a company problem." Mr. Milner reasoned.

"Alright, it's agreed then ... but is five hundred enough to purchase food for a crew of nine for, say, ten days?" the Captain wanted to know.

"Captain, we are in the Philippines ... that five hundred dollars will go a very long ways. If you will trust the purchasing to me I can get you the best value for your dollar, so to speak." Bobby responded.

"Hmm ... That might be a good idea ... if you take Richard here with you."

Bobby nodded agreement, then added: "Harry, could you please bring your pump up to the main deck and I'll have my boys pick it up."

"No worries," Harry answered.

"Now, Harry how much time do you need to get us running?" Mr. Patterson continued.

"I reckon we can have everything together by sometime tomorrow morning."

"So, Harry ... who do you want to help you?" I asked.

"Just Fred ... with my 50 gallon water separator ready to put into operation, we don't have all that much to do."

"Are you going to work during the night?"

"No way, matey ... I reckon we all need a night on the town, right?"

"That's what I'm looking forward to!"

Or to check out a certain beach!

Our first priority was the fresh water.

"Joseph, Laurie ... can you get out our long fresh-water hose; I'm going to find Mr. Cuscus so we can tie into an outlet." I instructed, suddenly filled with enthusiasm and feeling like a real 2nd Mate.

But Bobby intervened: "No need to bother Mr. Billatmor, the outlet is right over here ... the 'Laoang Shipping Company' uses it all the time.

The fitting was even the right size, about two and a half centimeters. Joseph volunteered to watch over the line and make sure we filled our two tanks.

Laurie and I didn't have anything else to do, so we decided to join Richard and Bobby Mundy in the quest for food.

"The first thing is to get our five hundred dollars from my bank account. My bank is right up the street. By the way, five hundred dollars Aussie converts to twelve thousand five hundred pesos, almost on the nose, or twenty-five pesos to the dollar."

If someone hadn't shown us, it would have been difficult to recognize the location as a bank ... the sign outside was small and almost hidden, and inside was indistinquishable from a regular office, except for one short counter with a single 'cashier's cage'. Once inside, we received a great deal of of attention. Bobby was apparently well known, and he and the office girls teased back and forth mercilessly. We found that they could all communicate in English, to differing degrees, and they thought Laurie and I were both American. Laurie made sure they were corrected for his part -- he was Australian! For my part I stuck to being American ... to be consistent with the Mayor's impression, and they seemed to love Americans, so what the hell. We exited the building amid laughs and giggles and promises to return.

"These people seem to like to tease and play?" My statement was also a question.

"Oh yes, these people are Waray, and that is definitely one of their most prominent characteristics," Bobby chuckled. "You're going to be amazed at how much food this can buy, mates. I guarantee we won't spend it all," he added, as he handed the peso notes to Richard.

And so the process started. Bobby led us a few blocks away to a large semi-open market -- really a conglomeration of many individual sellers, but all under the same patchwork expanse of rusted corrugated iron roof, which was easily two hundred feet square. Richard had a long list prepared, and Bobby started at the top.

"We need to hire a 'tricycle' mates." And so now I knew what these extraordinary vehicles were called. He managed to commandeer one that was designed for carrying cargo rather than passengers, and we proceeded to load it up.

Bobby handled the bargaining with finese, using a lot of strange words and phrases.

"What language do they speak here, Bobby," Laurie quizzed, curious as I was about the exchanges going on.

"The dialect here is Waray, but the national dialect is Tagalog. I don't bother much with Waray because they all understand Tagalog. Throughout the islands there are over 50 separate dialects ... really each is a different language."

"Something like New Guinea!"

"Nah, matey, not that different."

I started to see what Bobby was talking about when it came to value. Our total egg purchase -- Richard figured we needed twenty-five dozen to be safe -- was only 600 pesos, or less than one dollar a dozen. Fruits and vegetables were even cheaper. We bought an entire stand of bananas ... I counted 14 large bunches ... for only 80 pesos. Fish and meat were the last items. Northern Samar was a rich fishing ground, and Laoang specialized in prawns.

Richard was ecstatic. "Hey, blokes, I reckon this is even cheaper than in Rabaul."

We loaded up on the huge, succulent prawns; at twenty pesos a kilo Richard couldn't resist ... we took ten kilos. Then four large tuna, a couple of red snappers, and one swordfish. We bargained for two whole legs of pork and an assortment of beef cuts. I was surprised that beef was so readily available.

"Do they raise cattle here too?" I asked.

"Plenty ... Laurie, you'd feel like you were back home if you saw them ... mostly 'Brahmas', like in Australia ... you know the kind I mean: light grey-tan colored brutes with wide horns and a hump on their backs."

Our 'tricycle' was fully loaded ... to the max ... with no room for any of us, so we walked along beside as the driver slowly motorized our precious cargo back to the Trader. Being berthed at a wharf certainly made things easier, and it seemed this one had been deisgned with the Trader in mind, the height was close to ideal. By late afternoon we had transferred everything aboard, all stored properly according to Richard's instructions. He immediately began to prepare a meal.

"Captain, we are fully re-stocked and, sir ... I mean *well* stocked ... but we still have over four thousand pesos left ..." I held out the peso notes.

"Really?" He was pleasantly startled. "What do you think we should do with it?"

"Well, sir, it belongs to Lancey Shipping Company, I suppose ... but it would sure be nice to have some beer aboard."

He chuckled. "I'll make a deal with you: one bottle of my rum, one bottle of Johnny Walker's Scotch, and the rest for beer ... under one condition.

"Yes sir?"

"We don't touch any of it until we're out of the harbor."

"Great idea, Captain!"

Bobby helped us again. The J.W. and Bacardi took a good chunk of the money, but we were able to buy sixteen dozen San Miguel Lagers with what was left.

It had been a great afternoon!

At the same time that Joseph had completed filling the fresh water tanks and was coiling our one-inch hose, Richard's bell clanged out clearly and loudly. We invited Bobby to join us. It was almost our favorite: steak and eggs and yams.

"Sorry, no potatoes in Laoang," I apologized to Harry and Kevin.

Harry was a little put out when I explained about the beer ... he wanted a couple right then.

"Harry ... he just wants to make sure we get out of this harbor sober and in one piece. Besides, if we get into it now we won't have any left when we're at sea. You want to drink beer now, go buy some!"

"Up yours, Canuck!"

Ahh ... sounds like things are back to normal!

"But if it makes you feel better, Bobby here is taking us to that village at the beach we passed this morning, to get drunk on 'tuba ...'"

"Tuba?" Harry's face twisted into a questioning scorn.

"Yeh, matey ... it's a drink made from the juice of the coconut shoot ... but we can take along some beer too," Bobby interjected.

It was still fairly early, the sun had not yet touched down on Rawis across the channel, but we were all eager to go exploring, and the thought of a visit to a beach village sounded just great. And Bobby Mundy the pirate was our escort. The Captain and Mr. Milner had declined to accompany us. I was feeling just a little sorry for them when a 'tricycle' arrived on the wharf with Mr. Cuscus as a passenger. I was about to let the rest of the crew go ahead and escort him to the wheelhouse, but he insisted on finding his own way.

"It's alright ... I'm here to escort the Captain and Mr. Milner to the Mayor's house. I can find my own way."

Ah - hah ... an invitation to the Mayor's house ... interesting, I mused.

These Waray ladies don't fool around ... they're quick!

The eight of us made an interesting sight as we made our way through the town: one pirate, a tall athletic looking red-head with big freckles, a shorter Aussie with a dumb ass grin and protruding ears, a runty Canadian with blue eyes and 'strawberry-blonde' hair, and three dark-skinned hap-castes with Chinese eyes from New Guinea, one with a strange 'American Indian' hair style. We followed Bobby straight up the steep street from the wharf, which was the same street that went through the vertical cut in the hill, all of us remarking about it's uniqueness and the fascinating green growth of vines and moss covering the wall's surface, and we then turned left at its end. Two easy blocks on the level, then a right turn to take on the steep incline once again. We passed a school on our left, and finally came to the town's summit.

The sight before us caused me to catch my breath. Directly ahead of us was a park, one block square, pretty with a grove of assorted species of trees and an open grass area, green and well maintained. And to our left was the ancient cathedral I had spotted in the morning, even more ancient and magnificent from a closer view. We turned to walk past this grand artifact.

Its construction was massive ... rectangular, yet with distinctive arches in its windows and doorways. The front was two stories tall with a simple gable end, but with multiple insets framing a series of statues and images, their identities unfamiliar to me. To the left of the gable end-section was a four-story tower, rising in three stepped, rectangular shapes to house a bell-tower at its peak.

Midway was a wide balcony rounding three sides with a railing constructed of sculptured concrete. The exterior surface was badly in need of repair and new paint ... the mortor and stone were either bared or stained black by age and the wind and rain, or covered by mildew and mosses, with the surface deeply scarred by peeling and cracking. Yet all that seemed to intensify its elegance and magnificence, causing me to feel a reverence and a solemnity ... the cathedral was a monument to something omnipotent and everlasting, the antiquity of its beginnings accentuated by the structure's own great age.

The door was open, and I led the rest of our dubious gang into the cathedral's interior. My sensation of awe and veneration escalated. The interior was vast, with row after row of simple wooden benches leading to an alter at the far end, and on the wall behind was a twenty-foot high sculpture of Jesus on the cross. To the left the exterior wall consisted of a long sequence of high arched doorways, each splendid in itself, but the accumulation was truly astonishing. The exposed walls seemed impenetrable ... at least five feet thick.

Bobby was delighted by our interest. "This is the 'St. Michael the Archangel Church' ... it was built by Franciscan Friars in 1683 ... or rather the Filipino's slaved under their direction," he chuckled. "These churches were built to withstand the raids of Moro pirates ... when the town was being ravaged everyone would seek refuge inside. These massive walls withstood many of those murderous raids."

His words shattered my trance, but encouraged me to consider yet another facet of this awesome place.

From the cathedral we turned right at the end of the park, and passed several buildings which looked like they housed government offices. Sure enough, a sign on the first one read 'Office of the Mayor', and a plaque honoring the 'Mayor of Laoang, Mrs. Angeleine Dulay-Quibal'.

"Bobby, is the Mayor a widow?" I inquired.

"Yes, matey, she is ... quite a lady! Her husband died a few years ago. He was a senator ... and her father was once mayor of Laoang. And she is a former Miss Northern Samar. Yes, quite a lady ... sharp as a whip, but with a tongue like a whip as well. Not a lady to fool with."

Laurie was lagging behind, wandering a bit to the park side of the street. I was curious why, then saw the object of his attention. Mr. Dulay's daughter, Bernadita, was in the park, sitting alone at a picnic table about two hundred feet away, reading a book, but demurely glancing in Laurie's direction every few seconds.

Nope, these Waray ladies don't fool around at all!

Thinking of Joseph and Sandie in Lorengau, I decided to tease him.

"Well, it's your turn now, buddy ... I think she wants you to go over and talk to her."

"Yeh, I think I'll do just that ... catch up with you blokes later."

"Good luck. And remember ... keep the zipper up!"

He laughed. I didn't think he took my words serious. Not at all!

We were now walking downhill, which was a welcome change considering the beer we were carrying … we had stopped at one of the tiny shops on the way and had purchased a few six packs.

"What's the name of the beach, Bobby?"

"Onay ... Onay Beach ... a nice place ... there'll be plenty of tuba there, and some company ... might even be a girl or two.

We reached the bottom of the hill, then up and down a couple more, a left turn where the concrete pavement ended, a few hundred yards more, and we were finally at Onay Beach.

The sun had hidden itself comfortably behind the green hills of the Samar coast across the inlet, and twilight was settling gently around us. Bobby had brought us to one of the thatch-roofed cottages I had viewed early this morning, and we were all seated at a large picnic-type table, roughly constructed of wood and protected by a separate thatch roof of its own. He had introduced us to Manuel and Rojelio … Rojelio had gone to find us some 'tuba'. In the meantime we opened a round of San Miguel and watched the sunset. Several villagers came by and joined us … they were all very friendly, smiling and laughing, and chattering in what I took to be Waray. Among them were a couple of older ladies. Then the 'tuba' arrived: eight one-gallon glass jugs of an opaque, reddish colored fluid -- the kind of jugs with a little finger handle at the spout, so you could hook your first finger through the hole, toss the jug over your upper arm, and truly indulge.

Reminded me of one night in Edmonton, during the summer, when four of us had taken this half-Cree girl who could drink like ... a fish ... on a party of our own making out in the woods south of the city and we ran into these older guys who had forced each of us to drink their ultra cheap wine from a jug just like those ones until we were all drunk out of our minds and sick and we tried to make it home but I got a flat tire and I woke up in the morning flat on my back in a farmer's front yard where I had taken our date to find her a ride home and when I got back to my Chevy the four doors were all wide open, one of my buddies was asleep in the car and the other two were crashed in the grass in the ditch and then we drove the ten miles home on the flat tire … but that's a long story that I'd prefer to save for another time. Anyway, same jugs, and I've never been able to drink wine since.

"Bobby ... we are all curious as hell about you." I wanted to find out about this guy … Laurie and I had been busting with curiosity all day long.

"What would you like to know, mate?" Bobby Mundy smiled and settled back. I could tell he was getting ready to really lay it on.

247

"Well, for starters, we've been trying to figure out your nationality. I took you for Aussie, but Harry here says 'no way' … that maybe you've spent some time in Australia, but you weren't born there."

He chucked. "You're right, Harry ... my nationality is Australian ... I carry an Aussie passport, that is ... but I have lived in many countries: France, England, Germany, Spain. But I was born and raised in Holland. You and I have the same ancestors, Mr. Fletcher." He addressed the last part to me.

Now it was my turn. "Bobby, then you are Dutch-Aussie ... but I think you are really all ... pirate!"

That caused him to burst out in a long laugh. He looked at me appraisingly.

"Yes ... I am ... that I am!"

"What?" Three of us asked at the same time.

"First, you blokes have got to try this tuba. We have two kinds here: one jug of the 'fresh' tuba for the beginning taste, and the rest is 'aged' tuba … one week old. It's called 'bahalina'."

Glasses were found from somewhere and the crew of the New Guinea Trader tasted our first tuba. Harry spit his out. Kevin grimaced. Our New Guinea nationals smiled ... they liked it. That made me suspect that they were maybe used to something similar in Rabaul. I tasted mine. ". . eeuuhh!" Definitely not easy to swallow. It had a bitter plant taste, followed by a sticky dryness. I really didn't think I wanted any more.

"How do they make this stuff?" I asked, my eyes squinted near shut and my mouth twisted in a frown.

"Ahh ... from the coconut tree. You see there at the top, where the baby shoots for the nuts come out ... ?" He was pointing to the top of a nearby tree.

"What do you mean by 'shoot'?" Kevin wanted to know.

"The 'shoot' is a long tubular growth, out of the top of the tree, that eventually flowers and then the nut grows ... a young shoot."

"OK ... got you!" Kevin understood.

"Well, you climb the tree and poke that shoot with a tube ... any kind of tube ... and you tie a gourd or some kind of container to the tree ... and in about four hours time one shoot will give you over a liter of fluid. They then add some bark from a certain mangrove plant to give it its red color, and whatever else, and presto! If it's absolutely fresh it has no alcohol content. Afier one day it has a fair amount, and that's what you just tasted. But after one week … that's the good stuff … more expensive, though."

"How much?" Harry the miser was interested in price, even though he didn't like the taste.

"Twenty pesos a jug for the fresh, forty for the week-old."

CHAPTER TWELVE

Of Spanish galleons ...
and the Treasure of Solomon

**Above the belt is yours to enjoy,
but below is mine to keep.**

"So, Bobby, why are you here in Laoang?"

He looked at me coolly, and then the rest of us, deliberating on what he wanted to reveal.

"Would you like to hear a truly wild story ... which also happens to be the absolute truth?"

"Shoot!" I urged.

"Yeh, matey, lay it on," Harry added ... he had just tried the stronger tuba.

And now a word to the reader. The following is as it was related to us that night, and later, by the pirate, Mr. Bobby Mundy (pronounced Mundee), as best as I can recall. It *is* the truth ... I shit you not! Take it as you will.

"The reason I'm here, mates, is to watch over the 'Treasure of King Solomon'."

"I'm sorry?" Kevin suddenly came to life, startled by what Mr. Mundy had said.

"Yes! Yes ... the last of the Treasure of Solomon is hidden here in Northern Samar, and I am here to watch over it, and to claim it if and when it is recovered."

"What?" I said.

"Come a little closer, mateys, and let me explain. Have you ever heard of the Templar Knights?"

Everyone shook their heads. Everyone except Kevin, that is.

"But you know about pirates, of course, and 'Friday the thirteenth' and the old pirate's ditty that goes 'Ho ho ho and a bottle of rum, fifteen men on a dead man's chest' . . right?"

"Yes."

"Well, that's what the 'Templar Knights' are all about, my mateys. They go back many centuries to the time of the Crusades, those gallant and hard fought wars between the noble Christian armies of Euope and the Arab hordes, battling for Palestine ... the land of Christ and the old testament. The order of the 'Templar Knights' was organized in the aftermath of the First Crusade, in the year 1118 ... they were a small band of knights who took the three vows of povery, chastity, and obedience ... to dedicate their entire lives to the protection of pilgrims travelling to the Holy Land. There were originally nine of them, French and English, led by the first 'Grand Master', named Hugues de Payens ... nine knights who founded a great order of knights and a timeless legend ... who gained great fame and honor for their heroic expoits against the Arabs. The 'Templars', as it were, had taken their name from their original headquarters in an ancient mosque which had been built on the Temple Mount in the Holy City of Jerusalem, named the al-Aqsa Mosque, and which was the actual site of the original Temple of Solomon. Yes ... the very site. One of the Templar's secret objectives, we are told, was to re-build the sacred Temple of Solomon, built according to the specifications prophesied by Ezekiel, in the Old Testament. The Templars, intending to be builders as well as knights, modeled themselves after the warrior-masons of Zorobabel in the Bible, who worked holding the sword in one hand and the trowel in the other. Thus the sword and the trowel became part of their insignia, and also that of the society of Free Masons centuries later.

Following the crusades the Templar Knights became guardians of trade between the Far East and Europe, eventually becoming extremely wealthy and powerful, their form of guarding trade evolving from mere physical protection to include such things as insurance and finance. They massed incredible wealth, a part of which was the very 'Treasure of Solomon' itself, which they mysteriously came to possess. Some say it was found buried deep beneath their headquarters on Temple Mount. Others say it was part of their booty from the Arabs."

Bobby paused to take a long drag on the week-old tuba.

"What *was* the Treasure of Solomon?" Kevin took the opportunity to ask.

"Aahh ... I suspect that you know something about the things I am telling you."

"No ... not really ... I'm just aware that there are different 'versions of history' ... the conventional, formal history that we teach our children in school and that we all pretty much agree on, and 'other' versions ... one of which I think you are about to tell us."

"And therefore my version is a lie ... is not true?"

"Not at all. There's no doubt in my mind that the conventional version is full of a lot of garbage. There are vested interests that want to keep the story as it is."

"Aahh ... Kevin, you have stated it well! May I continue."

"Please do."

"To answer your question, the Treasure of Solomon was, and is ... books. Yes, books ... books of knowledge! I tell you the fair dinkum truth, my mateys! Not gold and silver and exotic jewels ... but books! Books of knowledge!"

The dubious crew of the New Guinea Trader stared at Bobby Mundy through incredulous eyes.

"Books? What were the books all about?" Kevin was intrigued.

"Ahh ... we will come to that, but first the story of the Templar Knights. By the end of the 13th century the wealth and power of the Templar Knights rivaled that of any of the major powers of Europe, and they were seen as an emerging threat. Especially to the Vatican, and especially because the Vatican wanted the Treasure of Solomon ... and the knowledge contained in those books. Things developed to a point, when, in the year 1307, Pope Clement the 5th formed an alliance with his 1st cousin, Phillipe le Bel, then the King of France ... an alliance to destroy the Order of the Templars and to capture the Treasure of Solomon. The Treasure and the headquarter of the Knights had converged at that time in Paris. The time of the siege was set ... it was to be on the morning of a Friday the Thirteenth, in the month of October. But in the darkness of the night before, the band of Knights who were the guardians of the sacred treasure, and who had been pre-warned, escaped down the Seine River in eighteen galleys. The small fleet held 300 Knights and their families, and 220 tons of treasure and possessions. The sail of the Templar Knights had traditionally been white with the blood-red 'Rose-Croix' ... the famed 'red cross patee' itself, the four ends splayed to form an eight-pointed cross ... but that night they blackened their sails to prevent detection, and this was the beginning of the forever-to-be-feared black flag of the pirates. The skull, two cross bows, and a sword came later."

Another pause for more tuba.

The San Miguel was all gone by now, as well as the more user friendly variety of tuba, so we were all heavily into the 'aged' variety, none of us seeming to mind its taste any more, for reasons of convenience and, perhaps, because of the spell that our pirate story-teller had cast upon us. It was now dark, with no moon yet, for we were now in a quarter-moon phase that rose in the east at about midnight. There was a great deal of activity on the beach, and I realized that the fishing boats were being prepared to launch out to sea. Each had one, sometimes two kerosene latterns attached to a pole high above their hulls.

"So the Templar Knights became pirates?" Kevin was anxious to continue.

"Yes ... the original pirates, in the classical sense ... yes, in the true classical sense ... you must understand that these were educated men of wealth and power. They were gentlemen. The English word 'pirate' is derived from the Greek word 'peiran', which means 'to boldly go'. Does that phrase sound familiar to anyone?"

We all shook our heads, not having the slightest idea what he was getting at.

"How about 'Star Trek?'"

Harry smirked. Kevin smiled. A couple of 'aahh's were heard.

"And in the end Captain Kirk defied the orders of the Federation and gave the command to 'head for the 2nd star on the left'. Our man Kirk was a pirate, true to the tradition!"

That was too much. I chuckled out loud. Bobby smiled at me, knowingly, and continued:

"Now ... you must understand that the order of the Templar Knights was very large indeed, and they were spread all over Europe. On that fateful day, that black Friday the Thirteenth, almost every Templar Knight in Europe was arrested and placed in chains ... to be charged with heresy and to be tortured, murdered, and even burned at the stake ... and their wealth extracted, of course. For this was the second stage of the infamous and hideous 'Inquisition', sponsored by the Holy Catholic Church ... the Church had already applied this evil on the Jews ... but history tells us that it was the wealth and treasure of the Templars that they were really after. The tortures and murders of the Inquisition continued for several years, ending with the burning at the stake of the Templar's last 'Grand Master', a Frenchman named Jacques de Molay. It is said that de Molay cried out the innocence of the Templars even as the executioners set fire to the wood pile at his feet, and he pronounced a curse on both Pole Clement V and King Philip IV, calling on them to meet him at the throne of God before one year was out. It is a matter of historical fact ... both the Pope and the French King died before the end of that year, in obedience to the curse of Jacques de Molay."

More tuba.

"But back to the treasure ... the one group in Paris had succeeded in escaping. They stealthily sailed their small galleys down the French coast to the port of La Rochelle, where the Templar Knights operated a naval station, and secretly regrouped their families and treasure into 22 galleons, and then separated in different directions, and for different purposes. Of the 300 Knights, one third -- mostly the older gentlemen -- sailed to Portugal and renounced the society of the Templars, and secretly re-organized as the 'Knights of Christ'. Another third, those with young families and less wealth, went to Northern Ireland. Their

252

successive adventures led them, shortly, to Scotland where they helped King Bruce defend his country against England. Legend has it that they were the very knights who led the Scottish to victory at the Battle of Bannock Burn. For a long time Scotland remained the official 'headquarters' of the Templar Knights, but eventually they were absorbed into the populace and disappeared as an organized society of knights.

Now, the final third undertook the quest of preserving the Treasure of Solomon, and literally vanished from the European world. Their original fleet consisted of 18 galleons with 18 captains, each dedicated to the mission of burying their portion of the Treasure in some remote place on the globe. Three of the 18 galleons were lost at sea, or in battles, but fifteen treasures were successfully buried in fifteen separate locations. We know that one was at Oak Island, in Newfoundland, and another close to the southern shore of Lake Ontario, at the head of the St. Lawrence River. Others were in various parts of the Americas."

At this Bobby Mundy stopped, and scanned me slyly, an expectant smile on his lips. But the significance of his questioning gaze was lost on me. Besides, I had a question of my own to ask.

"Newfoundland, the Americas ... in the 1300's?" I interrupted. This was not according to my history lessons.

"Ahh ... you believe all that nonsense about Columbus being the first? Total nonsense! Us 'peirans' had been travelling the globe 'unofficially' for a very long time before that gentleman came along. In fact, Columbus himself was a 'peiran' in the Templar Knights tradition. We know, for example, that as a young lad he had apprenticed aboard a pirate ship and that he was associated with the Knights of Christ, as were other famous Portuguese explorers of the same era, such as Prince Henry the Navigator, and Vasco da Gama. And, as proof of what I am saying, the Templar's original red cross patee was embrazened on the sails of the Nina, the Pinta, and the Santa Maria. The very same, as any history book will show."

I wasn't sure I was buying into all of this, but it was a good sailor's yarn and Kevin, for one, was absolutely captivated.

I noticed that a couple of younger ladies had joined us. I kept catching one's eye. She was slim and had bad teeth, but was still kinda pretty. In fact, she was getting prettier all the time. Several villagers were starting a fire on the beach, and the ladies were preparing prawns to be roasted over the fire.

We were invited to change our location. There was a general commotion as we all rose to comply, commandering our jugs with us and squatting down in the cool night sand, forming a circle around the fire.

The fishing boats were now all out on the waters of the bay and the mouth to the harbor, and had been joined by a large number of similar vessels from Laoang and Rawis.

"Hey, you guys, look at this ...." I pointed out towards the boats.

We all paused a moment to take in the scene ... a hundred and more lights dancing and flickering over the water, like a city at night, viewed from a distance.

"Yes, they're night fishing ... this is the time that the fish feed, and the lights attract them to the surface ... a pretty sight, isn't it?" Bobby explained.

"Hey, is *that* 'tuba'?" An outside voice interrupted. It was Laurie.

"Sit down, mate, and try some of this ... not so bad once you get used to it." Harry paused to take another sip, grimaced, and handed the jug to Laurie.

"This bloke has been telling us pirate stories. He's just about to rewrite the history of the world." Harry continued, sounding like he was well on his way to blissfull inibriation.

"Yes, let Bobby continue." Kevin urged everyone to get back to Bobby's story.

"Ahh, where were we ... the fifteen surviving captains had each buried their part of the Treasure, yes. Well, there had to be a way of recovering the buried treasures, and Scotland was now the 'head office' of what was left of the Templars. Each captain was instructed to prepare a careful map showing the site of his buried 'chest', and to somehow get that map back to Scotland. Here's where we begin to understand the ditty 'fifteen men on a dead man's chest' ... meaning the fifteen captains, each possessing a 'chest' of treasure bequeathed from the 'dead' King Solomon of old. To make a long story short, the maps and eventually the buried treasures all met different fates. We know that one or two reached Germany, and became the inspiration for the mystical order of the Rosicrucians, and their pursuit of magic and alchemy ... known for their crude attempts to use the knowledge of their part of the treasure to make gold from lead. We also know that one or two more became the possession of the order of Freemasons, which was a secret society formed from an assorted group of Templar Knights who had survived the horror of the Inquisition. The Roman Catholic Church was eventually successful in capturing several of the treasures, and they are even now hidden in obscurity within the thick walls of the Vatican sanctuary in Rome ... the knowledge contained in those treasures concealed from the minds of men. However, we of the 'Bretheren of the Coast' have remained guardians of several of those original fifteen 'chests' as well. Finally, two sites were later re-dug up by Templar peirans and re-hid in a far-away place ... in the Philippines ... here in Northern Samar. They are the last of the surviving fifteen parts of the Treasure."

"And that brings us to you?" Kevin quizzed.

"Yes."

"OK, explain that part."

Bobby Mundy paused, seemingly to ponder once more about what he was willing to reveal.

"Alright ... I will. Pirates have more or less survived down through the centuries, and have separated into many different groups. There are of course the ruthless bandits and thieves who are only cut-throats and who give us real peirans a bad name. But there has endured a true 'Bretheren of the Coast', and at present there are two groups who still follow the original ideals and who are direct descendents of the Templar Knights. One of the groups I discount and don't want to talk about, the second is the 'Order of the 13th', which was originally founded on that day in the year 1307, a Friday the 13th in the month of October. I, gentlemen, am the current 'Grand Master' of that order."

"Wow!" I blew out ... just then realizing that I had been kind of holding my breath.

"Why the Philippines ... and why Northern Samar?" Kevin wouldn't let up.

"Simply because it was as far away from the Vatican as you could get ... at that time at least ... and this area is the first natural landfall for voyagers from the eastern direction. Magellan for example, even General MacArthur during WWII, and of course the Spanish Galleons ... they all landed in Samar. But also because the Templar pirates found the Waray to be easy to get along with and of their own kind."

"Why do you say that?"

"The Waray were a seafaring people, actually pirates like ourselves, who used to plunder the Chinese junks and Arabic traders that passed through these straits, and we believe that the Queen of the Waray at that time assisted in hiding those last two chests of the Treasure of Solomon."

"Wow, what a story!" I was intrigued, wondering how much to believe.

"Can you answer my earlier question now. What were the books all about? And why did the Vatican want them?" Kevin pushed on.

"Ahh ... this is the most incredulous part ... I'm not sure you blokes could take this."

"Try us." Kevin was relentless.

Bobby took a long pull at a jug of tuba. One of the not-so-old ladies sat down beside him and started to tickle him. They obviously knew each other already. The girl with the bad teeth sat down between me and Kevin; she was smiling, but trying not to smile at the same time, being self-conscious about her teeth. The second younger Filipina squeezed in between Harry and Laurie. The two girls and two other older ladies then began roasting the prawns and feeding them to us.

"These ladies live lonely lives ... their husbands are out fishing at night, when they want to play, and then the husbands sleep during the day, when they are awake. But be careful, gents, the husbands are right out there!" Bobby cautioned.

Kevin wanted Bobby to continue, but our pirate was suddenly reluctant to talk more about the Treasure of Solomon. The spell had been broken. But I was very curious about lighter matters.

"Bobby, do you know much about the Manila Galleon?" I asked.

"Oh yes, the Manila Galleon is an important part of the history of pirates."

"Where did they land here ... we thought it was here at Laoang ... but it wasn't, was it?"

"No, it was at Palapag, which was originally located where Mapno is now.

But the town of Palapag was moved inland to give more protection from Moro raids ... that was during the late 1500's ... so Mapno is the actual harbor site. They came in through the deep channel between Batag Island and Laoang Island, on the other side."

"I see."

"You have to realize, the Manila Galleon was a good-sized vessel, and she was always accompanied by a fleet of between sixteen and thirty smaller warships. The waterway on the other side of Laoang was perfect. They would stop at Palapag to renew their fresh water supply, and then proceed to Capul, and then to Manila. Take note that 'Capul' is short for 'Acapulco'. So Palapag and Capul were the only two stops in the entire voyage."

"What did they carry?"

"Well, conventional history tells us that Manila had a flourishing trade with China and other parts of the Far East, and that these riches were taken to Mexico, to be then carried back to Europe, and the returning Manila Galleon carried silver and gold in payment. But what few people realize is that the Philippines was also rich in gold and silver. This archipelago is actually part of the Asian continent, and its geology is ancient. There's gold being panned in the tributaries of the Victoria River, at the other end of Northern Samar, right now. I know cause I've done a bit of it myself"

"Was the Manila Galleon ever attacked by pirates?" I wanted to know.

Bobby chuckled. "Oh yes, we pirates were very active ... we sank a large number of the Galleon's fleet ... but the Manila Galleon itself was taken only twice in the two hundred years it made its annual journey. Once at this end, when the entire fleet was sunk except for two warships, and once at the Mexico end, which is an interesting story."

"Tell us about it."

"The pirate's name was Roberts, and he had once served with the infamous Henry Morgan. He was actually only the 'quartermaster'. But in those days the quartermaster was the navigator and was actually more important than the Captain. Anyway, there were two pirate vessels under his command, and they had spent five weeks circling in the waters off Acapulco, waiting. The Manila Galleon, her name was the Santa Clara, and her fleet had survived two previous attacks and a couple of storms ... there were only eight companion ships left.

Four days out of Acapulco they encountered Robert's two pirate ships, and sank them both. But the surviving pirates had manned two of their own longboats ... there were twenty men in one and twenty-seven in the other ... and they rowed towards the Santa Clara. Now, you must realize that the Manila Galleon was manned and armed by over two hundred of her Majesty's finest. Well, the Spaniards were so frightened when the 47 pirates began scrambling up the sides of the Santa Clara that most of them fled by jumping into the sea. The Santa Clara was taken to Peru, stripped of her riches, and sunk."

By now we were all fully inebriated. It was a classical scene. Eight shipmates sitting around a fire on a sandy beach, listening to an old-timer spin his yarns of pirates and treasure, drinking a wild native drink served by pretty local ladies, all of us drunk out of our trees.

Laurie was having a terrible time with the tuba and wasn't very interested in the girl next to him, and wanted to go back to the Trader. Couldn't blame him really ... the girl was certainly no match for Bemadita. Harry was teasing one of the older ladies and trying to grab the girl beside him at the same time. She was constantly squealing and slapping at his hands ... and he was enjoying himself thoroughly. But he was also so drunk he could hardly stand up, or sit up. Kevin was disappointed that Bobby hadn't continued with his explanation of what was in King Solomon's books, and wanted to call it a night. As for myself, well, the girl with the bad teeth had my zipper down and was teasing me but *he* was too drunk to stand up either and I was having visions of being viciously murdered by angry Catholic husbands anyway. Maybe another 'Inquisition'!

I wonder if Catholics still burn people at the stake?

And then we ran out of tuba!
So we all slowly rose to our feet, thanking our guests as graciously as we could, in our condition, and I pulled up my zipper while the girl with bad teeth giggled, and we all began the long trek back to the Trader. Again we must have been some kind of sight ... the same strange assortment but this time noisily unsteady on our feet, wending our weary way home.

"You say that the Templar pirates were assisted by the 'Queen' of Waray? Do you know that it was a 'queen' and not a 'king'?" I probed Bobby, while we were walking.
"Yes, our information is that it was a queen ... and that fits what we know about society as it existed in the Philippines prior to the arrival of the Spaniards. Most of the Philippine cultures were matriarchal ... the women were dominant and held the power. In most of their religions the women were the 'priestesses', for example."

"I see ... I suppose that would explain a woman mayor and a woman president too. But it doesn't seem to fit in with Catholicism."

"Perhaps. But then Catholicism may not be as male dominant as one would think. Compare the significance of the Virgin Mary, for example, in Catholicism versus the Protestant dominations."

"Hmm ... Speaking of women ... what do you know of 'bar fines' and that sort of thing?" I slurred.

"Bar fines? Ahh ... I think I know what you mean. That's mostly in Manila, or near the American bases at Angeles and Olangapo, and Cebu. But we have a little bit of that here as well. Tomorrow I'll take you to Catarman ... and the 'Green Park Cafe'."

"OK ... sounds great!"

The Green Park Cafe ... has a nice ring to it, and the suggestion of promise!

"Yes ... and then maybe you can tell me what you know about the 'Urim and Thummim'. Bobby Mundee was eyeing me carefully.

"What did you say?" I was startled by his question, not understanding his choice of words, the tuba definitely not helping.

"The Urim and Thummim!" He laughed. "You're a Mormon and you don't know about the Urim and Thummim?"

"The Urim and Thummim?" I quizzed, still perplexed. Then I remembered. "Oh ... you mean the Urim and Thummim?"

"Yeh, Chad that's what I mean." Bobby was amused by my troubled memory.

"The 'stones' that Joseph Smith used to read the writings on the plates?" I added.

"Or that the Hebrews used to read the writings of their god ... that they carried with them in the 'Ark of Covenant' ... and that King Solomon used."

"What?" Bobby's question and implication overwhelmed me. And my fuzzy brain was not reacting quite up-to-par. But we couldn't continue our conversation, for we had reached the waterfront and I was caught up in the scramble to re-board the Trader. I waved back to Bobby, still standing on the wharf.

So how did he know I was a Mormon? And the Urim and Thummim??

As I passed through the wheelhouse I encountered Mr. Milner, sitting in a deck chair on the port deck.

"Chad ... come join me for awhile."

I sat down in the adjoining chair, not at all too soberly, which Mr. Milner was quick to notice.

"You boy's been drinking tonight?"

"Yup ... uhh ... yes sir ... we had our try at tuba ... a local coconut drink ... wild stuff."

"Chad, you can dispense with 'sir' ... if you like ... at least when we're not 'on duty', shall we say."

"Sure."

"Chad, do you mind if I tell you a few things?"

The question startled me. Even in my not-so-quick-to-think state. Mr. Milner had something heavy on his mind.

"Not at all, Mr. Milner."

"John ... how about just John ... we've been through a bit, you and I ... and you've been a friend. At least that's how I feel."

"Hmm ... thank you ... John ... uhh ... me too."

"I'm afraid I may have to leave the New Guinea Trader."

It took a couple of seconds for that to register, the information having to penetrate a dense mist of tuba, then I understood what he had said.

"What ... you mean leave the ship ... now?"

"Yes."

"But why?"

"Mr. Patterson told me that Mr. Fitzgerald had said that I would be put into custody when we reached Hong Kong ... by the police."

"What? On what charge?"

"It has to do with the matter of the captain on board a sailing schooner having been lost overboard."

"Oh ... yes ... I heard about that."

"You did? Hmm ... Mr. Fitzgerald also said that Lancey Shipping Company may add a charge or two of their own. Against the Captain as well."

"Wow!"

"Mr. Patterson has said he will stick it out till Hong Kong ... and face the music, so to speak. But for myself ... I'm afraid it's just not worth it."

"But what will you do?"

"I don't know ... stay here in the Philippines for awhile ... maybe right here in Laoang. I could live very well here on my remittance stipence. Maybe with this new event I can threaten to go back to England and thereby have the stipence raised," he chuckled. "And I have become interested in a certain lady here."

"Is this definite? And is the lady our Mayor?"

Mr. Milner was surprised at my mention of Mayor Dulay-Quibal. "Yes, it is ... and the lady is Mayor Angeleine ... she's quite a lady. How did you know?"

"Uhh ... I thought I could recognize some electricity between you two. And that's the second time today that someone said 'she's quite a lady'."

"What?"

"Mr. Mundy said the same thing."

"Ahh ... yes ... Mr. Mundy. We have a lot in common, he and I."

"You do?"

"Yes, we're both pirates, in a sense."

"You mean you think he's a real pirate? And things like ... The Order of the 13th actually exist?"

"Let's just say I know he's a pirate. He's a very well-to-do man, you know ... and I have heard of the 'Order of the 13th'. Has he been telling you tales?"

"Oh yes ... he kept us entertained all evening."

"Well, no harm ... I suppose ... but keep in mind that not all of what he says are only pirate's tales. And he may have a request to make of you. Remember that you can trust him."

"Wow ... but I'm not sure what you mean ... about a 'request'!"

"Never mind … but I do have one request of my own, Chad ..."

"Yes, Mr. Milner … uhh ... John."

"If this ever does come to anything ... if you are ever questioned … I know I can't ask very much ... but if you ... and the crew ... could put in a good word for me, so to speak. It would be nice if the entire 'mutiny' part was forgotten."

"Mr. Milner," I interrupted. "I will do what I can ... I don't think you have anything to worry about from us."

"Thank you. Now there are a couple of things I want you to be aware of. It has to do with Lancey Shipping Company, and Mr. Fitzgerald. I can't get rid of the nagging notion that they never intended for this vessel to make it to Hong Kong, and that there is still the possibility of some sort of interference to cause this ship to be lost. It is possible that Mr. Fitzgerald told Mr. Patterson what he did in order to encourage me to do the very thing I'm about to do, which is to abandon the voyage ... it's just a possibility."

"And with you out of the way the Captain would have the chance to shipwreck us?"

"No ... I'm not saying that. It *is* a remote possibility, I suppose ... and I used to think that at one time … but I've discounted that charge as just my drunken stupidity. I've come to know and trust Mr. Patterson. I don't think the man would ever do anything intentionally, and I don't think he has orders to do anything ... it's simply that without me around it is just that much easier for something to go wrong. The passage through the San Bernadino Strait and the rest of the way through the islands is one of the trickiest passages in the world, full of chances to be shipwrecked."

"Then you shouldn't leave us. Maybe what Mr. Fitzgerald says *is* a hoax, like you say."

"I'm sorry ... but I can't take the chance."

"But to finish the thought, let me say one more thing. From one perpective you could conclude that Mr. Fitzgerald and Lancey Shipping Company 'designed' this trip to fail. Maybe they didn't give anybody 'orders' to scuttle the vessel, or do something to directly cause a shipwreck, but the way the crew was put together and the choices regarding our equipment, especially our safety and navigation equipment, was done in such a way as to 'encourage' failure ... the voyage was designed to fail! One nagging thought that supports that idea is that not only did they choose what they thought was a totally incompetent crew, but also one with the least liability should there be any deaths."

"Least liability ... what do you mean?"

"I mean they chose a crew which would cause them the least problem and the least financial cost should a shipwreck and deaths actually occur."

"I still don't follow."

"Alright ... Mr. Morris had no family. Mr. Patterson and I learned that. The same with Mr. Patterson ... he has a daughter somewhere, but that's all. Harry and Laurie aren't married, not too much of a problem there. You and Kevin are foreigners. The hap-caste boys are also single. And I'm a crazy remittance man with a pending charge of murder over my head. And, not least, we are all non-union. The Australian maritime union is very strong, and a company pays dearly when there's a death. But not a single person on board belongs to a union."

"Wow!"

"Anyway, those are my thoughts, whatever they're worth. Just keep them in mind. And good luck!"

Once again I paused at the rail outside my cabin. What a day this had been. Mr. Milner leaving the ship. And the notion that our voyage was 'designed to fail'.

Is this part of your warning, Captain Rodney McKay??

And Bobby Mundy and his wild tale. And the Urim and Thummim. He had made a connection between his story and the Urim and Thummim, and Mormonism. What did he mean?

The night was black. A quarter moon had just lifted itself above the horizon in the east, but was yet hidden by the high hill that was the island of Laoang. It was the time of night when all slept in the small town and there was no one awake to witness mysterious events. Three figures moved darkly and silently across the concrete wharf to the Trader's edge, each weighed down with a sizable 'box' supported on one shoulder. They entered the entrance to the ship's superstructure, which was next to the officer's mess. A few minutes later they re-emerged, this time two of them supporting an orange painted object between them, which they hoisted over the ship's rail and onto the wharf, the entire procedure having been accomplished without sound. Before leaving the pier one of the three paused to wave back towards the Trader, to a fourth figure who stood watching from the starboard deck beside the wheelhouse.

"Clang - clang. . clang - clang!" I opened my eyes … they hurt. I turned my head … 'ouch'. I moved my legs o-o-o-o, very stiff. The tuba and the unaccustomed climbing up and down steep streets had left their mark. Food, coffee, breakfast? At least the coffee sounded good.

"Hell, you'd think we were still in the middle of that typhoon, judging by your sick-ass faces." I teased, but it hurt to talk and especially to be cheerful.

"Reckon it's all your fault, mate ... pirate stories and 'tuba'. I never want to see that stuff again ... even if it *is* cheap!"

Laurie and Kevin were snickering … both hadn't over-indulged in the evil liquid like Harry and I had. The Captain and Mr. Milner entered and sat down with us.

"You blokes don't look very healthy this morning!" the Captain observed. Mr. Milner was smirking.

"We were partaking of the island's hospitality, and trying one of their native drinks," explained Harry. "All of us except Laurie, that is ... and just how was she, mate?"

"What do you mean, how was she? We only talked ... keep your mind above your belt, Harry." Laurie was suddenly irritated.

"Whatever, mate!"

"Harry ... and Kevin. We have food and fresh water, and Mr. Mundy will have you a hand pump later today. When do we have two engines?" The Captain sounded a little anxious.

"This morning, Captain ... this morning."

"For certain?"

"Yes sir. When will Mr. Mundy take the pump?"

"He already has ... they came aboard early this morning and hauled it off."

We all looked bewildered. Are we all that badly hung-over, I thought.

Or is it just that Bobby Mundy is very good at being a pirate?

"Very well, then, we will leave from Laoang early tomorrow morning. Mr. Milner and I have discussed the details. We need you all to understand how tricky the passage in front of us truly is. Even with both engines our top speed is only eight knots. The tidal current running through that strait is extreme ... as fast as twelve or even fourteen knots, and the distance from one end of the fast ebb or flow to the other is 80 nautical miles. It is imperitive that we are in the correct position at the correct time, and go through on the flow ... with the current. That means we must leave here at first light. However, we now know that the channel will be too shallow at that time. We will therefore move the

Trader out past the channel at high tide this afternoon, which will be between 12 noon and 1:00 p.m.. That is our 'window'. You must all be present to assist in that operation. We will anchor there until morning, then weigh anchor at first light. We must have all you aboard at that time. Understood?"

"Yes sir," was heard around the table.

"I personally will sound Richard's bell just before dawn to make sure you are all aware of the time," he concluded his instructions.

"Well, mates, let's get to work!" Harry prodded his two assistants. "You heard the Captain.

Mr. Patterson had asked Laurie and I to top off the fresh water again, which we proceeded to do. Joseph went below to give the engine crew a hand.

About ten o'clock we heard th 'psst - psst' of compressed air, and one of the Perkins started. An hour later we heard yet another 'psst -psst' and Perkins number two came to life. We all cheered ... we were ready to roll.

We finished our topping-off, and were coiling our hose when Laurie stopped and excused himself. Bernadita was standing off the end of the wharf, near one of the first shops. Damn, she was a pretty sight: long shining black hair more than half-way down her back and bangs on her forehead, her smooth, full curves exaggerated by her petite size, her posture and bearing both sensuous and proud at the same time, with a touch of haughty self-confidence. This girl knew her own beauty, and revelled in her aristocratic heritage.

She also made me feel very warm just below the belt.

High noon arrived, and we were ready. The magnificent four were at our stations, ready to cast off, the Captain and Mr. Milner were at the bridge, in command, and our eager, responsive engineers anxious to give us power as needed. Mr. Patterson gave us the signal to cast off, the 'ding-ding' of the throttle pre-warned of the churning of white water at the stem, and we slowly pulled away from the wharf and made our way down the channel.

We went well past the transition line marking the end of the silt-laden river water and the beginning of the clear, blue water of the Pacific, and then lowered one anchor, purposefully keeping the anchor chain short, knowing that we would swing around the one anchor as the wind or current direction changed.

This all took time, and we hadn't had lunch, so Richard's call to a meal was welcome indeed. Our cook treated us to a plate of grilled tuna embellished with an assortment of steamed fresh vegetables, plus an elaborate selection of papaya, banana, some sort of cross between an orange and a grapefruit, and lychee.

"Bobby's going to take me to Catarman this afternoon, to the 'Green Park Cafe' ... anybody wanna come?"

"What's at the 'Green Park Cafe'?" Harry inquired.

"Well, I understand there's music, karaoke even, and girls, and dancing, and girls, and, oh yeh, plenty of beer ... even some imported Foster's, and ... bar fines!"

Harry grinned that wide dumb ass grin again.

"Count me in ... I still want to find out what King Solomon's books are all about." Kevin put in.

"I'm out, blokes, I have a date with a certain young lady ... she's invited me to a church party." Laurie excused himself.

"A church party?" I grimaced. "Jeeses, she's going to convert you to becoming a Catholic."

"Hell, matey, it might be worth it?" Laurie teased in return.

Kevin almost choked on his coffee.

Careful, Laurie, careful.!

"How about you two, and Richard?" I asked Fred and Joseph.

"Nah, we want to go back to the village ... we made some friends there, and Richard likes the tuba."

We all laughed. "Well, he can have it!" snorted Harry.

At least it's better than drinking vanila!

I was ready for our new adventure, and was waiting for Harry and Kevin, when Mr. Milner surprised me on the aft deck.

"Chad ... I wanted to say goodbye. I'll be going ashore in a couple of hours. It has been a pleasure to know you. Please give my regards to the rest of the crew when you get a chance. And good luck to all of you." We exchanged a long, firm handshake.

"And the best of luck to you too ... John."

"One last thing, Chad ... please take care of our friend, Mr. Mundy. Remember, you can trust him."

Before I had a chance to again question what he meant, or even to react, he turned and returned back down the passageway.

Yes, it's been an experience, Mr. Milner and a pleasure ... I will certainly remember you! Sure am curious about what he meant regarding our pirate friend, though.

Bobby arrived in his friend's outrigger to pick us up just as Harry and Kevin finished washing-up.

"Jump in, mateys."

Harry had to shout over the 'put -put' of the inboard: "Bobby, did you find a buyer for our centrifugal pump ... and where's my hand pump?"

"Hey, mate ... I got you covered ... no worries!"

"The hell you say ... we're leaving at first light in the morning!"

"Trust me .... everything's taken care of." Bobby grinned, holding his palms in front of him as if to say 'take it easy'.

The landing at Rawis was even more crowded than at Laoang ... the outriggers over-lapped and the canoes were two deep for most of the short waterfront, with the operators bantering noisily, vying for passengers and cargo. The total landing area was less than half of Laoang's and there were no concrete steps, and the shoreline was heavily littered with debris and rubbish. Most of the buildings were constructed of wood and were aged and deteriorated with rot and lack of repair and very little paint. The only feature exempt was a large bright red Coca Cola sign which read 'Welcome to Rawis' in English.

"It seems that these pump boats are the area's main form of transportation?" My statement was also a question.

"Palapag and the local coastal towns are served by water transport only ... Palapag doesn't have a road access, even though it's a major municipality on the Samar mainland. Our only highway is the coast road from Rawis here to Allen, which was built a few years ago by the Aussies."

"Aussies ... why the hell would they want to do that?"

"It was part of an international assistance program. Besides, they were planning to mine bauxite on Batag Island, but for some reason they abandoned the project."

"Oh."

We left the pump boat and walked down the access road to the waterfront. Small open-air shops lined the street on both sides, and I recognized several of the same kind of 'tricycles' I had seen at Laoang, plus a few that were simple man-powered pedicabs: a bicycle with two rear wheels instead of one, with a seat in-between encaged in a light frame with a canvas roof, wide enough so that two skinny people might sqeeze in.

I was then introduced to an even more exotic mode of Filipino transport. We

were walking towards the open rears of several mini-buses, their operators calling out where they were going. Bobby said 'Catarman' to one operator and we were immediately ushered into the back of one vehicle. We found ourselves inside the full-length cab of what was really an extended jeep, with the back of the driver's seat open to the passenger's compartment, which contained two long, narrow, thinly cushioned benches, one on each side. The sides of the cab were open above the back of the bench seat, with roll-down plastic 'curtains', presumably there in case of rain. I was captivated, and climbed back out of the vehicle to take a better look. The driver and his 'fare collector' joked about us, especially me. I walked completely around the strange vehicle, fascinated. Bobby started to explain:

"It's called a Jeepney' ... they build them from scratch, mostly in Manila and Cebu. Originally they were all WWII American jeep frames and engines, but now they fabricate even the frames, and use Isuzu diesel engines ... all have heavy duty suspension, big tires, and the body is mostly stainless steel.

"Incredible!"

But it was the finishing decor that had me spell-bound. The underlying paint job was bright sky-blue, but with red and yellow stripes and an overlaid orange flame design. Over the paint was added a vast assortment of stick-on vinyl decals, ranging all the way from small colorful flowers to American 'Wynn's' stickers and a large sign at the back which read: 'Watch My Rear-End, Not Her's'. Reflector tape was everywhere, as were extra side lights and clearance lights -- on the top and sides, on the front fenders and hood, and I even spotted a couple of blue ones aimed towards the road. I counted a total of 6 exterior mounted horns: two fire-engine-yellow conventional auto horns, and a row of four chromed 'Model A' type glaxon horns -- I assumed each played a different note.

And stainless steel and chrome everywhere in between. The vehicle was truly a work of art!

"Hey mate, time to go."

Harry had joined me on the 'round the jeepney tour' and was equally affected, although he thought a lot of the decoration was silly, especially the multiple tassles around the windows and the large figurine of the Virgin Mary on the dash.

"Reckon it's unusual, alright."

It was forty minutes to Catarman we were told, but our driver did it in thirty. I had never heard so much horn honking in my life, nor experienced so much swerving and braking to avoid other vehicles -- and pedestrians walking along the edge of the road. But our other passengers and the outside traffic seemed to take it all in stride. In fact, I recognized that there was a definite system to the apparent madness. Pedestrians knew to get out of the way, and were watchful … and if one vehicle was overtaking another the one being passed would pull over as far as he could, even slowing down to allow the faster vehicle to pass more easily. At one point enroute the driver indicated he wanted payment, and that the fare was twenty pesos each.

"I'll catch the fare ... you can all buy me a beer later." Bobby volunteered. "The Green Park Cafe is just beore Catarman, mates ... coming up soon."

I noticed that he pronounced Catarman with the accent on the 'ar', or the second to the last syllable. I had picked up that peculiarity in the local speech in Laoang. I supposed that was a characteristic of Tagalog and Waray … they tended to follow that pattern even when speaking English words.

"Dito lang," I heard Bobby tell the driver. We slowed to a stop besides a single story fenced-in compound, somewhat isolated, with no other buildings close-by. The exterior wall was white with a combination of thatched and corrugated steel roofs exposed above. A large sign reading 'The Green Park Cafe' swung from a tall pole outside the entrance.

"Here we are gents."

I watched as the jeepney pulled away. Including the four of us there had been 18 passengers. I shook my head in amazement as the jeepney's horns sounded off a litany of assorted notes and the driver worked through his gears, the vehicle lurching forward to it's next stop.

We found ourselves in an open-air collection of individual tables or groups of tables under separate thatched roofs, all arranged in an 'L' shape around two sides of a central building. A bar occupied the corner of the 'L' and a platform for live musicians was situated at the extreme far end on the right, equipped with a set of large speakers, an amplifier, three chairs, and a couple of music stands. One karaoke TV was supported by a shelf in the center of each of the two exposed sides of the central building, each atop a pair of tall speakers and auxiliary karaoke equipment.

One of the TV sets was on, tuned to a Manila program in Tagalog, and six girls were sitting at a large table, watching the show and exchanging small talk ... we were early, apparently ... there was only one other customer besides ourselves. Our entrance caused them to turn and watch us, they began a livelier chatter, giggling and motioning in our direction.

"We don't get many foreign visitors in Northern Samar ... you blokes are a celebrity the moment you walk in the door." Bobby explained.

Two of the girls sauntered sensuously to our table to take our order. Neither of them were outstanding beauty queens, not in comparison to, say, Bernadita, but they were OK, and I was definitely interested.

Harry was delighted to discover that they did, indeed, have Foster's ... he was even willing to pay the higher price. I preferred the San Miguel ... it was cheaper and I didn't want an Aussie beer anyway, just out of principle.

Hell .. we're in the Philippines now!

We were also relieved to find that our Aussie dollars were perfectly acceptable; Bobby did the quick math to let us know how much to pay. Our change was in pesos.

"Salamat," Bobby said when the drinks arrived. "The girls will sit with us if we buy them a drink, but at 40 pesos a pop let's wait until later."

"How much is the bar fine ... and where do we go?" I whispered.

Bobby laughed. "My, you are an anxious one ... all in good time ... but the bar fine is usually one hundred pesos, per hour, and the girl will either take you to a room back there, or you can book in at the Lanso Hotel, about a hundred yards down the road. That would cost about three hundred pesos. And the girl will want three or four hundred for herself, for either of the two options.

I see ... sounds more expensive than I had thought." I was totalling the different costs, and thinking that it was more than the fifteen dollars that our dear departed Mr. Morris had mentioned.

"So, Bobby ... I still want to know ... what are King Solomon's books all about?" Kevin clearly didn't want to waste any time.

"Hey, matey, I haven't even finished my first beer ... but alright. Let's see, where were we? What's written in the books? I suppose you blokes are familiar with the Bible, right?"

"Yes," Kevin answered, listening carefully. Harry and I nodded ... Harry was not overly interested.

And you understand the conventional story of creation ... Adam and Eve and all that jazz?"

We all nodded.

"OK ... now let's explore another idea. You've all heard of UFO's and the concept that extraterrestrial beings are real and that they regularly visit us. Do you think there's anything to that … any truth in all the stories of reported sightings, and so on?"

Harry and I shrugged.

"Maybe there's some basis to it all." The philosopher theorized.

"And have you ever heard the notion that perhaps those extraterrestrial beings had something to do with our 'creation'?"

"Whoa," Harry interrupted, "You're not saying we were created by a bunch of green extraterrestrials?"

Bobby smiled to calm Harry down, but continued: "Maybe ... you said: 'a bunch of extraterrestrials'. When you think about it, what's so different about that from the idea of a supernatural God, or Gods? Especially to the Hebrew nomads of the Old Testament."

Harry just looked at Bobby funny like, his forehead creased in skepticism.

"Or consider the concept of God, or an extraterrestrial being, not 'creating' us in the sense of from scratch, but maybe 'interfering' in our evolution a bit ... maybe the leap from being an ape to a homo sapien was a small modification, or even an inter-breeding, caused by God, or an extraterrestrial."

Bobby stopped for a couple of swallows of his San Miguel. Harry was obviously unhappy with Bobby's direction of thought. Kevin was fascinated.

"Alright, I don't want to go into this too much ... it's heavy duty stuff ... and I see Harry here doesn't approve of my line of thinking. To put it briefly, our creation, or evolution, *was* caused by interference from extraterrestrials. This is supported and even explained in the Bible. Next time you get near to a Bible, read what it says. Don't put all kinds of 'interpretations' into it … what your minister says this or that means … just read it literally, take the words to mean what they say, not what someone else says they mean. Then read the book of Genesis, about where it says right at the beginning that God is not one, but is plural; read about how the 'Lord' experimented, and failed a couple of times, about where other lesser 'gods' were co-mingling with the earthly females and causing a problem ... 'giants' being created as offspring, for example, and then especially read about King Solomon and his 'temple', and the Ark of Covenant. When you read about King Solomon's temple you are told that the 'Lord' came down and lived in that temple. Now I know that this is an 'interpretation', but you can't help but conclude that the temple was a foundation for an extrterrestrial home, or space ship, where the 'Lord', who was an extrterrestrial, lived for a time. King Solomon's Treasure is the knowledge revealed to Solomon by his extraterrestrial Lord, which was recorded in a strange and difficult to understand language, contained in many volumes of books."

"Wow," I expired.

"That's really something," Kevin reflected out loud. "But what kind of knowledge?"

"The story of man's past, and the experimentation by the extraterrestrials, knowledge of the earth and the universe, of all the things we now know from science, and much more that we don't know."

"And that's why the Vatican wanted, or wants those books ... because that knowledge undermines the religious story of creation, and even religion itself, and especially Catholicism." Kevin suggested.

"Exactly ... and that's why the Spanish came to the Philippines in the first place ... the Vatican was desperately searching for the last 'chests' of the Treasure of Solomon. And the missing Urim and Thummim."

Once again Bobby Mundy glanced slyly in my direction. And I realized that he was again talking about the same 'stones' that Joseph Smith, the founder and 'prophet' of the Mormon Church, had used to interpret the writings which he had found buried in the Hill Cumorah, near Palmyra, New York, on the southern shore of Lake Ontario.

On the southern shore of Lake Ontario?

But Bobby's attention was diverted towards Harry, whose eyes were making all kinds of weird movements.

"One last thing ... before Harry pops a cork," Bobby laughed. "The one piece of 'super knowledge' contained in those books was the explanation of how to travel beyond our planet, and solar system ... in other words, space travel. It explains how to construct space crafts, how to equip and maintain them, and, most importantly, how to power them. We already know that the source of power has to do with the harnessing of light ... yes, light itself ... but we don't know how. That is the last part of the ditty, 'yo ho ho and a bottle of 'rum' ... but it is meant to be 'light' instead of 'rum': '15 men on a dead man's chest, yo ho ho and a bottle of 'light'."

Harry sputtered in his beer. Kevin sat back, enthralled. I remembered what Mr. Milner had said: 'not all of what he says is pirate's tales'.

And is mister Mundy implying that Joseph Smith's buried plates was one of King Solomon's buried treasures??

Two men were approaching our table, a European and our friend Mr. Panganiban. The European was carrying a large carboard box.

"Ahh," Bobby exclaimed. "Come join us, mateys. You all know Mr ... uhh .

Villamor ... and this is Tony Cummins ... Tony owns the Flying Dog Resort on Dalupiri Island. And this carton here is your hand pump, Harry. Am I correct, Tony?"

"Correct you are ... brand new ... a 'Tokheim', the very best!" He set the container down on a chair and reached into his pocket. "And here's what's left after the sale of the centrifugal pump."

Harry's eyes lit up, and he reached for the carton. The two men sat down, while Harry was enthusiastically opening his Christmas present.

Bobby accepted the roll of notes from Tony, and counted them. "Not bad . here you are gents ... I reckon the person to give it to is your 2nd Mate." He counted out five of the notes which he put aside and then handed me the ones remaining ... I did some fast adding and subtracting.

"Harry, if your figures were right yesterday, how much should I have in my hand?"

Harry had to use a pencil, and he wrote on the carton. "Comes out to a net of eleven hundred dollars ... but I don't reckon we could get two thousand for our pump, it being second hand."

"Well, I have here in my hand eleven *American* one hundred dollar bills!"

At that he beamed. "Right on, mates ... reckon we need to say thank you ... and my apologies to you, Bobby, if I was being a little, shall we say, skeptical. Any chance we could use a tiny part of that money to buy these gents a drink?"

I hesitated. This wasn't our money to use. But then it could be considered part of the deal to buy them a drink. I was saved by Mr. Cummins.

"I insist that you don't, gentlemen. Your ship needs that money ... Bobby and I are just glad to help out."

Tony reminded me of Bobby, they could almost be brothers, except of course Mr. Cummins didn't look like a pirate. I decided to try out my observation.

"You two look like you could be brothers."

Both Tony and Bobby laughed.

"Not even close!" Tony negated the notion. "Bobby's too old and ugly."

"He's just jealous cause I don't have p.o.m.e. origins," Bobby countered. "An accident of location made him a London cockney at birth, and he's never been able to live it down ... he even tried to become Italian to get away from it."

One of the bar girls immediately sat down beside Mr. Panganiban, and ordered herself a drink.

"Mr. Cummins, tell us about your resort." Kevin prompted.

"Sure ... We have the best resort in the Philippines," he laughed. "At least we like to think so. It's a complete resort, with all the necessary amenities, designed around a simple village motif, with separate Filipino style bungalows, and we have a beautiful beach, an extensive reef for great diving, and we offer short excursions to other islands, mostly centered on observing and exploring wildlife and flora, and caves ... that sort of thing."

"Does Northern Samar have much to offer for tourists, I mean?" Kevin quizzed.

"Are you kidding? Northern Samar is a paradise yet to be discovered ... it is a magical land, full of mystery and intrigue, not to mention lush tropical forests and exotic islands."

I was feeling mischievous, and I wanted to test out Bobby's stories on another resident of the area.

"What, for example ... specifically?" I inquired.

"Alright ... let's see. I get to practice my tourist promotion role. Actually, there's so much to tell about. For one, this area is steeped with history, and antique hunting for artifacts going back to pre-colonial contact with the Chinese and Arabs and Javanese is popular, one good spot is right here in Catarman. Then there are the old Spanish churches and cathedrals, and remnants dating back to the days of the Manila Galleon, which used to stop in Palapag. We have undiscovered diving paradises like Bani Island, or totally exotic islands like Biri with its unique rock formations and unbelievable winter surf. Let's see now ... we take people on excursions into the rainforest near Victoria, and they can't believe their eyes at what they see. We even take people to pan for gold on.the Victoria River. Or even more exotic, we go on exploratory trips to search for the 'white monkey' or the six meter tall 'giants' or the people high in the mountains

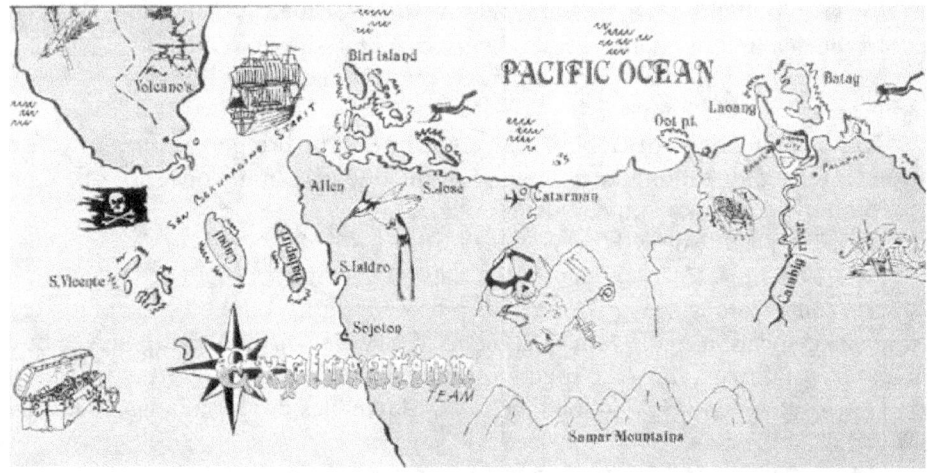

that look like the 'Hobbits' of 'Lord of the Rings'. I can go on and on. We can even hunt for lost treasure."

"Hunt for lost treasure?" Now he was getting to the part I was waiting for.

"Oh yes, there are many tales of buried or sunken treasure in Northern Samar. The sources go back to the Spanish Galleons, or even before to the piracy of Chinese junks and Arabic traders, and in more recent times the search for one of General Yamashito's legendary Golden Buddhas, supposedly hidden here during WWII. Just last year a group of Aussies spent a couple of months digging one hell of a hole on Biri Island. They had a map and were serious as hell ... as far as we know they didn't find anything, and we don't know which treasure they were digging for."

"And how about the 'Treasure of Solomon'?" I asked, glancing at Bobby.

Tony Cummins laughed. "Sounds like you've been listening to pirate's tales."

He motioned with his thumb in Bobby's direction. "But I don't know anything about that ... it would seem to me that we're a little too far away from King Solomon's part of the world."

Doesn't sound like I'm going to hear anything more about the Treasure of So/omon!

After his companion's second drink Mr. Panganiban made an exchange of peso notes and he and the girl left the bar.

"Now you see why I call him Mr. Billatmor!"

Everyone laughed ... I had already related the story of the meaning of 'bilat' to Harry and Kevin. I wanted to go the one step further and call him Mr. Cuscus, but then we would have to explain the story to Bobby and Tony, and that was too much.

"So he went next door to the hotel?" I asked.

Well, I guess I don't need to worry about him exposing my 'lie' anymore!

"Well, Harry ... Kevin. You game?"

"What, you mean taking one of the girls? Nah not tonight." Harry declined.

"Not me either." Kevin shook his head, which I think was still too full of Solomon's Treasure.

It was time for me to visit the men's 'head', and I asked Bobby where it was. He offered to accompany me, a little too eagerly I thought. Hell, he was probably busting to pee the same as I was! He led me through a gate to the back of the centrally located building. The area was poorly lit and we had to grope around a bit to find the toilet room, which lacked a commode or even a latrine ... instead we both stood together, aiming at the sorefully inadequate small 'hole' of the squat-down facility, the opening centered closely behind two 'foot prints' contoured in a concrete bowl on a slightly raised portion of the floor.

It sure is hell for a person who can't squat down on his heels ... like me," I chuckled.

I know just what you mean. When I first came to the Philippines I had to practice squatting as an exercise for a couple of months before I could finally manage it with any degree of success."

As soon as we had started on our return trip to the bar, Bobby took hold of me by the arm and stopped me. We were in a blackened, obscure part of the back 'yard' of the complex.

"Chad, there is a matter of utmost importance which I must discuss with you ... to explain to you ... but I must have your full trust and confidence ... can I swear you to secrecy?"

"Secrecy ... what are you talking about, Bobby?" I was impressed by Bobby's obvious sincerity, but once again I was being asked to form a 'secret' alliance.

"The story of the treasure that was Solomon's is not without substance ... what would you think if I told you that we have indeed 'come in possession' of part of that treasure, a portion of the two 'chests' that were hidden in Samar so long ago?"

"I wouldn't know what to think," I shrugged.

"Well, we do ... in fact, it's loaded onto your Trader!"

"What??"

"Yes ... it's vital that we get the 'treasure' out of the Philippines. Vatican spies have been watching us closely. Hong Kong is a good choice for a temporary location. We have been waiting for a long time for the chance to transport it there. Your Trader provides us with a good solution."

If *the Trader makes it to Hong Kong* ...

"You say the'treasure', or whatever it is ... is already aboard the ship?"

"Yes, matey ... it is stowed under the seat in your officer's mess, where you found the ketchup," he chuckled.

"Jeeses!"

"Chad, I need you to make contact with a 'Bretheren' in Hong Kong ... and I need a chance to explain some things to you. How about if you and I take a couple of girls to the hotel next door so we can talk. My treat of course."

"A couple of girls ... next door? You're treating? Yeh ... I guess so ... yeh, I'd like you to explain a couple of things too."

"It's a deal, then ... let's go back to the table, choose the girls, and split."

"You're on ... I'm right behind you."

"Hey, what took you so long, Canuck?" Harry wanted to know.

"Go and try to take a crap in that 'Samar' style toilet, and you'll find out ..." I responded.

I scanned the girl who had been serving me. Her name, she said, was Maribel, and she was, interestingly, from Laoang. I thought she was pretty: slender and graceful and walked with a rythmic, sensuous sway, rounded bulges teasing at the light fabric of her long, loose dress, suggesting a full, well-curved butt and ample breasts. She brought another San Miguel for Bobby and I, and lingered at my side for several seconds, her right hip gently caressing my arm. No words were spoken, only smiles and the suggestion in our eyes and a soft nudge exchanged between arm and hip. She borrowed a chair from the neighboring table and sat beside me, snuggling close. I indicated that I was willing to buy her a drink and she relayed instructions to one of the other girls in what sounded to me like a mixture of New Guinean Tolai' and Spanish. Bobby was making his choice in a similar fashion, and after a few minutes gestured to me that it was time to make our move.

"Would you come with me to the hotel next door?" I whispered in Maribel's ear. She turned her face towards me, showing surprise. She surveyed me closely, as if wanting to know if I was serious, and questioning her own willingness. Then she cocked her head to one side and smiled. "Yes!" she whispered in return.

"Gentlemen ... please excuse Chad and I ... uhh …. these two beautiful ladies want to show us around the hotel next door ... and I don't think we can resist ... but we shall return ... shortly."

With that the four of us exited the table, the girls making us wait while they scurried into the back to retrieve whatever it is that ladies think they need for excursions such as this, and Bobby exchanged pesos for the bar fines. We were thus forced to suffer Harry's snickers and Kevin's know-it-all grin.

"How much was the bar fine?" I quizzed. "Like I said, a hundred pesos each. We got only one hour."

Maribel glowed with an unexpectedly radiant smile as she and her companion re-emerged from the darkness of the mysterious back rooms, and took hold of my arm in a flowing, high stepped motion that gently propelled me towards the exit and out to the roadside. Bobby and his own escort followed close behind. The second girl's name was Liezel, and it seemed to me that the two of them had done this before. Together, I mean.

"Well, matey ... to the Lanso Hotel it is. We can speak freely, these girls appreciate the importance of 'confidentiality' of matters discussed by their, shall we say, 'clients', and their understanding of our lingo is limited, anyway."

"Uhh ... Bobby ... how did you know I was a Mormon?" As I spoke I felt an increase in pressure on my arm, as if to let me know that my attentions were to be more appropriately directed elsewhere.

"Ahh … John ... your Mr. Milner, that is, told me the story of the demise of your unfortunate Mr. Morris, and that you and Mr. Morris shared the same religious persuasion."

"I see ... but I am curious as hell ... in your story last night you implied that the writings that the Prophet Joseph Smith discovered in the Hill Comorah was one of the Templar's buried treasure."

"Well I'm happy to see that not all that I said passed unimpeded between your ears. He answered lightly, grinning at me with almost annoying mishchievousness.

Maribel squeezed me once again, this time more sharply, and I turned towards her to face an expression of playful vexation.

"Talk to me ... not him!!" she pouted.

We had arrived at the gate to the hotel. A gravelled roadway led to a large courtyard, the roadway encircling a round, concrete-walled planter in the center, with a parking area to the left. Our conversation was necessarily interrupted as we negotiated the path to the hotel entrance. I noticed that the structure-motif of the hotel was a two story, European 'Swiss chalet' style, with shuttered windows and dark brown wooden battens crossed over a white mortor exterior, and a duplex of high-peaked, shingle gable roofs.

"The hotel was built by a couple of Australians a few years ago," Bobby remarked, as if reading my mind.

A Filipino youth dressed in a blue security uniform greeted us at the small outside terrace, seated casually behind a black-colored wooden table. He met us courteously and rose to open one of the double entrance doors, scanning the four of us with knowing eyes. Yet his manner was hesitant, and revealed a measure of discomposure. If it wasn't for knowing that short time visits such as our were a common matter of trade, I would have thought that he was genuinely embarrassed.

The four of us filed through the doorway ... and then Bobby abruptly stopped dead in his tracks, the remaining three of us piling up behind him. The scene before us was both startling and perplexing, and explained why our doorman was embarrassed. Opposite to the entrance where we stood was what I assumed to be the reception desk, with a staircase heading to the upper floor close by. But in-between, filling a large open lobby, was seated a congregation of fifty or so people, and directly in our path a gentleman in a dark suit stood behind a portable pulpit, an open Bible in his left hand, and he was undoubtably delivering a religious sermon. Seated behind him were another half-dozen persons who I took to be other speakers and/or singers.

Jeeses, we've just walked into the middle of a church service ... !

All eyes turned towards us, even the preacher paused to glance in our directon.

"Shit!" I exclaimed under my breath. "Now what do we do?"

But Bobby the Pirate hesitated for only a second, and whispered "Follow me, matey," and then took advantage of the preacher's own pause to stride out boldly across the floor, the two girls and I queing ackwardly behind him. I could feel the redness rush to my face, and I struggled to show as much dignity as I could muster. But Maribel and Liezel were much less inhibited, and giggled to each other with their palms to their mouths throughout the entire passage. Fifty and more pairs of curious and admonishing eyes followed, and watched as an elderly woman with glasses hurriedly took Bobby's three hundred pesos and handed him a single key. She started to question why we wanted only one room, but then shrugged impatiently and pointed to the staircase, motioning that our room was on the second floor. The preacher had continued with his sermon, but I could make out a definite stutter and a lack of continuity.

"Hell, it's only Saturday ... must be Seventh Day Adventists ... screw 'em!! Bobby had whispered to me while negotiating for the key.

The room was large, with two almost-double-sized beds. I flopped on the closest, still overwhelmed by embarrassment. Maribel was pointing at my reddened face, giggling animatedly. Bobby sat down hard on the second bed and roared with laughter, falling backwards onto his back. Liezel quietly placed herself coyly beside him, already reaching for the top buttons to her white blouse, much less concerned than the rest of us over the episode just enacted, and wanted to get back to the business at hand.

It took a few moments for my emotions to adjust, and then I remembered the true purpose of our excursion, and the questions I wanted to ask Bobby.

"So ... Where were we. So you're saying that what Joseph Smith really found buried in the hillside was one of the eighteen parts of Solomon's treasured writings?"

"You got it, Chad ...

"And the Urim and Thummim?"

"Yes, the Urim and Thummim ... Joseph Smith had found the one burial that contained the stone-like apparatus that enabled one to translate the writings. There is only one Urim and Thummim, you know ... and you Mormons have it."

Maribel was squeezing my arm once again, and I was aware of her warm body adjusting to a prone position, snuggling closely. Liezel suddenly stood from the bed and walked briskly towards the door ... and turned off the lights. I could hear her giggle as she piled herself on top of my pirate associate.

"But that's not possible, Bobby ... the writings were about a Biblical people who had travelled from somewhere in Mesapotemia to the Americas ... and the Urim and Thummim ... Joseph Smith gave that back to the angel Moroni."

There was considerable russling of clothes before Bobby answered, and Maribel was working at my own clothes, trying to help me disrobe.

Bobby finally replied: "I know that's what you were told, Chad. What you have been told is part true, part conjecture, and part just fiction. For example ... we know that Joseph Smith kept the Urim and Thummim, because he used it a second time fifteen years later, when he translated a set of papyrus rolls which had been discovered along with four mummies in one of the catacombs of Egypt and which had been brought to the United States and put on display as part of a travelling show. Joseph Smith claimed that those scriptures were the writings of Abraham, and they became the basis of your second exclusive book, the 'Pearl of Great Price'."

I was trying to remember the Sunday School lessons of my youth.

"OK ... maybe. But we don't have it anymore. And how could the story of a people in the Americas be the writings of Solomon, in Jerusalem?"

"Chad ... you gotta put what you've been told in perspective and realize that good 'ol Joe Smith and his cohorts had used his buried find as the basis for a new religion. Maybe it was a set of records that was legit, but had somehow gotten back to the land of Israel. Or maybe it was mistakenly assumed that the setting was the Americas simply because that where the writings were found. Maybe it had been somewhere else closer to Palestine ... maybe Africa, or India. The story would fit equally well in those places. Or maybe the part that was the Book of Mormon was mostly fabricated, and the most important parts of the writings were kept secret, to be revealed only in discreet priestly ceremonies within the confines of your temples."

"Bobby ... that's just too far-fetched!!"

Maribel's movements were becomeing more aggressive, and I could now feel her bare breasts against my shirtless torso, her mounds firm, yet wondrously soft, her nipples hardened and protruding.

"Ahh, Chad ... OK. Please consider one or two puzzling facts. If the Book of Mormon was the records of the original inhabitants of the Americas, translated by a young American in the state of New York in 1815, why is the Book of Mormon written in King James English?"

Bobby's words were beginning to be inter-dispersed with heavy breathing.

"Or, if you were to investigate the early history of your religion you would learn that there was a strong complaint against the Mormons by the Freemasons, who complained that Joseph Smith had stolen the doctrine and especially the ceremonies from their own sect ... but Joseph Smith argued that he had received the teachings and rituals from his buried writings. Now, we know that the Freemason's had preserved the knowledge and ceremony of the Templar Knights, and that they also possessed part of Solomon's written treasure. So if Mormon doctrine and ceremony are similar, and it was obtained from buried writings, then it confirms that those writings were also part of King Solomon's ...! Do you follow my gist, mate?" Bobby's last words were heard as broken parts.

Jeeses ... he's talking to me and poking her at the same time ..!

Maribel was now all over me, and I was naked. But I was lying on my side faced towards Bobby, trying to understand what he was saying.

"Your Joe Smith was a clever rogue ... part con artist and part saint. He would ... have made a good ... pirate!"

With that troubled finale, Liezel let out a mournful squeal, and my good buddy Bobby made a great deal of grunting noises. And then only muffles and silence.

Maribel was agitated. And I think she was pissed. My mind had definitely been centered on something else than what she had in mind, and my response to her manipulations had suffered dearly as a result. But I couldn't help it. What Bobby had said was heavy stuff. He had been attempting to destroy the carefull indoctrination of my entire adolescence and youth in one sweeping blow, with only an incredulous sailor's yarn to take its place.

Or is it so incredulous ??

"Hey, matey ... it's time to go. Let's get dressed and get back to the Green Park Café. If our timing's right we can catch a ride back to Rawis with Mr. Bilatmor."

At the mention of the word 'bilatmor' Liezel laughed. But my own dear Maribel was not so easily humored. Especially not now, not after my failure to properly attend to her. I tried to make up and get some last minute loving by turning to her and starting something. But I was too late. Besides, Liezel turned on the light and we both scrambled to put our clothes on.

"Take what I have said for what its worth, my good friend ... but now I have a more important matter. As I mentioned before, I am trusting you to contact one of my fellow 'Bretheren of the Coast' in Hong Kong, and to deliver our 'cargo'. His name is Peewee, and here is the location where you'll find him ... the password phrase between you is: 'From the Templars of old, More precious than gold'. Can you remember that? It is imperative that you get the treasure safely unloaded. You will be amply rewarded."

I repeated the two lined ditty.

'From the Templars of old ... More precious than gold' Jeeses, what a phrase!

"Yeh, I guess I can remember that." I accepted the piece of paper from Bobby and put it in my pocket.

Somehow, I don't have a good feeling about this!

The hotel lobby church service had ended, and our congregation was nowhere in sight. Perhaps our interuption had hastened the end of their service. We casually retraced our path back to the Green Park Cafe, during which time I tried my utmost to make amends to maribel. But my clumsy efforts only made matters worse, and she finally started to cry.

279

Jeeses, can't you do anything right, Chad??

Then Bobby came to the rescue, pulling out a wad of peso notes, and giving each of the ladies five hundred pesos. Well, that seemed to do the trick. Maribel stopped crying, and when I added another hundred pesos of my own she suddenly reverted back to her old self and once again clung to my arm, warm and smiling.

"One last thing to keep in mind, Chad, watch out for our Mr. Bilatmor ... he's the spy for the Vatican. But we sort of have him in control, so to speak ... as you can see. And keep an eye out for mysterious characters ... we don't want the treasure of two and a half millennia to fall into the wrong hands."

We re-entered the Green Park Cafe admist cheers and extensive hooting. Harry and Kevin had taken full advantage of our absence and both had a girl on their laps and a Foster's in hand. Although we hadn't been away long enough for them to have become inebriated, and I had yet to see Kevin drunk anyway. Bobby and I and our escorts ordered a round of drinks. Maribel sat down beside me, her unhappiness forgotten ... and we joked and talked. She taught me some essential Tagalog. I learned that 'pretty' or 'beautiful' was 'maganda ka', 'how are you' is 'kumusta ka', to feel pain is 'arai', and if you say 'arai - arai' then everyone understands that that is the sound of a girl being made love to. Delicious is 'masarap' -- the only Tagalog word I ran into that was accented on the last syllable instead of the second to last -- and if I called a girl 'masarap' she understood exactly what I meant. And I also learned that goodbye is 'paalam', or 'paalam na po' if you were being especially polite.

Maribel had a story to tell me. We were now very comfortable with each other, massaging each other discreetly in interesting places, and our conversation had become both intimate and open. She related her story of how she had been disgraced by becoming pregnant when she was only sixteen, unmarried of course. In the Catholic community of Laoang this spelt total ruin for a girl, she explained bitterly. She was disgraced and condemned ... for life. There would be no normal future for her ... a husband was unlikely, especially a good one, and most channels for furthering her education and a successful working career were badly damaged, if not closed completely. She explained that her world of choices was to either stay in Laoang and settle with a third class future and make the best of her circumstance, or leave her baby daughter with her mother and move to another part of the Philippines and try to hide her secret, or better yet to marry a foreigner ... or go to Cebu or Manila, or near one of the American bases at Angeles and Olangapo, and become a prostitute.

Maribel left her daughter behind and went to Manila, ending up as a dancer and a prostitute in a Makati strip bar. She was popular, she said, and did very well. She even showed me a picture of her taken then, young and provocative in a sexy dance costume. With her high earnings Maribel had managed to buy a home for her parents and daughter in Laoang, and had regularly sent them money to improve their welfare. But now she was twenty-six and wanted a normal life -- a good husband and more children and a happy home.

I felt deeply sorry for her. There had been a strong hint in all of this that her and I could get to know each other better. But I was leaving at morning's first light. Her story reminded me of Deli, and the 'maris' in Rabaul. It occurred to me that this was a sad and unfortunate predicament for many young women all over the world, and was a manifestation of male dominance and exploitation at it's ugliest, and the cruelty of societies to their own ... and was particularly conspicuous in Catholic countries and communities.

Hmm ... sounds like a good idea for a novel!

It was time to say 'paalam'. Mr. Billatmor, or was it Mr. Cuscus -- now I'm getting all confused -- had just returned from his own adventure next door (I wondered if he had run into the same church group) and he had arranged for a special jeepney to be available at that hour, so we all climbed into another jeepney 'work of art' for the return trip to Rawis. Mr. Cummins said goodbye, he was headed in the opposite direction, back to Catarman.

Maribel and Liezel followed us out to the jeepney to say goodbye. Maribel's eyes had been just a little puffy from her short crying period on the way back from the hotel, but now they were suddenly even more puffy. I kissed her tenderly and whispered 'paalam na po'. Liezel and Bobby were feeling frisky and were teasing each other with reciprocating pinches on the buttocks. Finally loaded, the jeepney sounded its litany of

horn notes and lurched through the first and second gears. We gazed back towards the group of girls waving at us, and we all heard Liezel call out loudly: "Bobbee ... I luv you ... no shit!!"

I realized that we were fortunate, indeed, that Mr. Billatmor had arranged for the jeepney, for there was no traffic on the road, and no other jeepneys. We flew, and were in Rawis in no time.

There we found that we would have had difficulty finding a pump boat to take us to the Trader, as well, had it not been for Bobby. Rawis town was as if deserted, not a soul about. But Bobby knew where one of the boat owners lived, and in a few minutes we were motoring noisily down the channel towards the Trader.

Everything was death still on board. We said our final farewells to Bobby the Pirate and thanked him.

"I will never forget your 'new version of history'." Kevin shouted.

I just grinned and waved.

Harry muttered something about 'bullshit'. I didn't get it. But at the same time he was happily lugging the carton that contained the Tokheim hand pump.

"Clang - clang ... clang - clang!"

I was on my feet and out the cabin door in less than a second.

"Good morning, Captain."

Mr. Patterson was on the wheelhouse starboard deck, smoking his black pipe and watching the pre-dawn light slowly marking the beginning of a new day. Apparently he had been there for awhile.

"Morning, Chad," he replied. "Please have your crew ready to weigh anchor. Ahh ... Mr. Milner won't be with us. But I understand you knew that already."

"Yes sir ... I mean, yes, I knew."

"Please have Laurie available to take the wheel."

"Yes sir."

I went below to find everyone. I met Fred and Joseph in the passageway, bleary-eyed. Harry was washing up. Where was Laurie ... I stuck my head in the starboard crew cabin ... his bunk was empty.

"Hey ... Harry, Kevin ... where's Laurie?"

'Dunno ... haven't seen him."

"Hmm ... Fred, Joseph ... where's Laurie?"

"Haven't seen him this morning." Fred answered.

"Not since at the beach last night." Joseph added.

"What do you mean?"

"We were at the beach, and he came by with ... Bernadita ... is that her name? Anyway, they went off to the far end, and we never saw them after that."

"Oh shit!"

I took one last look around, to be sure, then raced up to the wheelhouse, again checking before I sounded the alarm. I certainly didn't want the same thing to happen as when I was pronounced 'overboard'. But he was nowhere.

"Captain," I panted, "Laurie is not on board.”

"What!"

"He's not on board, but I know where he is ... may I have permission to go get him?"

"Of course ... of course ... but please hurry, we must be on our way immediately."

I raced to my cabin and grabbed my shoes and socks. I'm going to need these, I reflected, remembering my run to the ship in Rabaul, and thinking about the rough concrete on Laoang's streets, purposefully contoured to provide traction to vehicular traffic. I raced below again.

"I'm going after Laurie. Fred, can you be ready to weigh anchor ... Joseph, I need you to man the dinghy."

The mighty Seagull went 'put-put', and we made our way to the closest end of the Laoang waterfront. Enroute I struggled with the socks and shoes.

"Joseph, wait right here for us ... and be ready to shove off lick-ed-dee-split!

I ran down the waterfront, then turned up what was now a familiar street. Straight up, a jog to the right and left to go around the school, and then straight up to the park.

The Trader was anchored just around the end of the short peninsula from Onay Beach, and sound carried easily across the still water in the quiet of a day not quite begun. Laurie's eyes bolted open at the 'clang - clang' of Richard's bell.

“Damn!" He untangled Bernadits's arms gently and jumped up.

"Bloody hell, they're going to leave without me."

Bemadita was rubbing her eyes, startled. Then she realized that it was almost dawn. She too rose to her feet quickly, a frightened look on her face.

"Oh ... oh! Looree, we must go ... *bilis*!

The two started back towards Laoang, walking fast and running in short spurts when they could. Back behind the village, up a hill, down a hill, finally coming up the final incline between the park and the Mayor's office, the cathedral straight ahead.

"*Tikang ka diin*?"

Bernadita heard a familiar voice coming from the park.

"Oh ... oh! Looree, it is my auntie ... I'm in big trouble."

"*Tikang ka diin*?" her aunt asked again, this time more firmly.

"Oh ... oh!" Bernadita's face contorted with sheer terror.

The woman walking towards them wore a shawl over what was obviously her night clothes -- a long white cotton dress -- and her feet were bare.

"Auntie, I was at the beach ... with Looree ... we fell asleep."

The woman's expression transitioned from harsh admonishment to wide-eyed shock. She crossed herself and asked:

"*Bata, virgin ka po?*"

Harry caught the word 'virgin' and guessed what she was asking.

The aunt grabbed Bernadita by the shoulders, shaking her, and demanding an answer, this time shouting:

"*Bata, virgin ka po?*"

Just then two men appeared, also in their bed clothes. One of them was Mr. Elias Dulay, Bernadita's father. He was walking rapidly, a viscious look on his face directed straight toward Laurie.

It was then that I reached the top of the hill, and the park. Laurie, the woman, and Bernadita were less than two hundred feet away. I saw the two men making it for Laurie, and in that instant I could read it all. Terrible visions of horrible murder and mutilation flashed before my eyes. It was time for Laurie to make a run for it.

"Laurie," I yelled ... not as loud as I could, but just about. Not a good idea to awaken potential assistants to the assassins.

"Run for it, buddy ... let's go!"

Laurie hesitated. Bemadita was in the firm grasp of her auntie, still being shaken, now crying, her face twisted with fright and anguish.

"*Bata, virgin ka po?*"

In a fraction of a second Laurie weighed the situation. He knew she was still a virgin. They hadn't gone that far. A shame, if he was about to die for it, he reflected. But that part would get sorted out. However, these two men had 'kill' in their eyes. And he had a boat to catch!

Bernadita had been teaching Laurie some Tagalog too. He quickly spit out 'paalam' and 'Bernadita, I love you, I think' and he turned and started running towards me.

"That-a-boy!" I whispered under my breath, "Faster, faster!"

Not a second too soon, for the two men were less than two yards away from their intended victim.

"*Tuku, tuku!*" both men started yelling, taking up the chase. I was surprised at their speed. Damn fast for such short, elderly gents! This was going to be a close one.

"*Tuku ... tuku!*"

Bernadita realized that Laurie was running, and that her father was in hot pursuit. She broke away from her aunt and chased after her father, yelling:

284

"*Tafay, waray nahitabo!*"

I was just glad I had my shoes on. Laurie paused to slip off his thongs ... his feet were going to suffer on the rough concrete pavement ... but better that than the sure and gruesome death chasing behind him.

It seemed we were forever presenting a curious scene to bystanders in this town. Well, I hoped this was the final one: Laurie and I racing down the hill towards the waterfront, Laurie yelling 'ouch', 'ouch' as the concrete bit the bottom of his feet, slowing him down, with two middle-aged men in rapid pursuit, surprisingly quick and agile for their ages, yelling:

"*Tuku, tuku!*" and "*Ar ikaw papfayon!*". And a gorgeous young lady further behind, running a little slower and crying out in anguish:

"*Tafay waray nahitabo!*" and "*Tafay, virgin la ak gihapon!*", her firm young boobies bouncing delightfully.

We reached the bottom of the street and the waterfront. And there was our good buddy, Bobby Mundy, waiting for us, a great wide grin on his face.

"*Tuku ... tuku ... Ar ikaw papfayon!*

"*Uutdan ta ikaw san imo bunay!*"

Bobby ran with us for a short distance.

"What are they saying, anyway?" Laurie wanted to know, urgently, in between gasps of air and yelps (because of his feet).

"Nothing much ... the father say's he's going to kill you ... oh yes ... he's going to cut off your dick and balls ... and the girl ... she says nothing happened ... that she's still a virgin ... so, mateys, nothing to worry about ... adios!

"Goodbye, Mr. Bobby Mundy!"

"Go for it, I'll try to slow them down ... goodbye, fellow pirates!"

Joseph was waiting for us. He had seen the commmotion and understood that we needed quick transport. We were in the dinghy in whirlwind speed, and our mighty Seagull powered us to our escape.

I needed to laugh.

"Mate, it is *not* funny!"

"The hell it isn't ... so she's still a virgin, ehh?"

I could see Fred at the bow ... they were raising the anchor! Bless their hearts. I guessed that the entire scene was visible from the Trader, and that the Captain didn't want to risk some last minute delay caused by an irrational father. Once again we were on the run. Maybe Bobby was right ... we *were* pirates.

We scampered onto the aft deck. Harry met us to give us a hand pulling the dinghy out of the water. He had that wide dumb ass grin all over his face again. Joseph ran ahead to help Fred with the anchor.

"Laurie, the Captain wants you at the wheel." I had just remembered Mr. Patterson's earlier request.

"OK"

We came to 1/4 forward speed, and began to arc around ... the ebb of the tide had swung our stern out towards the open ocean. Once our bow was pointed towards the entance of the San Bernardino Strait, the Captain brought us to Full Speed Ahead and we slowly began to leave the island of Laoang behind us.

"Put us on 300 degrees for now, Laurie"

As soon as we had reached full speed ahead, and were maintaining a steady course, Harry and Kevin and all three hap-caste boys came scrambling up the steps to the wheelhouse, wanting to hear what had happened. The Captain was interested as well, although he didn't say so.

"Sorry ... Captain ... we just fell asleep on the beach."

"And she's still a virgin?" Harry was busting for details.

"Yes, gentlemen ... she is still a virgin ... I did the honorable thing." Laurie answered indignantly, disgusted that Harry was still pushing the virgin bit.

"The police aren't going to be waiting for you in Hong Kong, then?" Mr. Patterson wanted to know, a smile on his face.

"No, no ... nothing like that ... it'll all be okay as soon as Bernadita has a chance to explain things to her father. But we did make quite a scene ... her reputation might be damaged a bit."

"So, you mean to tell me that you two spent all night on the beach, and you never got into her pants?" Harry still wanted details. Besides he was skeptical of Laurie's story anyway.

"Well, I never said that ..."

"Oh ... what do you mean?"

"Well, we did fool around a bit, but she told me she had a strict rule, the 'Golden Rule' she called it ... I could only go so far."

"What do you mean 'Golden Rule' ... what did she *say*? Harry was persistent, his curiousity piqued.

"She said 'above the belt is yours to enjoy, but below is mine to keep'!"

We all roared. All of us. Mr. Patterson too. Harry and I had to sit down.

"So, did you at least get a taste of cuscus?" Harry still wouldn't let up.

Laurie squirmed, holding the Trader's wheel. He was enjoying the notoriety, but this part was a touchy subject. His face reddened.

"Yeh, I guess you can now say that I've eaten cuscus."

"Hurray!" Harry shouted. And there was more laughter.

"Just one last thing, Laurie ... I gotta know, mate ... did she like it?"

"Yeh ... she liked it." He answered lightly, then paused, thinking about it. "She liked it a lot!"

More laughter. Harry got up and congratulated Laurie with a firm slap on the shoulder.

Jeeses, what kind of a place is this ... where the women are the priestesses and become the mayor and the president and the young girls tell their boyfriends 'above the belt is yours to enjoy but below is mine to keep'?

"By the way, guys ... I suppose you all noticed that Mr. Milner is no longer with us. He's left the ship, for personal reasons. But he asked me to give you all his best regards, and wishes us all luck.

Each accepted the news with different feelings, but no one had anything definite to say. They hadn't gotten to know him as I had, perhaps, still thinking of him as the madman who had taken over the ship, on that first day out of Rabaul.

Harry and Kevin returned to the engine room and I took the opportunity to say farewell to Laoang, making my way to the aft deck. We were a full mile past Onay Beach already, but I imagined I saw a beautiful Filipina girl standing on a rock at the end of the beach nearest to us, waving farewell to Laurie. For his sake I waved, long and steady, and whispered 'paalam na po', 'paalam na po'.

CHAPTER THIRTEEN

Unwanted ... but undaunted

> **"I require these items,"** he explained,
> **"Because I hate the sound of a screaming
> woman and I abhor the smell of burning
> rubber."**

It's going to be one hell of a ride, gentlemen ... I reckon the current will top 12 knots, and our own speed relative to the water will be 8 knots plus we will have a brisk northeasterly to our back. In a sense, we will be 'surfing' the San Bernardino Strait."

Mr. Patterson was outlining our strategy for passing through the infamous waterway. At the mention of 'surfing' Laurie smiled and leaned a little closer over the chart table. Joseph was listening from the wheel, and Fred had been invited to the briefing as well. Mr. Patterson was making sure that his three quartermasters and 2nd Mate fully understood what lie before us.

"Then we will be going through the strait with the current, plus the swells will be moving in the same direction?" Laurie was trying to see the picture of how everything was going to fit together.

"Yes, that's right ..."

"So then it really would be like surfing ... bloody hell. It would really be something if the swells were actually surfable ... with a board, I mean."

I remembered what Tony Cummins had said. "We might see some worthwhile surf when we pass Biri Island ... a guy we met at the Green Park Cafe mentioned that it was a famous site for big winter surf."

"Biri Island? I don't reckon I've ever heard that name ... I'd like to see it ... I haven't seen good surf for a long time." Laurie was nostalgic for his home area of Surfer's Paradise. He had remarked a couple of times before about his disappointment when he had come to New Guinea and discovered that the calm breezes of the doldrums just didn't generate good surf.

"Then a ship coming the other way would have it kind of rough?" I speculated.

"If a vessel was coming the opposite direction he would have a difficult time indeed, unless of course he had a high enough speed to overcome these forces. And when the tide starts to ebb against the wind and swells it would be a very choppy and unhappy sea."

"Do you think, Captain, that the difficulty of getting through this strait was one of the reasons that the Manila Galleon stopped at Palapag and Capul ... I mean, the two ports are at each end of the strait, and they were the only two stops the Galleon made on its entire voyage all the way from Manila to Acapulco, or on the return trip?"

Mr. Patterson smiled. "I can see you're developing some sea sense, Chad. Did our pirate friend explain that to you?"

"Not really. Or at least I didn't understand it that way."

"Well, imagine what it would be like to travel this channel with only sail for power. Look at all these islands here ... very treacherous ... and if you were forced to tack against a wind, and the current was perhaps double your maximum sail speed? I am sure the galleons often waited for days, maybe even weeks, for the right wind and tide conditions. Yes, Chad, I am sure that the San Bernardino Strait was the Manila Galleon's most troublesome waterway. And it is no wonder that this was a favored spot for piracy, for it would be here that a ship heavy with cargo would be the most vulnerable. I understand that over sixty sinkings have been catalogued in just this century alone."

"What is the danger to us, Mr. Patterson?" Laurie questioned.

"Our timing is right ... we are going through on the flow and we have a full day's light, and the weather is favorable ... we shouldn't have any problem as long as we keep track of where we are … and our engines keep running." The Captain paused to shuffle the charts.

"Now, Mr. Milner and I have plotted the individual segments of our passage through the islands. I want each one of you to study this and memorize the entire passage. See here: we pass throught the San Bernardino Strait to just northwest of Capul Island, then turn almost ninety degrees to the starboard and follow a heading of 304 degrees to the northern end of Ticao Island, then another hard turn, to port, to come between Ticap Island and Burias Island, then another right angle turn, with a small jog, to take us south of Marinduque Island, another jog to take us north of Verde Island and the beginning of the Verde Passage. But once past Verde Island we swing south to a heading almost due west to pass to the south of Maricaban and Golo islands ... we follow that route instead of continuing through the Verde Passage because we want to avoid the main shipping lane to Manila … we certainly don't need to be dodging other traffic. And once we reach this point here, we are finally free of the Philippine Islands and can swing to the northwest to a heading of 325 degrees for a straight route across the China Sea to Hong Kong

Any questions?"

"Interesting. I can see now that the Philippines really is seven thousand islands." I exclaimed.

"Most important, gentlemen, is that we keep track of just where we are at all times. We are short handed, we don't have a log to tell us how many miles we've travelled, or our speed, nor do we have a depth sounder, and these islands are strange to us ... with only a few lighthouses spaced uncomfortably far apart. I'm going to rely on you, Chad, for some serious coastal navigation, and for each one of you to keep your eyes open and to be able to recognize the different lighthouses and major landmarks. One last thing, we will be encountering other vessels ... keep your eyes open ... and I hope that each of you understand how to recognize a collision course ... do you?"

"If we are getting closer to another vessel, and their bearing from us remains constant, then we are on a collision course ... you and Mr. Milner explained that to us before." Laurie related.

"Yes. Now, we have been on a heading of 300 degrees for three hours. At eight knots that should put us right here." Mr. Patterson pointed to a location at the eastern entrance to the San Bernardino Strait. "Joseph, please bring us to port to a new heading of 245 degrees. This is it, gentlemen, no turning back ... this lighthouse, here, and Biri Island should be visible to us shortly."

It was now 9:00 a.m.. The Captain wanted Laurie at the wheel and for Fred and Joseph to get some rest, to be ready for later watches. But none of us wanted to rest, we were all excited and expectant ... this passage was critical.

The weather was near ideal, as the Captain had stated. Only a few white puffs clouded an otherwise unobscured expanse of light blue. The sea was not smooth, nor flat, for the brisk breeze coming from the northeast had generated a strong swell and was causing the water's surface to ripple and crest in small, temporary splashes of white.

True to the Captain's prediction, the silhouette of an island's topography slowly emerged throught the haze of the horizon, ahead of us and slightly to the port side. I was about to make the announcement, but Laurie had been observing it even sooner.

"That must be Biri Island up there now," he called out.

According to what we knew about the timing of the tide, low tide should have been about an hour and a half ago, and the flow in the westerly direction just starting. I thought I could detect a faster movement now, but there was nothing to guage our progress by except Biri, which was still only a distant outline.

"Chad ... I think I can see the San Bernardino Island lighthouse ... there's a flashing white and red light ... check the chart. "Mr. Patterson was studying the sea ahead, his binoculars held to his eyes.

"That's it, Captain ... flashing red and white." I stepped away from the chart to try and pick out the lights myself, straining my eyes. "Can you see it, Laurie?"

290

"Yeh, just barely ... straight ahead."

"Straight ahead?"

"If you can see it, Laurie, bring the Trader to port just a tad and aim for the middle between the lighthouse and the north end of Biri Island.

Both the island where the lighthouse was located and Biri Island were rapidly becoming more discernible. Our speed must be increasing, I thought. I took out the hand held sighting compass to take a bearing of our two landmarks, and just for practice plotted our position. Mr. Patterson came over to watch what I was doing.

"Good, Chad we must do that continuously all the way throught these islands."

I could now make out a series of unusual appearing smaller islands in front of Biri, unusual because each was similar in size and shape, yet individual, and formed a long, straight row ... maybe as many as six of them.

"We should be able to sight the skeleton of a shipwrecked fishing boat at the end of Biri," the Captain stated.

"A shipwreck?" I asked. We hadn't heard about this from our friends Bobby and Tony.

"Yes, Mr. Mendosa told us about it ... it just happened a couple of months ago, and the Northern Samar government was concerned about it because they were apparently fishing illegally. It's a Taiwanese fishing boat that ran aground on the island's northern tip. Instead of trying to salvage the vessel at the time, they simply abandoned her and the crew was quietly whisked away by a sister fishing boat."

We were picking up speed. Now that islands were in view we could use their relative position as a guage. Plus another curious factor: as our speed increased due to the current, the swells, and our own power, the breeze coming from behind us seemed to lessen, although I knew it was still blowing strong because of its effect on the sea's surface. I mentioned this phenomenon to Laurie.

He nodded, smiling. "This is really something. And if this ship was just a little smaller, and those swells a little higher, we really *could* surf."

Biri Island was now coming up on our port side. The row of frontal islands were now clearly in view.

"Laurie, check out those formations ..." We could now see that each was really one huge rock and could distingquish their formations of layered sandstone, clearly ancient in origin, carved by wind and surf in complex and eerie contours, each one rising perhaps two hundred feet above the sea and separated from the main island by a quarter mile of mangrove tidal water. I could now verify that there were six of them, standing solid and proudly protective, sentinel to Biri Island and the other islands more leeward to the winter northeasterly.

"Blood hell! Look at that surf ...!" Laurie gasped, excited. We had now progressed far enough so that the surf was no longer hidden from our view by the backs of the very swells that produced it, but we could now see the face of the swells as they rose up into high vertical walls, and crested in a smooth, expanding pattern.

"Surf like that ... and not one single surfer in sight! This is an undiscovered paradise. If I don't come back to Samar for Bemadita, I'm coming back for that surf ... see how it forms and curves ... that's classical. I bet it forms a pipeline on good days ... one thing, though, it's all rock in front ... definitely not for amateurs."

I reflected on the couple of months I had worked in Sydney at the British Motor Corporation plant, and had lived in Bondi Junction. My best friend on the Cap Finnisterre had been Richard, an American college student from Riverside, California, who had joined with us in San Francisco. When we landed in Sydney we had met another American named Darryl at a disco in King's Cross on our very first night. Richard and I were both broke, and meeting Darryl had been a life saver. He and his mother lived in Bondi Junction and he invited both of us to live with him temporarily. Well, Bondi Beach is one of Sydney's better surfing spots, and I received my introduction to serious surfing. Even had a chance to try it. Failed miserably, though, and my pink white skin just couldn't handle the required exposure to the sun. But I learned a little about surf, and the lingo, and came to appreciate that surfers are avid travellers and will go a long ways to find exceptional surf. I felt I knew what Laurie was talking about.

"And there's the shipwreck!" Laurie's sharp eyes picked out the black skeleton of an iron hull, wedged up between bare rocks at the end of the island, now visible because we had passed a more easterly peninsula.

"Spooky, isn't it?" I could feel a coolness in my lower back. "That could be the New Guinea Trader!"

"Don't even think such a thing," Laurie cringed.

Maybe she, too, had been an 'unwanted' vessel?

"Laurie, bring us a few more degrees to port ... we now need to aim between those two land masses ahead." Mr. Patterson directed, pointing ahead.

I checked the chart. Our next slot was where Luzon ended at Matnog to the starboard and Samar's Balicuatro Point jutted out from the south, on our port side.

"This is where the ferry crosses between Matnog and Allen ... keep an eye open for her." I cautioned, locating the two ports on the chart.

"Hell, we *are* moving. ." Laurie exclaimed.

I walked out to the deck's edge. It was uncanny ... I could see the waves and water's surface being ruffled by the wind , with the crests spitting white water, but I couldn't feel any breeze ... it was as if there was no wind at all.

"You know, Laurie, I can't feel any wind ... we must be doing close to twenty knots.

"There's the ferry ..." The Captain pointed to the Luzon side. "Keep your eye on her."

I took a bearing of the vessel with the hand compass, and marked my reading on a piece of paper.

I was watching the surface waters, and realized that something unusual was occurring. There was a great deal of seaweed in the water, and in between the swells and wave action I could see that the water formed frequent swirls and almost a churning of the surface, as if water was being brought to the surface from deep below. I mentioned this to Mr. Patterson, who had joined me for a moment.

"This area must be a very good fishing ground. What you're seeing is 'upwelling' ... it's the deep water from the Pacific being pushed into this channel and forced to surface, bringing the seaweed and other bottom nutrients with it," he elucidated.

"I remember you mentioned that even 'whirlpools' developed in this area ... is that a danger?"

Mr. Patterson chuckled. "I suppose whirlpools do occur, in extreme conditions, and sailors love to tell stories of giant, swirling holes openning up and an entire ship being gyrated down into its bowel, but I don't think we have anything to worry about."

I watched the swirling, eddying patterns a few moments longer.

Sure look like real whirpools to me!

I took another shot of the ferry ... the bearing had changed, she was now at a more northerly heading. Apparently we were moving at a greater rate of speed than she was.

Just then I felt an unwelcome sensation.

"Captain, Laurie, I think one of our engines is in trouble.

The miss that I thought I felt became reconizable to everyone. A moment later the miss developed to a full-on sputter, then the engine died completely.

"Damn! "

"Chad, go and find out what the hell is going on!"

I hurried down to the engine room. Harry and Kevin were both in a frenzy ... I could see that they were removing the fuel pump from the dead Perkins. Fred had arrived just before me to give a hand.

"Damn it to hell . .!" Harry swore. "I think this pump has had it ... it didn't look very healthy when we put it back together three days ago."

I looked at Kevin. I had come to understand that Kevin was a good nuts and bolts man; but he just wasn't very clever at solving difficult mechanical problems. Strange, I thought, since he was such a great philosopher. So no help there.

Unless the engine can understand philosophy, maybe!

And Harry was still reacting out of anger, no help there either. But Fred ... he had become our problem solver: quiet and cool headed. I grabbed his arm and brought him up to the main deck and fresh air.

"Well ... what do you think?"

Fred appraised me for a second. He knew exactly what was going on, and what was being asked of him.

"Chad, we could hook up both engines to the one good pump ... I'm sure it'll handle it."

"Good thinking," I patted him on the shoulder. Now it was my job to motivate Harry and Kevin into accepting the idea. No time for finese, I figured.

"Harry ... Fred and I have been talking about a possible solution. Can we hook up both engines to the one good pump?"

"How the hell can we ..." he started, then changed direction. "Yeh, we can probably do it, but we would have to stop the second engine for a few minutes."

"Can't you make the tie-in with the engine running?" I perceived that Fred was giving me a slight nod, to the side.

"No way ... but we'll get it all ready and it'll be only a couple of minutes."

"Let's do it!"

"You got it, mate!"

I hurried back to the wheelhouse with what I hoped was good news. Mr. Patterson was concerned.

"I don't like shutting down the second engine, Chad ... let me show you ... see here ..." He used the pencil to mark a point on our course which was just before Capul Island. "At this spot the tidal flow splits into two directions ... we need to make sure we are in the flow northward to round Ticao Island. If we get caught in the southerly split we are carried towards Capul and to these islands here, with the wind pushing us directly towards them ... a bloody good chance of ending up on those rocks ..."

He was going to say more, but the decision was taken out of our hands, for at that moment our second Perkins slowed to a quiet rest.

"Hell!"

"I'm sorry sir ... I'll go see if I can hurry them up!"

I raced below, but when I saw Harry and his two assistants working desperately I knew that anything I said would only have a negative effect. I kept my mouth shut.

Not an easy thing to do, is it Chad?

The Trader had come to a stop, relative to the water, but I could see by watching the landscape to either side that we were actually moving very fast. The Matnog-Allen ferry was close now. I wondered if we were in any danger of collision. I quickly returned to the wheelhouse.

"What about the ferry ... Captain, Laurie?"

Definitely not a good time to stop, but even with no engines we're probably faster than she is. She has to direct her bow against the flow in order to maintain her proper direction, so she's pretty slow. We'll miss her."

With the Trader once again dead in the water, the swells and the wind started to act on her hull. The swells wanted to bring the hull broadside, parallel to their length, while the wind fought to push our aft superstructure more downwind, so the end result was that our bow was pointed almost due north, the swell hitting us just a little to the starboard bow of broadside ... it was reminiscent of the same phenomena during the hurricane, five days earlier ... a cool chill passed up my spine.

The quartermaster of the the Matnog ferry must have realized that we were in trouble, for he altered his course slightly to give us better clearance, and passed by well over two hundred yards to our starboard. But we were now careening down the strait stern first, with no power, aiming directly for the norther tip of Capul Island, and already in the grasp of the southern tidal split ... which was the wrong one.

"Chad, we are definitely in trouble ... go back below again ... we must have power.

I fled. "Damn," I whispered to myself. I had been too optimistic. 'Shouldn't have agreed to stopping the engine'. I couldn't help but think it had been unnecessary. I flashed on Fred nodding his head. The connection could have been done with the second engine still running. Damn you, Harry," I rationalized that it was his fault.

Of course it is his fault!

Before entering the engine room I took a quick scan in the direction of where Capul Island was ... we were closing on it fast, its shoreline maybe only four nautical miles away.

"Damn, we're only fifteen minutes away from shipwreck." I spoke out loud to myself.

Fred was pulling on a couple of wrenches, connecting a tubing fitting with a 'T' fitting on the 'out' end of the good pump.

"Is that the last connection?" I asked, trying to keep the sound of desperation out of my voice.

"Yup!"

"However, mate ... the engine that conked out is going to take a bit more to get going ... we've got to bleed the bloody fuel line." Harry added.

"Well, I don't want to slow you guys down by causing a panic ... but I figure we are now ten minutes away from being shipwrecked!"

"The hell you say!"

"For real, Harry ... this is no time to joke! .. I *definitely* shit you not!"

Even though this was certainly no time for humor, I couldn't help but remember when Harry had made a similar sort of announcement a couple of weeks previously, only now the shoe was on the other foot. I snickered secretly to myself.

But Harry, please get that engine running!

The frenzy in the engine room increased. Kevin prepared to let loose with the compressed air, Fred gave a last turn with his wrench and waved his arm, Harry got ready to bleed air from the fuel line just before the injector pump, and signalled to Kevin.

"Psst - psst, psst - psst," and a sputter. "Psst - psst, psst - psst," and another sputter, Harry grabbed the throttle, giving it a jerk back and forth at the same time, there was another sputter followed by a series of loud knocks, and a roar. Perkins number one came to life.

I gave Harry the thumbs up, signalled with my palms opened upward to ask if we could have power ... he nodded affirmative. I raced to the wheelhouse. The Captain was waiting with his hand on the throttle. Laurie stood rigid at the wheel, his face white. I gave Mr. Patterson a thumb's up signal.

"Ding - ding!"

I thought I could hear crashing waves. I hurried to the edge of the deck, port side. We were perhaps three hundred yards behind a line of breaking waves, the rocky cliff of the windward shore of Capul directly beyond, its waterline strewn with bare, ugly boulders, the waves smashing down heavily with booming concussions, white water spewing and spitting angrily.

The single propeller began churning fiercely. Fortunately, our bow was already pointed in the appropriate direction, almost due north. But now it was a test of possession between two forces. I guessed that the current would actually sweep along the shore, not towards it, and might be helping us, but it was the wind that sought our demise on the rocky shore, blowing us directly towards it. Our propeller, at the same time, was trying desperately to pull us away from the island. but at an angle to the wind, so the two forces formed a vector, and our fate depended on which of the forces was the stronger. We continued to move downwind, yet made headway in a perpendicular direction as well.

We were at the most northerly tip of Capul Island, and as we lost distance downwind, we also progressed northward, coming closer to the island's end point. We were all holding our breath, knowing that disaster was imminent.

"Psst - psst, psst - psst!" Our gallant hero from down under was trying to start the second engine.

"Chad ... tell Harry to give us full power to the second propeller as soon as the engine starts ... don't wait for me to signal from here!"

I hurried below, expecting to feel the Trader lurch to a sudden stop any second, having crashed on a submerged rock.

"Harry ... no need for the formalities ... give us that second propeller as soon as the engine starts ... and hurry!"

"Psst - psst, psst - psst, cough."

"Psst - psst, psst - psst, sputter."

"Psst - psst, psst - psst, sputter, knock - knock, roar!"

I hurried back up top as Perkins number two joined her sister, and propeller number two began to beat at increasing rpms.

Capul Island was now directly to our stem. We had made progress to the north while the wind had persistently pushed us westerly -- the net effect was that we rounded the end of the island, only yards away from a rocky grave.

However, we were still in the grasp of the wrong leg of the tidal current. Our dual Perkins steadily pushed us northward, yet the current and wind continued to carry us westerly, towards another group of islands that were equally as treacherous and dangerous as Capul. I watched for several anxious minutes, then realized that the Trader was no longer moving westerly -- we had left the southern leg of the tidal split and were now being assisted in a northerly direction, back on course. The Luzon coast was in sight to the north, just to the starboard off our bow. Ticao Island was still hidden behind a hazy horizon. But now we were in open water. We had made it!

Richards's bell let loose with a loud 'clang - clang'. Laurie and I both glanced at the Captain, waiting for instructions.

"Go ahead, I'll take the wheel for awhile ... you both need a break after that little ordeal."

"Harry ... we were so close ... that close!" For a second time during this voyage someone was comparing our nearness to destruction to the distance between his thumb and first finger. This time it was Laurie.

"Who's idea was it to shut down our second engine, anyway?"

I wished that Laurie hadn't asked that question, and I was preparing myself for a few sparks. I tried to pretend I didn't hear, with my nose held close to my steak sandwich. But I was aware of a couple of fingers and at least one pair of eyes directed towards me.

"I cannot tell a lie," said Harry. "It was him!"

"Now wait a minute ... it was you who insisted on shutting down the engine ... I just gave the permission." I wasn't going down without a fight.

"How the hell was I to know we were being blown onto a bunch of rocks ... we're down there ..." Harry pointed to the floor." All we can see is an iron hull and those bloody engines!" Harry backlashed, but not without a measure of playfullness.

Bless his black heart!

I realized that we were all relieved that we had come through in one piece, and it was a dead issue ... no sense in arguing about it.

Not for now, at least

Laurie and I finished our lunch quickly and returned to the wheelhouse. Both Fred and Joseph decided to take a rest: Joseph was due behind the helm at 2:00, and Fred at 10:00 that night. Harry and Kevin were discussing how they would break up their engine room stints.

Ticao Island was now in full view on our port side, and our heading was 302 degrees, which would take us to the northern end of the same island. We could tell that we were still on the flow of the tide, taking advantage of its speed. We had one more factor in our favor: high tide came later at this end, the tidal volume needing time to flow, and react, and we would therefore still be able to take advantage of the current for two more hours, Mr. Patterson estimated.

Joseph came to relieve Laurie at 2:00 p.m.. It was clear that my freckled friend was one tired dude.

"Guess you need some sleep, guy ... don't figure you had much sleep last night, ehh!" I teased.

"Hell, I've been through a lot in the last ten hours ... almost got murdered, lost the love of my life, and then came an inch away from death by shipwreck. Reckon I need a rest, alright."

I laughed, the Captain and Joseph joined with chuckles.

Mr. Patterson suggested I rest as well, but I asked him if I could stay until we had completed the next two ninety degree turns to get us around the south end of Burias Island. Once we were on the open track to Marinduque I figured I could afford to rest.

At 3:00 the Captain had Joseph swing to a heading of 212 degrees, and we navigated the strait between Ticao and Burias islands. 5:00 p.m. brought us clear of Burias and we then took a turn to starboard and a new heading of 297 degrees. I borrowed the binoculars from the Captain and was able to pick out the three-second flash of the lighthouse at Bugui Point. I took a compass bearing of the lighthouse and the tip of Burias Island. We were now unaffected by tidal flows, and at 8 knots the next turning point would be at 10:00 p.m., five hours away, and the change of watch. I asked Joseph to wake me at that time, and headed for my cabin.

I stopped at my favorite spot at the deck railing beside the door to my cabin to gaze at the sea a moment and reflect on the days events. The San Bernardino Strait had been some experience, plus the stay in Laoang. We had passed through a piece of history, following the course of thousands before us. I could almost envision the Chinese Junks, the Arabic Traders, the Spanish Galleons, and even the Japanese and American warships of WWII, all of them having passed this way, most of them successfully, as we had somehow managed to do, and a lot not so successful, as the Taiwan fishing vessel reminded us, having met its rocky fate only two months before.

Joseph's hand shook my shoulder. "It's ten o'oclock, Chad."
"Thanks, Joseph ... everything alright? I guess I slept through the dinner bell."
"Yeh ... everythings OK. And you didn't sleep through the bell ... Richard never rang it, with you, Fred and Kevin sleeping. But he left dinner for you blokes in the frig."
"Thanks."
I went down below and was surprised to find Richard in the kitchen. He was warming up the plate that he had prepared for me earlier.
"Hey, Richard ... surprised to see you ... thanks."
"Reckon I gotta change my schedule to match you blokes ... right now four of you want something to eat."
"I see ... Harry and Kevin came in the mess together, both with heavy eyes ... one having just woke up, like me, and the other about to crash.
"We reckoned we'd switch to 8 on, 8 off, to coincide with the rest of you. Besides, six didn't work ... not enough time to get a good sleep and we were always missing meals." Harry explained.
"Sounds good by me!" I was anxious to get back up top and said 'paalam'.

The moon was just starting to poke its half crescent shape above the eastern horizon. It rose earlier now, and its phase was advancing to a half moon. We still had a northeasterly breeze, although much calmer now, and the sea was no longer freckled with white crests. It was dark all around, no lights of any kind visible. I studied the chart, concluding that we were too far away from any island to be able to see even the lights of a coastal town or village, and the next lighthouse wouldn't be until the Verde Passage.

Mr. Patterson had come to look over my shoulder.

"Where do you reckon we are, Chad?"

"Well, we're on a heading of 288 degrees, 51/2 hours from this point here, so at 8 knots that puts us right here," I placed a small x on the chart in pencil.

"Very good ... that's the same as I estimated. We can hold this heading for another 6 hours, which should place us here, just south of Marinduque. I'd like to get some rest now. Please wake me if there's anything ... anything at all ... understand?"

"Yes sir."

I settled in for a long night of it. Mr. Patterson had said there wasn't any need to take star shots, that we were relying on coastal navigation through these islands, but I took a series of four sightings anyway. I was pleasantly relieved to find that my result was a nice convergence almost precisely where our dead reckoning had indicated we should be. That not only made me feel good about my improving skill, but also added a sense of confidence regarding our location and safety.

Fred had been watching me. "How did your star shots work out?"

Fred had been present during almost all of Mr. Milner's 'lessons' of days before, and I supposed he had acquired an understanding of what we were doing and how the star sightings resulted in the plotting of our position on the chart.

"Close ... very close." I brought the chart over to the wheel. "See ... right here."

"That's good to know ... if you don't mind me saying ... I for one would like you to do that often ... finding our way through these islands is spooky, especially at night like this."

I was surprised by what he said ... and delighted as well. "Alright ... I will. I know what you mean ... makes me feel more confident too. Damn, when its dark like this we could be on top of a small island or reef before even knowing it was there. Yeh, it's spooky alright."

"You said it, mate!"

"Fred ... you figure we're going to have any more engine problems?"

"With that mess down there ... and our luck. I'm sure we will."

"Maybe we oughta think about that a bit ... maybe anticipate a potential problem like what are we going to do if that second pump gives out."

"Yeh, I've been thinking about that ... I think I've got a solution."

"Oh?"

"Those pumps are meant to suck the fuel from the tanks ... but now we have the 50 gallon water separator," he chuckled at calling our jury-rigged drum a water separator. "I reckon if we simply lift up that 50 gallon drum about one meter more, we'd have gravity flow to the injector pumps and could bypass the fuel pumps."

"Fred, you're a genius! Yes, that would do it ... keep it in mind, OK?"

"You got it!"

The sun had risen very early in Laoang because it was located at the eastern edge of the time zone. But as we continued westerly we were getting deeper into the same zone, and so sunrise was just a little later, by the clock. I therefore didn't expect any light at all at 4:30 a.m., when we should have reached the turning point south of Marinduque Island. That bothered me, because it was a narrow passage between the large mass of Marinduque and a pair of tiny islands to the south, named the Dos Hermanos Islands, with no lighthouse to help clarify our location. Our chart showed a couple of villages on Marinduque and another one on Bantan Island. I hoped that the villages would have some sort of lights to identify them by, and help me verify our position.

I reflected for a moment on what Mr. Milner had said about the Trader being poorly equipped for navigation. A modern freighter would have an electronic speed indicator and electronic depth sounder, would probably have radar, and her radio would be fully functional with an accurate, efficient direction finder, even capable of tuning in on the Loran system. I now fully appreciated what he meant.

Mr. Patterson joined me at 4:00 a.m., and I expressed my apprehension.

"Your concern is fully justified. And yes, watching for village lights is a very good idea. I've thought about why we don't have better navigational aids as well. You know, I asked Mr. Fitzgerald for a depth sounder before we left Rabaul. He said we didn't need one."

I was watching our bow as we were talking, and realized that there were lights directly in front of us, in the far distance.

"Captain, I see lights straight ahead of us!"

Mr. Patterson reached for his binoculars, and studied the tiny group of flickering dots.

"It's a vessel coming towards us, head on ... I can make out the red to our starboard and the green to our port." He handed the binoculars to me.

"That tells us we're right on course ... in the shipping lane." he added.

"Captain ... his heading is not changing ... he's dead ahead ... directly in our path .. or we in his."

"No problem ... bring us to starboard a bit, Fred ... we'll pass him on the right, with him to our port ... rules of the road."

The distance between us closed fast, and it was only a few minutes before the ship was broadside to us, moving very fast. It was too dark to make out the name and nationality, but we could see that she was a big freighter, her lights outlining two tall masts and an expansive white superstructure to the aft. She zoomed past. I did some quick mental calculations and estimated that she was six hours from this end of the San Bernardino Strait, if her speed was 20 knots, which meant that she would pass through at high tide. With her high speed that would be sensible timing ... but then again, with that kind of speed her Captain probably didn't care.

Now we were confident that we were still on course and not close to any small islands, which made me feel a lot more at ease.

At 4:30 Mr. Patterson directed Fred to alter his heading to 302 degrees. The horizon to the east was just beginning to show the first touches of the pre-dawn glow, its soft light gradually intensifying.

I could now detect the shadowy outline of a mountain peak off our starboard quarter bow, and knew that it was the four thousand foot summit at the southern tip of Marinduque Island, just inland from Suban Point. I felt another surge of reassurance. We should pass Tres Reyes Islands in approximately one hour, and we now had ample light to see them.

Richard's bell marked 6:00 a.m., and time for a welcomed breakfast. Laurie came up to the wheelhouse to relieve Fred.

"Go ahead and have breakfast, Laurie ... I can stay on for a bit longer." Fred offered.

Neither the Captain nor I wanted to leave the wheelhouse right then either ... we were both searching the sea ahead for the Tres Reyes Islands, sharing the binoculars back and forth between us.

"I see them ... ahead and to our starboard ... tiny buggers, and no height to them at all ... it would have been easy not to see them during the night." Mr. Patterson had spotted them first.

Again I felt that coolness in the small of my back.

"Go ahead and have breakfast, Chad."

But I waited just a few moments more, until I could make the islands out with my bare eyes, and a little bit more until it was clear that we would pass well to the south.

"This is tricky business," I sighed, sitting down at the mess table. Harry and Kevin were just starting into their pork chops and eggs, Laurie just finishing his.

"What do you mean, mate?"

"What I mean is that passing through these islands at night is treacherous as hell ... we don't have a log anymore, we don't have a depth sounder, nor a radio direction finder ... nothing except our eyes. It's just so damn easy to run straight into one of these small islands without knowing it's there ... damn easy. Most of them are uninhabited, you know, so no village lights, nothing."

"So you reckon Lancey Shipping Company sort of 'left out' a few necessities, do you?" Harry asked, with a sardonic tinge.

"I don't know ... it's an old ship and doesn't have a lot of modern equipment built in, and I guess they got along without those things in New Guinea ... they probably knew the waters like the back of their hands ... and it's partly our own fault. We were more interested in bluffing the Rabaul Harbor Master than in making sure we were safe and well equipped. I don't know."

"But how about that B.S. back at Laoang ... about being 'bloody well on our own' ... like they were unhappy we had made it?" Harry added sarcastically.

"Yes, there's that, alright."

I related what Mr. Milner had told me that last night we had talked, when I had come back from Onay Beach. They were all startled.

"Well, mates ... that puts a different light on things ... I reckon we've got a fight on our hands when we reach Hong Kong, " Harry concluded defiantly, his overly-vivid sense of the dramatic surfacing again.

"So, we are 'unwanted'," Kevin mused.

"But *undaunted*," said I.

"Reckon we'll be at Verde Island just before noon, and then round its northern shore, right here, shortly after," the Captain computed.

We were now fully aware that we were in a major shipping lane. Two more freighters passed, eastward bound, and another overtook us, moving in the same direction as our own, plus a small local coastal vessel crossed our track headed south, presumably for Cebu.

The narrow passage between Verde Island and the Luzon mainland was several hours away. I took the opportunity to rest, and dozed in my cabin for a couple of hours.

"Chad, you realize that we are entering another tidal flow ...?"

"Yes ... I was just thinking about that. This time the tide is coming from the China Sea, but the timing is the same as the San Bernardino Strait, except that we will want to go 'out' with the ebb rather than 'in' with the flow. Is that right, Captain?"

"That's correct, Chad ... except here the current won't be nearly as strong as in the San Bernardino Strait. We could make the passage at any time, really ... but it just so happens that it will be high tide when we reach Verde Island, and we'll be able to take advantage of the ebb all the way out to the China Sea. Couldn't work much better, really ... except that maybe we're a tad early."

Verde Island was typical of the many islands and shorelines we were encountering. Most were uninhabited, with a band of sandy beach at the water's edge on the leeward, or westerly shores, and short cliffs and a rocky shoreline on the east and north side, the topography rounded and deeply green with varied vegetation. Often I could discern that the greenness was coconut trees, assumedly harvested for their copra, but other times the plant growth was of undetermined species ... yet equally dense and generous.

At 12:30 Verde Island was directly to our south, and Mr. Patterson instructed Laurie to alter course to 270 degrees, due west. We were on our final leg to the China Sea.

"Laurie ... keep an eye out for another ferry. This time it's the one that round trips between Batangas and Puerto Galera." The Captain showed me the two loacations on the chart.

An hour later we were crossing the ferry's estimated route, and yes, we could see a ferry approaching us from the bay on our starboard side ... the port of Batangas in the far distance. On our port side we could see the northern shore of Mindoro, with the 8500 foot volcanic peak of Mt. Halcon rising symmetrically in a cone shape above the horizon's haze.

"Ahh ... I took that very same ferry a couple of times, many years ago," the Captain remarked.

"You did?" I responded curiously, sensing a story.

"Yes, Mr. Morris is not the only one of us who experienced Manila and the bar girls of Ermita. It was a common thing to take one of the girls for a two or three days excursion to Puerto Galera, if your ship was in port long enough, that is."

"Was there any special girl?"

"Not really ... I remember taking the trip twice ... but, yes, there was the one girl, come to think of it ... Marie," he chuckled. "It seems that about half of them were named Marie. But this particular girl was special ... we had a lot of fun together ... and she had this one peculiarity. She had a bladder problem and was always needing to pee ... and when she had to pee, she had to pee! Once it happened on the beach, once in a restaurant ... both times in front of everyone. And both times I laughed and laughed. That made her upset as hell and she wouldn't let me touch her ... it ended up costing me more money."

We both laughed.

"How do you think the Chinese girls compare with the Filipinas ... I mean, are we going to find anything like Ermita in Hong Kong?"

Hey, maybe we should be heading for Manila instead of Hong Kong!

Mr. Patterson laughed. "You don't have to worry about that, Chad ... Hong Kong is all one great big Ermita!"

Oh, it's OK then.

"I think I'm looking forward to that."

We could now feel the pull of the ebbing tide, helping to increase our speed, the landscape passing faster now.

Richard's bell let us know it was 2:00 p.m., our new lunch time. He had prepared a huge quantity of fried prawns and a mixture of vegetables, the prawns succulent and delicious.

"How's things going, navigation officer?" Harry wanted to know.

"We're not out of the woods yet, but almost." I answered.

Maricaban Island came and went ... to our starboard. Another heavy tonnage freighter appeared on the horizon, this time having approached from an angle of approximately 45 degrees to our starboard ... we were crossing the shipping lane now, choosing the less busy passage south of Golo Island rather than north, since Manila was not our destination. As the freighter came closer, the three of us at the wheelhouse suddenly became aware that our auxiliary had ceased to run.

"Chad ... please go below and find out what is happening this time," the Captain requested, nervous and agitated.

I hastened to the engine room. Harry had the auxiliary's fuel filter apart on the engine room floor, and was casually rinsing out the fabric element.

"Harry ... what the hell is going on?"

"Nothing much, mate ... just a good chance to clean the filter ... a bit of maintenance, that's all ... a stitch in time saves nine, they say. No worries about the refrigeration; I let Richard know and he's going to keep the freezer and reftigerator doors closed until I'm finished."

"Jeeses, Harry, you scared the shit out of the Captain and the rest of us!"

"Tell 'em no worries!"

Just Harry being 'dramatic' again!

"It's OK, Captain Harry decided to clean the filter, that's all ... I think he was feeling lonely and left out ... just wanted us to know he's still there."

"One hell of a way to do it!" he grunted.

"That's our Harry."

One hour later the auxiliary diesel came back on line.

"Chad, we'll stay on this heading until 8:00 p.m., when we'll swing to 325 degrees and aim straight for Hong Kong. Why don't you catch a few more hours rest ... then I can do the same later."

"You're on, Captain."

The fading light of the setting sun was my clue to return to the wheelhouse.

"Chad, let me bring you up to date. I was able to take a compass reading on both of these two lighthouses at the same time," Mr. Patterson pointed out the lighthouse on Golo Island and a second one on Cape Calavite at the extreme northwest corner of Mindoro. "So I got a good solid fix right here ... that was only one hour ago. So we are now here."

"I see ... we're right on our intended track ... is 8: 00 p.m. still the time for us to change course?"

"No ... I'd rather do it right now ... then we'll pass close enough to the lighthouse here at Cabra Island to get another fix ... at about 9 o'clock."

Following the Captain's instruction, Joseph brought the Trader around to 325 degrees ... it was now one long straight shot all the way to Hong Kong.

"Well, we made it, Captain!" I shouted exuberantly.

"Not yet, Chad ... not until we're anchored in Hong Kong Harbor."

"But that's duck soup ... we've made it through the hard part. How far are we from Hong Kong ... how many hours?"

"I've calculated it out ... we are 564 nautical miles to the entrance to Tathong Channel. At 8 knots it should take 68 hours ... four hours short of three full days."

"Sounds wonderful!"

Just before 9:00 p.m. I was able to make out the two-second flash at the Cabra Island lighthouse and took a series of compass headings at ten minute intervals until it was well to our aft.

"Clang - clang, clang -clang!"

This time Richard's bell held a special significance. Not only was it appreciated because it meant I could do something about the growing hole in my stomach, but it marked the completion of our passage through the 'seven thousand islands'. Apparently this significance was not a guarded secret, for just as I was about to go below to the officer's mess Fred showed on deck carrying a tray of plates, with Harry and Laurie right behind with several San Miguels tucked under their arms.

"Reckon it's time for a celebration," Harry announced.

Mr. Patterson joined us from his cabin, our noise having disturbed his sleep. But he had a smile on his face, and was clearly happy to join us. Within minutes everyone on board was on deck with a plate and a San Miguel in hand. All of us, that is, except the Captain.

"Captain, how about joining us with a drink of your rum." Harry suggested.

"Thank you, Harry ... but no thank you! You see, I don't drink rum any more ... but I will join you with a San Miguel beer ... but only one."

I suppose we had all been aware that we hadn't seen the Captain with his usual glass of rum in his hand for awhile, but with all the excitement we hadn't really caught its implication.

"Chad, Laurie ... here's the bottle of rum and scotch that you bought for Mr. Milner and myself in Laoang," he pointed to the bottles of Johnny Walker's and dark Bacardi rum, standing besides each other high up on the shelf next to the radio. I hadn't noticed. None of us had.

"You see, neither Mr. Milner or I have had a drink since Mr. Morris's death."

A silent reverence ensued among the crew. I personally was stunned. Stunned because I hadn't noticed, and also because it was amazing that the two men had actually stopped drinking.

"Uhh ... sir ... then I propose a toast to you ... and Mr. Milner ... that is truly commendable ... and remarkable."

"Hear, hear!" And we all toasted the Captain.

"Gentlemen, while we are feeling up to making toasts, I propose we all toast to Mr. Morris at this time as well ... perhaps it's fitting."

"Hear, hear!" Another round. I glanced at Harry, expecting him to show reluctance, but he had forgotten his former feelings of disgust for Mr. Morris's incompetence, or at least had put them aside.

Such a forgiving soul!

"Captain ... Speaking of Mr. Morris ... it has been a puzzle to me how he died," Kevin interjected, solemnly.

"How do you mean, Kevin?" Mr. Patterson inquired, equally somber.

'Well, he was drunk, and passed out ... but he never woke up ... it was as if he had decided not to wake up.

"Yes, I think you're right, Kevin ... that is the part that moved Mr. Milner and myself so much. We had just finished our very last remaining rum and scotch, you know ... and of course he knew it. I suppose he simply didn't want to wake up to a world without booze."

A long silence followed, we all sipped quietly on our San Miguels for a moment.

But Harry in particular felt that enough was enough for such sad thoughts. After all, we had come together to celebrate.

"And now, matey's, here's a toast to us ... we made it through the Strait and through seven thousand treacherous islands. I understand it's a clean shot now all the way to Hong Kong ... to Hong Kong and seven thousand beautiful Chinese maidens. No worries, right 2nd Mate!"

"Hear, hear!" We were all eager to consider happier thoughts.

"However, gentlemen ... we're not there until we're there ... but yes, maybe it's 'in the bag' so to speak."

"If you keep those damn engines running, Harry." I couldn't resist the opportunity to get in a jab.

"No worries ... no worries!"

"We almost didn't survive the San Bernardino Strait." Laurie reminded us. "You know, when those two engines were dead, and we were being blown straight towards those rocks ... well, I'll just have you know the insides of my shorts got kinda moist!"

"But we made it ... and that's gotta be some kind of achievement, especially since Lancey Shipping Company didn't expect us to." Harry added, in between snickers.

"Captain, do you think it's true ... they didn't intend for us to make it ... or at least were hoping we wouldn't?" Kevin wanted to know what the Captain felt.

Mr. Patterson became very serious. "Gentlemen ... I don't know ... I just don't know."

"Well, wanted or unwanted ... I reckon we'll do it anyway!" Harry proclaimed, defiantly.

"Unwanted ... but undaunted," Kevin laughed.

And despite your cursed warnings, Captain Rodney McKay!

We all had a couple more San Miguels. Except Mr. Patterson. He stuck to his word and stopped after that one beer. As I sipped on my own San Miguel and listened to the continuing banter and small talk, I realized that something meaningful had occurred: the comradeship between us had intensified, and it now included our Captain, Mr. Patterson.

Sixty-eight hours to Hong Kong! The Captain checked to make sure we were still on 325 degrees, and returned to his cabin.

I took four star shots at about 1:00 a.m., which included my 'ol buddy', Polaris, and was again pleased with the results. I left my calculations on the chart table for Mr. Patterson to review.

We were now into a main shipping lane again, and encountered two additional freighters in the distance. Fred and I closely watched their passage. One had apparently left Manila, heading for Hong Kong or a port further north -- maybe Taipei, or Yokohama -- the other was coming from across the China Sea from somewhere in Southeast Asia, perhaps Singapore or Bangkok or Bombay, and crossed our path diagonally, probably tansversing the Philippines on its way to the Pacific, and beyond. It thrilled me to imagine the many diverse ports that these travellers of the sea had just come from or were destined to reach.

Mr. Patterson came to relieve me at about 3:00 a.m., and I slept long and peacefully, aware of the 6 o'clock breakfast bell but choosing to ignore it.

I noticed the sky was partially clouded over when I finally did awaken, at about 11:00 a.m., and the northeasterly was still blowing.

"Morning, Captain ... at least I think it's still morning."

"Good day to you, Chad."

"Looks like our weather is changing ... sure hope we don't have to go through another typhoon."

"As long as we have the northeasterly we should be fine ... it's the southeasterly that signals a typhoon," he expounded.

"We're in a strange part of the world, as far as winds go," he continued. "If we were farther east into the Pacific the northeasterly would be a prevailing wind, the 'trades', and would bring good weather. But here the northeasterlies are thought of more as a winter wind, bringing rain. Then further west begins the southeast monsoon regions of Southern Asia and India."

"Thank you," I chuckled. "You're sounding like National Geographic again."

"Sorry .. I reckon I do at that. Do you mind?"

"Oh no, not at all ... on the contrary ... I love it!"

"Chad, you want to take over for awhile ... I'd like to get a few hours sleep."

"Uhh ... Can I grab a sandwich or something first?"

"Of course, of course," he answered.

Richard was in the kitchen, and offered to put something together for me: left-over fish and vegetables, with lots of yams. I took the plate to the wheelhouse, and Mr. Patterson retired.

"Hey, how's the philosopher?"

Kevin had come up to the wheelhouse, a San Miguel in hand, and made himself comfortable in one of the deckchairs.

"Sort of boring ... now."

Fred was being relieved by Joseph ... it was 2:00 p.m. and I was wondering when Richard would sound the bell. Instead, he appeared a few minutes later with a tray of food.

"Hey, you blokes want to eat up here?"

"Sure ... we didn't hear the bell." I said, thinking that he was bringing the plates to us because we hadn't gone down below.

"No need ... didn't want to wake the Captain. No problem."

Laurie went below, and returned a minute later with one open San Miguel plus a couple extra.

"Like a beer, Canuck?" he asked.

"Nah ... not when on duty ... but thanks anyway," I chuckled.

"Well Kevin ... any new thoughts about our pirate friend and King Solomon's Treasure?" I teased casually, mostly just to make small talk.

"Not really ... it would be interesting to spend some time in a good library and check out some of the events he referred to ... but I've never heard or read anything that either directly supports or refutes what he said."

Hey, maybe let him have a peek at what's under the seat in the officer's mess ... ?

"I'd like to look up a few of the Bible references he mentioned," I mused. "Especially that one where the 'gods' come down and co-mingle with earthly females. I've never heard of that part."

"Don't you ever think of anything besides sheilas?" he chuckled.

Laurie wanted to know what we were talking about. He had missed at lot of Bobby Mundy's story; so Kevin and I filled him in a bit. But our version wasn't nearly as convincing as the original, and he thought it was mostly just funny.

In between I reflected on how strange these ideas were to me. I was just an uneducated country bumpkin, raised in a strict religous environment that didn't allow much free thinking ... which I'd had a problem with and was rebelling against, sure ... but here I was on a wild ocean voyage listening to bizarre pirates tales of King Solomon's Treasure and Templar Knights and man having been created by extraterrestrials. And then there was Kevin's discussion on philosophy. It was all kinda heavy for me.

Oh yeh, almost forgot about Kevin's philosophy!

"Hey, Kevin, what about your philosophy? ... I had almost forgotten!"

Kevin chuckled. "Not *my* philosophy, Chad!"

"Oh ... OK then, the version you prefer."

"No, no ... you don't understand."

"OK, philosopher ... explain it to me!"

He smiled, and chuckled to me again. "I'll tell you what ... I'll give you a quick outline ... and then sometime you go and read up on it yourself, and see if you agree with my conclusions'."

"Shoot!"

"Where did we leave off?"

"Where you said we don't need an explanation ... and I said that that sort of leaves us in the wide open without much security."

"Oh yeh ... and I was going to tell you which philosophers talked about that."

"Yeh ... you said you'd have to give me a 'history of philosophy'."

"I said that? Big order, you know."

"Neither of us are going anywhere for three days." I joked.

"OK ... here goes! The philosopher who said we don't need an explanation, or at least the first one in modem times that made a good case for it was the German philosopher, Friedrich Wilhelm Nietzsche, during the late 1800's."

"His name was what?"

"Nietzsche ... N-i-e-t-z-c-h-e."

"Nietzsche?"

"Yes ... can I go on?"

"Yes."

"Nietzsche claimed that the history of philosophy had failed to come up with an irrefutable 'explanation'. So he said, simply, 'so what'! We're grown ups who can face up to that reality, if that's what it is, and go on without an absolutely irrefutable explanation, or the 'absolute' or 'irrefutable truth' on which to base that explanation. He described the individual who was strong enough, and sophisticated enough to accomplish that as an 'Upperman'. He argued that the need for an absolute explanation came out of weakness, that societies had traditionally used religion and claims of possessing 'the truth' as a crutch, and that declarations of 'godliness' or 'righteousness' were nothing but products of human vanity. Do you follow me so far?"

"Well, Kevin ... I'm having a hard time ... but I get the gist of it. I have a question, though."

"Shoot!"

"Kevin ... that's my line."

"Well, then ... go ahead."

"So, this guy Nietzsche says this. So, big deal. Is he just one guy out of ten million? Or what?"

"Ahh ... Well, Chad, this is why I said it was unfair to just drop you a name ... that I needed to explain the 'history of philosophy'."

"Well, shoot."

"No ... it's too much ... just a very brief outline, OK?"

"OK!"

"OK ... the part of philosophy which we're talking about is 'epistemology'."

"Kevin ... don't do this to me."

"I was going to explain ... give me a chance, alright. Epistemology is the the 'theory of knowledge', or the exploration of what we can or can't know, which we already talked about. Remember when we talked about color blindness, and the conclusion that our perceptions are different, that your world and my world are different, and that we can't know conclusively what the *real* world actually is?"

"Yeh, I remember that."

"Well, in a nutshell, the history of philosophical thought, at least as far as epistemology is concerned, came to this conclusion early in the 1800's. As one bloke put it, his name was Hegel, philosophy was 'bankrupt'. And it probably was. The Greeks had battled with epistemology and had gone the complete circle. Then the Western philosophers did battle with it and completed pretty much the same circle. Just remember two names, one from each of those great eras: Plato and Kant."

"Who? Kevin, you're not talking about cuscus all of a sudden, are you?"

"No, no ... idiot ... Plato and Immanuel Kant ... K-a-n-t ... Plato was a Greek philosopher, about 400 B.C., and Kant was another German philosopher in the late 1700's."

"So what about these guys?"

"What's significant about these two philosophers is that they each brought the discussion of the theory of knowledge to a conclusion for each of the two eras. Both argued that there was a 'real world' but that we could only perceive a 'shadow', or 'reflection', or 'dream version' of that real world. Plato said it was like we were in a cave, with the real world outside and all that we could see were the 'shadows' of that real world on the walls of the cave. Kant said we could only perceive a 'relection' of the true world, as if from a non-perfect mirror, or a 'dream version'."

"Hey, Kevin, I think I see what you mean now ... but you leave a great big question wide open."

"And what is that?"

"You say that if we can be 'Uppermen', and we don't need an 'explanation', that we can live without one. But without something as a solid base, how do we know what's right or wrong, or how to decide what's good and bad, or what we should or shouldn't do?"

"What you have just objected to was Nietzsche's biggest criticism. He was condemned as an 'anarchist', because his critics interpreted him as saying we could do anything we wanted ... but we know more now."

"We know more now?"

"Yes ... the Existentialists such as Sarte and Camus taught us that, contrary to most religous thought, which attempts to 'combat evil' and control us, common man generally seeks and demonstrates good, and finds good in basic survival. Another concept then … is that we can form an advanced version of Nietzsche ... we can choose a 'functional' explanation to guide us the way which we rationally have chosen to go. We can use reason and logic as our guide and choose a 'functional absolute', so to speak."

"Oh boy ... you're too heavy for me, Kevin ... what about finding a 'meaning' to life and existence?"

"Well, this is largely my own conclusion, but we can again choose a functional explanation, if we really gotta have one, or you can argue that the only thing we end up with is 'hope' ... but maybe that's enough. *I* think it's enough. We can't know for sure, and insisting that we are the stuff of gods or more than the grains of sand on the beach are just projections of our weakness and vanity, but we can humbly 'hope' that there's more, that there *is* maybe life after death, or that we have a soul, or that as mankind we are doing good and progressing, not regressing. And like one Chinese philosopher put it when he criticized western religous thought: if we would worry less about the hereafter and more about us as human beings, in this life and on this planet, we just might be able to make this a better world in which to live." He paused. "Well, that's the end."

"That's it, Kevin?"

"Yeh, that's it!"

"Jeeses, I was hoping … hah … there's that word … that you'd give me something really earth-shattering ... you know, something absolute, irrefutable."

"Well ... I'm terribly sorry to disappoint you, Chad."

"Kevin, you gotta do some more thinking, and when you come up with something real super, let me know." I laughed.

Kevin shrugged his shoulders and smiled.

Laurie had been listening all along and chuckled.

"So, Laurie, what do you think?" I questioned.

"I think I'm going to have another San Miguel."

I reflected on the notion that had flashed before me when Kevin and I were talking -- about showing him the 'treasure' under the seat in the officer's mess. I was busting with curiosity myself, and would love to check it out. But it was risky … almost impossible to do without the entire crew knowing. I almost wanted to let everyone know about it. But no, I was being trusted with a secret and a responsibility. No, better to simply forget that it's there. At least until we're in Hong Kong.

Good boy, Chad!

The 68 hours began to stretch out. The same northeasterly continued to tease the China Sea, endlessly rippling its surface and causing its swells to crest and spit white froth back at their tormenter, our sky remained overshadowed, with an occasional shower, and the Trader maintained its rythmic rumble constantly pushing through the purple sea at a consistent 8 knots, the bow folding back the water's surface in a white curl on both the port and starboard sides and leaving behind a long, straight wake, the swirling, churning water slowly blending back to its previous state, eventually hiding all evidence that we had passed.

Kevin and Laurie had finished their San Miguels some time ago, and had crashed, and Mr. Patterson had joined me on the wheelhouse deck. Joseph finished his watch, and Fred was at the helm.

"Captain ... do you figure Mr. Milner will be alright?"

"I'm sure of it," he smiled, "He's a survivor ... and there was strong feelings between him and Mayor Dulay-Quibal. I wouldn't be surprised if something long term came of it. Might be what the man needed."

"Do you think maybe something really did happen on that schooner from Hong Kong?"

"Oh, something did happen ... the Captain was lost overboard."

"I mean, do you think Mr. Milner murdered him ... threw him overboard?"

"Well, you saw for yourself how crazy he could get when he was drunk ... especially before ... if you remember the incident with my glasses. There may have been an argument ... and perhaps an accident ... but no … not murder."

"Hmm ..."

"Mr. Milner was a man who chose to run away from a life of responsibility and adherence to a strict code, and traded the life of a nobleman for freedom and adventure," Mr. Patterson continued. "He resented authority, and yet the one thing he wanted most was to become a ship's captain."

I took another four star sightings and worked carefully through the calculations. I guess I was getting pretty good at this, for again my intersections were close. Mr. Patterson checked my work.

"You're developing some skill at this, Chad."

"Thank you, sir."

The breakfast bell woke me. I wanted to sleep more, but my stomach was begging me to take advantage of Richard's great morning meals, so I agreed.

"Good morning, Captain," I tossed off casually on my way past the wheelhouse, my eyes still only half open.

"Good morning to you, Chad."

Laurie was at the wheel, with a grin on his face. I was still wondering why when I reached the mess. "Well?" Harry asked.

"Well what?" I answered. Something strange was going on, I sensed. I checked myself to make sure it wasn't because I forgot to put my shorts on, or my fly was undone, or some such thing. Nope … everything checked out.

"You mean you never noticed?" Harry smirked.

"Harry ... what's going on ... never noticed what?"

"The Captain ... you just walked past him ... how could you *not* notice?"

"Harry ... I haven't the foggiest what you're talking about!"

"Chad ... Mr. Patterson shaved off his goatee."

"He what?" This I could not believe.

"Yeh ... go see for yourself ... he shaved it off."

Richard was at the door with my plate: red snapper fillet, eggs, and yams.

"I'll be right back, Richard." That plate looked good. "Don't go away." I added. I hurried up the steps to the upper deck.

"Yes, Chad ... what is it?" Mr. Patterson smiled.

"I didn't believe them ... had to come and see for myself

Mr. Patterson's long white goatee was truly gone. I mean it just wasn't there anymore. Instead was a clean, pink chin. He had chosen to keep the full moustache. The effect was dramatic.

"Captain ... you look like a brand new man ... and ten years younger."

"Well ... thank you, Chad." Mr. Patterson was both pleased and a little embarrassed.

"Uhh ... well ... I guess I'll go have breakfast."

I woke up with Jeri Miller and Angie Harris heavy on my mind again. It led to an argument with Harry.

"Harry ... I miss Deli ... had another god-damn wet dream ... but this one was for real." I had to clearify what I meant; I could see he was already starting to smirk.

"Yeh ... I miss Liza too. She was such a playful thing ... and the only girl I'd ever met that never said no ... I mean *never*." He sounded genuinely nostalgic.

"That was because she was only sixteen," I laughed. "And you're such an old fart ... you probably couldn't keep up with her!"

"The hell with you, Canuck. I could keep up with her just fine. As a matter of fact, it was *you* who couldn't keep up with Deli."

"And what do you mean by that?" I couldn't believe he had said what I'd just heard.

"You were so drunk most nights, you couldn't do anything!" Harry bantered.

"Yeh, I was drunk a lot ... but that never interfered with my sex life." I was starting to get angry.

"Are you kidding, mate ... you used to be so drunk you'd pass out on the floor."

"Pass out on the floor? Harry, you're a god-damned liar. It was Deli who used to end up on the floor, if anyone."

"Oh no, matey, you have it all wrong. You'd come home stoned, pass out on the floor, and then Deli would put you in bed ... then sometimes you were so obnoxious and stinky, she had to sleep on the floor to get away from you."

"Deli put me in bed? ... no ways, mate ... you're full of it, Harry!"

"Canuck ... I know, cause I had to help her a couple of times!"

I was pissed. I stood up and left the officer's mess. Jeeses, I wanted to take a crack at the son-of-a-bitch. His nerve ... saying that Deli put me in bed cause I passed out on the floor!

It may *have been true, Chad!*

Later, watching the sea slip past, I recalled how it had been the last few weeks in Rabaul. When I first started working at CDW, I used to have a few South Pacifics almost every evening after work. Then I graduated to screw drivers and bloody marys, mostly because of the hang-overs. It had become a daily routine. Again, like Dennis, 'ol buddy' had joked ... I was going 'down the drain'. Yeh, there had been a few bad- nights. The couple when I was so drunk I drove on the 'right' side of the road and almost killed myself. Or one night when I passed out at one of Walter's parties. Or another at some other person's house when a visiting Australian chick called me a 'bloody drunk'. She was good looking and it had stung. Now Harry tells me that I used to come back to the CDW camp so drunk I would pass out on the floor and Deli would pick me up and put me in bed?

Maybe it was true. I didn't like it, but I realized then that it probably was true.

Atta-boy!

We were now twelve hours from the entrance to Tathong Channel. It was just past midnight, Fred and I were at the wheelhouse, the Captain was in his cabin, and everything was quiet except for the steady drone and vibrations of the three diesel engines. Without warning, the two Perkins suddenly ceased to run. No sputtering, no coughing, no miss ... they just simply and quietly died.

Mr. Patterson was on the deck within seconds. There was a commotion below, both Harry and Kevin were scrambling to get to the engine room ... I guessed that neither of them had been on duty ... everyone wanted to know what had happened.

I looked towards Fred.

"Both engines conk out at the same time? No missing, no sputtering? Just running out of fuel'? Guess we both know what it is. Go ahead and take care of it, Fred."

"Chad, what's going on?"

"It's a problem Fred had anticipated ... he already has a solution worked out. It's the single fuel pump working for both engines ... finally gave out. But Fred is going to raise the 50 gallon drum so we have gravity flow and can by-pass the pump."

"Chad ... Harry won't listen to me ... I can't do anything."

"Let me talk to him." I was still feeling sore with Harry since our little argument. Maybe now was a chance to even the score.

Even though he had been right?

"Harry, you can be a bone-head Aussie all you want, but Fred and I know that the one fuel pump simply petered out with the double load and the simple solution is to raise that s.o.b. drum up high enough to create gravity flow and by-pass the fuel pump with the lines. Please proceed accordingly, you dumb shit!"

I turned and fled, chuckling all the way back to the wheelhouse. "The hell with you, Canuck!" echoed repeatedly behind me. I loved it!

Chad, you are beyond hope!

Two hours later both Perkins were back on line, and Fred returned to his position behind the wheel, a smirk on his face.

I took a final set of star shots just before sunrise. We would reach the entrance to Tathong Channel at approximately 3:00 p.m., and this would be my last chance for a fix. I had taken four readings and worked through the computations as carefully as I could. The resulting intersections were OK ... we had a good position. I double-checked the dead reckoning projection ... the ETA of 3:00 p.m. was also good. We did need to alter our heading, however.

"Fred ... please change our heading to 322 degrees."

"Clang - clang, clang - clang!" Richard's bell announced the 6:00 a.m. breakfast. We all knew that Mr. Patterson had requested Richard to sound his bell, and we were all asked to be present.

"Good morning, gentlemen." The Captain was in good cheer, and well rested. This was a big day for him. For all of us. We were just about to enter Hong Kong Harbor, and anchor the New Guinea Trader at her final destination. Her final destination as far as we were concerned, that is. Anticipation and excitement were running high.

"Gentlemen, I have only a couple of things to say ... we are almost there, I will save congratulations for when we finally do anchor. However, we should be at the entrance to Tathong Channel at approximately 3:00 p.m.. The channel is clearly marked and we shouldn't have a problem. We will probably be met by a pilot and immigration/customs vessel part way down the channel. There will be some formalities. Please remember we are gentlemen. The pilot will lead us to an anchorage in Hong Kong Harbor, somewhere around here." Mr. Patterson had brought the chart of Hong Kong with him, entitled 'Eastern Approaches to Hong Kong', and he indicated an area just outside Kowloon Bay, perpendicular to the airport runway.

"Now for an urgent matter." He sat down and urged us all to do the same, our curiosity piqued. "Mr. Fitzgerald informed me that we could expect to be boarded by the Hong Kong police, in regards to a matter concerning Mr. Milner, and possibly myself. If they do board, there will be many questions asked. Specifically, they may ask about the incident during our first day out of Rabaul when Mr. Milner locked me in my cabin and took command of the ship, and there may be a question or two about the 'level of competence' displayed by Mr. Milner as well, and Mr. Morris ... and myself." He paused.

317

"You are all grown men, and you have your own minds and your own convictions about what is right and wrong, and your own feelings about the things that I'm talking about ... I cannot tell you what to say. However ... gentlemen, this is difficult. I hope you will have good things to say about the three of us. Even Mr. Morris, Harry. And I want you to know that as far as I'm concerned the incident with Mr. Milner never happened. So I would like to know how you gentlemen feel.

A long silence followed, none of us knowing quite what to say.

"Mr. Milner taking command of the ship? Locking our Captain in his cabin? I don't recall anything like that happening!" Harry had that dumb ass grin all over his face again.

"I'm with you, Mr. Patterson ... it never happened." I gladly obliged.

Laurie and Kevin both nodded in agreement.

Richard spoke for the three New Guinea nationals: "Hell, we don't even speak English!"

The somberness of Mr. Patterson's discussion quickly passed ... our thoughts swiftly returned to our anticipated arrival in Hong Kong.

"When do you reckon the 'meat boat' will show up?" Harry asked, out of the blue.

Mr. Patterson smiled.

"What did you say?" I quizzed, perplexed by what I thought I had heard.

"Yeh ... the 'meat boat'! You mean you don't know what the meat boat is?"

"No, Harry ... I don't know what the meat boat is?"

"Well, I have it from an unquestionable source that we will probably be met by a 'walla-walla' loaded with beautiful Chinese ladies, and they will come aboard to service us right here on board the Trader."

"You gotta be kidding?"

"It's dinky die!"

"Harry's right," Mr. Patterson interjected, a twinkle in his eye. "However, you gentlemen ... ahh ... must be properly prepared." He added, with an excited edge to his voice.

"What do you mean, 'properly prepared'?" Laurie wanted to know.

"Well, each of you have your own 'methods' and idiosyncrasies, I am sure, but we each must have our special equipment ready."

"Captain ... what *are* you talking about?" Laurie asked, bewildered.

"Excuse me ... I will show you." With that, Mr. Patterson left the mess, presumably going to his cabin to fetch something.

"He probably means that we should all have a good supply of top quality condoms," Harry suggested. " I got mine."

"Can I borrow a few?" I requested.

"I'd be glad to give you as many as you can handle, Canuck ... let's see, that'll be a total of one!"

"Up yours …!"

Mr. Patterson returned to the mess, sat down, and placed one Trojan condom, a pair of rubber ear plugs, and a wooden clothespin on the table. We all watched, expecting an explanation, all wondering what this was all about.

"Well, gentlemen ... I hope you all have your special equipment ready. As you can see, I have mine." He motioned towards the condom, the ear plugs, and the clothespin, and waited.

"Excuse me, sir," Laurie couldn't control his curiosity. "We know what the condom is for … but what about the ear plugs and the clothespin?"

"You don't know?" the Captain replied. "Why, these are to put in my ears, and this is to hold my nose closed."

"But sir, why would you want to do that?"

"Well, like I said, we all have our individual idiosyncrasies. Mine is that I can't stand the sound of a screaming woman, and I abhor the smell of burning rubber!"

Harry was on his back on the floor, holding his stomach, his legs kicking in the air. Laurie just looked puzzled. Fred was giggling and explaining it all to Joseph and Richard.

Mr. Patterson sat back in the bench seat, a satisfied grin on his face.

I was laughing hard, but thinking at the same time that this was not the same man I had met in Rabaul some four weeks before.

CHAPTER FOURTEEN

Hong Kong

"So engrossed was he in his labor that it was only for the brief moment when he chased the boulder back down the hill could he reflect on the absurdity of his efforts."

"Joseph, you will have the honor of bringing the Trader through Tathong Channel, and into Hong Kong Harbor. We should be here, at the entrance to the channel, at approximately 3:30 p.m." Mr. Patterson had invited the crew up to the wheelhouse for a final briefing.

"It is simply a matter of following down the right side of the channel, keeping these channel markers to our port."

"Ahh ... like driving on the 'right' side of the road . . where 'right' is right, like people in sane countries drive ... Canada and the U.S., for example ... and unlike in that strange land 'down under'!" I couldn't resist the opportunity to elaborate on one of my pet peeves.

"Yeh, and you know where you can go, Canuck!" Harry responded, with a conspicuous lack of humor.

I noticed that the sea was gradually changing color, from a deep blue to a greenish-blue, and seemed to be becoming increasingly green.

"Mr. Patterson, I can appreciate now what you mean by 'navigating by the color of the water' ... the color is changing right now, and I see on the chart that the water depth is becoming more shallow at the same time."

"Yes ... it's the green color of the shallow China Sea. Your're right."

Off to our port side I thought I could see a sail, in the far distance. I continued to watch ... the vessel was travelling due south.

I think you're seeing your first Chinese Junk, Chad. Here, take a look with the binoculars."

I accepted the glasses, and trained them on the sail. Yes, it was a Chinese Junk. Or at least it looked like the pictures I had seen of Chinese Junks, with their distinctive sail and rectangular hull, the aft section raised high with a square cabin. I was fascinated, and wanted to get a closer look.

"You'll soon be seeing many, many of them." Mr. Patterson had read my mind.

I then spotted a group of fishing boats off on the starboard side: small open craft, again also rectangular, and with a single quadrilateral sail supported from the top by a gaff spar.

"Those fishing boats have small inboard diesel engines as well as sail, but they prefer to trawl under sail ... they reckon they catch more fish without the noise of the diesels."

At almost the same instant I caught sight of lights from what I thought were two lighthouses.

"Captain, I think I see two sets of lighthouse lights."

Mr. Patterson motioned for me to return the binoculars, wanting to see for himself.

"Please check the chart, Chad ... the one to our port has two flashing lights, the one dead ahead has a single light."

"Mr. Patterson, that would indicate the lighthouse at Waglan Island to our port and the first channel marker to Tathong Channel, straight ahead."

"Good ... that means we're right on course ... your heading adjustment this morning was justified ... good work!"

It seemed as if all of a sudden there were vessels and islands everywhere. Another Chinese Junk passed to our port, but I was too busy to be able to watch it closely. I could now make out a group of tiny islands to the starboard which were named the Ninepin Group. The island of Po Toi was visible behind the Waglan Island lighthouse, and the DiAguilar Peninsula, which is part of Hong Kong Island, was recognizable by its 'dragon back' topography and its two lighthouses at Cape DiAguilar and at Tai Long Pai.

"Do you see the channel marker ... dead ahead, Joseph?" the Captain inquired.

"Yes sir ... I see it now ... I just keep to the right?"

"Yes ... like Chad says: 'right' is right," he chuckled. "At sea, at least."

We were approaching from the southeast, and the entrance to the channel was due west.

"Joseph, give the marker at least a one hundred meter clearance, and as soon as we have the marker on our port broadside, bring the Trader fairly hard port to about 270 degrees. The second marker is approximately one mile further down the channel.

A vessel was approaching in the outgoing lane. It was still a long ways away, in the next leg of the channel, so that our view of her was slightly to her port side.

It was huge -- the largest ship I had ever seen -- a tanker. Another Chinese Junk went by. Several more fishing boats were outside the channel lane, going in both directions. One more junk appeared to our starboard; its sails were battened down and she was motoring ... it was overtaking and passing us! I couldn't believe its speed, and size ... well over one hundred feet in length. She must have one hell of an engine, I mused.

But I didn't have much time to gaze. Too much was happening too fast. And yet it was difficult not to be spellbound by the sights. The tanker was now swooping past us. The vessel was easily four hundred yards away, but I had the sensation that I could reach out and touch the surface of her vast black hull. Coming back to earth, I rationally estimated that her length was at least ten times ours, and I had to look upwards to her main deck. I started to fall into a trance again, mesmerized by her enormous size. Mr. Patterson tapped me on the shoulder.

"Chad," he admonished. "We have to keep an eye on our own progress, not hers."

I flashed back to the sign on the rear bumper of the jeepney in Rawis: 'Watch my rear end, not hers!', and I snickered to myself

"Uhh ... yes sir ... I'm sorry ... it's just that it is so huge."

We reached the second marker and the Captain instructed Joseph to come to starboard about twenty degrees. He pointed out an island ahead and to our starboard which we could use as a guide.

"That's Fat Tong Chau, or 'Junk Island' ... aim for its southern shore. We should have a pilot visiting us any time now." he explained.

It was as if he had already seen the craft, for we were immediately aware of a motorboat coming alongside, on our starboard. The vessel looked like a small tug, a rugged looking vessel with heavily protected gunwales and a sizeable enclosed cabin, tall and kind of squarish, complete with an extraordinary assortment of auxiliary lights and official looking writings on the sides of the cabin, mostly in Chinese characters, but also included bold lettering in English, reading 'Hong Kong Port Authority -- Immigration and Customs'.

Laurie was Johnny-on-the-spot, with our boarding ladder ready in place. Two Chinese gentlemen scrambled up the ladder, with a Chinese sailor dressed in navy blue and a sailor's cap immediately behind. A second and third sailor stayed aboard the visiting craft, standing by.

Laurie escorted the two gentlemen to the wheelhouse. Without introductions or forewarning, the first official announced in an authoritive voice:

"Gentlemen, this is most unusual. Why didn't you contact us via radio? And you are not on our list of expected arrivals. Please explain."

I expected Mr. Patterson to be both embarrassed and abashed by this confrontation, but he was neither. He stood stalwart in front of our visitor, and explained in a calm, dignified tone:

"Sir ... I am Captain Patterson, and this is the New Guinea Trader. We have just come through Typhoon Denance. We have lost two of our officers and much of our gear. As you can see by our list, we are damaged, and I'm afraid part of the damage we suffered included our radio. We were unable to contact you. We have come to Hong Kong for a refit, but we are many days late, which would account for us not being on your list. Our owners have probably given us up for lost."

I flashed on the idea that maybe the Captain and Harry should put their talents together ... look out, Errol Flynn!"

Hmm ... Errol Flynn again!

The Chinese official seemed to have been robbed of his bureaucratic wind. I suspected that what the Captain had said gave us special 'distress' status.

"Well ... uhh ... we are glad to assist you, of course. I am Mr. Henri Cho, your customs and immigration representative, and this is your pilot, Mr. Soon."

"Good day, gentlemen," Mr. Soon motioned with a movement that was partly a nod and partly what I took to be a Chinese bow, and positioned himself to Joseph's left side.

"May I see your ship's papers and your crew's seamen credentials," Mr. Cho requested, recapturing some of his authoritative tone.

The Captain presented him with the same package that he had given Mr. Cuscus in Laoang, and our visitor began his examination.

"You have a cargo of scrap iron, Mr. Patterson?"

"Yes, sir."

"Can you please have your crew pull back the tarps and open your holds ... I would like to take a look."

The Captain turned in my direction.

"Mr. Fletcher, please instruct Laurie and Fred to open the two holds ... and please return as soon as you've done so."

I hurried down to the main deck.

"Laurie, Fred ... the customs guy wants to inspect our holds ... can you two remove the tarps and open the holds."

"How do we do that?" Laurie was perplexed.

"Open the holds, you mean? Beats me ... figure it out best you can."

I flashed on an absurd idea during the return trip to the wheelhouse: what if Lancey Shipping Company had loaded us with something illegal. Then another possibility occured to me: could that be part of the warning from the mysterious Captain McKay? We would have never known. Anything could be hidden in that hold. Almost anything at all. I imagined a black vision of all eight of us rotting away in a Hong Kong prison.

Jeeses, Chad ... snap out of it! Don't be so paranoid.

Mr. Cho spent what seemed an uneccessarily long time going over our documents, asking Mr. Patterson many questions. He was particularly meticulous when he came to my seaman's card. It was the same as the others that had been issued in Rabaul: an off-white piece of folded poster board with typed lettering, a passport size black and white photo pasted on with Elmer's glue, and a blue stamp. But mine declared that I was the Trader's Second Officer. Scanning me suspiciously over the top of his glasses, he questioned: "*You* are the 2nd Mate?"

"Uhh ... yes sir ... I'm the 2nd Mate."

"Where are your Second Officer certification papers?" he demanded, his voice taking on a cross-examining temperament.

"Mr. Cho ..." Captain Patterson interrupted. "Mr. Fletcher is not a certified Second Officer ... certification is not required for him to fill the capacity of 2nd Mate on this ship, which is in accordance with maritime law."

"Hmm ... do you have any other documents, or papers?"

Mr. Cho reminded me of the stereotype Communist Chinese interrogator in movies such as the 'Manchurian Candidate', and any second I expected for him to insist I sit in a chair and for him to suspend a bright light close above my head and tie my hands behind my back.

"Only my Canadian passport, which you have there ... among those papers."

He found my passport, and spent a very long time examining its pages, noting the stamps for entry to the U.S., New Zealand, and Australia. Finally, he turned to me with a wry smile.

"It seems you are a young adventurer ... welcome to Hong Kong."

I sighed inwardly, with no small measure of relief

"Captain Patterson, I am going to require that you file a report for the death of your Chief Engineer and the departure of your First Officer ... I hope he recovers from his malaria.

Malaria?

While I had been suffering Mr. Cho's interrogation, the Trader had reached its anchorage site under the guidance of the Pilot, Mr. Soon, and Lauire and Fred had lowered our starboard anchor.

"Please make sure your anchor is secured firm, with a short chain ... our wind and tide are variable and you will need to be able to rotate about." Mr. Soon had explained.

Our two deck hands had succeeded in opening both holds. It turned out that each wooden covering had a small section that was easy to remove, affording a good view for inspection, and was probably designed for just that purpose. Mr. Cho spent several minutes peering into each hold, but never ventured to climb down inside. He was finally satisfied.

"Captain, you and your crew are free to visit Hong Kong ... but I am requiring that you visit the Harbor Master's office no later than tomorrow ... is that understood?"

"Yes, Mr. Cho."

And then they were gone. I, for one, sighed with great relief, and was finally able to dispel my anxiety and vision of a dark, dungeon-like prison and torture by sadistic Chinese interrogators.

Richard's surveillance and sense of timing was again par excellence. His bell announced the moment we had long awaited: anchorage in Hong Kong Harbor ... and substance for our craving bellies as well, of course.

The mess table was forested with a number of San Miguels ... we were told we were close to the end of that critical commodity, by the way, and Richard had laid out three large trays: one of fried prawns, another of cut steak, both embellished with an assortment of steamed vegetables, plus a third tray of mixed fruit ... the last fruit still not spoiled from our Laoang shopping spree. The intention was for us to choose what we wanted, buffet style. We dug in.

"Now, gentlemen, we can toast to the successful completion of our voyage."

Mr. Patterson raised a glass. "I personally congratulate each of you ... and thank you for your hard work, your ingenuity, and your perseverance."

"Hear, hear!"

I was then cognizant of a pause, and an expectation aimed in my direction. I supposed that because I was 2nd Mate it was my duty to return the toast.

Ahh, I suppose rank does have its responsibilities!

I hurried mentally to come up with something half-ass suitable.

"Uhh ... and I propose a toast to you, Captain for having guided us through it all and including Mr. Milner, who I do hope recovers from his malaria ... and Mr. Morris too ... of course!"

"Malaria?" Two or three voices asked in unison.

Mr. Patterson chuckled. "Yes, at least that's the official story!"

Everyone laughed. I took a long drag on the San Miguel and settled back in the bench seat. We were finally here in Hong Kong. Our anchor was securely dug into the harbor's bottom, the twin Perkins had been brought gently to rest, and the New Guinea Trader had definitively reached her final destination. We had made it … unwanted, but undaunted!

But the feeling of relief and joy at having reached our goal also prompted the question 'what now?'. And so I asked:

"Alright, gents ... but where do we all go from here?"

The question had been in the back of all our minds, but our preoccupation with the tasks at hand had preempted any discussion about 'what after'.

"Gentlemen ... I do have something to say regarding that question. I may be breaching my loyalty to my employer, Lancey Shipping Company, but I want to do what I can to ensure that you are all properly taken care of. Are you aware that Lancey has an obligation to do just that?"

"Captain ... I'm glad you brought this up. From what we know already, I reckon we're going to have a fight with Mr. Lancey ... and Mr. Fitzgerald. Do you agree?" Harry questioned.

"I honestly don't know, Harry. But I do know that the first thing all you need to do is come with me to the Harbor Master's office tomorrow and properly 'sign off'.

"What do you mean, Captain?"

"Well, according to internatonal maritime law, the shipping company must repatriate you to the port where you signed on, once your service has been terminated and you are signed off. So if you officially register with the Harbor Master, and receive a 'discharge', then that locks Lancey Shipping Company into an obligation to repatriate you back to Rabaul."

"But I don't want to go back to Rabaul!" I objected.

"Chad ... think for a moment ... there is no air connection between here and Rabaul except via the three-quarter circle through Singapore and Sydney. And there are no regular ships from here to New Guinea either. That air route is a very long and expensive one. I reckon you could bargain for an air fare to just about anywhere in the world."

"Alright!"

That speculation sparked several ideas.

"I reckon I'd like to get back to Sydney," Harry pondered wistfully. "Maybe go back to work on the Snowy Mountain project."

"Where do you want to go, Canuck?" Laurie asked.

"Don't really know. How about you ... and you, Kevin?"

"I want to visit Hong Kong for awhile ... but eventually I'd like to return to England." Kevin responded, obviously having already thought about the question. Laurie was still browsing the alternatives.

"England ... that's maybe not a bad choice," I contemplated out loud.

Richard, Fred, and Joseph remainded silent. I was wondering why, then remembered my conversations with Fred. I realized that their options weren't the same as ours.

Any further discussion was halted, however, by a very important event.

"Toot - toot!"

"What was that?" Harry exclaimed, jumping up and leaving the mess cabin to investigate. Our Captain's face broke out in a wide, knowing grin.

"Bloody hell ... it's the 'meat boat'!"

We all scrambled to the deck to take a look.

I leaned over the rail to get a better view. A vessel had pulled alongside, and I could see about ten Chinese females of different ages, shapes, and degrees of attractiveness waving to us, obviously seeking permission to come aboard. And of course we were encouraging them to do exactly just that. With startling dexterity they all scaled the same ladder that our pilot and 'interrogator' had used only an hour before.

The vessel caught my attention, briefly, in between my more pressing evaluations of our female visitors. It was an open, wooden vessel with a full width canvas canopy for a roof, the hull was similar to a large Boston Whaler, except more rectangular, and I judged that it had a flat bottom. This, I assumed, was what Harry had called a 'walla-walla'.

Our first lady reached the top of the ladder and straddled the rail. Mr. Patterson, our gentleman, was beside her instantly to assist. She was rather stout and big bosomed for a Chinese, I surmised, but then she was a little old too.

"Oh ... thank you, sir!" she whispered with pretended shyness. She turned and rattled off something in Chinese to the rest of the girls ... I took it that she was their 'leading lady' of sorts.

One by one they reached the top.

"What do you think, Laurie?" I quizzed in a low voice.

"I hope this isn't the best that Hong Kong has to offer!" He mirrored my sentiments exactly. But I guessed that they weren't. Coming out in the harbor to climb aboard rusty old freighters and dealing with rowdy, lower sloblovian sailors on their own turf was probably not considered the option of choice by Hong Kong's more desirable queens of the evening. But then that was just a wild guess on my part.

One was a frolicsome, bubbly miss that I guessed was in her late twenties, a little on the chubby side and with her black hair piled in an extraordinarily high and stiff-looking affair on the top of her head, but her friendliness and impromtu giggling set her apart … she and Harry naturally gravitated together. She was snuggling up to him as we all filed back into the officer's mess, he grabbing her and pinching her on the butt, she squealing and giggling.

Only one struck me as possessing enough charm to invest in: she was younger, and not really the prettiest, but she had attractive long, straight, raven black hair and an athletic appearance, with definite curves and a healthy, earthly face … a girl that if I took home to mom, mom would be disappointed because she was not really pretty, but would be truly delighted that I had chosen a robust, hard working, and down-to-earth girl.

Laurie was thinking the same thing. We glanced at each other, both of us wanting to know if the other was going to make a move.

Our leading lady's name was Mimi … her real name, she said … and she got down to business immediately.

"Well, gentlemen, don't you like any of these beautiful ladies? We're all yours, you know!" she fluttered. Her English was understandable and actually pretty good, but with an accent not yet familiar to my ears.

"If you don't mind me asking, ma'am ... uhh ... how much would it cost?" Harry was worrying about his budget, as usual.

"Oh ... oh, that ... well, gentlemen, you make your own deal with the girl you choose, but it begins at twenty Hong Kong dollars."

"How much is that in Australian dollars?" I wanted to know, whispering to Mr. Patterson.

"The exchange rate is seven Hong Kong dollars to one Aussie dollar," the Captain informed us.

"Well?" Mimi asked again.

Harry was squirming, desire written all over him.

Then Mr. Patterson had a proposal. "Harry ... I have a great idea ... if the rest of us agree ... if you do it right here in front of us, we'll pay for it!"

"Oooh," the bubbly lady responded. "That would cost much more ... at least double."

"Let's see, that would be six dollars Australian ... or one dollar each ... we would be giving her *seven* dollars."

"Bloody hell ... right here on the table in front of everyone?"

"Now, let's see ... that's forty-nine Hong Kong dollars," calculated Mimi.

"Ooohh . ." agreed the bubbly lady.

Harry laughed, and stood up, undoing his shirt buttons.

"OK, mates ... dish out!"

We all frantically searched our pockets for a dollar bill … this we simply could not pass up … one or two of us made a quick trip to our quarters.

The table was cleared in an instant, and the bubbly lady climbed on top.

Mr. Patterson had been making eyes at another of the older ladies. He reached for her arm, and excused the two of them.

"Gentlemen ... please excuse me and the lady ... and of course don't be alarmed by screams and the smell of burnt rubber." We all took time out from watching the bubbly lady to roar in laughter. The crew, that is ... the Chinese girls were wondering what it was all about.

"Please leave the Trader intact ... if you don't mind," were his final words as he left.

Meanwhile, the show went on. Between the other bodies in the crowded mess cabin, I caught glimpses of bare flesh and bare body parts, and of a cuscus with no hair. I couldn't stand it.

"Laurie, you know it's my turn right!" I reached for the girl with the wholesome face. "May I have the honor, ma'am?"

She flashed a radiant smile, and I quickly led her away from the iniquitous scene taking place on our eating table.

"Oooh ... ooh. " I heard as we made our way to my cabin.

"Oooh ... my hair ... ooh ... my hair! " followed soon afterwards.

"Oh ... oh ... oooohh ... Harry!" very soon after that.

"Ooh ... aren't you finished yet?" a few half-seconds later.

I discovered that her name was Ling Fu Chan, and that she was married.

"You do this, and you're married?" I asked incredulously.

"My husband doesn't know ... he thinks I'm working in a factory ... we are very poor." She tried to explain in her limited English. "We come to Hong Kong one year now ... I have two children."

She had told me this after our swift love making. I wondered if I would have been able to go throught with it if she had revealed those things earlier. I paid her double what she asked, or six Aussie dollars.

We were in another world. I was sure we had somehow been transported to another part of the universe. This was unlike anything I had ever experienced, or even imagined. Our Chinese ladies had left well over an hour ago, just before the sun had melted into a red haze to the west, leaving behind a black sky with no moon, yet the blackness existed only at the extreme zenith, for all around us were lights. And even though we were in a mile-wide waterway, with the nearest shore or neighboring ship several hundred yards distance, there was visible movement in every direction ... the pulsating movement of humanity itself. A large, brilliantly lit ferry crossed from what showed on the chart to be Kowloon, to Victoria, on the island of Hong Kong. Boeing 747's and a mix of many other aircraft made repeated and frequent use of the airport runway, which was about three quarters of a mile away, the runway extending directly out into the harbor itself. A strange, futuristic appearing hover craft swooped by, heading out the Tathong Channel. I guessed it was the hover craft ferry to Macau, the Portuguese gambling center south of Hong Kong. Chinese Junks passed, and this time I was able to watch them carefully. I was astonished by their variation: some were enormous, easily a hundred and fifty feet in length, tall and broad, and very fast in the water, often with a mast and boom at the center of its cargo carrying space for loading and unloading. Others were small and delicate looking. Here in the harbor only one or two were under sail, but I could see that their sails varied greatly as well ... some were very rectangular, others more a quadrangle, and yet others were divided into several triangular shapes, pieced together with battens. Most made use of a gaff spar at the top of a single mast. Others didn't, and there could be two and even three masts. Even the material that the sails were made of differed. One smaller one seemed to make use of a traditional matting, probably bamboo, I guessed. While others, especially the larger ones, appeared to use a modern dacron, or canvas. But regardless of each of the vessels size or function, all in the harbor were filled with people, each to the point of overflowing, it seemed, as if the entire mass of Hong Kong's millions were at that moment fleeing to another destination, crowding aboard every craft, regardless of where it was going.

I wanted to wave down a walla-walla right then, and travel to the nearby shore, eager to begin exploring, but the Captain had reasonably suggested that we wait until the following day, after a good nights sleep ... we had already experienced a great deal of excitement for one day. Hong Kong could wait ... and the disposition of Bobby Mundy's 'treasure'. I pulled out the piece of paper he had given me one more time. It said to contact a man named 'Peewee' at the 'Aberdeen Sampan Company', on Pok Fu Lam Road in Aberdeen, using the ditty that Bobby had given me as a 'password', of course.

"Harry, you put on quite a performance ... thank you ... kinda quick, though, wasn't it?"

He grinned falsely and told me to shut up.

"And how was *your* young lady, Canuck?" Laurie wanted to know if he had missed anything.

"I still miss Deli," I grumbled. Harry laughed.

"Don't *any* Chinese girls have hair on their cuscus?" I asked, taking a survey.

"Well, you all saw miss giggles's." Harry glibbed, struggling over the plural 's'.

"You might have something there, Chad ... because it was all bald as far as I could tell." Kevin threw in.

Captain Patterson smiled contentedly, satisfied just listening to our banter.

"Well, gentlemen ... we have a big day tomorrow, and I'm bushed ... see you all in the morning."

It was the middle of the night, but I was awake, thinking about Bobby Mundy, and whatever it was that was down there under the seat in the officer's mess.

Leave it be, Chad!

But my curiosity was killing me. I just have to take a look, I concluded. I slipped out of the bunk and proceeded to make my way down to the main deck, barefoot, trying my best not to make a sound. 'Like a pirate!' I giggled under my breath. I closed the door to the officer's mess ... the damn thing let out a tiny squeak. I stopped, motionless, for a full minute, half expecting Richard to come charging in wanting to know what was going on. Hell, I calculated, I could simply tell him I came down to get something to eat. Yeh, that's what I could say.

The first seat top came off easily, and silently. It was because I had done it once before ... I remembered when Laurie and I had discovered the cases of ketchup. I fumbled in my jeans pocket for the package of matches I had brought, and lit one. There it was ... the treasure! Except it sure as hell didn't look like any kind of treasure you would imagine. It was simply a box, or perhaps more a crate, because the exterior was framed in wood, and was solidly put together. There were three of them. I would have to break open the wood exterior if I wanted to see what was inside. Which of course created a dilemna ... I didn't have any tools, and prying off one or two of the wooden pieces would require extreme care if I intended to replace them without noticable damage, and it would make a lot of noise. I sat down to think.

The door again make a small squeak as it was opened. I damn near jumped out of my skin ... and fumbled to replace the seat top.

"Who's there?" A voice asked. And then the light came on.

Jeeses!!

I motioned fantically to Kevin to turn the light off and to be quiet. He obliged.

The light went off, a small squeak was heard one more time, and he crouched down beside me.

"What's up, Chad??" There was a lot of curiosity in his voice.

"This is not the time to explain ... here, help me get this crate out of here ... I'll explain everything to you tomorrow." I promised.

"OK ... but what the hell is it?"

"Shhh ...!"

With Kevin to help we silently lifted the one crate out from it's hiding place and I hoisted it on top my right shoulder.

"Thank you, Kevin, and good night."

"Not so fast ... what's in the crate?"

" Shhh ... I'll explain in the morning, " I whispered.

"If you must know, it's the 'Treasure of Solomon'!"

"What??"

"Shhh ..."

"Let go of your cock, and grab a sock ... it's daylight in the swamp!" Harry bellowed through my cabin door, causing me to bolt upright in my bunk, my eyes wide open and unfocused.

"Harry ... what the hell?"

"Hey, mate, the sun's almost up, and we have all of Hong Kong at our doorstep!"

"OK ... OK ... you got me up."

As soon as he left I checked to make sure the wooden box was still hidden under a pile of my clothes. Yes, the 'treasure' was secure.

But Harry was bullshitting again. It wasn't even sunrise yet ... there was only a diffused glow to the east. But I was glad he had wakened me. I too felt the excitement of being in this place, and I wanted to explore, to experience. And of course I had an important matter of business to take care of ... 'Peewee'. With a name like that, I imagined that he must be a giant of a man ... probably a ruthless smuggler and a cut-throat pirate. Not the sort of individual to take lightly. The thought made me a little apprehensive, and nervous.

Even at this early hour the movement of Hong Kong's humanity was already well underway. I wondered if it had stopped at all during the night. A walla-walla passed close, its operator watching us to see if someone was wanting to go to shore. Several fishing boats were grouped together, heading out to open sea, and an early morning arriving flight was just then gliding down through the haze, a large BOAC DC10. 1 wondered if the haze that had prevailed last evening and this morning was a typical event.

It seemed I was the last one to make it out of his bunk, for the officer's mess was full, and Richard was serving breakfast.

"Jeeses, what time it it, anyway?" I asked, to no one in particular.

"It's already five o'clock, mate!" Harry informed me, acting like a jittery race horse at the starting gate.

Even Mr. Patterson was up.

"Well, then, what's on the agenda?" I still was feeling grumpy about the way I had been awakened.

"I need to call Sydney as soon as possible, of course," the Captain said. "Sydney is two hours ahead of us ... it would have been useless to have tried calling yesterday evening, but the earlier I try this morning, the better."

That made sense, and was a good reason why we were rising so early, I rationalized. I suspected Harry of collusion with our Captain.

"And the trip to the Harbor Master's office is going to take awhile ... we are close to the Kowloon side, while the office is in Victoria, on the other side. We will need to take a walla-walla to Kowloon, then walk to the ferry terminal, then take the Star Ferry to Victoria."

"I see." So the earlier we get started the better.

Richard had prepared something special this morning: a choice of poached or scrambled eggs, pork chops, and baked yams. But he was concerned about our food supply for the next few days.

"Captain, we are out of beer and fruit, and we're low on almost everything."

"Alright, Richard, wait until I talk to Lancey . We still have eleven hundred dollars from selling the pump, if we need it."

I dug out one of my two pairs of long jeans, my best shirt, and put on socks and shoes ... we were no longer in a shorts and thongs climate, or environment ... and met the rest of the crew on the main deck. As a consequence of being visited by the harbor pilot our ladder was now on the starboard midships, and no one had bothered to return it to the stern. It was equally functional where it was, I supposed.

Harry had flagged down a walla-walla, and we all climbed aboard, saying good morning to the Chinese operator, who grinned happily, scanning us with inquisitive eyes, pausing on our hap-caste crew mates. He said something in Chinese that seemed to be directed to Joseph, but Joseph just smiled at him.

"Joseph, don't you speak any Chinese?" I quizzed, surprised that there hadn't been any communication.

"I know a few words in Hokien, but these people speak Cantonese ... I don't understand a thing."

"But most understand and speak English," Mr. Patterson interjected. "After all, this *is* a British Colony."

The walla-walla's inboard diesel, a small, bright red, two cylinder Yanmar, gruffly putt-putted us toward the nearest shore, dodging a fishing boat and two other walla-wallas on the way. As we came closer to our destination I was shocked by the apparent density of buildings and people on the shore. It seemed we were approaching a solid layer of humanity, with a wall of man-made structures rising above.

The walla-walla brought us bow first to the crowded concrete landing, and we disembarked. Captain Patterson picked up the tab, the operator settling for one dollar Australian.

"We gotta exchange our Aussie dollars for these Hong Kong ones quick like, I reckon." Harry suggested.

"Gentlemen ... stick close together and let's walk to the next street, then turn left ... I believe that'll take us to the ferry terminal. Please keep together."

Good advise, I thought, but it wasn't easy to do. Movement among the solid mass of people was like trying to get into a football stadium right after the game ended.

"I reckon quite a few Chinese live here, ehh, Canuck." Laurie chuckled.

"I reckon they *all* live here, Aussie," I joked in return.

We made it to the main street which Mr. Patterson had somehow known was there ... he certainly couldn't have seen it through all the human interference ... and turned left. A sign on the corner of a building at the intersection informed me that this was Salisbury Road. Remarkably, the crowding thinned out a bit and progress became a little easier. I was now able to appreciate some of the details of the scene around us. I couldn't keep my eyes still, there was so much motion, so many things to focus on. Now that we had left the waterfront I noticed a change in the dominant style of clothing, from mostly a black, two piece short legged pants and blouse combination to more colorful variations, and a tendency towards Western dress. The term 'sampan outfit' came to mind for the dress of the people on the boats and waterfront, and was only slightly different for men compared to women ... the male top was a full buttoned shirt, cut straight around the bottom, while the woman's version was a pull over blouse with a short 'tail' both in the front and back. Almost all had been black, with only a few of the ladies wearing yellow or orange tops, which seemed to be their only other colors of preference. But here on a Kowloon main street there was a much greater profusion of color, and diversity of style. Still, I noticed a strong showing of the 'sampan' style.

However, it was the people themselves that were the most intriguing. Everyone seemed to be in a hurry, each intensely absorbed with their singular chore at hand, all with expressions of solemn determination. There were no smiles, no giggles or laughter here, only people consumed with a somber purpose. The observation both surprised me and caused me to wonder why that was so. Coupled with this was the realization that I didn't see any young people ... no children playing in the street or running playfully and mischievously in between the adults, and no teenagers either. I saw only adults. Some younger, some older, but all adults.

"Gentlemen, this is the terminal." The Captain's announcement startled me out of my tourist's trance.

Our timing couldn't have been better ... one of Star Ferry's double-decked, green and white vessel's was just unloading and would be receiving passengers in a couple of minutes ... we were in luck, or so I thought.

"But we don't have any Hong Kong money." I didn't have any small Aussie bills left either.

"Well then, let's change some, gents. Right this way." Laurie pointed to a kiosk on the exterior of the terminal building with an 'Exchange' sign above it's cashier's cage facade. Of course! Hong Kong, the international city ... and the main ferry between Kowloon and Victoria ... just the place to expect to find a foreign exchange vender. We each exchanged everything we had in our pockets, and quickly returned to the ferry turnstiles. The fare was 30 cents H.K. for the trip, per person.

The Star Ferry seemed to be a continuation of the flow of the throngs on the Kowloon streets. The only difference was that a segment of that flow was held in limbo for a few short minutes ... I discovered that the crossing took only seven minutes, and loading-unloading approximately five, so the longest anyone had to wait for a Star Ferry was twelve minutes. So it hadn't been 'luck' that had afforded us the timely arrival. The ferry itself was also designed with a rapid flow of people specifically in mind, I conjectured, for it was symmetrical ... it featured a bow at each end ... and therefore didn't turn around. The throng quickly crowded on at one terminal, paused in time briefly, then swiftly continued on their way at the oposing end.

Seven minutes to watch more of the fascination that was Hong Kong. We left Kowloon with its level waterfront area and relatively low-rise buildings, and approached Victoria, with the triple peaks of Mount Cameron, Mount Kellett, and Victoria Peak in the background, and a perpetual forest of high rise buildings terracing the steep Victoria landscape below. One building stood out in particular ... a majestic tan colored landmark standing singularly behind and just to the left of the Victoria ferry terminal. Mr. Patterson informed that it was the Bank of Shanghai building, and that the more modern tower a little to the right of it was the new Hong Kong Hilton.

Now that we were in a deeper part of the harbor we could see past the Kowloon peninsula. The view that unfolded totally astonished me.

"Laurie ... look at this ... look at all those junks ... all those boats." I gasped.

Mr. Patterson was standing close by. "That's one of Hong Kong's several typhoon shelters, Chad ... a floating city ... you'll want to take a closer look at one when you get a chance ... according to my map and guide that one is the Yau Ma Tei shelter."

It was an amazing sight: the closest vessel was over a half-mile away, but I could still judge the size of the 'city'. It extended along the Kowloon shoreline for about a half mile, and reached out into the waterway perhaps a quarter of a mile ... 400 yards.

"How do the inshore vessels ever get out?" I questioned, dazed by the proliferation of entangled water craft.

"A lot of them never do ... and a person can be born there and live their entire life without either stepping on shore or going out to sea."

Is that possible?

"By the way, Captain ... where is Aberdeen?" This was a good chance to find out.

"Aberdeen? That's on the south side of Hong Kong Island, directly across from Victoria. Of course you have to travel around the western end. It also has a typhoon shelter ... the largest in Hong Kong, in fact."

"Hmm ... sounds interesting ... I'd like to visit the place." I tried to sound casual.

"Not difficult to do ... will take a little time, though."

So I need to make the trip during the day, I calculated, and allow some time.

This is not going to be so easy to do!

Our ferry reached Victoria, and we were carried with the flow of humans towards the exit.

"It has been many years, gentlemen ... but I think I can find the Harbor Master's office ... our customs officer verified the address for me. It's just off Harcourt Road in the 'Admiralty' complex." Mr. Patterson paused to get his bearings.

We jogged around a couple of streets (no, not running) and to the left of the Star Ferry terminal, remaining close to the waterfront, and reached our destination with unnatural timing ... the office had just opened.

"May I help you gentlemen?" the clean-cut young Chinese clerk on the other side of the counter asked.

"Yes, we are the crew of the New Guinea Trader, which just arrived late yesterday afternoon. I am Captain Patterson. I have been asked to file a report with the Harbor Master ... and my crew is here to register and be discharged."

"I can take care of your crew's registration ... and if you'll follow me, I will introduce you to our Harbor Master," the clerk responded, in immaculate English.

There ensued a series of formalities and forms to fill out. The Captain was politely ushered into a back office for a personal interview with the Harbor Master.

I briefly wondered about Mr. Fitzgerald's threat ... would the Captain be arrested?

This may be the last we will see of our Mr. Patterson??

At one point I was singled out by a young Englishman, who had come forward to take the place of the clerk. He introduced himself as the Harbor Master's 'junior assistant', whatever that was.

"This form says you were the vessel's Second Officer. Do you have any papers to show your qualification as a Second Officer?" The young man was clearly puzzled and more than a little suspicious.

Oh no, not this again!

"Sir, I was hired on as 2nd Mate ... and ... uhh ... served in that capacity. You can check with Captain Patterson."

The youthful official looked at me hard, debating what he should do with me, then shrugged.

"What the hell," he snorted in resignation, a twisted smile on his face, "I'm sure we'll never see you again." He handed me the yellow form, my official 'discharge' from the New Guinea Trader as Chad Fletcher, Second Officer.

We waited for the Captain. Harry had been whispering some nonsense about Mr. Patterson being questioned about Mr. Milner, and we were worried.

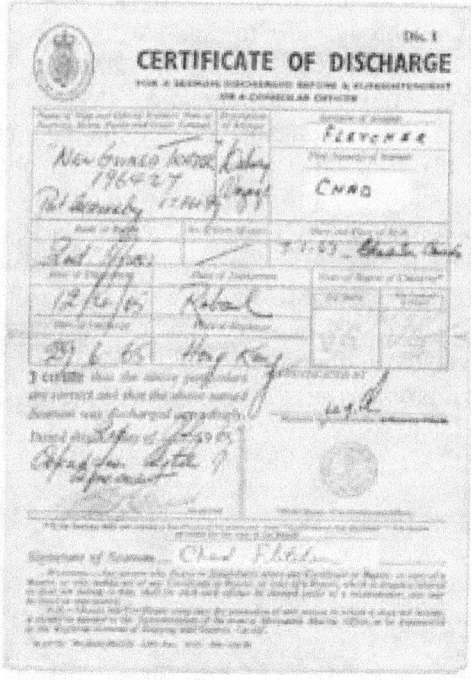

7

He finally emerged from the back office.

"Do you all have your discharge papers?" the Captain asked.

"Sure do, Captain ... except they didn't want to give Canuck his. I reckon they figured he was too ugly to be a 2nd Mate!" Harry chuckled mischievously.

"But you did get it?"

"Yup ... right here," I showed him the yellow form.

"Captain ... Were there any questions about Mr. Milner? Charges being filed against him ... anything like that?" I questioned, concerned.

"No ... nothing. Now, I must call Sydney. I didn't want to call before you received your discharges, you know. I was afraid they might give me instructions not to sign you off. If you gentlemen will wait, I can call Sydney from here."

Strange ... so the threat ftom Mr. Fitzgerald and company was B.S. ??

We decided to wait outside ... no sense spending more time in such a drab office.

The building housing the Port Authority offices was on a slight rise, near the waterfront between the Star Ferry Terminal and an area called 'Wanchai', I remembered from our chart. From outside the main entrance we had a view of the entire harbor from the Star Ferry terminals to the Tathong Channel. Wanchai, to the right, was apparently a naval base, for there were four British navy vessels in the area, two berthed at a wharf and two anchored close by. All four looked like destroyers. Across from Wanchai, to the right a bit, was the airport runway ... and we could make out the Trader, resting as if exhausted at her anchor, her heavy list to the starboard side clearly discernible. She looked old, and tired, and sorely neglected. I wondered what her fate would be, now that we had brought her to this place. A refit, then returned to New Guinea and put back into service? I hadn't thought about it before, but just then it occurred to me that a refit would be impractical. Maybe a different fate awaited our aged lady.

Mr. Patterson emerged through the double entrance doors.

"Well ... that's done!" he sighed heavily, as if having just completed an incredibly arduous task.

"What did they say, Captain?" Harry blurted out, but asking the question for all of us.

I talked to Mr. Fitzgerald. Surprisingly, his attitude was greatly improved compared to when I talked to him in Laoang. He was actually friendly, and jovial. He congratulated us and said he'd be here on the first arrangeable flight ... he'll probably arrive here tomorrow. Mr. Lancey will be following him a day or so later.

"Mr. Lancey himself." Harry raised his eyebrows. "Are we *that* important?"

"Not *us*, Harry ... the New Guinea Trader. She's still worth a few dollars!" I corrected my not-so-bright friend. Mr. Patterson chuckled. Harry showed me an vertical forefinger.

I also contacted the company that'll be unloading our scrap iron ... they want to start immediately ... we need to get back to the Trader as soon as we can."

We began retracing our steps back to the ferry, across to Kowloon and towards the same landing where our walla-walla had dropped us off earlier.

"Richard, if I give you four hundred dollars of the money we received from the sale of the pump, could you and Joseph shop for some of the things we need?"

Richard's eyes widened. "No problem, Captain. But that's a lot of money. Can Fred give us a hand too ... and can I buy the crew some beer?"

"Of course!" But you'll have to exchange the dollars somewhere ... and save some for the walla-walla fare."

"We can handle that."

The Captain pulled out four U.S. one hundred dollar bills and gave them to Richard. A couple of walla-wallas were waiting for fares at the landing, and we were on our way across the water in minutes. Just in time, it worked out, for a large open barge was just pulling up alongside the Trader as we boarded.

I didn't want to miss the unloading of the Trader's cargo. I was curious, and concerned ... curious to see if there was anything unusual about the cargo in the hold, and concerned about the welfare of our 'treasure'.

"Captain Patterson, my name is Alvin ... Alvin Yat Sen, and we are here to unload your scrap iron. I'm the crew foreman."

I was surprised at the man's youthful appearance ... he couldn't have been more than twenty-three or twenty-four ... a good looking guy with an energetic air about him, and he spoke English clearly with a noticeable British accent.

His crew were swarming over the Trader within seconds. We didn't have to do a thing. They pulled back the tarps and opened the holds, and manned our mast and booms to unload the assorted shapes and sizes of rusting iron that was our cargo. I was amazed at how quickly and efficeintly they worked, and how many of them there were.

At one point, while his crew had everything under control, I had a chance to approach the young foreman.

"Your men are very efficient." I praised, hoping to start a conversation.

"Oh yes," he responded eagerly. "We have a good crew."

"This is my first time in Hong Kong; I'm curious about a few things. I may want to live here for awhile. If you don't mind my asking, how much do you and your men get paid?"

Alvin paused, assessing me before he answered.

"What is your name," he inquired, first wanting to establish some kind of a relationship before he answered such a sensitive question, I supposed.

"Chad ... Chad Fletcher."

"How do you do, Chad," he extended his hand. "To answer your question, we don't get paid very much. Labor is very cheap in Hong Kong. My crew and I work twelve hours every day ... every day ... I am the foreman because I can speak English, and because I was lucky enough to finish secondary school. Conditions are very hard, and we must all struggle to make a living. My men make about thirty dollars a day ... I make fourty ... that's Hong Kong dollars ... and that's good pay by Hong Kong standards."

I did some fast arithmetic. It certainly wasn't very much.

"Where do you live?"

"It's expensive to live in Kowloon, impossible in Victoria, so I live in the territory. It takes an hour and a half to travel to our work place in the morning, the same to return at night. So I have maybe eight hours with my wife and two children."

"Damn! That's kinda rough!"

"What's your nationality, Chad? You sound like you're an American."

"I'm Canadian. That's why I could probably stay here, because I'm a 'British Subject'."

"Ahh ... I wish I was able to have a British passport ... and to leave Hong Kong. Of course, that's what everyone here would like ... a chance to immigrate somewhere else."

"Are you originally from China ... Communist China?"

"Yes, of course ... and even though it is difficult in Hong Kong, it is much better than in mainland China."

Now I was beginning to understand some of the things I had seen, like the solemn expressions of fatigued determination that seemed to be on everyone's faces. And I was also thinking that it would be difficult to stay here and work, with those kind of hours and wages ... maybe I'd better be thinking about another destination.

It seemed that they had just arrived, but all of a sudden they were finished, and the covers to the holds were replaced, the tarps expertly tied back in place, and the boom gear returned to their prior positions. I had been watching the entire operation fairly closely ... the only thing that I had seen come out of the hold was scrap iron, scrap iron, and more scrap iron. Of course I could have missed something. Who knows?!

Thinking about the inscrutable Captain McKay again, Chad?

I shook Alvin's hand goodbye, and he left.

"Hey, blokes, how about a hand?"

I recognized Richard's voice. About time, we were all feeling hungry. Richard and Joseph started handing up the packages of foodstuff while Fred, Laurie, Harry, Kevin and I formed a chain to get everything on deck. The distance from the deck rail to the water had increased enormously, now that we sat higher in the water, and for the first time the Trader sat vertically straight, with no list. The packages kept coming and coming. Like in Laoang, the American or Aussie dollar apparently went a long ways. One of the items was beer ... lots of it ... some San Mguel and also a few cases of Fosters.

"Hey, right on, mates!" Harry shouted with delight. "I could use a couple of those right now."

We helped sort everything out and again followed Richard's meticulous directions for storage, and then all lounged in the mess to wait for a late lunch, Joseph offering to give Richard a hand.

"What now, mateys?" Harry sat back in the bench seat, relaxed, and happily caressing a Fosters.

"I for one want to check out Hong Kong's bars and night spots ... and be a tourist." I was eager to grab another walla-walla back to shore and continue exploring. And of course to seek out my 'Bretheren of the Coast' contact, as soon as possible.

Mr. Patterson had already been in the mess, using the table to go through some paper work.

"Maybe I can offer you a couple of tips. The bar area on Hong Kong Island is Wanchai, which is also where the naval base is ... the bars cater to the navy boys and are more expensive, and the girls are more, shall we say, aggressive. Kowloon is cheaper and has more to offer. I suggest you start there."

Richard surprised us with a Chinese dish, his version of a chow mein, with some left-over pork chops cut up in small pieces, and some doughy rolls with sweet pork inside that he had bought ready-made. He called them 'manapua' but said that the Cantonese had another name for them.

"These were the world's first 'hamburgers'," he claimed.

"One thing, gentlemen, at least one of us must remain on board at all times. This morning was an exception, because I felt it was critical to take all of you to the Port Authority. But we cannot take that kind of risk in the future."

Richard volunteered to stay on board that night, but only because he had work to do, he said. Tomorrow night had to be different.

"I think we can remove these two pieces right here." I accepted the pry bar from Kevin and carefully worked the chisel end in between the wooden 'one-by-threes'. The crate was well constructed, and resisted my efforts.

"Try here ..." Kevin suggested. "And tap the end of the bar with the hammer."

The new approach worked ... one piece came off, and another. Exposed beneath the wooden frame was a wrapping of thick black plastic sheeting. But we were lucky ... we had opened a side where the sheeting overlapped, and we were able to fold it back a few inches.

"I'll be damned!" Kevin exclaimed softly, catching his breath. "It really *is* books ... ancient looking too. Can we take one out?"

"Let's try ... but be careful."

The center one came out. It was about the size of a large phone book, only twice as thick, and with a hard cover of some sort of stiff material, engraved with a complex design and strange writings. Kevin sat on my bunk, holding the book excitedly in his hands, yet with great care and reverence. He opened the cover and scanned through several of the thick pages. The writing was completely foreign to both of us, and was interspaced with frequent drawings.

"It's like Bobby had said ... written in pictographs." I said.

"Fascinating ... of course we can't understand any of this ... but I'm sure there are scholars who can. Absolutely amazing!" Kevin was enthralled.

"Kevin ... you gotta help me get the three crates to Bobby's contact. I must go to Aberdeen to locate him as soon as possible."

But I would need a few hours of sunlight ... time to find my way around Hong Kong Island. Tonight was our first evening in Hong Kong, however, and it was already late. It would have to wait.

Our evening excursion party boarded yet another walla-walla and headed towards Kowloon's shore. The sun was low in the western sky, reddened by the low lying blanket of haze. We chattered happily, in anticipation of witnessing a sample of Hong Kong's notorious night-life.

We again found Salisbury Road, the main street that had led us to the ferry terminal, then wandered among a couple of side streets. Once again I marvelled at the continual hustle and bustle, at the constant motion and diversity of activity. We walked around open carts displaying food and a great variety of other goods for sale, and dodged rickshaws and pedicabs, or stepped aside to allow the occassional motorized vehicle to beep its way noisily through the throng.

We passed one or two bars, small and empty, but Mr. Patterson waved us on. We finally reached one that seemed larger, with strings of flickering lights outside and a giant neon sign telling us that this was the 'Red Lips Bar'. The sound of laughter and mixed male and female voices came from inside.

We queued through the doorway, all seven of us, and stood awkwardly inside the entrance, pausing to adjust our vision to the darkened interior. As soon as my eyes were able, I saw that I was standing directly in front of a mystically beautiful Chinese girl, petite and with long flowing hair, shimmering black, and a very tightly fitting silver dress with a long slit up one side, revealing a curved and succulent thigh. I knew immediately that I was in heaven. There were at least five other girls standing close by, their attentions directed to other members of our crew.

We were graciously ushered to a long table with a high-backed, luxuriously cushioned bench seat on both sides. I slid onto the seat, shifting towards the other end until I bumped into Laurie coming from the opposite direction, very aware that the succulent thigh in the silver dress was right behind, her hand reaching out to me the whole time, the hand finally resting on my own thigh. She said her name was Moon, and she asked for a drink, and there was no way that I was going to disappoint her. I discovered that my San Miguel ... I had come to like the brand ... would cost three dollars and her glass of tinted water six. But I didn't mind. I didn't mind at all. Not even when she asked for another when my own rapidly disappearing San Miguel was still half full. But her teasing hand, the view and feel of that one succulent thigh, and the pair of gorgously black Chinese eyes melted all resistance ... and common sense.

I was aware of Harry snickering on the other side of the table.

"Take it easy, mate," he cautioned. "You're going to blow your life savings in the first hour."

Moon glared mischievously at him. He was pinching the not-nearly-so-delicious young lady beside him, and she was squealing and slapping at his hands. I noticed he hadn't bought her a drink yet.

Variations of my own experience were taking place around the table. After Moon's sixth drink my sensibilities were slowly coming back to earth, and I was wanting to slow her down. It was now my chance to return Harry's snicker.

"Harry ... don't you think she deserves at least one drink for all the bruises you're giving her?"

"Mind your own business, Canuck!"

Fred and Joseph were noticably uncomfortable and Kevin was a little bored, unhappy with the heavily made-up girl beside him.

"Gentlemen," Mr. Patterson interrupted. "I think it's time to explore further."

We regrouped outside the entrance, the echoes of Moon's pleas to stay ringing in my ear, plus the lingering sensation of that last squeeze in a vital spot.

"Jeeses ... what a rip-off!" Laurie exploded.

"A rip-off, you say ... I never noticed." Harry was bragging about being a tight-ass.

"Gentlemen, that was a little too quick a tempo for me ... I'm headed for the maritime officer's club in Victoria, if anyone would care to accompany me to

Hong Kong Island. The club is for certified officers only, however ... we have to show papers at the door."

"Joseph and I are cutting out," Fred said, making it clear that the two of them wanted to explore on their own. "That's too expensive for us."

"Hey, we passed a place just back there that had a Fosters sign outside ... looked like it was more of a pub than a girlie joint ... how about we try that?" Harry suggested.

"You're on!" Laurie agreed.

Harry had read the place correctly. It was called the Oasis Club. There were several girls inside, nice looking too, but there was no pressure to have them sit beside you or to buy them a drink. Harry was much happier with a Fosters in his hand and no girl to hassle him. At least for the moment. Kevin was of the same mind. But after a few minutes Laurie and I each chose a girl to sit with us, but I immediately made a bargain with mine that she could match me drink for drink, but no more ... and if I said no, it meant no. She was even prettier than Moon, and with just as succulent a thigh, I noticed. But I felt I was now an experienced old-timer and played it cool.

"Tomorrow Mr. Fitzgerald arrives ... what do think is going to happen?" Harry opened up the question that had been on all our minds.

"You know, I was so eager to leave Rabaul that I didn't think much about what was going to happen when we reached this end ... and I never talked about it with Mr. Fitzgerald. I suppose I assumed that I was on my own once we got here." I explained.

"How about you, Harry?" Laurie queried.

"Yeh, Mr. Fitzgerald and I mentioned it briefly. I took it that they would send me back to Australia, to Sydney."

"And you, Laurie?" I asked.

"Same as Harry, I reckon."

"Kevin?"

"We never discussed it. I was planning all along to stay here for awhile," he responded.

"But if we can force them to give us all onward air fares ... why not ... and how about our New Guinea boys ... the poor bastards!" Harry argued. I could see what he was getting at, and after my discussion with the Chinese foreman, Alvin, bargaining for an onward passage was maybe a good idea.

One of the girls reminded me of Ling, from the 'meat boat', because of her use of less make-up and a more down-to-earth look. She kept making eyes at Kevin, and I thought I recognized an opposite attraction as well. It was only a matter of time before she was sitting beside him, and they exchanged light conversation.

"What do you guys figure is going to happen to the Trader? I was thinking this morning that she's not worth refitting ... and somehow I don't think Lancey will take her back to New Guinea." I expounded, passing on the thought that had occurred to me earlier.

"Funny you mention that. I was thinking the same thing." Harry agreed.

"How long would a refit take?" Laurie quizzed, trying to figure something out.

"Depends on how much they did, I reckon. But you saw how these blokes worked today. I don't reckon more than a couple of weeks ... one month at the max." Harry speculated.

"Then if they really wanted to refit the Trader and take her back to Rabaul, wouldn't it be cheaper and less trouble for them to just keep us on for the return trip." Laurie reasoned. Now I understood what he was getting at.

"Yeh ... you would think that, wouldn't you ... yeh." Harry was now deep in thought.

"That bothers me, somehow ... Harry being in deep thought, I mean!

"And why isn't there a company out there right now, starting on the refit?" Laurie continued.

"Yeh ... yeh?" I thought I could detect a whisp of smoke rising out from Harry's protruding ears ... portentous smoke signals.

Laurie suddenly snorted, and started to laugh. "Wouldn't it be something if the Trader was simply scrapped, after all we've been through to get her here. It'd be one big joke ... a joke on us ... like all we had accomplished was for nothing ... nothing more than an exercise in futility ... in absurdity!"

"Absurdity?" Kevin's eyebrows popped up, and he took on that philosopher's look. "That's a word I've heard quite a few times on this voyage."

"Oh - oh ...! Kevin's going to tell us more philosophy." I warned, in jest.

"Why ... what's the philosophical lesson to be learned from this, Kevin?" Laurie asked.

"Yeh ... 'the absurdity of man's efforts'." he started. "Reminds me of the story of 'Sisyphus', or the 'Myth of Sisyphus'."

"The who?" I asked.

"The Myth of Sisyphus!"

"OK ... Kevin ... tell us about the Myth of Sisyphus!"

"Oh, not much to tell ... short and quick and to the point. Sisyphus was a minor Greek God, the legendary ruler of Corinth, who had angered his more superior Gods, and was therefore condemned to rolling a huge boulder up a hill throughout eternity. So engrossed was he in his labor, pushing that boulder up the hill, that it was only for the brief moments when he chased the boulder back down the hill could he reflect on the absurdity of his efforts."

I clapped my hands. "Kevin, that's the best thing I've heard from you yet. And damned fitting."

Laurie agreed, and was chuckling softly. Harry nodded, grinning that dumb ass grin of his.

"Well, mateys ... I reckon the boulder stops here!"

I laughed, but there was something more to what Harry had said, and how he said it, that rang an ominous note.

Hariy has something up his sleeve!

The girl sitting beside Kevin had listened carefully to our conversation, and Kevin's contribution to the history of philosophical thought. She was looking at him with great interest, and respect. Is it possible, I pondered, for her to be falling in love with our good friend, with a diabetic with one-inch thick glasses?

Of course, idiot ... some girl might even fall in love with you someday!

We talked a long time, enjoying our beer, and each other's company, and the girls. A couple of times Kevin and I exchanged secretive glances. I knew he was busting to tell the others about our 'treasure', but we had both agreed that we must remain tight-lipped, not wanting to risk the wrath of the giant cut-throat pirate named Peewee.

Harry eventually resigned himself to buying one of the girls a couple of drinks, her name was Vicki, and Kevin was getting along very well with miss down-to-earth. Later we found out her name was Shan Li. And the girl sitting beside me was Chong Mii. It seemed to be my night for picking out the not so down-to-earth ones. But she massaged me well, and I truly enjoyed her succulent thigh. And we, or at least I, had drunk far too much beer to seriously consider anything else ... it was time to head back to the Trader.

More hours had gone by than I realized ... it was almost midnight ... and I was astonished by the scene which now confronted us. Hong Kong's Chinese did sleep at night, we discovered. In fact, the side streets we were walking along were now strewn with prone bodies. Men and old ladies were lying on mats on the sidewalk, some beside their food cart, others in doorways. A few had blankets, most didn't. We literally had to step over and between the sleeping figures in order to transverse the street. One intriguing realization occurred to me: in the midst of all this humanity and poverty we felt perfectly safe ... it was unthinkable that we would be attacked or mugged. Such was their pre-occupation with their own chores, their own struggle for survival, and their indifference to the foreigner.

The walla-walla operator was sound asleep as we approached, but immediately jumped to his feet, eager to take on our fare.

Once again I paused at my favorite spot at the poop deck rail, scanning this magnificent harbor and the lights of both Kowloon and Victoria. Such a place, so much humanity. Tomorrow I wanted to explore more. And I felt an urgent need to complete my responsibility to my friend Bobby Mundy as well. I resolved that tomorrow I must seek out the pirate named 'Peewee'!

"Clang - clang, clang - clang!"
Good 'ol steak and eggs and yams. I wondered when I would see a potato again.
"Hong Kong doesn't have potatoes either?" I asked Joseph, as we all started in on our breakfast.
"We never saw any," was his reply.
"What are you going to do today, Canuck?" Laurie quizzed.
"I'd like to do some serious exploring," I answered, thinking about how I was going to be able to go on my own to Aberdeen.
"Gentlemen ... before you make any plans for the day, I have a proposition."
"Yes, Captain?" Two or three responded.

Oh ... oh?

"I realize you're officially signed off, but that was done so you have some, shall we say, 'leverage'. We still have this ship to take care of. Mr. Fitzgerald will probably arrive this afternoon. I propose that we spend today giving this vessel a thorough clean-up in order to put our 'best foot forward' for Mr. Fitzgerald."
'Well, that shoot's the hell out of going to Aberdeen today,' I cringed to myself. Maybe I could get away in the afternoon.
"But why would we want to do that?" Harry questioned stubbornly.
"Harry, this vessel is a mess ... especially down there in your engine room." Mr. Patterson matched his stubbornness. "And if you want to bargain with Mr. Fitzgerald, I think it would help your case immensely if you demonstrated that we have at least taken good care of their freighter and are a worthy crew."
"Hear, hear!" Laurie interjected in support of the Captain, sensing an unhealthy resistance coming from Harry. Mr. Patterson was right ... we needed to present ourselves and the Trader in the best possible light.
Harry shrugged in resignation, and the Captain continued: "I propose then, that Richard take Joseph to assist him in cleaning the kitchen, pantry, and officer's mess, that Chad, Laurie, and Fred begin swabbing the entire ship from the top to bottom, and that you two, Harry and Kevin, clean up the engine room.

Harry, you can have Joseph and Fred to help you when they can be freed from the other work. Any questions?"

There was a general concensus of agreement, although somewhat reluctant.

"Alright, then let's get started. If we need anything, let me know and I will go ashore and buy whatever's required.

And so we all dove into our assigned chores. It was kinda fun; Laurie and I and Fred thoroughly soaking each other with the fire hose. The Captain did go ashore for some cleaning items, mostly for Harry, who grumbled pretty much all day.

Mr. Fitzgerald arrived by walla-walla at four o'clock in the afternoon. All of us were still working at our individual tasks, my swabbing crew had progressed down to the main deck and we were almost to the aft deck, which was now the lowest end in respect to elevation due to an empty cargo hold, and was therefore the logical place to work towards. Fred spotted him first, seeing him standing on the port side gunwale of the walla-walla as it approached. Laurie and I stopped work to greet him as he came up the ladder.

"Hello, Mr. Fitzgerald," I greeted him as he climbed over the rail, and shook his good right hand as soon as he had established comfortable footing on deck. Laurie and Fred also shook hands with him. By that time Mr. Patterson had joined us and followed suit.

"Gentlemen, I am sure you can understand that Mr. Patterson and I have some matters to discuss ... will you please excuse us.

The two men went to the wheelhouse port deck to talk, and we continued our work. Richard took them up some drinks … the non-alcoholic kind. Harry had come up from the engine room, curious about their meeting.

"Richard ... how are they doing up there ... are they arguing ... or what?" He quizzed in a low voice.

Richard shrugged. "I reckon they're arguing alright. I think Fitzgerald is mad as hell!"

Harry snickered. I was now doubly glad we were all doing something useful, and acting like real sailors. I sensed that we were in for an uphill battle with our Mr. Fitzgerald.

Their discussion continued for a long time, and our day's chore was coming to an end. We started to clean up; Richard let us know that he was preparing an early dinner, which would be ready shortly. We all filtered into the officer's mess, one by one, and waited for Richard … and news from the two gentlemen up top. Harry and I grabbed a beer, each of us choosing our separate brands, of course.

Mr. Fitzgerald and the Captain finally joined us. I perceived a redness to Mr. Patterson's complexion, and an arrogance in Mr. Fitzgerald's manner, a characteristic which I had never seen in him before.

"Gentlemen ... I am glad to see you're taking good care of the Trader ... and congratulations on the success of your voyage. I understand it has been an eventful one." Mr. Fitzgerald greeted us cordially, not without praise.

Richard brought Mr. Fitzgerald a Fosters, and then started serving our meal. Joseph again excused himself to give him a hand.

We drank, and ate, and exchanged small talk. No one was venturing to ask what we all really wanted to ask. Although I was very aware that Harry wanted to do so: he kept squirming and clearing his throat. Finally, he couldn't hold it in any longer.

"Mr. Fitzgerald ... can we ask about our pay?" He blurted out, clearly being more blunt than he had intended.

Mr. Fitzgerald was startled, and took a moment to reply. "Harry ... uhh ... I will have to do a little accounting to figure out what is owed. But I didn't bring any money with me for that. Payment will have to wait until Mr. Lancey arrives, which will be tomorrow.

"I see ..."

I looked briefly in Mr. Patterson's direction, wanting to find out if he was going to be part of our bargaining for wages and repatriation, but I was disappointed by his apparent disattachment. His expression was a mask of forced indifference. I deduced that whatever had transpired between him and Mr. Fitzgerald made it difficult for him to give us active support.

"And what are your plans for us ... Mr. Fitzgerald ... are we still working as crew, and stay aboard the Trader, or will you make arrangements to repatriate us?" Harry persevered, continuing to press Mr. Fitzgerald. I noticed that Mr. Fitzgerald jumped ever so slightly at the word 'repatriate'.

Oh - oh!

"Harry ... that question will have to wait until Mr. Lancey arrives as well ... I can't answer it. Of course ... any of you are free to leave the Trader, if you so wish."

Harry's face reddened, but he kept his cool.

"I see."

"Well, gentlemen, I have a great deal to do. If you will please excuse me." Mr. Fitzgerald abruptly rose from the table, excusing himself. I noticed that he hadn't finished his plate of food. Mr. Patterson also excused himself and followed Mr. Fitzgerald ... he glanced in my direction as he left, motioning with a slight shrug.

"Hey ... let's go back to the Oasis Club again," Kevin suggested. "At least for starters." Harry and Laurie agreed that it was a good idea. I managed to get by without making a commitment.

"Kevin ... cover for me. I"m going to go to Aberdeen right now. I'll meet you all at the Oasis Club later ... if I can."

"You got it, mate . . take care! "

CHAPTER FIFTEEN

Dynamite and boulders

> **"Well, mateys . . I reckon the boulder stops here!" he promised, ominously.**

The street signs told me that Pok Fu Lam Road was the main route going through Aberdeen. 'Shouldn't be too difficult to find the Aberdeen Sampan Company', I reflected, as I stepped off the red, double-deckered bus. I was directly across from the beginning of Aberdeen's 'floating city', having just come down the hill that was the western entrance to the municipality. I crossed the road, curious and wanting to take a closer look.

I was again overwhelmed with the sense of being confronted with a massive concentration of humankind. People were everywhere, and everywhere there was motion. For the first time, I now saw children. A lot of them. A few were playing, in the sense of chasing after each other, squealing and yelling and crying, like young children do. But in Aberdeen that sort of exuberant play was the exception, I perceived, for most of the children were busy -- busy working. They were helping their mothers, or taking care of yet younger children, or washing things, or helping an adult male with their work … each contributing their small share to the family's struggle for a livelihood.

The vessels secured in Aberdeen's typhoon shelter seemed endless. As I had seen from the top deck of the bus as we came down the hill, the entire inlet was jammed solid with boats, with only a few narrow pathways kept open for in-and-out traffic. In some places the craft were tethered together in double rows with water channels in between, so that conceivably each vessel

could separate itself from its neighbors and sail free out into the open waterway south of Hong Kong Island. But in other areas this was clearly impossible, for the craft were many deep, each tied semi-permanently one to the other. I guessed that in many instances perhaps as many as twenty or thirty craft would have to be untied to allow just one to find its way clear. But I imagined that rarely happened; the vessels closer to shore coveting their better location and never daring to risk their place.

The craft were of all varieties ... ranging from tiny rectangular sampans to spacious ocean-going 'junks', each crowded with live-aboard occupants. Most had some sort of protective covering to provide at least minimal defense against the sun and rain, and the typhoons: there were canopies of colored canvas stretched in a half-circle over bamboo frames, or simple tarps stretched tent style between poles, and even crudely constructed roofs of rusting corrugated steel. And everywhere were clotheslines laden with washed laundry.

I kept walking on Pok Fu Lam Road, not really wanting to ask anyone for directions. I figured it would be wisest to maintain as low a profile as possible. I reached the inland end of the typhoon shelter, and was about to consider another direction, when I spotted a sign above a single-storied building which told me I had found my destination. The building was old and poorly maintained, with no windows and only one door facing the street, which was closed shut. My stomach was brimming with butterflies, and my brain was imagining all sorts of scary aberrations. I wasn't sure if I should knock, or just walk in.

My indecison, however, was annuled by the sudden opening of the door from the inside. A diminutive, swarthy complexioned European with rimless spectacles stepped out. He looked upwards towards me, startled, and then smiled amicably.

"Good day to you ... can I help you?" he asked in an open, friendly manner.

"Yes ..." I replied, easily more startled than even he was. "I'm looking for a man named 'Peewee'."

"Well, you've found him ... I was just about to go across the street to fetch a bite to eat, but come on in ... and how can I help you?"

I was shocked. '*This* is Peewee??' I puzzled to myself, totally perplexed. But I had expected someone much different ... he was neither huge nor 'pirate-like', and he expecially didn't appear dangerous and blood-thirsty.

And what did you expect? And why?

I was about to repeat Bobby's ditty, but changed my mind. It just didn't seem necessary, or even fitting.

"I'm a friend of Bobby Mundy ... and I've just arrived aboard the New Guinea Trader.

"Ahh ... no need to say more ...! Well ... uhh ... let me show you around. My business is sampans and walla-wallas, as I am sure you have already surmised. I have a fleet of both, and we have runs throughout Hong Kong and the Territories, and to Shenzen and Quangzhou.

The interior of the building was a large open office, with a work or storage room behind. Two not-so-young Chinese secretaries were busy with paperwork at separate desks, and several Chinese men in work clothes were milling in and out. The man named Peewee led me to the rear of the building and out into an enclosed yard which sloped down to the typhoon shelter's shoreline, and a wooden pier. The land portion was crowded with sampans and one of the larger walla-wallas, all in various stages of repair, and more were secured at the pier, two and three deep on both sides. Peewee escorted me to the water's edge at one side of the property next to a high brick wall that was the adjoining building, where we were presumably out of earshot from everyone else.

"I suppose he gave you some silly ditty to tell me," Peewee laughed, with a mischievous gleem, suggesting that it wasn't really necessary for me to repeat it, but he would like to hear it just the same.

"Yes ... it went: From the Templars of old, More precious than gold." I repeated.

"Now, where is your vessel anchored, and when can I send a walla-walla to pick up the 'shipment'?" Peewee queried. "It should be at night ... preferrably in the late evening."

"I see. Then it can be a night when I will be the one left on board to watch the ship. I will have to let you know when."

"Fine," the small man smiled. "But as soon as possible ... alright?"

"Of course."

With that our business was finished, for the time being, and I followed Peewee back towards the building. At the rear entrance I was suddenly stopped short, having confronted a colossus figure blocking the entire doorway. He was Chinese, and seemed to fill the door opening completely, both in width and in height, with bare arms and chest, and muscles bulging in every direction. He was just like in the movies. A hired Chinese bodyguard: massive, with a bald head and bare above the waist, and with loosely fitting trousers, which were secured by a red colored sash band. He looked indestructable, and deadly. My eyes were searching for the sword and buccaneer's pistol.

'Jeeses,' I gasped under my breath. 'Well, this is it, Chad,' I was paralyzed by a sense of impending doom. 'This is Peewee's paid assassin, a sadistic, blood thirsty killer, and you have just met your Waterloo.'

But then the mountain of Chinese muscle smiled graciously and stepped aside, politely. "Oh ... I'm sorry, sir ... please excuse me."

353

The whole of my terror and anxiety must have shown on my face, for Peewee quickly came to my rescue, smiling broadly, and chuckling with roguish amusement.

"Chad, this is Tin, my yard foreman."

It was still early when I made it back to Kowloon, and the Oasis bar. I figured my threesome friends from the Trader must have just arrived a short time before.

"How was she, Chad?" Harry snickered.

What??

I caught a signal from Kevin.

"She's really something else, Harry … thank you for asking." I replied sardonically. I guessed that Kevin had told them I had taken off on a secret rendevous with a girl I had met, and so I slipped into the role.

Hey, Harry ... I can play at being an actor too!

"So the girl from the meat boat was that good, ehh Canuck?" Laurie added, with just a touch of jealously. "What was her name?"

"Uhh ... yeh ... Ling Fu ... and she's a nice girl. Not nearly as nice as Bernaditta, of course." I added the last part in order to make him feel better, and to end the interrogation.

Shan Li was smiling at Kevin generously, clearly delighted to see him again. Chong Mii was there as well, but I teasingly held her at bay, telling her that she had to wait until my second beer before I would buy her a drink. She sat beside me and resigned herself to the wait, positioning herself so that her succulent thigh was both well exposed and pressing against me, her hand in my lap. I had forgotten the power of these simple gestures, and she had a drink in front of her well before the end of my first San Miguel.

"The nerve of that bastard!" Harry erupted, finally able to let it out. "Any of you are free to leave the Trader, if you so wish!" he mimicked. "I don't think our Mr. Fitzgerald or Lancey Shipping Company has any intention of paying us or repatriating us anywhere." Harry was pissed. I wanted to feel as strongly as he did, but it just wasn't in me, not yet anyway.

"Well, let's see what Mr. Tom Lancey has to say tomorrow ... maybe we're getting excited for nothing." I tried to calm our exciteable friend.

"I don't reckon so, mate ... I can see the writing on the wall ... mark my words …but like I said yesterday, the boulder stops here."

I chuckled. "See what you've done, Kevin, now *Harry's* become a philosopher."

"Bloody unlikely," Harry grumbled, smoldering yet grinning at the same time.

"Laurie, I feel like a little action ... let's go exploring." I suggested.

"Good idea ... yeh, let's do some exploring. How about you two?" Laurie extended the invitation.

"I'm good right here," Harry responded. Kevin just smiled, Shan Li tightening her grip on his arm.

Laurie and I started walking. It was about nine o'clock and Kowloon was in full swing. It seemed that every street we turned into had at least one bar, the neon signs and lights making them glaringly obvious. And everywhere were food stands, some small and specializing in only one item, other's large ... so large that I wondered if they were actually portable ... displaying all varieties of rice and noodle dishes, soups and chop sueys, and meats. I came to a sudden stop beside one, and grabbed Laurie's arm.

"Jeeses ... look at what's hanging around the top of that cart ... those are cat and dog carcasses!" I blurted.

Laurie stared. "Bloody hell ... I reckon they are. I've heard of the Chinese eating cat, and dog ... but ...?"

We both stood there, frozen in revulsion, both silently resolved never to eat from one of those carts.

Several places we passed had 'hustlers' on the street in front, soliciting us to go inside. After we had refused two or three we decided 'what the hell', at least we could take a peek inside to see what they were all about. We discovered real soon that Kowloon offered a great range of establishments catering to the needs of male visitors and the more well-to-do Chinese.

At one we found ourselves in a long well-lit room, with a full-length bar on one side where we were encouraged to have a drink, and on the other side sat an equally lengthly line-up of girls. The system, we learned, was to have a drink of short duration while we chose the girl of our dreams and then off we would go to indulge in heavenly bliss. We both felt this was just too brazen for our romanticist souls, and we drank our one drink and fled, admist a flurry of intensified solicitations and insults, among them I heard 'hey you, cheap Charlie' and 'what's the matter ... you cherry boy?'. We laughed and giggled for a full street block.

Another was a dance hall where you purchased tickets to pay a girl of your choice to dance with you, one ticket would pay for one dance ... or the length of one song or tune. And of course the girls were available for a more intimate short term relationship. That was OK, but when Laurie chose this one girl, she must have been only fifteen or sixteen, she began to cry ... sobbing great tears and making a terrible scene. We didn't understand what was happening; I suspected that this was some sort of scheme to make Laurie feel sorry for her and therefore cost him more money. But an older girl came to the sweet thing's rescue, explaining that yes, she would go with Laurie if he insisted ... she was under contract to her employer to do so. But it would be her first time, and she was terrified, especially, she said, because Lauire was so big. And she was referring to length and diameter, not height! Laurie understood ... he truly felt sorry for the girl and said it was OK, and that no, he wouldn't take her out. The delicate sweetheart beamed in gratitude, and once again we beat a quick retreat.

Yet another place had go-go dancers and so we stopped there for awhile, enduring a constant barrage of attempts to hustle us for drinks. One girl who just wouldn't leave me alone was a not-so-good-looking college student. She explained that education in Hong Kong was expensive, that parents had to pay for tuition after the elementary grades, and that she was desperately trying to complete a college degree so that she would have some sort of a future, hopefully to be able to immigrate to some other country. I felt very sympathetic towards her, only because she was so unattractive that, yes, an education was her only chance of being rescued.

When we finally concluded that the girls were not going to go bottomless and that their tops were woefully inadequate as well, we hit the trail once again.

"Laurie ... I hate to say this, but these Chinese girls just aren't all that great, are they?"

"I was thinking the same thing ... not much shape to them, ehh."

"I'll bet the reason they didn't go bottomless back there is because they're shy about their bald cuscus's." I laughed. "How was Bernadita ... I mean ... did she have hair?"

"Oh yes ... and lots of it!"

"Hmm."

Maybe the Trader should have stopped in Manila after all!

We were searching for more of Kowloon's night life when we discovered that we were back at our starting place ... we had unknowingly completed a full circle.

"Hey, let's see if Harry and Kevin are still here.

They were. Shan Li was snuggled even closer to Kevin than when we had left, and Harry was caressing another Fosters, as well as the girl named Vicki sitting beside him.

"I'll bet he still hasn't bought her a drink!" I whispered to Laurie.

I was cognizant that Kevin was drunk. This was the first time I had seen him in that state, and it startled me.

"Kevin, you'd better take it easy ... diabetes and booze don't mix well."

He opened his mouth to say something in rebuttal, but slumped back in his seat and smiled. He was enjoying himself.

"I had forgotten ... you said your mother was diabetic ... so you know a little about diabetes, and diabetics."

I was instantly sorry I had said anything ... I really didn't like to talk about my mother, and diabetes.

"But you said she *was* diabetic, so then your mother's no longer alive?" He asked, suddenly interested.

"No, she's still alive, but she's no longer diabetic."

"Chad ... diabetes is not curable; if you're a diabetic, you're a diabetic!"

"OK then, she 'controls' it, and doesn't need to take insulin anymore."

"She was Type 1 diabetic? She took insulin? And she doesn't take insulin anymore? I don't believe it!" Kevin was slurring a bit.

I shrugged. "Kevin, you're drunk ... and I don't really want to talk about it ... but it's true."

Kevin straightened himself up in his seat. I had touched on something of vital importance to him. He was interested, and not about to let it go.

"How?"

"Mostly through diet, if you have to know, and with the help of supplements and exercise." I replied reluctantly.

"What kind of a diet, and what supplements."

"Kevin ... can we do this another time ... like tomorrow ... or next year?"

"No way ... what kind of diet and supplements?"

"OK ... OK! According to her the trick was to control your blood glucose level without the help of the pancreas, and also to try and repair the pancreas. As far as the supplements went, she took an all-around vitamin and mineral multi with plenty of B vitamins and chromium ... and selenium. Oh yeh ... no milk." I rattled this off the top of my head, trying to remember the details of my mother's many 'lectures'.

Kevin was listening intently, a look of incredulity on his face. "Sounds like you know what you're talking about, but I still don't believe it."

"Kevin ... I think it's time to go back to the Trader."

Kevin laughed. "Hey ... this is not like you ... why don't you want to talk about diabetes and your mother?"

"Because it was such an embarrassment to me ... and I guess I rebelled ... I suppose I still am."

"You were embarrassed because your mother was diabetic?" Kevin looked at me astonished, and condescendingly.

"No, not because she was diabetic but because she was a 'health food nut'. It was bad enough being a Mormon, but our family were health food nuts on top of it. There I was, in a new high school, trying my best to be a normal guy, and find new friends and that sort of thing ... with our Mormon church two blocks away from the school in one direction and my mother's health food store in the shopping center two blocks away in another direction ... I was constantly being teased .

All three of my crew mates laughed. Kevin had succeeded in breaking the barrier I had tried to maintain. So I decided to lay it on. I related the instance when I had brought a new friend home with me for lunch and my mother had prepared 'meatless' hot dogs on whole wheat buns ... no ketchup, pickles, or mustard allowed. The new friend couldn't wait to get to school to tell everyone and make a big joke out of it. And the time when I'd had a cold and had called good 'ol mom at the health food store to get some advice on how to cure it. She had recommended I take some garlic, but she didn't say how much. There was a bundle of it in the refrigerator, and I figured if a little was good, then more was better, and so I stuffed as much as I could betweeen slices of bread and ate the whole thing ... about four whole cloves. Again I had been the laughing stock of the entire school ... everyone held their noses and teased me by fleeing from me in the hallways, and refusing to sit near me in class. The principal finally suggested I stay home for a few days.

"So your mom had her own health food store, which was because she was diabetic?"

"Kevin, normally I'd refuse to say anything more ... I've always been embarrassed as hell about it. But I'm telling you about my mother and her method of dealing with diabetes, only because maybe it'll help you."

"OK ... tell me more ... shoot!"

"Kevin, you're stealing my line again."

"OK ... go ahead."

"I'm going to spare you the long story of my mother's history, about how she missed a year of grade school because she had her appendix removed and there was an infection that wouldn't heal ... you know that that's a symptom of diabetes, right ... and her years of taking insulin, and I remember times when she hemorrhaged, and once when she went into a coma because we were so poor at the time that she couldn't afford the insulin. Or about her going to nursing school and becoming an R.N. because of her interest in medicine and in finding a cure for her diabetes. Or about the failure of conventional medicine to deal with diabetes, and her disillusionment and frustration with doctors, and even anger, and finally how she looked up an old friend from nursing school who had become a health food nut, and how she finally was able to control the diabetes through diet and stopped needing to take insulin, and then opened up her own health food store ... OK?"

"If you insist." Kevin grinned. "Just tell me what I have to do so I don't need to take insulin ... if you could do that I'd kiss your royal butt every morning for eternity."

"Please don't ... that would be a worse fate than Sisyphus's. But OK. My mother used to give lectures on this and I heard them many times ... this is what she used to teach. If you're Type I diabetic, that means your blood glucose level is too high because the beta cells in your pancreas don't secrete insulin, or not enough. Science says that the insulin increases the ability of the cells to absorb glucose from the blood stream and thereby regulates the blood glucose level. So you must take insulin shots to make up for the lack of supply from the pancreas. OK?"

"That's what I've been told." Kevin nodded.

"OK. My mother says just blindly taking insulin ignores a few things. First of all is the question of why our blood glucose level surges in the first place ... and she blames that on consuming simple sugars and carbohydrates that have a high glycemic index rating.

"A what?" Kevin interupted.

"Glycemic index. That's a ranking of how much a sugar or other carbohydrate raises blood levels of glucose ... after ingestion."

"Oh ... yeh ... I think I heard of that ... go on." Kevin was being a little bleary.

"To get to the point, the trick is to eat foods that digest slowly and don't cause radical fluctuations in blood glucose levels. That means a diet with a higher protein level than normal, and less carbohydrates in general, and especially limiting the highest glycemic rankers, such as simple sugars, rice, breads, and potatoes."

"Rice, breads, and potatoes ...?" Kevin questioned, startled.

"Yes. It is surprising that the foods with the highest glycemic index are *not* only simple sugars, but include some complex carbohydrates as well. There's a lot to the glycemic index ... you gotta do some research on your own."

"Oh."

"Is that enough ... or do I have to continue?" I really did want to end this.

"Please continue ...!" Kevin insisted.

"OK ... my mother then asks *why* the pancreas isn't producing enough insulin ... which is produced by the beta cells in the pancreas. She insisted ... and I kinda question this part ... that there is a correlation between drinking cow's milk and diabetes, 'cause something in cow's milk causes the body's own immune system to attack the beta cells. There's supposed to be some research to support that. Or it could be genetic. Or poor nutrition ... a lack of the B vitamins, for example."

"Cow's milk?" Another interuption.

"Yeh ... that's what she claimed." I shrugged.

"Then, she argues that the body has other ways of regulating glucose levels ... that the minerals chromium and selenium are important in promoting and regulating glucose take-up by the body's cells, and that exercise and weight control are important. She also stressed that the problem is sometimes not 'too little insulin', but 'too much *glucagon'*, which is produced by the alpha cells in the pancreas and has an opposing effect to insulin. But that condition is mostly evident in Type II diabetes."

I took a deep breath … so much talking made me run out of oxygen.

"Well," said Harry, "I reckon we've underestimated Canuck ... all the time we should have been calling him 'Doctor Canuck'." Harry snickered.

"Yeh ... well, Laurie and I found a new name tonight for you too!"

"And what's that?"

"Well, I forget exactly ... help me out, Laurie. I know it rhymes with 'Cheap Charlie'." I returned his snicker.

"Cheap Harry!" Laurie exploded, laughing.

I slept for just over two hours, and woke suddenly, spontaneously, my mental alarm clock responding correctly to an earlier programming. It was time. The ship was deathly quiet, and even the harbor was still, the silence broken only by the soft putt-putt of a distant walla-walla and the occasional throaty sound of a ship's horn, far away. Once more I hoisted the heavy wooden crate onto my right shoulder, and started on the journey down to the main deck, and to the officer's mess. Everything was pitch black. But I had become so familiar with the Trader and this particular route that no light was required, even during the delicate chore of replacing the box to its previous hiding place under the removable seat. 'I'm getting good at this,' I joked to myself.

Harry woke up in the morning knowing that something was seriously amiss. It had to do with his private parts, with 'Neb' … that's short for Nebuchadnezzar, which in Babylonian means 'little king'. The name he had given to that particular organ was one of his private jokes. A pusy fluid came out the end when he squeezed him, and it hurt to pee. He immediately became concerned. This was Hong Kong, a port notorious for sexually transmitted disease.

"Oh shit … oh shit!" He kept saying to myself.

"Gentlemen ... I think I got some kind of VD!" Harry explained his symptoms. Both Laurie and I roared in laughter. Harry definitely wanted to kill both of us.

"Hey, mates ... this is *not* funny. I do not appreciate you jerks making a joke out of it. A very important piece of my anatomy is at stake."

"So ... when did it happen?" I queried, thinking that I wasn't aware of him going all the way with any of the bar girls.

"The girl from the meat boat ... I guess."

"The girl from the meat boat? Harry, didn't you wear a condom?" I questioned, amazed.

"Yeh, I did ... but something must have happened. I can't wear those things anyway ... they keep coming off. Besides things were a little excited right then.

The opportunity had presented itself ... I just couldn't resist. "Why do they keep coming off, Harry ... does it have something to do with ... size?"

"No ... jerk ... because I'm not circurnsized. They just weren't designed for my style of equipment."

Laurie and I couldn't stop laughing. Harry finally got up and walked out, scowling and cursing under his breath.

We were aware that the Captain was preparing to leave the ship. There had been a few articles of clothing hanging out to dry in the wheelhouse when we had returned from shore the night before ... they looked like they had been hand washed. And he was up well before breakfast, moving around in his quarters. What clinched it, however, was when he arrived in the officer's mess wearing slacks and a dress jacket, and he had carried down his large brown suitcase and matching briefcase.

We waited for an explanation.

"Gentlemen, I'm scheduled on the nine o'clock Qantas flight to Singapore, and then Sydney."

"Mr. Fitzgerald didn't waste any time, did he?" Harry sneered.

"I'm sorry, Gentlemen ... I'm under strict orders not to even talk to you ... I'm threatened with all sorts of charges. Let it be enough to let you all know that you have rights ... if you don't get paid, in full, or they refuse to repatriate you ... go talk to the Harbor Master. I've done all I can to help you. I'm out of the picture, so to speak."

He pulled out a white envelope from his inside jacket pocket and slid it across the table in my direction.

We had all listened intently to Mr. Patterson, suddenly very saddened that this man was leaving.

"Sir, I know I speak for all of us when I say that it has been our pleasure to have known you and worked with you, and the very best of luck to you ... thank you for your help, and for having brought us through this voyage." I expounded, humbly and sincerely.

There followed a round of quiet 'hear, hear's'.

"One last thing though, Captain." I added. "How about Mr. Milner? Will you be contacting him ... and did Mr. Fitzgerald have anything to say about him?"

"It's curious, Chad, but there has been no mention of Mr. Milner, other than my telling Mr. Fitzgerald that he had contracted malaria and was in the Philippines. Nothing. He didn't even ask where in the Philippines. I will be sending Mr. Milner a letter letting him know."

I rose to shake the Captain's hand as he prepared to depart. We all accompanied him on deck while he waited for a walla-walla, and remained waving until he was almost to the Kowloon shore.

Goodbye, Captain Patterson!

"What's in the envelope?" Harry wanted to know.

"You know what it is, Harry. It's the money left over from the sale of the pump." I tried to pretend that the realization should have been obvious, but I had felt through the paper and could make out the outline of the one hundred dollar bills ... seven of them I figured. "So what are we going to do with it?" I smiled at Harry's ready inference that is was 'our' money. "Let's talk about it." I held him at bay.

We all went back to the mess, to finish our breakfast and to consider this new event. I opened the envelope, and read the short note out loud:

"Mr. Fitzgerald doesn't know about this money. I told him we spent
 everything on food supplies. The best of luck to you all,
Your Captain,
Mr. Frank Patterson
P. S. Please destroy this note."

"I figure we ought to divide it up between us, according to rank." Harry suggested, excitedly.

I couldn't believe my ears, but it was Harry true to form. I was curious as hell about how he thought 'according to rank' should be, however.

"And how, exactly, should that be, Harry?"

"Half between the crew, and half between you and me!"

Don't you just love the way this guy thinks!

"And why should the 2nd Engineer get the same as the Navigation Officer?"

"Navigation Officer my ass!"

Laurie and Kevin were visibly annoyed. The New Guineans weren't too happy either. I turned to our cook.

"Richard ... how are our food supplies?"

"Great ... for now."

"How many days can we go with what we've got?"

"At least a week ... two if we had to ... and we're down to seven of us now."

"Well, I'm all for splitting it up even, with the understanding that we have to all pitch in if we need to buy more food ... or that we're on our own in that event. And we wait until tomorrow to see what Lancey is going to do." I reasoned.

"No way!" Harry cut in. "How are we going to be sure you don't blow that loot on Chinese sheilas tonight?"

"Take it easy, Harrry ... what do the rest of you think?" I asked.

"Split it up even ... the sooner the better. Lancey might find a way to take it from us." Kevin argued, logically, everyone except Harry nodding agreement.

"Do you agree, Harry?"

Harry paused, scanning the faces around the table. "Majority rules ... I reckon." He finally shrugged in resignation.

I spread the hundred dollar bills on the table and each took one.

"Now what?" It was becoming a frequently asked question.

"Well, Lancey will probably be on the 3:00 p.m. flight, like Mr. Fitzgerald. But they've got to get to a hotel, and talk, and so on ... I don't think we're going to see them today." I speculated.

"And I don't reckon there's any sense in doing more work on board, not after what Mr. Fitzgerald said to us yesterday." Harry was quick to find justification for canceling out more work.

"I want to explore Victoria, maybe take the cable car up to Victoria Peak." I announced.

"Sounds good ... can I join you?" Laurie joined in.

"Sure ... anyone else?"

Kevin had a date with Shan Li, the New Guinea threesome had their own direction, and Harry reckoned that he needed to locate one of the free Hong Kong health clinics. The Captain had mentioned that there were several, and that they specialized in the treatment of venereal diseases, which was a serious problem in Hong Kong.

It worked out that we were all ready for the walla-walla at the same time, so shared one for the trip.

"You and Shan Li seem to be getting pretty close, Kevin." I was curious as to what sort of a relationship was developing.

"Yes, we are ... we're going to look at apartments today."

"Apartments? You mean to rent an apartment?"

"Yes, Chad ... to rent one."

"Wow ... so you really *do* plan to stay in Hong Kong?"

"If I can find a reasonable job, yes."

"Well, good luck."

Once we had reached Salisbury Road we all split up into our separate directions. Laurie and I wished Harry luck.

"Hope they don't have to cut it off!" I teased.

"Go to hell ... both of you." Harry tossed back at us, still sore about the money, I reckoned. We both laughed.

The clinic wasn't difficult to find at all, and was only a few blocks away from the regular shore landing. Harry was met by a Chinese receptionist, an older lady who was exceptionally efficient but neither very friendly nor good looking. Harry was informed that they needed to extract a blood sample, and he was placed in the care of an enchanting Chinese nurse who he reckoned was better looking than any of the bar girls he had seen ... and he was comparing her in the harsh clinic lighting, opposed to the darkened red lighting of the bars, which made even godzilla look attractive. She did, however, extract a vast amount of blood, and Harry was wondering if she might have a sadistic streak. He was then introduced to Doctor Swift.

"You state here that you have just come from Papua New Guinea, and may have been exposed to malaria ... very interesting. We already know you are suffering from a mild 'virus', which explains the discharge and the pain when you urinate. It's minor, and this salve and these pills should take care of it within a few days. It's not gonorrhea or anything like that. With gonorrhea we have to insert a wire 'brush' down your urethra tube and 'scrape' the sides ... not pleasant at all ..." he explained, unnecessarily descriptive, Harry thought.

"Doctor, if you're tying to scare me, you're doing a right good job."

"Scare you? Of course not. But you *will* use a condom next time, right?"

"Yes sir ... no worries ... from now on it's condoms all the way."

"Now, please return tomorrow ... we won't have the results from your blood sample for twenty-four hours. But it is imperative that you return ... understand? Here's a note for your Captain. See you tomorrow."

Laurie and I headed for the Star Ferry, walking slowly and taking our time.

"Chad, mind if we stop off at the Australian Embassy ... I want to apply for a passport.

"Laurie, that's a great idea. I hope you don't have to wait a long time to get it ... like a couple of weeks."

"Yeh ... I should have done it yesterday."

Let's do it first, then. Hey, if you have a passport, then you could go to England."

"That's just what I had in mind."

"Do you have everything you need ... birth certificate, photos?"

"Photos? I forgot about that. Hey, let's stop by some place and get a set."

It took us awhile ... finding a phone book for an address, stopping in a shop to take a set of instant photos, another to get a street map, then a long walk to locate the right building and office. But it was great fun, just experiencing the city. Victoria seemed much cleaner, better organized, and more modern than Kowloon. The streets weren't nearly so crowded with people, there were London style red double-decked buses on the thoroughfares, and taxis rather than rick-shaws and pedi-cabs, and there was much more color and variability in the pedestrian's clothes, with more Western style dress. We even saw a few men and women in business suits.

The personnel behind the counter at the embassy were Chinese, except for one Australian, a lady from Melbourne who was very friendly and helpful. She would do her best, she said, to have Laurie's passport in two days. Laurie was delighted, and relieved. I was surprised that it could be done so quickly.

"Hey, that's alright, Laurie!" I was impressed. "Your embassy actually has an Aussie behind the counter ... one who doesn't speak with a phony British accent."

"Why ... is that what the Canadian embassies are like?"

"Yeh ... at least the ones I've visited." I told Laurie about my visit to the Canadian Embassy in San Francisco. I had been so annoyed with this one English lady -- she was a recent immigrant to Canada, I found out -- who flaunted a pseudo high-nose attitude, exaggerated her British accent, and fluttered about like she was in Buckingham Palace. I was so pissed I decided to put on a show of my own. I made like I thought I was lost, looking around, and said something like: 'Oh, I'm sorry, I thought I was in the Canadian Embassy, not the British Embassy". It was at the end of my visit, of course, after I had already found out they couldn't give me the information I wanted. The English snob had turned hysterical.

We proceeded to the peak tramway, which was a few blocks from the Star Ferry terminal ... past the Bank of Shanghai building and up behind 'Government House'. For the first time we found ourselves rubbing shoulders with genuine honest-to-goodness tourists. The red-colored tram climbed the incredibly steep railway, taking us to The Peak, which we discovered wasn't the real peak at all ... Victoria Peak was still a considerable distance further ... but accessible to us only by walking up Mount Austin Road, which we chose to do. 'Hell', we figured, 'if we've come this far a short walk to the top is nothing'.

We were glad that we had. The walk was invigorating and the views spectacular. We passed the Governor's House, which was of course unaccessable to the public. The spectacle from the top was unbelievable. Victoria Peak is more towards the Chinese mainland end of Hong Kong Island, and the panorama unfolded before us was a 360 degree sweep of the island, the entire harbor, and beyond ... from past the airport to the Star Ferry, towards the Territories, and then around the end of the island and to the other side, to Aberdeen and Stanley ... all of which was a world of scattered islands and deep inlets on all three sides, sprinkled thickly with all varieties of vesseIs, many of them Chinese Junks.

On our way down I reflected that it was amusing to watch the tourists. At one point I realized that I hadn't seen real tourists for a long time, especially a large group like this. There hadn't been any in Laoang, to be sure, and they were a rarity in Rabaul as well. But on the tram we had been surrounded by a sizeable group of the genuine article: several American couples, a few Aussies, I heard German being spoken, and French, a group or Arabs, and I thought I could pick out the Canadian baroque.   We had heard the French from a pair of acceptable-looking French college co-eds, who we tried to strike up a conversation with. But we failed miserably … their English was strained and all I could say in French was 'je non parle par Francais', and 'au revoir'. But the death blow had been when we proudly pointed out the rusty colored New Guinea Trader in the distance, and tried to explain that we had brought her through all kinds of hell all the way from Papua New Guinea. Their already limited interest immediately dropped below zero, and we were dismissed as some sort of lowly riff-raff merchant marine types.

"Guess they just can't appreciate real adventure and travel, ehh," I said, trying to cover my hurt feelings."

Neither did they appreciate the true beauty that was our gallant vessel.

"That's their problem." Laurie sneered.
We laughed … still damaged and disappointed, however.

I was reading one of the tourist hand-outs -- a guide to shopping in Hong Kong -- and it explained how to say 'how much does it cost' (*Gai doe chin*) and 'it's too espensive' (*Tai quay*) in Cantonese. We had come back down to Victoria and had wandered over towards the Wanchai district. We passed the Hong Kong Police barracks compound and were on the edge of what we assumed was the bar district when I spotted a popular looking place named 'The World of Suzie Wong'. Years before I had read the story, and remembered Nancy Kwan in the movie version. Laurie said he had seen the movie.
"Hey ... we gotta check this out." I insisted.
We entered … it was still early in the afternoon, too early for heavy duty hustling, we reckoned. But no sooner had Laurie and I sat down at the bar did two girls come to ask us for a drink.
"The Captain was right when he said Wanchai girls are more aggressive. Laurie, I gotta try this out ... don't say a word, OK?"
"Shoot!"
The two girls arrived at our sides, all smiles, hands reaching out to squeeze our arms and thighs. I turned to the one closest to me and asked:
"Gai doe chin?"
The girl's face exploded into reddened fury. She took two quick steps back and stomped her right foot on the floor, hard, with arms straight by her side and fists tightly clenched.
"One thousand Hong Kong dollars!" she screamed.

"Tai quay!" I answered back, calmly.

Her fury doubled in intensity, she stomped one more time, even harder, and then turned and fled.

"Jeeses ... it works!" I said.

"A little *too* good," Laurie suggested, feeling a pang of sympathy for the girl, then added: "Nah, just right!" and laughed.

We wandered around Wanchai for several hours, trying out a couple of bars and strip joints. But we were uncomfortably aware that there were quite a few British sailors around, plus a few Americans as well, and decided to return to the Trader reasonably early.

While on the ferry I was thinking about Mr. Lancey's arrival.

"Mr. Tom Lancey is here now ... I wonder if he and Mr. Fitzgerald visited the Trader." I asked Laurie, thinking out loud.

"I seriously doubt it. The way I read it, they're going to hope that at least some of us just 'leave the ship' ... especially after what Fitz said." Laurie reasoned.

"Hmm ... hadn't thought about it that way." I mused.

Harry woke with a cold sweat on his forehead. He was having a bad dream. The details were fading fast from his conscious memory, but it was the Chinese girl, Vicki, and they were just about to make love. He remembered seeing her gorgeous thigh, both of them in fact, and then she had screamed horribly, with her hands over her face. Harry had looked down to see why, and there was this gastly mess of pus and gangrine and little white worms. Bloody hell!

He told himself, firmly, that it was only a virus ... temporary and not serious ... that was what the good Doctor Swift had said.

"Clang - clang, clang - clang!"

That's gotta be one of my most favorite sounds, I decided. Third day in Hong Kong! 'What is going to happen today?' I wondered, stretching before putting on shirt and shorts. I reminded myself that I had to 'schedule' a night with the guys when I would be the one left on board to watch the ship.

"So what did you find out?" Laurie quizzed, a mile-wide grin on his face.

"So far it's just a 'virus'." Harry responded quietly.

"A virus!" Laurie and I exploded with a full-on spasm of mirth.

"Harry's dick has a cold!" I exclaimed noisily, laughing even harder.

"Canuck ... shut up!" Harry was thinking that Chad was making Neb embarrassed.

Breakfast was once again terrific.

"Richard ... I'm going to miss you when this is all over."

Richard stopped what he was doing, and looked at me full on, moved by my unexpected sincerity. So was I, to tell you the truth, I had blurted it out kinda spontaneous like.

"Thank you, Chad!"

We had just finished our breakfast when Mr. Fitzgerald arrived. He was by himself, and had come to the mess before any of us realized that a walla-walla had pulled alongside.

"Good morning, gents."

I was cognizant that he had used the term 'gents' instead of his usual 'gentlemen'.

"Good morning, Mr. Fitzgerald." Harry greeted him cheerfully. "Any good news?"

"Yes ... Mr. Lancey is here now."

Harry's perplexed expression told me that that wasn't exactly what he had in mind.

"But what about us, Mr. Fitzgerald?"

"What about you, Harry?" he answered, evasively.

"Well, what about our pay, for starters?"

"Harry ... we're working on it ... but we feel we aren't required to pay you until your duties on this vessel are finished and you're signed off. And although Mr. Patterson had you sign off with the Port Authority, which he did without the permission of the owner, you are still working. In fact, I would like us to get started immediately on a long list of things that need to be done, starting as soon as you've all finished breakfast."

Harry's startled expression said all, for the rest of us as well. 'What the hell is going on,' I wondered silently.

Mr. Fitzgerald knew all about our jury-rigged 'water separator'. He wanted Harry and Kevin to dismantle the system and remove the engine's fuel pumps so he could take them ashore to be repaired. He also, ingeniously, I have to admit, worked out a scheme whereby they would pump all of the ship's remaining fuel into one fuel tank, then clean the inside of the empty tank and epoxy seal the leak when it was found, and then pump the fuel back into that tank, filtering it and removing the water and fungus at the same time. Even Fred couldn't have come up with a better idea, I conjectured.

In the meantime, the three quartermasters and myself were to begin dismantling all the rigging that was part of the Trader's single mast and boom equipment, and clean and grease everything, especially applying a coat of a black, sticky combination of grease and graphite to all the steel cables. Which was a major undertaking. And it was hinted that as soon as we finished that we would begin chiseling out rust and repainting ... the entire topside deck and hull.

Harry approached Mr. Fitzgerald as soon as he had completed outlining our work, and explained his little problem with his private parts, especially emphasizing his urgent need to return to the clinic that morning. I couldn't help thinking it was a beaut of an excuse, and even wondered if Harry was making the whole thing up, just to get out of work.

"You're just a tad early," Doctor Swift informed Harry when he reached the clinic. "Please sit down. We'll have the results in a half hour or so," he continued in his thick British accent. The good doctor was elderly, with a pink English face and white moustache, and long, equally bushy sideburns that reminded Harry of movies where the setting had been in a British colony during the 1800's, in colonial India or Africa.

Harry waited, occupying his time by reading the literature on venereal disease, of which there was an abundance in the waiting room, conspicuously displayed. He reckoned it was all part of their educational drive, mostly to scare men like himself into using condoms and restraining their promiscuity. Well, it worked, Harry reflected, still feeling shaky over his nightmare the night before.

"Mr. Fiddler, please come into the doctor's office," the pretty Chinese nurse requested. As Harry entered his office he found himself once again comparing her favorably with the bar girls. He was especially infatuated with her unstinting smile. 'It would be nice if her tight white nurse's dress had a slit down the side, though,' he amused himself. 'What was the word that Chad used? Oh yes -- 'succulent'. I'd wager her thigh was at least as succulent as Vicki's.'

Doctor Swift leaned back in his leather recliner, smiling at Harry thoughtfully.

"Mr. Fiddler ... you have syphilis."

Harry's eyes opened full wide and his face exposed his sense of terror. He gulped.

"I have syphilis?" He asked, incredulous, hoping that he had heard wrong.

"Yes, Harry, your blood test showed that you have contracted that distasteful disease ... and we also found an indication that you do, indeed, have a touch of malaria as well. But not to worry. Are you allergic to penicillin?"

"Allergic to penicillin? Not that I know of."

"Then it's a simple treatment: two shots of penicillin each week for five weeks ... we'll give you your first one this morning. How long will you be in Hong Kong?"

"Doctor Swift ... I don't know. But I think it will be only for a few days ... then I'll be returning to Sydney."

"If you go to Sydney you can continue the treatment there ... so no problem. But yours is an interesting case ... reminds me of my years in the British Foreign Service. I'm an old-timer, you know, and I spent many years in the tropics in places much like Papua New Guinea, where there was a lot of typhoid, and yellow fever, and of course malaria." He paused, happy to have the chance to reminisce.

"Yeh? I reckoned that you were the sort of doctor that lived in places like India, or Aftica."

"Oh yes ... I have spent many years in both areas. But back to your case. Are you aware that during the years before penicillin was available, we used to treat syphilis with malaria?"

"What ... syphilis was treated with malaria?" Harry repeated, thinking that the proposition sounded strange.

"Yes ... you see, malaria kills syphilis, and in those days we could treat malaria, but not syphilis. So, granted we had the time and resources of course, we could induce malaria into a person with syphilis, and thereby destroy the syphilis, and then we could treat the malaria. Not very many doctors know about that ... it goes back into history a bit, and it was reserved mostly for royalty and member of our 'upper class'," he laughed. "But I'm an old-timer, like I said."

"I see, and I happen to have both syphilis and malaria." Harry interjected.

"Yes ... fascinating, isn't it?"

'Oh yes, super fascinating!' Harry whispered wryly to himself.

"Well, not to worry, young man, we'll take care of you."

"But I *do* worry, doctor ... last night I had one hell of a nightmare about it."

The doctor laughed again. "Good ... then use a condom from now on ... and be a little more 'selective' about your choice of partner." He was ushering me out of his office as he talked.

"Yeh, like your nurse," Harry muttered, not intending that the good doctor hear.

"Aahh, yes," he laughed again. "But she's off limits, I'm afraid ... aahh, to be young again. Miss Sung, please introduce our Mr. Fiddler to the wonderful world of penicillin shots ... he'll have his first right now."

She beamed at Harry, just a little mischievously. He soon found out why ... the needle was at least a yard long, and a half inch in diameter, with a gallon sized syringe attached to one end, or so it seemed to Harry.

Miss Sung asked Harry to drop his pants, and his shorts. His infatuation with this Chinese beauty was rapidly waning. But he followed her instructions, bending over the doctor's table, and she jabbed that monsterous spear deep into his buttocks. Harry let out a loud yelp.

"We have to find a nice soft spot," she explained. "One with lots of flesh to absorb this volume ... you'll be bruised just a little.

"And I have to take ten of these shots?"

"Yes ... isn't it wonderful? It'll be all over in only five weeks!"

Mr. Fitzgerald was on board off and on all day, making frequent trips to shore. Harry arrived back on the ship just before noon. Mr. Fitzgerald was on shore at lunch, and we had a chance to exchange thoughts.

"You reckon Fritz is trying to encourage us to quit on our own, to save him the cost of repatriating us, or maybe even so he doesn't have to pay us?" Harry asked, making the suggestion at the same time. Harry was very unhappy with his new work load, and other things.

There seemed to be a general concensus of agreement with his assessment.

"One thing for sure ... I don't see no refit crew out here. My guess is that the Trader is up for sale ... the work we're doing fits that idea." Harry projected.

Another round of nods.

"Well, like I said before, gents, the boulder stops here ... I reckon I got a plan in mind to fix our Mr. Fitzgerald and Mr. Lancey."

Oh - oh, this doesn't sound good!

"Harry ... what do you have in mind ... I don't think I like the tone of your voice." I quizzed, suspicious that Harry had some crazy-ass scheme in mind.

"Just don't you worry, mate ... I reckon I can turn things around."

Oh ... by the way, Harry ... how did it go at the clinic?"

Harry was a little reluctant to explain the new complication to his plight, but with Laurie's help I teased it out of him.

"Did you hear that, gentlemen?" Laurie gibed merrily. "Harry's 'cold' has developed into 'pneumonia'."

Harry was developing a thick skin and didn't take the razzing too bad. Or maybe he loved to be the center of attention, regardless of the cost. He also explained Doctor Swift's description of how malaria was used historically to treat syphilis.

"So, Canuck ... reckon you don't have to worry about syphilis ... your malaria will take care of it."

"Thank you just the same, Harry ... but you can keep it all for yourself."

We continued our labor until four o'clock, when we judged that we had put in a good full eight-hour day.

Mr. Fitzgerald had become more sour-faced as the afternoon progressed. We weren't really sure why. And he scowled when everyone stopped work.

We all cleaned up ... I went to my cabin to grab a towel. I realized something was not right as soon as I entered the cabin. Someone had been through my bags, and had even removed the bunk mattress, looking for something. Things had been replaced, neatly. But there were tell-tale signs, mostly because now things were too neat. Definitely not my style.

I was feeling panic. What were they looking for, and who? Was it the 'treasure' they were after? Who? Why? I couldn't help wondering if it had been Kevin.

Nah, Chad, not Kevin!

It was a good thing I had returned the crate to the hiding place in the officer's mess. I resolved to check on them as soon as possible.

"Hey ... were any of you guys in my cabin?" I demanded to know.

Everyone was startled at my accusation, and all shrugged a negative response.

"Look ... someone was going through my stuff ... so who's going to own up. I was starting to get a little irritated.

Kevin gave me a startled, worried glance, coupled with a tiny shrug.

"Maybe it was Fritz. "Harry suggested. There was just the slightest trace of a smirk on his face.

All right, Harry, tell me what it's all about!

"Harry ... what's going on?" I demanded, knowing that something was happening, and that he was at the center of it. But I wasn't going to find out any more … he wouldn't talk.

Tonight was to be Fred's stint to stay on board the Trader. I was wondering how I was going to be able to arrange an evening when only I was aboard. But tonight it was the Oasis again, and I wanted to find out what was going on … the matter of someone going through my cabin bothered me, and Harry was definitely up to something.

"Kevin ... I never had a chance to ask . How did your apartment hunting go?" I asked.

"We think we've found a place. Shan Li will know tomorrow."

The two looked like a great pair. I was starting to develop a good feeling for them, hoping their relationship would work out.

"Now, Harry ... I want to know what you've got up your sleeve." I finally got around to the question that had been bugging me.

"Up my sleeve?" Harry teasingly made a gesture of looking up both of his shirt sleeves. "Not a thing, mate ... not a thing."

But my suspicion was intensifying. Harry went to the 'head', and Kevin leaned over the table.

"I don't know what Harry is doing, but he's definitely got some kind of scheme going. Today he took Mr. Fitzgerald aside in the engine room and they talked secretly for quite a few minutes. Mr. Fitzgerald seemed very worried."

"Well, maybe that explains Mr. Fitzgerald's dark mood this afternoon." Laurie suggested.

Chong Mii's succulent thigh was as warm and smooth and enticing as ever. Maybe more so. We enjoyed our beers and company. But we were all too tired to make it a long night. We returned to the Trader without further exploration.

I waited in the officer's mess until I was sure that everyone had hit the sack. Then I casually lifted up on the seat and quickly surveyed underneath. One, two, three crates, just as they had been before.

We continued with the same project as the day before. I was glad we had Fred with us … he was a joy to work with; damn handy with the wrenches and constantly figuring out how to make a particular job easier.

Mr. Fitzgerald persisted with his darkened mood, and I caught him glancing at me suspiciously a couple of times. I wanted to walk over to him and ask what it was all about. But I didn't. I wondered if Harry was right, that it was Mr. Fitzgerald who had been in my cabin. But if so, what was he looking for, and why?

After one of Mr. Fitzgerald's repeated trips to Kowloon, he returned with our two Perkin's fuel pumps. Harry and Kevin complained bitterly about the task of cleaning out the fuel tank, and wanted Fred and Joseph to help them, but there was no way I was going to let that happen. Not until we had completed the rigging portion of work, at least. We stopped work at 4 o'clock again, and Richard adjusted dinner time to five, knowing that most of us would likely want to go ashore.

Laurie and I made a big joke out of Harry's 'infirmity'. Everyone did, for that matter. We quarantined him to the remote end of the mess table, and his plate and utensils were kept separate. Bodily contact was discouraged, and he was asked, not politely, to refrain from breathing directly towards any particular person.

Harry was depressed. He had visions of his sex life coming to a terrible end, permanently. It was no use going ashore in his condition, so tonight he opted to stay on board. Anyway, he was sure that if he went to the Oasis Club Kevin or Laurie or Canuck, or all three of them, would continue his harassment and no girl would sit down beside him, let alone anything else. The only bright side was that he sorely needed to do some laundry, and so this was a great opportunity. His pants and shirts were getting so they could stand in the cabin corner by themselves. It never occurred to Harry that Kowloon was one big Chinese laundry and that he could have everything he owned expertly laundered for two Hong Kong dollars.

"Reckon I'll watch the ship tonight gents ... you all can go ashore without me."

I was actually feeling a little sorry for him. "Harry you watch the ship tonight and I'll play watch-man tomorrow ... how's that?" I tried to make it sound like I was doing him a favor.

"Alright, Canuck ... you're on! He replied, sounding a little more cheerful.

So tomorrow night is the night!!

Kevin was listening, and understood my true intent. "So when are you going to see your sweetheart again, Chad?"

"Yeh, I've been thinking about her ... I think I'll go see her tomorrow morning ... yup, that's a good idea."

I noticed that Harry had picked up on that, and was strangely interested.

I had decided that the only way for me to leave the ship alone was to depart early, before the rest of the crew was up and about.

"Has he left yet?" Harry asked.

"Yeh ... the walla-walla just pulled away." Joseph said.

"OK ... here's the plan. We all go and visit our Mr. Lancey at the Hong Kong Hilton .... and we present him with our demands: we want to be paid, now, and we want to be signed off the Trader and given fare to our next destination ... all agreed?"

"Hear, hear!"

"OK ... let's go!" Harry ordered.

Laurie wasn't sure they were doing the night thing. It all seemed more of a dramatic 'plot' than a 'negotiation'.

"And why isn't Chad going with us?" Fred asked. He and his two fellow New Guineans had been part of Harry's scheming earlier that morning, but this part was still unclear to them. Fred thought that it should be Chad leading this confrontation with Mr. Lancey, not Harry.

"Because Chad is our 'ace-in-the-hole', mate. It's a long story, but Mr. Fitzgerald knows that Chad has six sticks of dynamite, with caps, on board the Trader, and I've made Fitz think that Chad will use those half dozen sticks to scuttle the ship ... blow a hole in its hull ... if we don't get what's rightfully ours."

"And that's why Mr. Fitzgerald was searching through Chad's cabin day before yesterday?" Joseph asked, perplexed.

"That's right!"

"So why don't we let Chad be a part of it and he come with us?" Fred quizzed, still not satisfied.

"Because he wouldn't go for it … he's too chicken-shit. And besides, it's better that they think he's back here on the ship, ready to set off the dynamite."

"Bloody hell," Laurie blurted. "It sounds crazy ... but what the hell!"

So … Harry's dauntless brigade started on it's expedition to penetrate the Lancey fortress on Victoria Hill and to do battle with that terrible tyrant, Thomas Lancey. Surprisingly, they met almost no resistance throughout the course of their intended siege, even at the entrance to the Hilton citadel itself, and one of the stronghold's sargent-at-arms quickly surrendered the room number and location of the Lancey bulwark without a fight. They mounted the castle's elevator and rode together to the thirteenth level … and banged on the barricaded entrance to number 1413, the tyrants unlucky refuge (the real number was 1313 , of course, the actual 13th floor being numbered 14).

"What the bloody hell?" the short, middle-aged man with the balding hair blurted, wearing only a towel around his generous mid-section, the pretty face of a similarly clothed Chinese female peering over his shoulder. Upon seeing the formidable force besieging their entrance she squealed in terror and retreated deeper into the Lancey refuge.

"Mr. Lancey, I am your 2nd Engineer, Harry Fiddler, and this is the rest of your crew of the New Guinea Trader. We have come to demand wages and repatriation."

'Hell,' Laurie cringed, silently, 'This is too much!'

"Well ... this not the time … nor place!" Mr. Tom Lancey retorted, reddening in the face, being instantly on the defensive.

"I'm sorry sir," Harry said, cutting him off. "But this *is* the time and place! We won't leave until we are dealt with!" Harry leaped to the offensive.

"I'll deal with you, all right ... with the help of the Hong Kong police ... Mr. Lancey counter attacked.

"Then you'll leave us no recourse but to take our complaints to the Harbor Master ... and there is your 2nd Officer and six sticks of dynamite to consider as well!" Harry rebounded defiantly, and with great gallantry, bringing his ace-in-the-hole brazenly into play.

Mr. Lancey was shocked by the revelation of this new secret weapon -- he knew he didn't stand a chance -- he was beaten. His defenses having crumbled, he retreated to the only way to save grace in this deadly conflict -- a negotiated peace.

"Alright give me a few minutes to get dressed and call Mr. Fitzgerald. Please wait for us downstairs in the lobby. We can talk there."

The heroic half dozen strategically withdrew to the fortress lobby, and waited to apportion the spoils, already confident they had won the battle.

Mr. Fitzgerald and Mr. Lancey arrived together, Mr. Lancey now more reasonably attired and carrying a briefcase. Mr. Fitzgerald greeted the crew cordially, even with a smile.

'My god,' Laurie pondered introspectively, 'Mr. Fitzgerald is actually amused by all of this.'

"Gentlemen, I think you are all grossly over-reacting," Mr. Fitzgerald began. "But what do you want from us ... can you present us with a proposal, Harry?"

Harry was deflated by Mr. Fitzgerald's surprisingly auspicious attitude ... his sail had been partially robbed of its wind ... but our noble warrior-hero was quick to regroup:

"Mr. Fitzgerald, we would all like to be paid our agreed wages, today, and we would like to be repatriated."

"Well, I was going to pay you all tomorrow, but it can be done today ... if I can have an agreement, that is."

"What sort of agreement?" Harry asked warily.

"Very simple ... we would like you to complete your present projects ... the re-working of the rigging, and the work on the fuel tanks. And of course we will require you to sign a 'settlement agreement' when we pay you."

"I don't see a problem with that, I reckon," Harry agreed. "How about the rest of you, mates?"

The other heroes all nodded.

"And the repatriation?" Harry continued as chief negotiator.

"What do you propose?"

"Fred, Joseph, and Richard need to get back to Rabaul. I would like to go to Sydney. And Laurie, Chad, and Kevin would like an onward fare to England. Kevin would like to have his 'open' as he may be in Hong Kong for awhile."

"Well, Harry, that is pretty much what we had in mind ... if you had just given us a chance. We've found passage for you three on a freighter that's leaving for Papua New Guinea the day after tomorrow ... is that agreeable?"

The three hap-castes looked at each other, and Fred took the initiative as their spokesperson.

"Yes, that's fine, Mr. Fitzgerald."

"Good. Then we have an agreement?"

A series of nods ensued.

"If you all get back to the Trader quickly, you may be able to finish the agreed-on work today. And please, Harry, tell Chad to safely dispose of that dynamite, OK?"

"Uhh ... how would he do that?"

Throwing it into the harbor would suffice ... without the caps, of course."

Mr. Lancey had opened his briefcase and pulled out seven white envelopes and seven agreement forms. The forms were signed and the envelopes distributed. Mr. Lancey gave Chad's to Harry, telling him that the form was inside ... it was trusted that Chad would follow through with the signing.

And our conquering warriors, having confronted the terrible tyrant and successfully completed the mission impossible, now victoriously returned to their battleship and home base, the New Guinea Trader.

The return trip to Aberdeen was uneventful, and I made the ferry crossing and bus connections easily. I was becoming familiar with Hong Kong. I felt like I was already a seasoned 'ex-pat'. I was wondering how long I would stay here, concluding that it really depended on what we could negotiate with Lancey. Right now things didn't look good. Maybe I would end up making Hong Kong my home for quite awhile.

The Aberdeen Sampan Company was a beehive of activity. This time the front entrance door was swung wide open with a rubber 'door jam' at the bottom to secure it in that position. The sound of hammering and other repair noises came from the rear yard, and the various workers in the office were chattering loudly in Cantonese. One of the secretaries was on the phone, shouting to be heard above the general clamor. Tin appeared through the back of the office and looked in my direction. He smiled, which somehow was incongruous with his appearance and my mental vision of his purpose, and motioned with his hand for me to wait. A minute later Peewee worked his way among the desks towards me.

"Good morning to you, Chad ... do you have a time set?" he asked casually, still surprising me with his open friendliness.

"I'll be alone on the Trader this evening."

"Good ... how about nine o'clock?"

"Great!"

"Then it's done. We'll be there ... I'm sorry, but I'm terribly busy now, please excuse me."

I was able to make it back to the Trader about mid-morning. The walla-walla pulled alongside the Trader. I hadn't seen anyone working on deck, and there were no sounds ... the ship was ghostly quiet.

'Hell, the lazy s.o.b.'s are probably lounging in the mess,' I chuckled to myself. But no, the mess cabin was deserted. There was no one on board. Not even Richard.

'What the hell!' I shrugged. I fixed myself something to eat, and prepared to wait.

I rubbed at my eyes and sat up on the mess's bench seat, having been awakened by the rowdy return of the rest of the crew.

"Here's your wages, mate!" Harry triumphantly slapped the white envelope on the table. "Please sign the 'agreement' letter and I will see that Mr. Fitzgerald gets it." he added, with exaggerated pomposity.

I opened the envelope, and my eyes widened. I had been aboard the Trader for just over four weeks. I had been told I would be paid a net of one hundred dollars a week. I had been paid for five weeks.

"Hey, we got work to do. Let's see if we can finish today." Harry presented us with the challenge.

Laurie filled me in on the details of what had happened, while we were working. I laughed and laughed.

"So then it was Mr. Fitzgerald who was going through my cabin ... and he was looking for the dynamite that Harry had told him I had?" I quizzed Laurie, still not believing that this was all Harry's scheming.

"Yeh ... reckon it was Fitzgerald alright!"

We all worked furiously, smelling the scent of new adventure, and wanting to end the chore. We were all excited about having been paid five weeks wages, and about where we would be going after leaving the Trader. Except maybe our New Guineans. I wondered about them. Was the prospect of taking another freighter back to Rabaul a disappointment, or were they looking forward to it?

Our rigging was all back in place, and we had only a couple of minor things to do to be completely finished.

"Fred, Joseph ... Harry and Kevin would sure like you to help them. Laurie and I can finish this ... would you mind helping them out?"

"Sure, Chad," they both agreed. "We can't get any dirtier than this anyway."

We worked till dark, Richard held off dinner until we had all called it quits.

"I reckon it's done, mates." Harry boasted as soon as we sat down. "Both tanks are cleaned, we patched the leaks, and the fuel had been strained and the water removed ... and the chemical added."

"Yeh, and I heard the full story from Laurie about your theatrical confrontation with Mr. Lancey ... and the dynamite. You know, Harry, I honestly can't believe you did that!" I'd had some time to react, and I was now pissed about how he had used me in his scheme.

"I reckon that's mighty ungrateful of you, Canuck. You've got five hundred dollars in your pocket, don't you?"

"From what I hear we would have gotten it tomorrow anyway." I argued.

"You don't want to believe it was because of me ... and the way we went right up there and stuck it in Mr. Lancey's nose ... then that's your problem. But it was Harry Fiddler who made sure the men got paid and repatriated." Harry boasted, having a little trouble with the last word.

"Like ... the boulder stopped here ... thanks to Harry Fiddler!" I chuckled. I couldn't stay angry with this guy for more than a few minutes. I was enjoying his showmanship. Kevin and Laurie laughed, remembering the Myth of Sisyphus story.

"That's right, mate ... the boulder stopped here!"

The moon wasn't due to rise for another hour or so. Hong Kong's night-time haze was in place, and the evening light had faded into a murky blackness. It was a 'pirates' night, and an ideal time to unload the Trader's secret cargo -- the last of Solomon's Treasure.

I thought I heard the putt-putt of a walla-walla's diesel close by, and hurried to the starboard rail to take a look. Sure enough, a darkly colored walla-walla quietly emerged from the mist and pulled alongside. Peewee's face grinned up at me. He scaled the rope ladder quickly, leaving the other members of his pirate crew behind.

"Are the containers small enough and light enough for you and I to handle them?" he questioned in a soft tone.

"Yes ... follow me. "

I hadn't dared to bring the three to the open main deck prematurely. Peewee and I entered the officer's mess and quickly carried the three crates to the rail, passing them to the waiting hands of his Chinese crew. I spotted 'Tin' watching from the stern of the walla-walla.

"Here ... this is for helping the Bretheren of the Coast, Chad ..." Peewee whispered as he slipped a small cloth bag into my hand. Whatever was inside was shaped tubular, like a roll of notes I surmised.

"And if you're ever in need ... anytime, anywhere ... you can always seek out a fellow Bretheren ... just remember Bobby boy's ditty. Fare-thee-well, matey, and our thanks."

As quietly and mysteriously as they had arrived, they were gone.

"Clang - clang, clang - clang!"

I woke to a new day. I had been dreaming sweetly of Jeri ... through it all she was the everlasting girl of my dreams. I wondered what had become of her. As far as I knew she was attending the University of Alberta. Maybe if I got back to Canada sometime in the next couple of years I could look her up ... maybe re-kindle the old fire. I'd go to university, like her ... just to be worthy of her if nothing else. And if I ever wrote the story of this crazy adventure I was now a part of, I would dedicate it to her.

Richard loaded it on this morning, like it was our last supper. We had steak and pork chops and ham and eggs sunny-side up and eggs scrambled, and we had yams and yams and yams.

"Richard ... you are the greatest!" I cheered. He beamed. But my own reference to a 'last supper' now worried me. Richard had demonstrated an uncanny abitlity to time things, almost to predict. I was wondering if he wasn't perhaps psychic.

No sooner than we were reaching the maximum of our abilities to comsume more of Richard's great breakfast, Mr. Fitzgerald strode through the door.

"Good morning, gentlemen. I have good news. Since you have all completed your end of the bargain, it's only fair that Mr. Lancey and I complete ours."

Mr. Fitzgerald opened his briefcase and brought out several envelopes.

"Mr. Fitzgerald ... how did you know we had completed our work?" Harry wanted to know.

The man chuckled cheerfully. "Well, just a small secret between you and me, but we have a clear view of the harbor from Mr. Lancey's room, and with my binoculars ... well."

We all laughed. But then I had the impromtu realization that they maybe could have witnessed the unloading of the Trader's treasure the evening before. The notion made me feel uneasy. But then again, I pondered, it had been dark and hazy.

"Tomorrow morning I will escort Richard, Fred, and Joseph to the 'Madang'. She's a Burns Philip boat, and will be leaving for Papua New Guinea in a day or so. It just so happens that she was here for a refit. I would like to ask you three if you would care to work for Burns Philip. I feel that each of you has been an outstanding hand, and the Madang has a few openings ... what do you say?"

All three indicated an enthusiastic affirmative.

"We all reckon that would be great ... thank you, Mr. Fitzgerald." Fred again acted as their spokesperson.

"Kevin, here is an open BOAC airfare to London, good for one year."

Kevin stood, and accepted Mr. Fitzgerald's extended hand.

"Thank you," he said, somewhat shyly.

"And Harry, here is a Qantas ticket to Sydney ... you're booked on tomorrow's 10:00 a.m. flight."

"And for you two, Chad and Laurie ... here's two airfares, also to London with BOAC ... you're both scheduled on tomorrow's noon flight.

Harry took Mr. Fitzgerald's one good hand and shook it vigorously. "Thank you, Mr. Fitzgerald!"

Jeeses, an actor to the end, ehh Harry?

Laurie and I also shook his hand, but with more genuine sincerity, I hoped.

"Oh, by the way I'm moving on board this morning. I've brought my luggage." Joseph instantly volunteered to help Mr. Fitzgerald with his bags.

Kevin was the first to 'abandon' ship. We had all gotten ready to spend our last day as tourists in Hong Kong, but when we gathered on the main deck to wait for a walla-walla, Kevin showed with his suitcase and a small duffel bag.

"Shan Li and I have found an apartment ... she's already moved in."

"Hey, right on, Kevin ... and the best of luck to you ... to you both." I patted him on the shoulder.

I sat next to him on the walla-walla, wanting to say more words of farewell.

"Kevin ... I figure I learned a lot from you ... about philosophy ... and things."

"And Chad ... you should go back to school ... go to college ... if nothing else, just to satisfy that over-blown curiosity of yours and maybe you could study some philosophy on your own."

"Yeh, what were their names ... Nietzsche, Plato, Cuscus.

He laughed. "Immanuel Kant, you idiot ... and I'm going to try your mother's remedy for diabetes, too … after I do a little research, that is."

"Really?"

"I shit you not!"

We both laughed.

"And what about the 'treasure'?" Kevin suddenly whispered, sure that no one else could hear.

"It's safely delivered." I whispered in return.

The walla-walla reached the landing. At the first street we all shook hands again, and Kevin climbed into a rick-shaw … suitcase, duffel bag and all, and we watched as he quickly disappeared amongst Kowloon's early morning throng.

"What now?" Again we pondered our future.

"I'd like to take the train trip into the Territories," Laurie announced. "Maybe go all the way to the China border."

"That sounds like a great idea ... mind if I join you?" I asked.

"Sure."

"What about you three?"

"We'd like to take the cable car up to Victoria Peak."

"Oh!" Laurie and I both chuckled.

"Watch out for the French girls!" I shouted meaninglessly, as they headed towards the Star Ferry.

"Where to, Laurie?"

"Chad, I gotta pick up my passport. Can we do that before catching the train?"

"No problem ... let's go."

The Melbourne lady greeted Laurie with a generous smile. Today we seemed to be receiving smiles in every direction.

"Where are you travelling to?" she questioned as she handed him his passport.

"We fly to London tomorrow," Laurie answered, the delight showing on his face, scanning through the document.

"Well then, you won't have any problem ... you don't need a visa or anything for entrance to the U.K.

We crossed the harbor one more time. The train terminal was located towards our usual landing for the walla-walla to and from the Trader, and a few blocks inland.

"You want to take a couple of rick-shaws?" Laurie quizzed.

"Sure ... let's go for it!"

So we corralled two rick-shaws and headed for the station, feeling like tourist fools. I marvelled at my operator's strength and endurance ... so much of both in such an old, thin, tiny man. I almost felt ashamed, thinking that I should be pulling him, not the other way around.

The station, and the train, seemed ancient. They reminded me of the trains in Queensland, when I had worked for the Queensland Railroad in Townsville. The cars were all colored a dark green, and were constructed with an open design. The seats were wooden and uncushioned. If they had a first class, we never knew about it, for we found ourselves in a class where people brought everything with them: produce to sell or which had been newly purchased, goods to take back to the territories, extended belongings, whatever. The aisles were stacked high with these carry-ons, and people filled every space between.

The train moved slowly on the aged rails, making frequent stops. We had been told that the trip to the border would take three hours.

We both studied the scenery as the train passed through Kowloon and entered the Territories. What astonished us was the rapid transition from the high density that was Hong Kong to a rural environment. We left the narrow streets and clusters of high rise apartments to suddenly find ourselves passing through open farmland and small villages. The villages and small towns were spread out and the few modern buildings in sight were only two or three stories high, with red tile roofs. All available land was a patchwork of carefully tended rice paddies and plots of vegetable gardens.

We were curious about the communist border, and took the train all the way. But we were disappointed. We found that the border itself was inaccessible to us, and was only a single-story building complex constructed unattractively in concrete. The complex straddled a high wire fence which stretched into the distance on both sides, with a water filled canal on the China side. We were not allowed to enter the complex, and had no choice but to purchase another pair of tickets and return to Kowloon.

It was already late, the sun having exhausted it's red glow shortly after we left the border. We hoped we might find Kevin or Harry at the Oasis Club. About a block before the club we passed a newstand and a headline on one of the English language newspapers caught my eye.

"Laurie, wait a minute ..." I stopped to take a closer look. The headline read: 'Australian Opposition Party Advocates Immigration Reform'. I quickly bought a copy, fascinated.

"Laurie ... your opposition party is advocating abolition of the 'white immigration policy'."

"That's nice." he said.

I had forgotten that I had never talked to Laurie about the Aussie immigration policy. Come to think of it, I hadn't talked to an Australian about the subject since Townsville, when I had shared an apartment with three Aussies. I had learned then that it was best to keep my mouth shut because they were so bone-headed on the subject. I'd had to conclude that most Australians had an indoctrined fear of their nation being swarmed over by Asian hordes.

"Sometime I'd like to educate you about this," I half teased, half probed. "But this is *very* important news for our hap-caste boys."

"What are you talking about, Canuck?" Laurie didn't understand the connection.

"Never mind ... never mind." I answered.

Harry was indeed at the Oasis Club. Already drunk out of his tree, and he was buying drinks! Not just for one girl, either ... Harry was buying drinks for four of them. It was like walking into a one man bordello. He was pinching and squeezing and everything else he could get away with, while all four girls were squealing, and giggling, and fighting over drinks. This was one picture in a million, if only I had a camera. But I hadn't owned a camera since I pawned my last one in Townsville.

"Isn't that kinda dangerous ... with him having syphilis?" I questioned.

"I don't really know ... but I reckon it could be." Laurie was feeling maternalistic, and wanted to rescue Harry.

"Laurie ... let the man be," I held him back. "It's his last night in Hong Kong. Ours too for that matter. Let him enjoy himself ... but I guess we gotta stop him if it gets too far." I laughed, remembering his syphilis.

"Come on, Chad ... these girls are going to rob him blind!" Laurie pleaded.

"Laurie ... tell you what. Why don't we sit down and join them?" I suggested. "You mean join Harry?"

"No ... I mean let's help the girls rob him!" I snickered.

"Hey, knock it off ... you can be a s.o.b., you know that!" he protested.

"And you're too damn soft-hearted, you know that!"

So we settled on a compromise ... Harry paid for the drinks and we fended off the more serious gouging into his pocket by the ladies. And we had to step in at one point and prevent Vicki from taking him into the back room ... for her sake, of course.

We helped Harry stagger back to the Trader, carefull to minimize body contact.

"Clang - clang, clang - clang!"

I laid back for a couple of minutes. 'Yes, I gotta do something about you, Jeri', I whispered to myself. And then I thought about what lay in front of me -- today. I cupped my hands behind my head and reflected: 'Today is the first day of the rest of my life'. And today I would be flying to London. Wow ... London!!

But then an immediate sadness swept over me. It was just great to look forward to an exciting future, but I had come through a fantastic experience with a wonderful bunch of guys ... I didn't want to forget that.

I had guarded my newspaper all through the previous night's 'wilding', and I now took it with me to the officer's mess. I laid it out reverently on the table. Fred was already there. Joseph came in shortly, and Richard stopped to read it during one of his round trips. An excitement developed amongst them, and each in turn smiled in my direction, nodding acknowledgement. Mr. Fitzgerald was there as well, and I realized with great surprise that he both understood, and condoned.

The man has depth ... there is more to the man than any of us had envisioned!

Mr. Fitzgerald was going to escort our New Guinean mates to the Madang right after breakfast. We all gathered on the main deck to see them off ... all three of us, that is. I had a special message for each of them.

"Joseph, go take care of Sandie. She is truly special, and will make your life. And if you don't, you s.o.b., I will." Joseph broke tradition, and gave me a full-on two armed hug. My eyes were wetting.

I turned to Richard. "Richard, you are the best god-damn cook in the world!" He shook my hand long and hard. I noticed that his Mohawk haircut was growing out.

"And Fred ... I just wish you the best of luck. You are without a doubt an amazing mechanic. I hope you can really do something with your skill." He shook my hand in a proud, manly manner, paying me the honor of considering me as his equal.

They boarded the walla-walla and I stood watching as the craft grew small in the distance.

Harry was of course late. He had been long-faced and hung-over at breakfast, and was now desperately trying to get his luggage together. It was still only half past seven, but it was a timely trip to the airport and he had to get moving.

"Bloody hell ... what happened last night ... I spent over two hundred dollars, Australian!"

I somehow knew that would be his biggest worry!

"You know what else, Harry?"
"What, Canuck ... what?"
"Well ... you and Vicki had sex last night ... we couldn't stop you!"
"I did what? ... oh no!" He was actually panic-stricken. Which surprised me ... the man has a conscience after all, I mused.

Harry ?? Is that possible ??

"Nah, you didn't," Laurie felt he just had to intervene, cause Harry's face was sheet white. I chuckled. Laurie did the same.
"You bastard!"

It took awhile, but he finally got his stuff together, and was ready to leave. It was down to the three of us, now, as we stood on the main deck, waiting for the walla-walla which we had already waved down.
"Canuck ... one last thing. I almost forgot. I promised Mr. Fitzgerald you would dispose of the dynamite. He suggested you just throw it overboard, without the caps."
I laughed. "Harry ... what dynamite, and what caps?"
"The six sticks you have on board ... the six sticks you took from your Hadson and brought with you ... that's what I'm talking about!"
"Harry ... remember that day in Rabaul when you saw those sticks of dynamite in the back seat of the Hadson?"
"Yes ... of course ... those are the ones I'm talking about."
"Well, Harry, if you will remember, there were only three sticks ... and I didn't have any caps ... and I put those three sticks in the trunk, or 'boot' as you would say ... right?"
"Yes ... so what have you done with them?"

"Harry ... I left those three sticks in the trunk of the Hadson. I'm sure Walter found them a long time ago."

"Is that the dinky die truth, Canuck, or are you shitting me?" Harry eyed me suspiciously.

"I shit you not!"

The walla-walla pulled alongside. Harry shrugged and smiled, and then turned towards the ladder.

"Well ... you two ... have a good one!"

I was wondering what he meant. He had already reached the walla-walla.

"A good one what?" I yelled.

Harry grinned that dumb ass grin of his one more time, it covering his whole face, with his ears protruding like a panda's.

"A good life!" he yelled back, and waved heartily as the walla-walla headed for the shore.

Laurie and I boarded the BOAC 747. We had asked for a window seat, starboard side.

"Uhh ... we mean 'right' side," we had corrected.

"It's OK," the cute Chinese girl at the ticket counter counter had explained. We use the same terms for aircraft too."

Laurie claimed the window.

The plane gained speed, and we felt the abrupt ceasation of vibration as it was suddenly airborne, immediately banking to the starboard to a heading of about 230 degrees, I reckoned, and we had a brief view of the airport end of the harbor.

"Hey ... there she is!" Laurie exclaimed, pointing to her tiny, but familiar outline.

I looked over his shoulder, and we could see her ... small and alone ... unwanted but undaunted. And then, for no reason in particular, I momentarily fantasized that I could see the ghostly Captain Rodney McKay pacing the Trader's deck ... alone ... finally her captain once again ... now that we were gone.

"What do you reckon, Chad ... do you think it's true that Lancey Shipping Comapny never intended for us to make it?"

I sighed. "Damned if I know, Laurie ... I mean I really don't know. But you wanna know something. I really don't care either ... I mean I really don't give a shit. But hell ... it was great fun, wasn't it?"

Epilogue

When did the story take place?

The reader was probably confused at several points about the dating of the related events. This was partially intentional, because I was attempting to make the setting of the story as timeless as possible. However, when I had completed the writing I realized that this was an unrealistic ambition. This conclusion was especially reinforced when, after completing the writing of this first draft while I was in Thailand, I travelled overland through Laos, Vietnam, and southern China to Hong Kong, and witnessed the dramatic change that China and Hong Kong has gone through in recent years.

The actual voyage took place in the months of May and June, 1965. Since that time each of the three locations – Papua-New Guinea, Northern Samar, and Hong Kong -- have gone through economic, social, and political changes so significant that my written observations are valid only for that specific era.

Then and now: Rabaul

My son, Chad, and I visited Rabaul in December, 1992. Physically the town and surrounding area was much the same as it had been in 1965, except that the 'Cosmos' hotel had burned down in 1986 and the location was left as a grassed park. Papua New Guinea finally achieved independence on September 16th, 1975, and with independence came a multitude of economic and social changes.

The story accurately reflects the attitudes of the Australians and the different segments of the Papua New Guinea population during the era prior to independence, particularly in reference to the Australian 'White Australia Policy'. The New Guinea immigrant Chinese were actually granted the right to possess passports, and theoretically to become naturalized Australian citizens, in 1957. The same status was officially granted the hap-caste population in 1960. These privileges were dolled out by the Australian government very guardedly, however, until the reversal of Australia's 'white immigration policy' in 1974, and the independence of Papua-New Guinea a year later. Between 1960 and 1974 the Chinese and hap-caste population could obtain passports without too much difficulty, which allowed them to visit foreign countries and do such things as work in the merchant marines, but it was very difficult for them to obtain rights of entry to Australia, and Australian citizenship was granted to only a select few.

The restrictions imposed by the Australian government on the Papuan New Guinea natives were even harsher. Before independence the Papuans and New Guineans were classified as 'protected persons' under the trustee control granted to Australia by the United Nations following World War 11. They could not hold passports and were not allowed to travel anywhere beyond the Territory, except with special status. For them it would have been impossible to be a member of the crew of the New Guinea Trader on her voyage out of New Guinean waters.

Debate in Australia concerning the immigration of non-whites is still on-going. Pauline Hanson's crusade of a few years ago to return to a whites-only policy is an example. Fortunately, her efforts largely failed, although her "Pauline Hanson's One Nation" party had as many as 40,000 members (1997). Historically, the reversal of the White Australia Policy in 1973-74 was largely in response to the need to find homes for Vietnamese refugees after the pull-out of American, Australian, and New Zealand forces in 1973, and was directly a result of Australia's unfortunate participation in the Vietamese conflict itself.

With the reversal of Australia's white immigration policy in 1974 the Rabaul Chinese and many of the hap-castes left the Territory, and thus when I visited in 1992 the many small Chinese shops and an occasional glimpse of a pretty Hokien girl were no more. The CDW camp was still there, but had become the 'Rabaul Department of Public Works', operated solely by the Rabaul New Guineans. Chad and I were able to talk to a few old timers ... we were lucky enough to find and share a couple of beers with Walter Schnaubelt, my old foreman. I had forgotten about the 'sticks of dynamite story'; with his exceptional memory he reminded me of that episode and gave me a great deal of detail about many things that I was vague on. He hadn't changed a bit, it seemed.

The raunchy pursuit of young New Guinean 'maris' was of course no longer possible with the change in politics. Walter told us about a period of time just before independence and shortly afterward when the New Guineans were exercising their new-found power and authority. Things had been very touchy for the white men who had chosen to stay, and for the Chinese and hap-castes as well.

Aunty Freita had died, and the name Deli Matak was unfamiliar to all of those I asked.

On September 19th, 1994, Vulcan and Taranguna craters erupted violently, dumping up to one meter of hot ash and grey volcanic mud over the entire town and environs. Local authorities declared Rabaul closed and abandoned, and the official intent was for it to remain so. A similar eruption had devastated Rabaul once before in 1937, and the townsite was therefore deemed to be permanently unsafe. Upon hearing the news, I assumed that Rabaul town was gone forever. However, a phone call on December 15, 1996, got me through to the 'Hamamas Hotel', which had recently re-opened, and the receptionist informed me that people were slowly returning, that several shops had been rebuilt, and the harbor was receiving ships. Burns Philip, however, had not yet chosen to reclaim their former shore facilities. What Rabaul is like now I will leave for the adventurous reader to discover

Then and now: Northern Samar

The Australians improved and paved the road from Rawis to Allen long after the New Guinea Trader had made its landfall at Laoang, and the Green Park Cafe hadn't been thought of yet. I discovered these improvements when I visited in 1996. Most other things, however, were very much the same, for Northern Samar has remained a distant provincial outpost and has been largely left out of Philippine mainstream progress. In 1996 the sight of a foreigner still caused young children to flee behind their mother's skirts, wide-eyed and with their fists held to their mouths. Young Filipinas still romanticised that marrying an Aussie or American is a dream come true, but are now much more discerning and cautious. The American bases at Angeles and Olongapo (Clark Air Force Base and Sepic Bay Naval Base) are now closed, and Mayor Lee of Manila shut down 'Ermita' with a loud bang in 1993. But in Laoang 'Onay Beach' is still as it was in 1965, and I spotted several potential 'Bernadittas' while climbing up and down Laoang town's hillside streets.

Then and now: Hong Kong

In November, 1996, I entered Hong Kong through the back door, having travelled overland from Vietnam. As the bus approached Quangzhou (Canton) I was startled by the transition from rural China to an ultra modem city with toll expressways and an incredible density of new high-rise buildings. There were no rick-shaws in Quangzhou, not even bicycles, and only a few motorcycles. A five minute taxi fare cost as much as my bus fare for twelve hours of hard travel through rural China; a hotel cost over a hundred dollars U.S., compared to my hotel charge in Guanging the night before of 100 remimbi ($12.00 U.S.). I sensed that I was being prepared for Hong Kong.

When I did cross through the multi-leveled, super-modern border facility I discovered that my premonition had been correct … I discovered a Hong Kong that held no resemblance to the Hong Kong of 1965, or even the Hong Kong of 1975, when I had been there with my daughter, Kim. The changes were astonishing. Gone were the aged dark-green railroad cars of the three-hour train trip through a rural Territories from the border to Kowloon. Instead was an incredibly smooth and fast subway system that even the citizens of Tokyo would be jealous of, ultra modem in every respect. The trip from the border to Kowloon took only twenty minutes. Gone were the rice paddies and checkered fields of diversified truck gardening in the Territories. Instead there were only cluster after massive cluster of grandiose high-rise, interconnected by dense networks of highways and rapid transit.

Ships no longer anchor in the narrow harbor between Kowloon and Victoria, narrow because reclamation projects have transformed large areas of the waterway to provide for land-based expansion; and the naval base at Wanchai is no more. Victoria is now called 'Central', and the Bank of Shanghai building is no longer a prominent landmark standing proud and alone, visible all the way from Kowloon ... instead it is hidden behind several new towers of shaded glass. And the neighboring Hilton had out-lived its usefulness several years ago, and also is no more. Two tunnels under the harbor now provide new pathways for the subway and motorized traffic. A new eighty billion dollar (U.S.) airport was being built on Chek Lap Kok Island. The antique green and white Star Ferrys still cross the channel in seven minutes, however, though are mostly a tourist attraction now. Before leaving I watched an amazingly swift hover-craft pull in at the pier beside the Star Ferry terminal and realized that during three days of touring Hong Kong I had yet to see a genuine Chinese Junk of days gone by. And there are no more walla-wallas.

Even more astonishing was the change in the living standards of the Hong Kong citizenry. There was no longer a 'floating city' of impoverished boatpeople in the Yau Ma Tei typhoon shelter, only expensive yachts and fiberglass speedboats. Gone were the rick-shaws, the portable 'food stands' and the black 'sampan outfits'. Instead there were only taxis and the sleek autos of the well-to-do, a MacDonald's or Kentucky Fried Chicken or other fast food outlet, seemingly one in every block, and everwhere were young Chinese in a consumer-buying frenzy, clothed in the latest Western fashions. Nathan Road in Kowloon is now called the 'Golden Mile', a wide, busy street, it and its side-streets lined with shop after shop after shop selling jewelry, expensive clothes, hand-bags, and other luxury items. Yes, there were foreign shoppers present, but the Chinese shoppers outnumbered the visitors one hundred to one, filling the sidewalks to capacity from 9 o'clock in the morning until 9 o'clock in the evening.

It had been rumored that Europeans were working on the new airport as tradesmen -- it had been joked that hungry-for-work imports from the British Isles had replaced the Chinese as laborers in Hong Kong -- and I ventured to Chek Lap Kok to check it out. Thought I might even apply for a job as a grader operator. I was surprised to see only a few Chinese workers on the project, mostly in the offices and as engineers. The laborers were either Nepalese or Filipino, and the heavy equipment operators and other tradesmen were British or, again, Filipino. I asked why there were so few Chinese, and a British superintendent informed me that the Hong Kong Chinese were no longer willing to work as menial labor. I was told that they tended to be lazy ('you couldn't get more than 4 hours work out of them') and if a 'Britt' boss scolded them they would simply 'walk off the job'.

More shocking, I spent one full evening exploring the bars of good 'ol Wanchai ... it was still the main bar area. But during that adventurous evening I found only one Chinese bar girl, and she was from Shanghai. The rest of the girls were either Filipina or Thai. The owners, however, were Chinese. I was curious about expectations among Hong Kong Chinese regarding the changeover to Communist Chinese rule at the end of June in 1997, only seven months away, and I thought the bar owners would be especially nervous. But the three 'mama-sans' I asked only smiled knowingly, and answered: "nothing will change!" In Kowloon I walked into an establishment which was clearly a bar, or lounge ... and it looked interesting ... only to be told politely that, sorry, the bar was for Chinese only. Curiously, when I glanced past the gentleman's shoulder I saw that the girls working in the bar were ... Chinese. It occurred to me that the Hong Kong Chinese were actually looking forward to June ... perhaps to finally be freed of the British colonial yoke.

It is now 2011, and Hong Kong has been under communist control for a full fourteen years. I do not know what changes have transpired since I was there in 1996. I leave that observation for you, the future adventurer.

Miscellaneous

There are a great many things which have changed over the years, of course. One of the changes closely related to the story of the New Guinea Trader has been the advances in navigation. Every modern Navigaton Officer must still learn the basic Marcq Saint-Hiliare method of finding a position line, and the more modern and streamlined models such as the H.O. 214 are still based on that method. But we now have incredibly advanced technology that makes the sextant, chronometer, and the Nautical Almanac useful only in primitive situations, or as emergency back-up. For example, satellite navigation has advanced to the point where the GPS, or 'Global Positioning System' can be used to pinpoint a position any time of the night or day under all weather conditions with an accuracy of plus or minus a few feet, or even inches, all with an instrument sold over yachting equipment sales counters for as little as two hundred dollars. We sure could have used that kind of technology on the New Guinea Trader!

I made reference in the story to Errol Flynn, which for one reason or another I never completed. Mr. Flynn was a well known character in New Guinea during the late '20s, prior to his going to Hollywood. One of my foremen on the Kokopo Road project in Rabaul, an older man named Frank, claimed that Errol Flynn was a friend and a drinking buddy of his during that era. He told me a few stories about the famous actor, how he was such a fun-loving young man, forever getting into trouble, especially of a financial nature, and was a boozer and a womanizer. And he didn't seem to mind what color of skin the belle of the moment possessed. Errol Flynn had originally come to Papua New Guinea as a 'peace officer', but had left that occupation to pursue more adventurous objectives. He had been successful as a gold prospector in the New Guinea highlands, somewhat as my friend, Mike, had done, and then had squandered his small fortune. Prior to the time Mr. Flynn left Papua-New Guinea he had borrowed extensively from his friends over a long period of time and he owed a great deal of money. Frank related that after his famous movie, 'Captain Blood' (1935), a group of his old creditor budddies got together and sent him a letter, and a bill. Errol Flynn responded with a return letter containing only a photograph of himself, autographed.

Yes, Hong Kong has changed. And so has Laoang and the Philippines, and Rabaul is a town in ruins. Politics and economics have changed the way people live and think, and technology has even changed our methods of navigation. And so, regrettably, my story must be dated. And yet, as I tell my son Chad, equal adventures still await in abundance for those who dare 'to boldly go'.

Of Solomon's Treasure

Which brings me to the story of the Templar Knights and the Treasure of Solomon. Now, Bobby Mundy was a real character, and the story is his. For those of a more inquiring nature, the history books will confirm much of what I have related, such as the history of the the Order of the Templar Knights, and their troubled end, of the curse of Jacques de Molay, and the disappearance of 22 galleons from the Templar naval yard at La Rochelle … never to be seen again … and the connection between the Templar Knights and the Freemasons and the Rosicrucians. Or of their aid to King Bruce of Scotland and their reorganization as the Knights of Christ in Portugal.

The possibility that the treasured writings of King Solomon was originally recovered by the heroic Knights Templar on Temple Mount in Jerusalem during the great Crusades and later buried as eighteen separate treasures shortly after that fateful Friday the Thirteenth, during the month of October in the year 1307, is historically plausible. The things said of the Mormom religon are valid as well. That Joseph Smith's find in the Hill of Comorah, near the town Palmyra on the southern coast of Lake Ontario, was one of those eighteen Templar burial sites, is also plausible.

How real it all is, and what future revelations will disclose, I leave to the reader, his inquisitiveness, and to the Bretheren of the Coast.

A final note:

I truly regret that my original diary and a whole host of photos taken during the voyage were not available to add substance to the telling of this adventure ... they were all stolen from Laurie and I's A51 Austin which we had parked on the beach in Torimolinos, Spain, some months after we had arrived in London aboard that BOAC flight from Hong Kong. We had worked in Wraysbury, Buckinghamshire, on a huge water reservoir project ... then had a riotous trip in the Austin to Torimolinos ... and we were about to split ... Laurie was heading north with some new Aussie friends to Paris ... he wanted to experience snow, he said, for the first time ... and I was about to enter Morocco, on yet another adventure. But *that* is another story.

Regrettably, I have never seen nor heard of, or from, Laurie since. None of the other memorable characters in the Trader episode either, for that matter. Maybe the writing of this story will prompt a renewal of old aquaintances, and friendships. Just maybe.

About the Author

The author once argued with a close friend that 'life is *not* an endurance race' (she was an adamant jogger and marathon runner), but is an *adventure*, and should be lived as such. He is convinced that if there is any real purpose to our existence, it is to experience, and to use that experience to further 'good', however one defines that. His younger sister sends him an email once in awhile to ask what he is currently doing ... because he is constantly seeking out a new adventure.

Brent's younger years are touched upon in this true life tale of one adventure as a young traveller, and explains that he was born and raised in Canada. After having returned home from his travels, he met his mixed-race wife from Hawaii while attending Weber State College in Ogden, Utah, and then made Hawaii his home base for over thirty years. His son and daughter and ex still live in Honolulu.

"I have worn a lot of different hats!" Brent says, to describe the assortment of things he has done through the years. One passion was to operate heavy equipment, and he was especially fond of Caterpillar motor graders, and owned a total of six ... which he all named "Sophie", and rented himself and his Sophie under the company name Grader For Hire. He founded and was president of Bateman Construction in Honolulu, building roads, U.S. Army maintenance yards, and even a golf course. In between he helped pioneer light-gauge steel framing for homes, and spent a time working for Reda Pump Company in Mexico and Canada, with two stints in the Waha oil field in Libya.

Now just turning 69, however, Brent says he is finally 'settling down' and thinking about retiring. A stroke four years ago did actually slow him a bit. But he still runs a shop building hand-crafted North American style wooden canoes and kayaks in picturesque Sangkhlaburi, Kanchanaburi Province, Thailand www.sanghaleicanoeandkayak.com, and continues to write ... mostly about nutrition.

Yes, nutrition ... Brent has spent fifteen years of his life pursuing his love of learning in an academic setting, first earning a BA in Economics from the University of Hawaii, then a BSc in Human Nurition from the same school a number of years later, and finally a MSc in International Nutrition from the prestigious Institute of Nutrition at Mahidol University, Thailand. He is currently writing a series entitled *The Nutrition Factor: A Bold New Perspective* and is on his third book of the series, with at least two more to come. He is also the editor and agent for Rex Gunn's *They Called Her Tokyo Rose, Suddenly ... On A Sunday Morning*, and another of Rex's manuscripts which he hasn't published yet.

www.ingramcontent.com/pod-product-compliance
Lightning Source LLC
Chambersburg PA
CBHW060148260626
47160CB00001B/167